D0348537

WILD RAIN

CHRISTINE FEEHAN

JOVE BOOKS, NEW YORK

THE BERKLEY PUBLISHING GROUP
Published by the Penguin Group
Penguin Group (USA) Inc.
375 Hudson Street, New York, New York 10014, USA
Penguin Group (Canada), 90 Eglinton Avenue East, Suite 700, Toronto, Ontario M4P 2Y3, Canada
(a division of Pearson Penguin Canada Inc.)
Penguin Books Ltd., 80 Strand, London WC2R 0RL, England
Penguin Group Ireland, 25 St. Stephen's Green, Dublin 2, Ireland (a division of Penguin Books Ltd.)
Penguin Group (Australia), 250 Camberwell Road, Camberwell, Victoria 3124, Australia
(a division of Pearson Australia Group Pty. Ltd.)
Penguin Books India Pvt. Ltd., 11 Community Centre, Panchsheel Park, New Delhi—110 017, India
Penguin Group (NZ), 67 Apollo Drive, Rosedale, North Shore 0632, New Zealand
(a division of Pearson New Zealand Ltd.)
Penguin Books (South Africa) (Pty.) Ltd., 24 Sturdee Avenue, Rosebank, Johannesburg 2196,
South Africa

Penguin Books Ltd., Registered Offices: 80 Strand, London WC2R 0RL, England

This is a work of fiction. Names, characters, places, and incidents either are the product of the author's imagination or are used fictitiously, and any resemblance to actual persons, living or dead, business establishments, events, or locales is entirely coincidental. The publisher does not have any control over and does not assume responsibility for author or third-party websites or their content.

WILD RAIN

A Jove Book / published by arrangement with the author

PRINTING HISTORY
Jove mass-market edition / February 2004

Copyright © 2004 by Christine Feehan.
Excerpt from *Mind Game* copyright © 2004 by Christine Feehan.
Cover design by Lesley Worrell.
Cover art by Daniel O'Leary.
Book design by Kristin del Rosario.

ISBN: 978-0-515-13682-1

JOVE®
Jove Books are published by The Berkley Publishing Group,
a division of Penguin Group (USA) Inc.,
375 Hudson Street, New York, New York 10014.
JOVE® is a registered trademark of Penguin Group (USA) Inc.
The "J" design is a trademark belonging to Penguin Group (USA) Inc.

PRINTED IN THE UNITED STATES OF AMERICA

30 29 28 27 26 25 24 23

For my son, Mark,
a clever man to provide me with my beautiful
granddaughter Erin
and my wonderful grandson James.

Acknowledgments

Special thanks to a wonderful writer, Lisa Cach, for helping me with research and to Brian Feehan for always being so willing to discuss fight scenes in the rain forest!

1

THE small launch chugged up the fast-moving river at a pace that allowed the group of travelers to see the surrounding forest. Thousands of trees competed for space, as far as the eye could see. Creeping vines and plants hung low, some sweeping the water's surface. Brilliantly colored parrots, lorikeets and kingfishers flitted continually from branch to branch, so that the foliage appeared to be alive with movement.

"It's so beautiful here," Amy Somber said, turning away from the forest to look at the others. "But all I can think about is snakes and leeches and mosquitoes."

"And the humidity," Simon Freeman added, unbuttoning the top two buttons of his shirt. "I'm always sweating like a pig."

"It is oppressive," Duncan Powell agreed. "I feel like I'm suffocating."

"That's strange," Rachael Lospostos said. And it was strange. The humidity didn't bother her at all. The heavy trees and creeping vines sent blood singing through her veins, making her feel more alive than ever. She lifted the heavy mass of thick dark hair from her neck. She'd always worn it long in memory of her mother, but had sacrificed it for the sake of a very good cause—saving her own life. "I really love it here. I can't imagine anyone lucky enough to live here." She exchanged a small smile of camaraderie with Kim Pang, their guide.

He nodded toward the forest and Rachael caught a glimpse of a noisy troop of long-tailed macaques leaping from branch to branch. She smiled as she heard the rasping call of the sap-sucking cicadas even above the roar of the water.

"I like it too," Don Gregson admitted. He was the acknowledged and respected leader of their group, a man who often visited the rain forest and raised funds for medical supplies for regions in need.

Rachael stared into the rich, lush forest, longing growing in her with a strength that shook her. She heard the continual call of the birds, so many of them, saw them flitting from branch to branch, always busy, always in flight. She had a mad desire to dive out of the boat and swim away to disappear into the dark interior.

The boat hit a particularly choppy wave and threw her against Simon. She had always had a good figure, even as a young girl, developing quickly with lush curves and a woman's generous body. Simon pressed her close when he caught her courteously, her breasts mashing against his chest. His hands slid down her spine unnecessarily. She dug her thumb into his ribs, smiling sweetly as she extracted herself from his arms.

"Thanks, Simon, the currents seems to be getting stronger." There was no annoyance in her voice. Her expression was serene, innocent. It was impossible for him to see the smoldering anger at the way he took every opportunity to touch her. She glanced at Kim Pang. He saw everything, his expression every bit as tranquil as hers, but he had noted the position of Simon's roving hands. "Why is the river becoming so wild and choppy, Kim?"

"Rain upriver, there is much flooding. I warned you, but

Don consulted with another and was told the river was passable. As we get farther upriver, we shall see."

"I thought a series of storms was coming," Don defended. "I checked the weather this morning."

"Yes, the wind smells of rain."

"At least with the wind blowing so hard, the bugs leave us alone," Amy said. "I am waiting for the day I don't have fifty bites on me."

There was a long silence while the wind tugged at their clothing and whipped through their hair. Rachael kept her gaze on the shore and the trees with their branches raised to the rolling clouds. Once she saw a snake coiled around a low-lying branch and another time she spotted flying fox hanging in the trees. The world seemed a rich and wonderful place. A place far from people. Far from deceit and treachery. A place in which one might be able to vanish without a trace. It was a dream she meant to make a reality.

"The storm is coming. We have to take shelter fast. If we're caught on the river, we could all drown." Kim Pang delivered the ominous warning, startling her. She'd been so absorbed in the forest she hadn't been paying attention to the darkening sky and spinning clouds.

A collective gasp of alarm went up from the small group and instinctively they huddled closer together in the power launch, hoping Kim could get them upriver before the storm broke.

A surge of adrenaline rushed through Rachael's bloodstream, triggering a rush of hope. This was the chance she'd been waiting for. She lifted her face to the sky, smelled the storm in the wild wind and felt droplets on her skin.

"Be careful, Rachael," Simon advised, tugging at her arm, wanting her to hang on to the edges of the boat as they whipped through the choppy water toward the encampment upriver. He had to shout the words to be heard above the roar of the water.

Rachael smiled at him and obediently caught at the

boat, not wanting to appear different in any way. Someone was trying to kill her. Maybe even Simon. She wasn't about to trust anyone. She'd learned that lesson the hard way, more than once before it sank in, and she wasn't about to make the same mistakes again. A smile and a word of warning didn't mean friendship.

"I wish we'd waited. I don't know why we listened to that old man saying today was the best day for travel," Simon continued, yelling the words in her ear. "First we wait through two nearly clear days because the omens were bad and then on the word of some man with no teeth we just all climb in the launch like sheep."

Rachael remembered the old man with shifty eyes and great gaps where his teeth should have been. Most of the people they met were friendly, more than friendly. Laughing and always willing to share everything they had, the people along the river lived simply yet happily. The old man had bothered her. He sought them out, talking Don Gregson into leaving in spite of Kim Pang's obvious reluctance. Kim had nearly backed out of guiding them to the village, but the people needed the medicine and he guarded it carefully.

"Is the medicine worth money to the bandits?" She shouted the question to Simon above the roar of the river. Bandits were reputed to be commonplace along the river systems of Indochina. They had been warned by more than one friendly source to be cautious as they continued upriver.

"Not only the medicine, but we are too," Simon confirmed. "There's been a rash of kidnappings by some rebel groups to supposedly raise money for their cause."

"What's their cause?" Rachael asked curiously.

"To get richer." Simon laughed at his own joke.

The boat bumped over the water, jarring them all, shooting sprays of water into their faces and hair. "I hate this place," Simon complained. "I hate everything about this place. How could you want to live here?"

"Really?" Rachael looked into the jungle as they rushed by. Tall trees, so many blurring together she couldn't tell one from the other, but they looked inviting. A refuge. Her sanctuary. "It's beautiful to me."

"Even the snakes?" The boat pitched wildly and Simon grabbed for a hold to keep from being thrown overboard.

"There are snakes everywhere," Rachael replied softly, unheard above the roar of the river.

She had been careful to disappear from her home in the States, had planned out each step carefully, with patience. Knowing she was watched, she had gone casually to the department store and paid a huge sum of money to a stranger to walk out wearing her trendy clothes, dark glasses and jacket. Rachael paid attention to details. Even the shoes were the same. The wig was perfection. The woman strolled slowly along the street, window-shopping, picked a large store, changed clothes in the rest room and walked away a good deal wealthier than she had ever imagined. Rachael should have disappeared without a trace right then.

She purchased a passport and identification in the name of a woman long deceased and made her way to a different state, joined a church group on a medical relief tour of the remote areas of Malaysia, Borneo and Indochina. She managed to escape the United States undetected. Her plan had been brilliant. Except it didn't work. Someone found her. Two days earlier a cobra found its way into her locked room. Rachael knew it wasn't a coincidence. The cobra had been deliberately planted in her room. She had been lucky to see it before it had a chance to bite her, but she knew better than to depend on luck. Anyone she met could be a paid assassin. She had no choice but to die, and the storm would provide the perfect opportunity.

Rachael was comfortable in a world of deceit and treachery. She knew no other way of life. She knew better than to depend on anyone else. Her existence would have to be solitary if she managed to survive. She kept her face averted from the others, loving the feel of the wind. The humidity should have been oppressive, but she felt it as a shroud, a blanket of protection. The forest called to her with the fragrance of orchids, with the cry of the birds and the hum of insects. Where others cringed at every sound and looked around fearfully, she embraced the heat and the moisture. She knew she had come home.

The boat rounded a bend and headed for the rickety pier. A collective sigh of relief went up. All of them could hear the roar of falls in the distance and the current was increasing in strength. The men worked to maneuver the boat to the small dock. One lone man stood waiting for them. The wind tore at his clothes. He stared into the surrounding forest nervously but stepped onto the shaky muddy platform that served as a landing, raising his hand to catch the rope thrown to him by Kim Pang.

Rachael could see beads of sweat on his forehead and dripping down his neck. His shirt was stained with sweat. It was humid, but it wasn't that humid. She looked carefully around, her hands automatically reaching for her backpack. She needed the contents for survival. She noted that the man tying off the rope to their launch was shaking, his hands trembling so much he had difficulty with the knot. He suddenly dropped flat, his hands covering his head.

The world erupted into a nightmare of bullets and chaos. Amy's high-pitched screaming sent birds shrieking out of the treetops, rising upward toward the boiling clouds. Smoke mixed with the veil of mist. Bandits poured out of the forest, waving guns wildly and shouting orders that couldn't be heard above the roar of the river. Beside her, Simon suddenly slumped down into the bottom of the boat. Don Gregson bent over him. Duncan dragged Amy to the bottom of the boat and reached for Rachael. Eluding Duncan's hands, Rachael quietly pulled on her backpack and snapped the safety catch around her middle. Kim frantically tried to cut through the rope tying them to shore.

Whispering a silent prayer for the others and for her own safety, Rachael went over the side of the boat, slipped into the fast-moving water and was immediately swept downstream.

As if on cue, the heavens opened up and poured down a wall of water, feeding the strength of the river. Debris churned and raced by her. She kept her feet drawn up in an effort to avoid any rocks or snags. It was difficult to keep her head above the choppy waves, but she struggled to keep the water from her mouth and nose as she allowed the current to carry her away from the bandits running toward the launch. No one saw her in the swirling rush of tree branches, leaves and foliage being carried rapidly downriver. Again and again she went under and had to fight her way to the surface. Coughing and choking, feeling as if she'd swallowed half of the river, Rachael began an attempt to catch at one or two of the larger trees the force of the water had toppled. The first one she missed and her heart nearly stopped as she felt the pull of the water dragging her downward again. She wasn't certain she had enough strength left to fight the monstrous suction of the river.

Her sleeve caught on a snag below the surface, jerking her to a standstill while the water swirled around her. She clawed frantically for a branch. Leaves came away in her hand. The water tugged relentlessly, pulling at her clothes. One boot flew off and spun away from her. Her fingertips found the rounded edge of a thick branch and dug in. Her shirt ripped and the water claimed her, pouring over her head, forcing her toward the bottom. Somehow she hung on to the stationary branch. Rachael wrapped both arms around it and hugged it tightly, once more breaking the surface with her face, gasping for air, shivering with terror. She was a strong swimmer, but there was no way she could stay alive in the raging waters.

Rachael clung to the branch, fighting for air. She was already exhausted, her arms and legs leaden. Although she had gone with the current, trying to keep her head above water had been a terrible fight. Even now the water fought to get her back, pulling at her, dragging at her body continually. When she was able she edged along the fallen tree until she was wedged between the trunk and the branch and could pull herself up enough to gain the massive root system. She was on the far side of the river now, away from the rebels and hopefully too difficult too see in the downpour.

Concentrating on each inch she could gain, Rachael began to scoot onto the closest branch. A snake struck her hip and was swept away. She couldn't tell if it was alive or dead but it set her heart pounding all over again. Cautiously she stretched her body along the root, pulled herself up out of the water, lying there panting, afraid of her precarious position. One wrong move could send her toppling back into the water. The tree shuddered as the water tried to pull it free of its anchor.

The branch was slick with mud from the embankment where it had torn lose, but it formed a bridge of sorts to the shore. It seemed a million miles away. All the while the rain poured down, adding to the slippery surface. Rachael wrapped her arms around the root and slowly scooted, inch by inch, over the twisting, curving limb. Several times she slipped and had to hug the root, her heart pounding until she regained her courage and could continue forward. An eternity later she managed to step onto the bank. Her foot sank into mire that sucked at her boot when she tried to pull it free.

Rachael took the remaining boot off and threw it far out into the water, away from the trees where it might get stuck and call attention to where she had managed to get ashore. Her one hope was that the tree, holding on by a few precarious roots, would be swept downstream, leaving no trace of her escape.

Barefoot, mud squishing between her toes, soaked and shaking with fear, Rachael crawled over the marsh to the edge of the tree line. Only then did she try to see what was happening on the opposite shore. She had been swept hundreds of yards downstream and the pounding rain formed a nearly impenetrable curtain. Rachael sank down behind foliage, peering through the sheets of rain as she donned her spare boots, brought along for the very purpose of sacrificing her other pair should she have the opportunity to go overboard. She hadn't counted on such a wild current, but the chance to make an escape, in spite of the danger, was too good to turn down.

The bandits seemed to be angry, herding those remaining alive into a small shivering group. They were all shaking their heads. Several men paced along the riverbank looking for something . . . or someone. Rachael's heart sank. She had a sneaking suspicion the raid had been aimed at killing her. What better way to insure her death than to have her meet with a stray bullet while they rounded up prisoners to ransom? Kidnapping was a common enough occurrence and the bandits could be bought easily to perform an assassination. Rachael adjusted her pack, took one last look at the river and headed into the jungle.

She couldn't stop shivering as she raced through the forest, searching for a faint path leading into the interior. She had spent nearly a year preparing for this moment. She ran every day, lifted weights and climbed rock walls. She was not a particularly small woman but she learned how to turn every pound into muscle. A private instructor worked with her on self-defense, throwing knifes and stick fighting. She had gone so far as to search out survival books, committing as much as she could to memory.

The wind whipped the feathery canopy in all directions, showering Rachael with leaves and twigs and a multitude of flowers. In spite of the wind, the dense canopy helped to shield her from the rain, breaking up the solid wall of water so that it fell with a dull thudding rhythm. She hurried as fast as she dared, determined to put as much distance between the river and her destination. She was certain she could build or find one of the old native dwellings. A hut with three walls of leaves and bark and a sloping roof. She had studied the design and it seemed simple enough to follow.

In spite of continually shivering, Rachael moved with confidence and hope. For the first time in months the terrible weight pressing down on her shoulders lifted. She had a chance. A real chance at living. She might have to live alone, but she could choose how she would live.

Something crashed in the brush off to her left but she hardly glanced in that direction, trusting her warning system to alert her should there be a real threat. Water squished in her boots, but she didn't dare take the time to change into dry clothes. It wouldn't do any good; she had to cross several waist-deep streams, some with strong currents. She was forced to use creepers to drag herself up a steep slope to hold her course. Rachael Lospostos was gone forever, tragically drowned when she tried to take medical supplies to a remote village. In her place, a new, independent woman was born. Her hands ached from the many times she dragged herself up the steep rocks to push deeper into the forest.

Night began to fall. The interior was already dim and without the occasional ray of sunlight pushing through the clouds, the world around her changed radically. Tiny hairs on the back of her neck rose. She stopped walking and took time to look up into the network of branches running over her head. It was the first time she really looked at her surroundings.

The world was a lush riot of colors, every shade of green vying with vivid brilliant colors erupting up and down the trunks of trees. High overhead and on the forest floor, flowers, fauna and fungi vied for space in the secret, hidden world. Even in the rain, she could see evidence of wildlife, shadows flitting from branch to branch, lizards scrambling into foliage. Once she spotted an elusive orangutan high up in the trees, tucked in a nest of leaves. She stopped and stared at the creature, amazed at the wonder she felt.

Rachael found a very dim path, barely discernable in the wealth of thick vegetation covering the forest floor. She dropped down on one knee, peering intently at the trail. Humans had used the path, not just animals. It led away from the river, deeper into the interior. Exactly what she was looking for. Following the faint route slowed her down, but she stayed on it, her step lighter as she moved toward the heart of the forest.

Something in her was coming alive. She felt it moving inside of her. Awareness. Heat. Joy. A mixture of every emotion. Maybe it was the first time she felt she had a chance at life. Rachael didn't know the reason. She was exhausted. Every muscle ached. She was tired and sore and soaked to the skin, but she felt happy. She should have been afraid, or at the very least, nervous, but she wanted to sing.

As darkness blanketed the forest, she should have been blind, but her eyes seemed to adjust quickly to a different kind of vision. She could make out things, not just the tall tree trunks with the multitude of fauna climbing up them, but tiny details. Frogs, lizards, even small cocoons. Her muscles hummed and vibrated in tune with nature around her. A fallen log was no obstacle but a chance to leap, feeling the steel in her muscles, an awareness of how smoothly they worked beneath her skin. She almost felt as if she could hear the very sap running in the trees.

The forest was alive with insects, great spiders and fireflies. Beetles busily moved along the earth and over trees and leaves. A world within a world, and all of it surprising, yet familiar. The rush of wings overhead was audible as night birds flitted from tree to tree and owls went on the hunt. A noisy chorus of frogs began, loud calls as males searched for females. She caught sight of a gliding snake, zigzagging from one branch to another.

Smiling, Rachael continued, knowing she was on the right path. Knowing she was finally home. Far off, she heard the sound of gunfire, muffled and faint, dimmed by the steady rhythm of the rain and the distance she was from the river. The sound seemed intrusive in her paradise. It brought with it a strange ominous warning. With each step her joy diminished and dread began to grow. She was no longer alone. She was being watched. Stalked. Hunted.

Rachael looked carefully around her, paying particular attention to the network of branches above her head, looking for shadows. Leopards were rare, even here in the rain forest. Surely, one hadn't found her and padded silently after her. The idea was frightening. Leopards were deadly hunters, swift and merciless and able to bring down very large prey. Her skin prickled with unease and she used far more caution as she moved along the path toward whatever destination fate had decreed for her.

THE rain fell steadily, not a slow drizzle, but sheets of pounding rain so dense visibility was nearly nil. Thunder shook the trees, reverberating through the high canopy of the forest treetops, all the way down to deep canyons and gorges cut into the Earth by an overabundance of water. Lightning lit the forest floor, revealing huge ferns, dense foliage and a thick carpet of needles, leaves and countless decaying matter from hundreds of species of plants.

The unexpected light fell across the hunter, throwing the hard angles and planes of his face into sharp relief. Water glistened in the thick, wavy black hair falling across his forehead. Despite the heavy weight of the large pack on his back, he moved easily and silently. He didn't appear to be bothered by the vicious rainfall drenching his clothes as he followed the dim path. His eyes moved restlessly, continually, forever seeking movement in the dark of the forest. Artic cold, his eyes showed no mercy, held no life, were the eyes of a predator seeking prey. He showed no sign that the spectacular display of nature bothered him. Instead, he seemed to blend in with fluid, animal grace, very much at home in the primitive forest.

A pace behind him, like a shadowy wolf, a fifty-pound

clouded leopard prowled, eyes gleaming, every bit as alert as the hunter. Off to the right, scouting first ahead, and then their back trail, a second leopard, twin to the first, had smaller forest animals quivering in alarm at his passing. The three moved together, a uniquely trained unit.

Twice, the hunter deliberately reached out his hand and twisted a large leaf, allowing it to spring back into place. Somewhere behind them a twig snapped, the sound carried on the unrelenting wind. The lead leopard swung around, baring teeth, a hiss of a threat.

"Fritz." The single word was enough of a reprimand to keep the animal pacing at the man's side as they worked their way through the wet vegetation on the forest floor.

The mission had been a success. They had snatched back the son of a Japanese businessman from the rebels, hightailed it across the border, his team spreading out and melting into the forest. Drake was responsible for getting the kid to the waiting family and out of the country while Rio deliberately drew the pursuers away from the others, leading them deep into territory known for cobras and other unpleasant and highly dangerous creatures. Rio Santana was comfortable in the vast jungles, comfortable with being alone surrounded by danger. The forest was home to him. Would always be his home.

Rio picked up his pace, nearly jogging, heading for the swollen bank of the furious river. The water had been rising steadily for hours and he had little time if he wanted to get the leopards across with him. He led his enemies through the forest, circling several times, but staying just out of reach to keep them coming after him. One by one his men reported in. The radio was mostly crackle in the storm, but with each burst of static, he breathed another sigh of relief.

The continuous noise of rushing water was too loud, drowning out all sound so that he had to rely on the pair of cats to sound the alarm should his tenacious adversaries catch up with him sooner than he planned. He found the tall tree beside the embankment. The tree had a silvery gray trunk topped with a feathery bright green crown and it rose high above the bank, making it an easy landmark. Water already swirled around it, moving fast, dragging at the roots surrounding the wide trunk. He signaled the cats to follow as he went up it fast, high, into the canopy, leaping easily from branch to branch, every bit as agile as the clouded leopards. Near the top, concealed in the foliage, was a pulley and sling he had secured long ago. The pack went first, crossing high above the river. It was far more time-consuming to take the cats. There was no network of branches to bridge the river and it was moving far too swiftly to swim. The cats had to be placed one by one into the sling and hauled across the river, something neither of them was too fond of doing. They knew how to crawl out of the sling onto the branches. It was an escape they had performed and perfected many times.

On the opposite bank Rio hunkered down in between the roots of a tall menggaris tree and peered through the driving rain across the swollen river. The wind tore at his face and ripped at his clothing. He was impervious to the weather, night vision glasses raised and focused on the bank across from him. He had them in his sights now, four of them. Faceless enemies furious over his interference with their plans. He had robbed them of their prey, kept them from their ultimate goal, and they were determined to bring him down. He eased his rifle into position, adjusting the scope. He could take two of them before the others could get off a shot. His position was fairly protected.

The radio tucked inside his jacket crackled. The last of the signals he'd been waiting for. Keeping a steady eye on the four men across the river, he pulled the small radio from his inside pocket. "Go ahead," he said softly.

"All clear," the disembodied voice proclaimed. The last of his men was safe.

Rio wiped his hand over his face, suddenly weary. It was over. He didn't have to take another life. For once the

isolation of his existence was inviting. He wanted to lie
down and listen to the rain, to sleep. Be grateful he was
alive for one more day. He tucked the binoculars into his
pack, his movements slow and easy, careful not to draw
attention. His signal sent Fritz crawling backward out of
the tangle of roots, deeper into the timberline. The small
leopards blended perfectly with the leaves and jungle floor.
It was nearly impossible to spot them.

Lightning flashed directly overhead, the clap of thunder booming through the forest. Rio didn't know if it was
the thunder or the cats that startled a fully grown bearded
pig into crashing through the undergrowth. At once the
sky erupted with bursts of red flames, a stream of bullets
bridging the river and blasting into the network of roots.
Splinters of bark peppered his face and neck, fell harm-
lessly against his thick clothing. Something bit at his hip,
skidding over flesh and removing a small chunk as it continued traveling.

Rio cradled the rifle on his shoulder, his targets already
chosen, and squeezed off two deadly accurate rounds in
answer. He followed with a burst of fire, laying down rapid
cover as he scooted back to follow the cats. His pursuers
wouldn't be able to cross the river, and with two dead or
wounded, they would drop the search for the moment. But
they would be back and bring reinforcements. It was a way
of life. Not one he had necessarily chosen, but it was one
he accepted.

Scattered shots zinged through the shrubbery, angry
bees without aim. The river drowned out the threats hurled
at him, the promises of retribution and blood. He shouldered his rifle and slipped into deeper forest, allowing the
creeping greenery to shield him.

Rio set a hard pace. The storm was dangerous, the wind
threatening to topple more than one tree. The cats shared
his life, but had the freedom to go their own way. He
expected them to seek cover, to ride out the storm under
protection, but they stayed close to him, occasionally taking

to the trees to travel along the highway of interlocking branches. They looked at him expectantly, wondering why he didn't join them, but eventually settled into his steady, ground-eating rhythm.

Miles of rain-soaked travel passed. Close to home, Rio was beginning to relax when Fritz raised his head, suddenly alert, swerving to brush the man who instantly stilled, becoming nearly invisible, a shadow among the tall trees. Behind him, the second cat slunk to the ground, frozen, a statue with glowing eyes. Rio hissed softly between his teeth and made a small circular motion with one hand. Fritz immediately disappeared into the forest, moving cautiously, halting beside a tree. The animal circled the large trunk once, then, like a silent wraith, returned to the man. Together, all three approached, making no more noise than the single clouded leopard had. Taking no notice of the ferocious storm raging around him, Rio made a thorough inspection of the tree. A rope reached from one trunk to another.

"It isn't a garrote," he murmured aloud to the cats. "It's just a piece of rope, not even hidden. Why would they give away their presence like this?" Puzzled, he examined the ground, clearly expecting a trap of some kind. It was impossible to find a track in the soaked vegetation. He signaled the animals to spread out and continued with more caution along the faint trail.

Rio was always careful to use different routes to reach the tree beside the river. If someone did a thorough inspection of the tree, they would most likely find the claw marks of a leopard, or think any scarring had been caused by the makeshift ladders, pegs, going up the tree to a wild honeybee nest. He left little or no sign, and always carried the pulley system away with him. Still, if his route had been compromised, it was possible the rebels had sent an assassin to circle ahead and lie in wait for him. Although his identity was a mystery, he had been at the top of the hit list for a long time.

His home was deep in the interior of the rain forest. He used many different routes to get there, often taking to the trees to leave no trail, but still, someone could have found him had they been persistent enough. He was more than adept at tracking and a few of his kind sold out if the money was good enough.

Roots from the trees were tall and fanned out wide, taking in considerable territory as if claiming it. The large networks of roots created a mini jungle. Along the trunks hundreds of other species of plants and mold grew to create a myriad of colors. In the tremendous deluge the fungi growing on fallen, rotting logs glowed in the dark with eerie luminous greens and whites. Rio's restless gaze observed and catalogued the phenomenon, dismissed it as unimportant until he registered a small smear on a log, then a tiny print on a root. A twist of his fingers sent a silent signal to the cats. The animals quartered the area, crisscrossing back and forth, hissing and spitting in warning.

He approached his home from the south, knowing that was the side most blind and therefore most vulnerable should the enemy be lying in wait. The house was built into the trees, a structure running along the higher, thicker branches, up off the ground and not easily seen in the thick foliage. Over the years fungi and creeping orchids covered the walls of his home, making it nearly invisible. He had encouraged the growth of thick vines to further hide the house from prying eyes.

Rio lifted his head to scent the air. With the rain it should have been impossible to detect the faint odor of wood burning, but he had an acute sense of smell. He was seventy-two hours without sleep. Two weeks of bone-weary, hard travel. A knife had sliced across his belly and still burned like a hot poker. A bullet shaved skin from his hip. Neither wound was noteworthy. He certainly had suffered worse over the years, but left untreated too long in the forest such injuries could spell disaster. He squared his shoulders and stared up at his home with hard resolution.

In spite of the river flooding, in spite of all his careful precautions, it appeared as though the enemy had circled around to get in front of him and lay in wait in his own home. A very stupid and costly mistake.

The cats approached from either side, slinking along the ground, moving toward the trees where the house was located. Rio shrugged out of his pack, easing it onto the ground against a thick tree trunk. All the while he stayed low, knowing he would be difficult to see in the driving rain. The wind howled and moaned through the trees, shaking leaves and hurling small twigs and branches in every direction. He remained still, studying the house for a long moment. A thin trail of smoke rose from the chimney to be dissipated quickly in the high canopy. A dim flickering light cast from a low fire onto the woven blankets hanging over the windows could be glimpsed through the ever-moving foliage. There was no movement in the cabin. Whoever had been sent to assassinate him was either certain he was still a good distance away, or they had set an enticing trap. Rio hissed between his teeth to draw the attention of the cats, gave a hand signal, a quick flick with his fingers and the three of them, like dark phantoms, scouted the ground below the trees for whatever tracks the fierce rain had not obliterated.

They moved in an ever-tightening circle until they gained the large network of roots and branches. Rio's muscles bunched, contracted, rippled beneath the layer of skin as he leapt into the tree, landing in a crouch with perfect balance. The cats crept silently into the thick network of tree branches to gain the verandah. The branches were slick from the downpour, but the trio of hunters maneuvered up to the house with familiar ease. Rio tested the door. Finding resistance, he drew the knife from the leather sheath concealed between his shoulder blades. In the flash of lightning, the long, wicked razor-sharp metal gleamed brightly. He slipped the blade in the crack of the door and slowly, inch by inch, forced the heavy metal bar on the inside upward.

As the door opened, then closed furtively, the sudden cold draft sent the flames of the fire blazing high, dancing and crackling before settling back down. Rio waited a heartbeat for his eyes to adjust to the change in lighting. He moved stealthily across the wide expanse of floor, carefully placing his feet, avoiding every squeaking board. A shadowy figure moved restlessly on the bed.

Rio went to the floor, on his belly even as the wildness flared in him, ripping through his body, heightening his senses. His skin itched, his bones aching and his muscles contorting. He fought it back, forcing his brain to work, to think, to reason when his body sought to embrace the change. For a moment his hand rippled with life, with fur, fingers bursting as claws clicked on the wooden floor, then retracted painfully.

He remained motionless, flat on the floor, knife in his teeth, trying to breathe through the pain, breathe away the urge for transformation. The cats separated without visible instruction, both low to the floor, two sets of burning eyes on the figure beneath the blanket. Rio could make out the shotgun against the wall beside the bed, within easy reaching distance. In the fireplace the log disintegrated into bright red coals. Light flared in the room, illuminated the bed briefly and was gone.

2

RACHAEL came awake, instantly aware of impending danger. The smell of wet fur mixed with the scent of something feral, something dangerous. There had been no sound, but the feeling was so overwhelming she instinctively reached for the shotgun. Fingers circled her wrist in a vise-like grip, crushing bone against tendon. The shotgun was torn from her hand easily, her attacker strong beyond her wildest imagining. She jerked her captured wrist toward her as if to struggle against his hold. Simultaneously, she brought up her left hand, gripping the short rattan-filled stick and slamming it with sickening force against her assailant's head. She rolled sideways away from him to drop to the floor, the bed between them.

To her horror, Rachael landed inches from glowing red eyes, hot breath in her face, gaping, hideous jaws filled with teeth coming straight at her. Not just any teeth, she was staring at what looked like a saber-toothed tiger. Thrusting the stick between the dripping fangs, she scrambled away, desperate to reach the fireplace and a weapon, any weapon to defend herself. A hand grabbed at her, missed, slid off her legs. She nearly made it across the room, reaching out for the heavy metal poker just inches from her fingers. Another step, a lunge and she'd have a chance. Something caught her ankle in a savage trap, tearing at her flesh, dragging her down, slashing mercilessly with sharp teeth.

Rachael imagined it was like being hit by a shark. Hard. The force of a freight train. She could hear someone swearing, animals breathing loudly, a terrible chuffing noise. Something hissed. Panic overwhelmed her, nearly shutting down her brain. Red-hot pain shot through her entire body, the agony taking her breath away. Gathering itself for another attack, a second leopard leapt at her. Gritting her teeth, Rachael threw herself forward, a scream ripping her throat as the lance-like teeth pierced and shredded flesh to crunch on bone. Her fingers curled around the poker, swinging it at the animal with desperate strength. A hand caught her wrist, abruptly stopping the vicious cut in midair.

A man loomed over her, dark and powerful, his face that of an avenging devil, thrust close to hers. To her horror the face contorted, fur bursting through skin, teeth filling the strong jaw. A leopard's hot breath blew in her face, the teeth at her throat. Not a small, clouded leopard, but a huge black leopard. The leopard's gaze fixed on her with merciless intent. Rachael saw the piercing intelligence in the brilliant yellow-green eyes. The haunting stare, smoldering with fire, with deadly danger, was etched into her mind. She closed her eyes, willing herself to faint, yet she could not shut out the focused stare.

Rio struggled against the beast rising in him. Too many wounds, too many days without sleep made it difficult to maintain control. He fought the change before he could make a kill. He breathed in and out. Drew the air deeply into his lungs. Forced the wildness in him back down, to settle somewhere deep inside until he was once again completely ruled by his brain and intelligence.

"Release," he snapped. The cats obeyed, letting go of

his assassin's leg, dropping to the floor, still on guard. "Now you. Give it to me."

Rachael was incapable of letting the poker go. Her fingers were locked around it, her mind numb with horror. She could only stare at him in shock. Terror held her mute.

"Damn you, drop it," he hissed, increasing the pressure on her wrist, knowing he could easily snap the bone if she continued to resist. His free hand clamped around her throat like a vise, instantly cutting off her air, elbow digging into her breast, knee across her thighs. His body effectively pinned hers to the floor with his superior weight. "I could break your neck," he pointed out. "Drop it."

Rachael would have cried out, screamed for help, for salvation, just screamed for the hell of it. She was more afraid of the man, or whatever he was, than the cats and their evil eyes. He'd successfully choked off all sound, but the pain radiating up her leg seemed to engulf her so that she had the incredible sensation of melting into the floor.

Rio swore again as he felt her go limp beneath him, the poker clattering to the floor. He shoved it out of her reach and as he did so, his hand encountered a warm, sticky substance. Instantly his hands moved down her leg. He muttered an expletive at his find. Clamping a hand over the wound, he jerked her leg into the air. "Don't you faint on me. Is there anyone else here? Answer me, and you'd better tell the truth." He was fairly certain they were alone, someone else surely would have revealed their presence during the short but intense fight. The house held no other human scent, but he wanted no more surprises.

A shudder ran through her body, trembling in reaction to the terrible wound on her leg. There was hard authority in his voice. A distinct merciless edge that carried inherent danger. "No." She managed to gasp out the word through her bruised throat.

Rio signaled to the clouded leopards. "I hope to hell you're telling me the truth because they'll kill anyone they find."

He applied a field tourniquet quickly, knowing the animals would alert him if they found another intruder. He couldn't imagine who would be stupid enough to send a woman after him. Rio lifted her with ease, carried her to the bed and set her on it. She didn't look capable of murdering anyone, her face white and her eyes too big for her face. He shook his head and went to work on the ugly wound in her leg. The puncture wounds were deep and had done considerable damage. The cat had savaged the leg as she'd tried to get away, tearing deep gouges out of her flesh, an unusual wound for a clouded leopard to make. It was an ugly mess and needed more skill than he possessed.

Rachael could barely breathe through the pain. In the darkness, the man looming over her appeared invincible. His shoulders were wide, his arms and chest powerful. He carried most of his upper body weight in sheer muscle. There were bloodstains on his clothes. Blood trickled from the ugly gash near his temple. He was drenched, his clothes torn and soaked completely through. Water dropped from his hair onto her leg as he bent over her, the droplets cold on her hot skin. He had a dark shadow along his jaw and the coldest eyes she'd ever seen on a human . . . or a beast. Brilliant yellow-green eyes.

"Stop shaking." There was impatience in his voice.

Rachael took a deep breath and forced her gaze down to her mangled leg. A single sound escaped and her world began to blur.

"Stop looking at it, you little fool." He caught at her impatiently, jerked her chin up so that she was forced to meet his glittering stare.

Rio studied her pale face, so drawn with pain he could see lines etched around her mouth. Beads of sweat dotted her brow. The marks of his fingers showed around her throat, swollen and purple. His gaze dwelt for a moment of speculation on her right wrist, noting the swelling, wondering if it was broken. It was the least of his worries.

"Listen to me, try to follow what I'm saying." He bent

close to her, his face inches from hers. His voice started out gruff, but even to his own ears, it gentled as his gaze drifted over her.

Rachael pressed back against the mattress, terrified that his face would contort and leave her staring at a beast rather than a man. She was floating in a sea of pain. A veil of haze blurred her vision, until she felt at a distance from everything. A look of resolution hardened his expression, warning her. She made an attempt to nod, to indicate she was listening, terrified of the intensity of his unblinking stare, afraid if she didn't respond he would suddenly grow a mouthful of teeth. All she really wanted to do was slide down in the bed and disappear.

"Infections start fast here in the rain forest. We're cut off by the river. This storm is a bad one and the river is over its banks. I can't get you help so I'm going to have to take care of this the primitive way. It's going to hurt."

Rachael pressed a hand to her mouth to stifle the hysterical laugh welling up. Hurt? Was he crazy? She was caught in the middle of a nightmare with no end. She was in a tree house with a leopard man and two mini leopards. No one knew where she was and the leopard man wanted her dead. Did he think her leg didn't already hurt?

"Did you understand?"

He seemed to bite the words out between strong teeth. Rachael tried not to stare at his teeth. Tried not to imagine them lengthening into lethal weapons. She made herself nod, tried to look intelligent when she was certain she was insane. Men didn't change into leopards, not even in the middle of the rain forest. She must have lost her sanity, there was no other explanation.

Rio stared down at her face, shocked at the way his stomach lurched at the idea of what he had to do to her. He'd done such things before. He'd done far worse things. It was the only chance they had of saving her leg, but the thought of hurting her further sickened him. He had no idea who she was. Chances were good she'd been sent to

kill him. He was a wanted man. It had been tried before.
Rio snapped his teeth together and swore silently. What the
hell difference did it make if her eyes were too big for her
face and she looked so damned vulnerable?

The rain poured down onto the roof. The wind howled
and lashed at the windows. He was uneasy, hesitant even,
something very unusual for Rio. He looked down, saw his
fingertips brushing damp tendrils of hair from her face, his
touch almost gentle, and jerked his hand away as if her
skin burned him. His heart did a peculiar somersault. Rio
pulled the small vial from the field medical kit strapped to
his belt. One hand clamped around her leg to hold her still.
He poured the entire contents over the gaping wound.

Rachael screamed, the sound tearing up through her
ragged throat to pierce the walls of the house. She tried to
fight him, tried to jerk into a sitting position, but his strength
was implacable. He held her down easily. "I can't tell you
anything. I don't know anything." The words were strangled
between trying to breathe through the pain and her swollen
throat. "I swear I don't. Torturing me isn't going to do you
any good." She looked at him, pleading, tears swimming in
her dark eyes. "Please, I really don't know anything."

"Ssh." Distaste for hurting her was bile in his mouth and
he didn't know why. Most tasks were done without feeling.
Rio had no idea why he would suddenly develop compassion for a woman sent to kill him. He filed her blurted revelations away for a better time to study them. The need to
reassure her took precedence and that worried him. He was
a man who always wanted knowledge. Information. He
wasn't the type to offer sympathy—especially for someone who had tried to take his head off. "It's only to kill the
germs and fight infection." He found himself murmuring
the words, his tone odd. Unfamiliar. "I know it burns. I've
used it on myself more than once. Just lie still while I try to
repair the damage."

"I think I'm going to be sick." It was the last humiliating straw. Rachael couldn't believe it was happening to

her. She had planned everything so carefully, worked so hard, come so far. Everything was lost now. This man was going to torture her. Kill her. She should have known she couldn't escape.

"Damn it." He held her head while she was sick over and over into a bucket he dragged out from under the bed. She didn't want to think what the bucket was used for. She didn't want to think how she was going to get away from him with a mangled leg, in the middle of a storm with the river flooding.

Rachael lay back, wiping at her mouth with the back of her hand, trying desperately to force her brain to work. Weakness was an insidious enemy, creeping through her body so her arms felt leaden and she didn't want to lift her head.

"You've lost a lot of blood," he said tersely, as if reading her mind.

"What are you?" The words came out a whisper.

The wind stilled for a moment so only the rain could be heard pounding on the roof. Rachael held her breath when he turned the full impact of his cold, merciless eyes on her. He didn't blink. She saw that his pupils were dilated. She saw that same piercing intelligence, glimpsed the dangerous fire smoldering. Her heart pounded in time with the driving rain.

"They call me the wind of death. How could you not know?" His voice was as expressionless as his eyes. A faint, humorless smile drew attention to his mouth, failing to light his eyes. "They didn't send you here with much information. Not very smart for an assassin. Maybe someone wanted you dead. You should give that some thought." He dragged a chair to the side of the bed, lit a lamp and dug into his field kit for more supplies.

Something in his voice gave her pause. She studied his profile. There was acceptance in his voice of who and what he was, not bravado or bragging. "Why would I be sent here to kill you?"

"Weren't you? It's been tried many times and I'm still alive." He was telling her the truth. She didn't understand what he was telling her, but she heard the honesty in his tone. He had a needle in his hand and bent very close to her leg.

Involuntarily she jerked away. "Can't you just tape it up?"

His hand clamped around her thigh, pinning her to the mattress, holding her still. "Damn cat made a mess of you. It's all the way to the bone. The lacerations need stitches. There's nothing I can do about the puncture wounds. I don't like the look of this. It isn't helpful with you shaking so much."

"I'll keep that in mind." Rachael muttered the words resentfully under her breath. She closed her eyes to block out the sight of her own blood. All the while, in spite of everything, she was acutely aware of his hand wrapped around her bare thigh. "You're obviously one of those he-men seen only on film who can take forty-seven kicks in the ribs and keep on fighting. Don't mind me for being human."

"What did you say?" His head swung around, his eyes focusing on her face.

Rachael could feel his gaze stabbing at her but she refused to give him the satisfaction of looking at him. Or at the needle. She'd already thrown up once; she didn't think a second round would win her any points. "Was it my imagination or did you turn into a leopard?" Not just any leopard. Not a clouded leopard like his two companion cats. "Not like those little cats either. I'm talking a big, for-real large, predatory, man-eating leopard." She could have groaned the minute the words left her mouth. It was utterly ridiculous. No one turned into a wild animal. Now he was going to think she'd lost her mind completely. And maybe she had. The image of his face contorting, the hot breath, the wicked teeth so close to her throat was very vivid. She'd even felt the brush of fur. And those eyes. She would never forget those eyes. She couldn't possibly have made up that predatory stare. Unable to prevent herself, her gaze lifted to his, regarding him as if he had two heads. She could see she was really making an impression.

"It's a bad habit of mine." He said it casually. Easily. As if it didn't matter. As if she really were crazy. And actually she thought he might be right.

Rachael watched him take a breath, let it out and take the first stitch. She tried to jerk her leg away from him, her breath hissing out between her teeth. "Are you insane? What do you think you're doing?"

"Hold still. You think this is easy for me? You've lost too much blood. If I don't repair the damage, you're not just going to lose the leg, you're going to die."

"I thought that was the idea."

"What was I supposed to think? You were here, waiting in my house for me."

"I was in bed asleep, not lurking behind the door ready to bash your brains out." She glared at him.

Rio turned his head again to look at her. Rachael had the grace to blush. Blood trickled down his temple to the dark shadow of stubble growing on his face.

"I thought you were trying to kill me. You were, weren't you?"

"If I wanted you dead, believe me, you'd be dead and I'd be burying your body in the forest. Hold still and cut the chatter. In case you haven't noticed, I'm soaked and have a few wounds of my own to take care of."

"And all this time I thought you were he-man and didn't care about the little things like wounds."

He muttered something under his breath she was certain was uncomplimentary before once more bending over her leg.

Rachael gave up the idea of being a true heroine straight out of the movies. She'd been trying bravado just to concentrate on anything beside the excruciating pain in her leg, but he wasn't helping with his tiny little needlework. It felt like he was sawing at her leg with a dull blade. She couldn't just grab the pillow and suffocate herself because her hand wasn't working properly. She could hear someone crying. An obnoxious, annoying sound that wouldn't stop. A high keening kept breaking her concentration, making it impossible to lie still.

Grim-faced, Rio held her down as he worked. He was grateful when she finally succumbed to the pain, lying motionless, her breathing rapid, her pulse pounding. Her soft moaning set his teeth on edge. Ate at his heart. "Damn you, Fritz. Did you have to take her leg off?" It took him close to an hour in the dim light, tiny stitches, working on the inside. Straightening, he sighed, wiping the sweat from his face with the back of his hands, smearing her blood over the stubble on his face. Now he could add torturing women to his long list of sins.

He brushed back her hair, frowning down at her white face. "Don't you die on me," he ordered, feeling for her pulse. She'd lost a lot of blood and her skin was clammy. She was going into shock. "Who are you?" He dragged blankets over her and built the fire back up to heat a large pot of water and added a smaller kettle to make coffee. It was going to be a long night and he needed a boost.

The cats lay near the fire, already asleep, but woke when Rio examined them for injuries. He murmured to them, nonsense really, showing his affection for them roughly as he removed parasites and ruffled their fur. He never admitted to himself he felt affection for them, but it always pleased him when they chose to remain with him. Fritz yawned, showing his long sharp teeth. Franz nudged him sleepily. Normally playful, the two leopards were worn out.

As he washed his hands, Rio became aware of how uncomfortable his soaked clothing was. Every muscle in his body ached now that he was allowing himself time to think about it. He had to clean and stitch his own wounds, and the prospect wasn't a pleasant one. His pack was still outside lying against a tree trunk and he needed the contents of the larger medical kit he always carried.

While he waited for the water to boil he searched his
home for some evidence of who she was and why she was
there. "Little Red Riding Hood, were you just walking in
the woods?" He went through the backpack containing her
clothes. "You come from money. A lot of money." He recognized the designer labels from rescuing more than one
rich victim. "Why would you be wandering alone in my
territory?" His gaze shifted to her face, a silken thong
crushed in his hand. He didn't want to give life to the
question in his mind by murmuring it aloud. Why did he
ache every time he looked at her pale face? Why did it feel
like a blow to his gut each time he saw his fingerprints
around her throat? How the hell did she manage to make
him feel guilty when she was the one invading his home,
lying in wait for him? He shied away from the questions,
tossing the silly little thong back in the pack. He would
take care of washing clothes tomorrow. He was about out
of steam at the moment, and he still had a long haul ahead
of him.

Coffee warmed his insides and helped clear the fog in
his brain. He stood over her, sipping the hot liquid and
studying her face. She thought he wanted information
enough to torture her for it. "What information? What do
you know that someone might want bad enough to hurt
you for?" The idea of it set a demon rising in him.

She stirred at the sound of his voice, moving restlessly,
pain flickering across her face. He brushed back her hair
with a gentle touch, wanting to soothe her, not wanting her
to surface when he couldn't ease her suffering.

Electricity ran through her body to his, sparked through
his fingertips and whipped through his bloodstream. Every
muscle in his body contracted. Wary, he took a single step
back. He felt the change rise in him, threaten to take him in
his tired state. He leaned over her and pressed his lips
against her ear. "Do not make the mistake of bringing my
emotions to life." He whispered the warning, barely audible in the pounding of the rain on the roof and the howling

of the wind at the windows. It was the only warning he would give her.

Rio ejected the shells from the shotgun, pocketed them and put the empty weapon in a small alcove out of sight. The moment he opened the door, rain lashed at him, piercing his soaked clothing. The storm showed no signs of abating, the wind ripping ruthlessly through the trees. The tree branches were slick, but he moved across them easily in spite of the heavy deluge of water.

Rio knelt beside his backpack to try his radio. He doubted if he could raise anyone there in the dense forest with the storm raging, but he tried repeatedly. He didn't like the look of her wounds and she was going into shock. The forest had a way of deciding matters and he wanted her safe somewhere under a doctor's care. When static was the only reply he glanced up at the house with a worried frown, cursed the leopards, the woman and everything else he could think of. Abruptly he gave up, shoving the radio inside the pack before returning to his house.

Rachael thought she must be asleep, caught in the middle of a nightmare, a horror film playing over and over. There was blood and pain and men turning into leopards with hot breath and wicked teeth. There was a strange floating sensation, as if she were removed from whatever was happening to her, but the pain was pushing closer to her, working its way through her body, insisting it couldn't be ignored. She let her breath out slowly, afraid of opening her eyes, afraid if she didn't, she would be trapped forever in that nightmare world. And she was tired of being afraid. It seemed she'd been afraid all of her life.

A rush of cold air announced she wasn't alone. The door closed abruptly. Rachael's fingers curled around the blanket, tightening into a fist. She lifted her lashes just enough to see, striving to keep her breathing even.

Her attacker dropped a heavy pack beside the sink and rummaged around in it, pulling out several items and laying them out on the table with care. His back was to her as he dropped his jacket near the pack. He wore a shoulder harness housing a lethal-looking gun. Between his shoulder blades lay a leather sheath with the handle of a knife sticking out. He took both weapons and hung them on a peg to the side of the fireplace.

The man turned slightly as he sat down in one of the chairs, grimacing as if it hurt to move. From his boot he pulled another gun, checked the load and placed it on the table near his hand. Only then did he peel off his shirt. She caught a glimpse of a barrel chest, very heavily muscled. He appeared to be an ordinary man. There was no excessive hair, no fur, just blood and bruises. Some of the tension seeped out of Rachael.

He groaned, the sound nearly inaudible. There was a hint of distaste. His chest and stomach carried bruises. There was a raw-looking wound seeping blood across his stomach and a small brown leech attached to his skin. He turned his back to her.

Rachael let out her breath, her stomach muscles clenching. He had scars on his back. Lots of them. And he had another leech. "You have another one on your back. Come over here and I'll take it off for you." The thought of touching the leech was disgusting, but it sickened her to see the thing sucking on him like the parasite it was.

His shoulders stiffened. Not a big movement, but one that told her she'd surprised him and he didn't like surprises. He turned his head, a slow, animal-like movement. Rachael's breath caught in her throat. His eyes glowed, much like that of a cat in the dark. The flames from the fireplace leapt in the yellow-green depths. There was a long moment of silence. A log hissed and shifted. Sparks flew.

"Thanks, but I'll pass. I'm used to them." Rio sounded gruff and abrupt and surly even to his own ears. Hell, all she'd done was ask to help him. He didn't need to bite her head off. "I think your wrist is broken. I haven't had time to splint it." He couldn't remember anyone offering to help him before. He rarely spent more than a few minutes in the company of others, and her close proximity was unsettling. She made him feel vulnerable in a way he couldn't understand.

Rachael looked with some surprise at her swollen wrist. The pain radiating up from her leg consumed her to the point she hadn't noticed her wrist. "I guess it is. Who are you?"

She watched him take his time before answering, pulling the leech from his stomach with the ease of practice and disposing of it. His strange eyes immediately focused fully on her. "Rio Santana." He obviously was expecting a reaction to his name.

Rachael blinked at him. The intensity of his gaze made her heart pound. She'd never heard his name before, she was certain of it, yet something about him seemed familiar to her. She shifted position and pain knifed through her.

Impatience flickered across his face. "Stop moving around. You'll start bleeding again, and I haven't even cleaned up the first mess."

"You spend a lot of time working on your manners, don't you?" she observed.

"You tried to bash in my head, lady. I don't think I need you to lecture me on manners." He stalked across the room to draw the knife from the sheath.

Her heart jumped, then settled into a steady pounding. Everything about the way he moved reminded her of an animal. The flames from the fireplace made the blade of the knife glow an eerie red-orange as he held it up.

"Stop looking at me like I have two heads," he snapped, sounding more impatient than ever.

"I'm looking at you like you're waving a big knife around," she said. Her leg was throbbing with pain, forcing her to grit her teeth and try to relax. How was she supposed to keep from moving around when it felt as if someone was using a dull saw on her flesh? "And I didn't exactly try to bash *your* head in. It wasn't personal."

"The knife is to remove the leech from my back. I can't reach it any other way," he explained, although why he felt compelled to explain what should have been perfectly obvious, he didn't know. "And I always take it personally when someone tries to remove my head from my shoulders."

She made a face. A silly, feminine expression of exasperation. And she did it with little white lines of pain etched around her mouth. It fascinated him, that wholly feminine expression. His stomach did a weird flip.

"You don't hear me complaining that your little pet chewed off my leg. Men are such babies. It isn't even that big of a gash."

He had the urge to laugh. It came out of nowhere, blindsiding him, bursting over him unexpectedly. He didn't laugh, of course; he frowned at her instead. "You put a hole in my head."

"You're going to put a hole in your back with that knife. Stop being macho he-man and let me take that horrible thing off of you."

His eyebrow shot up. "You want me to put a knife in your hands, lady?"

"Stop calling me lady, it's becoming annoying." Pain was beating at her so strongly now that she wanted to throw up again. It was definitely making it hard to think. She kept fear at bay with her usual chatter, but she wouldn't be able to keep it up for much longer. And she dared not think what might happen then.

"I don't exactly know your name. Where I come from, lady is a compliment."

"Not in that tone of voice," she objected. "Rachael Los . . ." she trailed off, casting around for a name, any name. She couldn't think clearly; she'd already forgotten her new name, but it was imperative she hide her identity. Pain throbbed in her head, beat at her body. "Smith."

If it were possible, his eyebrow went higher. "Rachael Los Smith?" His mouth softened for the briefest of moments, a rusty attempt at a smile. Or a smirk. She couldn't tell. Her vision was beginning to blur.

Rio moved closer to her, his mouth once more twisting into a frown. "You're sweating." His palm settled on her forehead. "Do *not* get an infection. We're stuck here without help for the duration of the storm."

"I'll make sure I follow your orders, Rio, because I have the power to determine that, you know." Rachael's gaze followed the path of the knife as it moved close to her. "If you don't let me help you now, I don't think I'm going to be able to at all." Her voice was funny, tinny and far away. "That awful leech is going to just stay there, getting high on your blood. Maybe it's a girl leech and she's going to have babies and they'll all live on your back, sucking your blood. A little leech community. How perfectly lovely."

He muttered something under his breath.

"And don't swear at me or I'm going to cry. I'm doing my best here and you aren't giving me anything to work with."

His fingers were gentle in her hair even though he didn't mean to touch her. "Don't you dare cry." The thought was more alarming than someone coming at him with a gun. Her tears might turn him inside out. "The morphine is wearing off, isn't it? I didn't give you very much because I was afraid you'd go into shock."

A small humorless laugh escaped. She sounded on the verge of hysteria. "I am in shock. I think I lost my mind. I thought you turned into a leopard and tried to rip my throat out."

He slipped the tip of the knife between his back and the leech, flicked it to the floor and hastily disposed of it. "Leopards don't rip throats out. They bite the throat and suffocate their prey." He dipped a cloth into a cool bowl of water and sponged her face. "They're tidy killers."

"Thanks for the information. I wouldn't want to think my death would be a messy one."

Rio was uncomfortably aware of her gaze studying his

face. Her eyes were large, too old for the rest of her. There was something sad in the dark depths that tugged at his heart. Her lashes were incredibly long, spiky from her tears. He actually felt as if he were falling forward into the depths of them, a corny and totally ridiculous notion he was impatient with. His heart began to pound in his chest. Anticipating—what, he didn't know. He deliberately wiped the cloth over her eyes, a gentle stroke to save himself from falling under her spell.

"Are you always this sarcastic, or should I put it down to you being in considerable pain?"

Rachael tried to laugh but it came out a gasping sob. "I swear it feels like my leg is on fire."

"It's swelling. I'm going to give you a little more painkiller and splint that wrist for you." Rio's fingers trailed in her hair, a thick mass of silk. There was a strange color surrounding her body, like a shadow that wouldn't go away. No matter how many times he blinked, or swept his hand over his eyes to clear his vision, the strange surrounding color remained.

"I think you need to take care of yourself," Rachael said, her gaze drifting over his face. He had the physical sensation of fingers touching him lightly in a caress. She didn't seem to notice the effect she had on him, and he was grateful.

"You look tired. I honestly can't even feel my wrist at the moment, although I think a painkiller is a good idea. Maybe a huge dose of painkiller." Rachael tried to smile at him, tried to make it a joke. If he didn't find something to stop the pain she was going to ask him to knock her out. He had a big enough fist.

She was shaking beneath the blanket, a sure sign of fever. He had packed the wound with antibiotics earlier, but it obviously wasn't going to be enough. Rio shook pills into his hand and helped her lift her head to swallow them. She pressed her teeth together, but a small sound, much like that of a wounded animal, escaped. "I'm sorry, I know

it hurts, but you have to get these down." If she had come
there to kill him, he was making a hell of a fool of himself,
but it didn't matter to him. He had to remove the despera-
tion from her eyes. She looked so helpless it twisted his gut
into hard little knots. He gave her another small dose of
morphine along with the antibiotics and waited until her
eyes clouded over before splinting her wrist. Her skin was
hot, but he didn't dare leave his own wounds much longer
or they both would be in trouble.

Rachael felt herself drifting away. The pain was there;
she didn't want to squirm around and provoke it, but she
could handle the intensity floating above it. Rio moved
away from her with his curious animal grace. He intrigued
her. Everything about him intrigued her. She couldn't keep
from staring at him, although she tried to think of other
things. The wind. The rain. Leopards leaping at her throat.

Her lashes drifted down. She listened to the rain and
shivered. Before she had been burning up; now she felt
inexplicably cold. The sound of the rain driving down on
the rooftop added to her discomfort. She couldn't hear him
moving around the house. It wasn't that the storm drowned
out the sounds, he was simply that quiet. Like a great jungle cat.

3

RACHAEL forced her eyes open to keep him in sight. She felt dreamy, disconnected with reality. Rio stood several feet from her, close to the stove. Casually hooking his thumbs in his wet jeans, he eased them from his hips, slowly exposing his firm buttocks and his long, muscular back to her. She tried not to gawk as he washed up, using hot water from the stove. He was thorough about it, his muscles flexing as he worked. He reminded her of the statues she'd seen in Greece, the defined muscles and well-proportioned ultra-masculine body. It occurred to her that he was completely at home without clothes. He seemed to have forgotten she was in the room, displaying no modesty whatsoever.

He lit a match and held it to the needle he'd used to sew her leg before performing the same task on his arm. Rachael heard him swear when he doused his hip with the same evil liquid he had used on her. Evidently he kept large supplies of it to refill his little vial. He turned slightly as he sewed his hip and she got a frontal view. Twin columns for thighs and looking every bit as good or better than the anatomically correct statues.

"You have a beautiful body." Rachael would never have called attention to the fact that he was naked. The words slipped out before she could censor them, or maybe someone else said them. She looked around to see if they were really alone. She had said it after all, and she meant it. The honesty in her voice didn't even make her blush or turn away when he looked over at her with his penetrating, focused gaze.

Rachael stared at him openly, inspecting him the way she might a beautiful sculpture. She smiled dreamily. "Don't mind me. I think it's the drugs talking. I've just never seen a man with a body as beautiful as yours is."

There was no come-on in her voice, no deliberate seduction, just simple honest admiration. And that was what made it so damned sexy. He hadn't even been thinking about sex. Or soft skin. Or full breasts. Or silky hair. She smelled like a damned bed of flowers. He hurt like a son of a gun. He was tired and edgy and he didn't understand what was happening to him. And now his body was reacting to her voice. Or her words. Or her smell. Who knew? Need punched him in the gut and hardened his body like a rock. He was furious with her. With himself. With his lack of control. Now he had a hell of a hard-on and a sick woman in his bed. And damn it all, if he had to endure it, she could just look at it.

He finished stitching his hip, all too aware of her unwavering gaze. It didn't seem to bother her that he was primed and ready and they were completely alone. Her eyes were overbright, her skin flushed with heat in spite of the continual shaking. Fortunately, the pain from the ugly gash on his hip drove the heat from his body so his lust wasn't so brutally exposed to her.

Rio didn't look at her but he felt her eyes on him. Hot. Staring. Devouring him. The thought made him ache all over. He swore again. Even with the pain of stitching his own wounds, her gaze, staring at his hardened body, set jackhammers tripping in his head and his temples pounding.

"Are you going to stare at me all night?" He growled the words at her. A threat. A promise. Retribution in the lines of his body. He turned his head then faced her down, allowing naked desire to flare just to scare the hell out of her.

She smiled serenely. "I'm sorry. Was I staring? It's just that you're the most beautiful man I've ever seen. I thought if I did die, you might not be such a bad thing to take with me as a last image."

She disarmed him just like that. The power she wielded was frightening. Nothing touched him the way she managed to. With a look, a single word. Just the tone of her voice. He was drowning and it made no sense. And it made him angry. He just wasn't sure whom he was angry with.

She was still staring, her eyes huge. Rio stalked over to her and pressed his palm against her forehead. "You're burning up."

"I know." He was standing right up against the bed, his groin level with her eyes. Rachael thought him extraordinary. She floated in a dreamy haze, where nothing seemed very real. Except Rio and his incredible body. She reached out to touch him, not believing he could be anything but a dream.

Her fingertips brushed the head of his penis and nearly sent him through the roof. Her touch was feather-light, barely there, but he felt it vibrating through his entire body.

"You are real." She sounded awed and her breath was warm along his shaft, tightening every muscle in his body. Her fingers trailed over his heavy erection, slid across his balls and down his thigh and the feeling was unlike anything he'd ever experienced.

"It's a damn good thing you're hurt," he snapped, turning away from her, afraid she might go further. Afraid he might let her. And he'd never forgive himself if he stooped that low. He had never wanted a woman so much. It was the way she looked at him. The sound of her voice. The honesty. Intellectually he knew it was the fever talking, taking away her natural inhibition, but he couldn't help reacting. Fever or no, she liked what she saw. Walking was torture, his body so hard he was afraid each step would shatter him, but he moved away.

Rio filled a bowl with cool water and caught up a cloth. When he turned around she was staring at him again. He sighed.

"You swear a lot, don't you?"

"You have a way of making me feel like I need to," he said and dragged a chair to the side of the bed. "I have to get your fever down."

Rachael laughed softly. "You'd better put on clothes then. I don't think anything else is going to help."

"Do you even know what you're saying?"

She frowned at the tone of his voice. "I don't know. Should I lie to you?"

"Do you always tell the truth?" It was a challenge.

Her eyes met his. "When I can. I prefer the truth. I'm sorry I made you uncomfortable. You just seemed so at home without clothes. I didn't think you could be real. I thought I made you up." Her gaze drifted over his chest, dropped lower to inspect his flat stomach, the dark brush of hair and his thick shaft, moved over the strong columns of his thighs. "I'm not actually certain where I am or how I got here. Isn't that strange?"

She sounded lost. Vulnerable. His belly did that strange somersault he was beginning to associate with her. "Never mind." Rio wiped her face with the cool damp cloth. "You're safe with me and that's all that matters. I don't care if you want to stare at me. I suppose it's flattering to have a woman like you admiring me."

"What kind of woman am I?"

"A sick one." He peeled back the cover, wishing he hadn't fed the fire in the fireplace, not even for hot water needed to cleanse her wounds. For both their sakes he needed to cool the room down. "I'm going to open the door for a few minutes. The wind should help. Don't move."

"I wasn't planning on it. I feel odd, sort of heavy, like I can't move."

Rio ignored her comment, opening the door to allow the wind to clear the room of the smell of blood and infection. Of flowers. Of the scent of a woman. The cool air rushed through the room, whipped at the blankets covering the windows, tugged at Rachael's hair. In the soft glow of the lantern, he could see that her face was flushed, her body too hot.

"Rachael," Rio said her name softly, hoping to bring her partially back so she understood what was happening to her. "I'm going to open your shirt. I'm not making a pass at you, I'm just trying to cool your body down."

"You look so worried."

"I am worried. You're very sick. I don't have a lot of medicine with me. I have a small knowledge of herbs, but I'm not nearly as good as the local medicine man from the tribe." He sat in the chair and leaned over her, his fingers brushing soft skin as he slipped the buttons from the holes to open her shirt. Her full breasts beckoned to him, the call much stronger than he had anticipated. Touching her felt familiar and right. Rio dipped the cloth in the water and bathed her skin, trying to be impersonal when nothing about touching her seemed impersonal.

"My leg hurts." Rachael tried to reach down to feel the wound, but Rio caught her hand.

"That won't help, try to think of something else." He needed to think of something else. The cold water turned her nipples into hard, inviting peaks. "Tell me what you're doing here."

Her eyes widened. "Don't I live here?" She looked around her, her gaze moving over the room and back to him. "Didn't we move here? I thought you wanted to live someplace where we could be alone and stay naked all day long together."

Her words struck a chord deep in his memory. A vision of another time and place. Rain falling softly against the roof. A breeze ruffling the curtains at an open window. Rachael turning over in an ornately carved bed, her dark, chocolate eyes filled with love. With that same honest admiration. Soft laughter played like a movie in his head. Her voice. Soft and sultry and sinfully tempting.

Emotion choked him. He didn't know what he felt, only that it was all-encompassing. "Did I say that?" The cloth moved over the swell of her breast, lingered in the valley and slipped along the soft underside. "I surprise myself sometimes. It sounds like a very good idea."

"When I look at you, there's a light surrounding you." Her expression was mischievous, teasing. "I'd say a halo, but certain parts of your anatomy seem to be keeping you from sainthood."

"Or elevating me to that status." He had no idea where the words came from, or that teasing, familiar tone. He was always gruff and surly with strangers, yet Rachael didn't feel like a stranger to him. He dipped the cloth in the bowl of water and allowed it to trace the soft swell of her breast. Even that felt familiar to him. He knew her body intimately. He knew there would be a small birthmark right above her buttocks on the left side if he turned her over. He knew the feel of dipping his tongue into her enticing belly button and making a slow foray lower. He knew exactly what she would taste like. It was in his mouth, a honeyed spicy tang that always left him craving more.

"Do you know me, Rachael?" He leaned close, his gaze capturing hers. "When you look at me, do you know me?"

She flung out her hand so that her fingertips rested intimately on his bare thigh. "Why do you ask me that? Of course I know you. I love just lying in bed with you, your arms around me, listening to the rain. Listening to the sound of your voice and the stories you tell." Her smile was far away, dreamy. "It's always been my favorite thing to do."

She was burning up with fever. Her body was so hot to his touch he was afraid the cloth was going to burst into flames. He bathed her wrists and the back of her neck, beginning to feel desperate. The wind cooled the room but her body was flushed a bright red. Her leg was a mess, swollen and infected, blood oozing from the wound. His stomach lurched.

"Rachael." He said her name in despair. Her palm was burning a hole through his skin where it rested.

"You're afraid for me."

"Yes," he answered honestly. Because he was. For both of them. He was as confused as she was. Abruptly he rose and prowled across the room to stand in the open door. The wind was dying down, a lull before the next wave hit. He was moody and restless and uncomfortable in his own home. The forest beckoned, the treetops swaying, leaves nearly silver as they rustled all around him with their own strange melody. He found the sound soothing in the midst of his uncertainty.

Rio knew Rachael intimately, yet he'd never laid eyes on her. Certain things were familiar, more than familiar, nearly a part of him, like breathing. He pushed a hand through his hair, needing the peace of the jungle.

Rachael's gaze followed him wherever he went. "Look." He didn't turn around, didn't want to meet the blatant appreciation in her gaze when she looked at him. He didn't like the fact that the heat between them was a tangible thing when she was so obviously ill.

"I am looking." She sounded amused and for some reason, his stomach did that idiotic flipping thing he knew to associate with her.

"Go to sleep, Rachael," he ordered sternly. " I'm going to try the radio again, see if I can get you some help. I may be able to pack you out of here to an open area where we can bring in a chopper to take you to the hospital."

Rachael frowned, shook her head in obvious alarm. "No, don't do that. I'll stay here with you."

"You don't understand. You could lose your leg. I don't have the proper medicine or the skill you need. As it is, you're going to have a mass of scars—and that's if I manage to save it."

She continued to shake her head, her bright eyes pleading

with him silently. His gut tightened. Abruptly, he stepped outside into the night, dragging air into his lungs. She was tying him up in knots. He didn't know why. Didn't understand it. Didn't like it or want it. He didn't know who she was or where she came from. He didn't need the complication or the danger.

"Damn woman," he muttered as he stretched his arms up to the driving rain. The drops fell on his hot skin, cool and tantalizing. His veins sizzled with life, thrummed with need. Even away from her, he felt her presence.

He was not wholly human, nor was he leopard. He was a separate species with characteristics of both. And he was dangerous; capable of killing, capable of great jealousy and outbursts of temper. The animal in him often dominated his thinking, a cunning, intelligent creature, but very flawed. He needed to be alone, a secretive solitary being by choice. Few things touched him in his carefully guarded world. There was something about Rachael that made him restless. Moody. Fear shimmered in him, blurred the edges of his control. "Damn woman," he repeated.

He stretched again, wanting the freedom of the change. Wanting to go out into the night and simply disappear. The wildness rose in him like a gift, spreading so that his skin itched and his claws lengthened. He felt the muscles running like steel through his body. He smelled the feral scent of the cat, reached for it, embraced it. An extraordinary means of leaving behind Rio Santana and all that he was, all that he had done. Fur rippled over his body. His muscles contorted; bones cracked as his spine became supple, flexible, as his body took the form of the leopard.

The leopard raised its head and scented the night. Inhaled the smell of the woman. It should have repulsed him, yet it drew him, just as strongly as in his human form. The cat switched the tip of its tail, padded around the verandah beneath the windows, and then leapt to a neighboring tree branch. In spite of the pouring rain, the leopard ran easily along the network of branches, a highway above the forest floor. The wind ruffled his fur and blew in his face but it couldn't rid him of the woman's enticing scent. Every step he took away from her brought uneasiness.

The leopard gave a soft grunting cough of protest, followed it with a sawing roar of temper. She would not leave him alone. Everywhere he went, she went with him. In his mind. In his churning belly. In his groin. He raked claws along a tree trunk, ripping the bark in a fit of foul temper, shredding it into long strips. She clung to him, would not let him go. The rain should have cooled his hot blood, but it did not nothing but fan the embers smoldering inside of him.

Rio should have been able to shed his human concerns and escape into the mind of the animal, but he could taste her. Feel her. She was everywhere he went, everything he did, the very air around him. There was no logic to it or explanation for it. She was a total stranger, without a real name or a past, yet she somehow had consumed him. It was alarming to him. He didn't trust her, and worse, he didn't trust himself.

He made his way back to the house in silence, padding slowly along the forest floor to give himself time to think. It shouldn't matter so much that he thought about her. It was natural. He hadn't had a woman in a very long time— now one was lying in his bed. Rio told himself that had to be what it was. A simple case of lust. What the hell else could it be when he didn't even know her? Satisfied that he'd worked it all out, he leapt into the trees and returned to his house using the safer and much faster route.

RACHAEL floated somewhere between sleep and consciousness. She couldn't understand where she was. Everything looked strange, not at all like her home. Sometimes she thought she heard voices yelling at her, shouting at her, demanding things she couldn't tell them. Other times she thought she was lost in a jungle with wild animals stalking her. She tried to move, tried to drag herself out of the strange, hazy world she seemed to be locked inside of.

"Like a bubble," she said aloud. "I live in a glass house and if someone throws a rock, I'll shatter right along with the walls." She looked around, frowning, trying desperately to remember how she got to such a strange place. Her voice sounded different, far away and not at all like her.

And the pain was ripping through her with every move she made. Had she been injured? Tortured? Someone was trying to kill her. Why hadn't they just finished the job instead of leaving her half alive? She had always known it was going to happen sooner or later.

Something moved outside the window. The woven blanket covered the glass, but she knew something heavy passed by. Straining to hear, she looked wildly around for a weapon. Had they finally come for her? Her heart began to pound with alarming force and her mouth felt like cotton wool. A lethargic apathy had seized her body. She could hear the crackling of the fire, the steady rhythm of the rain. Thirst was overpowering, making it necessary to get up, but it was difficult, as though wading through quicksand. Attempting to sit up sent jagged pains racing up her leg. She found herself on the floor, her leg buckling beneath her.

Surprised, Rachael looked around the room, trying to remember where she was and how she got there, trying to bring the room into focus. What was wrong with her? No matter how hard she tried, her mind refused to function properly. The lamp was burning brightly. She didn't remember lighting it. Her gaze shifted to the door. The bar was no longer across it.

Rachael swallowed, the tight knot of fear blocking her throat, and reluctantly looked down to inspect her useless leg. Her calf and ankle were unrecognizable, swollen almost to the point of bursting. Bright red blood seeped and oozed, making her stomach lurch. She'd been attacked by a wild animal. She clearly remembered the eyes. The cunning intelligence, the piercing danger. Terror welled up, nearly paralyzing her. It was only then, as she looked around the room, that she saw the two leopards curled up near the fireplace. One was watching her with a steady stare. The other appeared to be asleep.

She began to drag herself across the floor. It was purely instinctive, driven by fear. Rachael couldn't focus her mind enough to know what was happening. It terrified her to remember the hot breath in her face. The feel of needle-sharp teeth tearing into her leg. The eyes staring at her with deadly intent.

She clawed her way up the wall, gritting her teeth against the sobs bursting from her throat, sweat blurring her vision. Tugging the gun from the leather, she leaned against the wall, the only thing holding her up. Her arms felt leaden and it was nearly impossible to aim the gun at the leopard, she could barely see it.

The door swung open as Rio stepped inside, arms filled with wood, his eyes immediately riveting to hers. His hair hung in wet strands, his naked body covered in droplets. Unhurriedly he closed the door with his foot and crossed the room to put the wood down carefully, almost directly in front of the leopards. "Put the gun down, Rachael." His voice was very low, but it carried a hard authority. "It has a hair trigger. You breathe and it could go off."

"They're right behind you," Rachael answered, clutching the wall for support. "Don't you see them? You're in terrible danger." She tried to remember who he was, someone very familiar to her. Her beautiful naked man. She remembered the feel of his skin beneath her fingertips. "Hurry, get away from them before they attack you." She inspected his body, saw the bloody streaks on his belly, his hip. The gash on his temple. "You're hurt."

"I'm fine, Rachael." He kept his voice calm, soothing. "Give me the gun."

"It's hot in here." All at once she sounded like a forlorn child. "Isn't it hot?" She wiped the sweat from her face with the back of her hand to clear her vision.

Rio watched her through narrowed eyes, silently cursed as the gun swept close to her face. The blood on her leg was too bright, suggesting the need for immediate action. The muzzle of the gun wavered, far too close to her temple. She swayed slightly. He moved, casually maneuvering into a better striking position. "It's all right, Rachael." Deliberately he used her name, his voice soothing, persuasive. He gained another step. "They're just pets. Clouded leopards. Small cats, really."

Her eyes were overbright. She frowned at him. She kept wiping her eyes in an attempt to get rid of the blurring. "Look what they did to my leg. Come away from there and don't turn your back on them."

He moved with unexpected speed, slapping the gun away when it swung in his direction, his body slamming into hers, shielding her protectively as a deafening explosion reverberated in the small cabin. His body pressed hard against hers, her soft breasts pushing into his chest, her face against his shoulder. Her legs went out from under her and she began to slide to the floor.

Rio swung her up into his arms, cradling her close to his chest. She was burning up with fever. "Everything's okay," he soothed, trying to ignore the ominous thud of the bullet striking metal and what it meant to them. "Don't struggle Rachael, you're safe."

She moved against his wet skin restlessly, the pain making her feel ill. His skin was so cool in comparison to hers she wanted to press herself closer. "Do I know you? How do I know you?" She frowned up at him, squinted through her spiky lashes to peer at his face. She made an effort to lift her hand, to trace the strong line of his jaw, his cheekbones, his mouth.

With great care, Rio laid her on the bed, trying not to jar her. He framed her face with his hands, forcing her to stay focused on him. "Can you understand me? Do you know what I'm saying to you?"

"Well of course I can." For a moment her eyes cleared

and she smiled at him. It wasn't sexy, it was more angelic, and he felt it all the way to his toes. "In case you haven't noticed, you're not wearing clothes." Rachael sank back against the pillow. "Turn off the light please Elijah, I'm really tired."

There was a small silence. Something deep inside him began to burn. Something dark and dangerous. Rio reached for her left hand, his thumb sliding over her ring finger to find it bare. He brought her fingers up to insure there wasn't a tan line proclaiming she'd recently removed a ring. He had no idea why relief swept through him, but it did. "Rachael, try to follow what I'm telling you. It's important." He carried her hand to his chest, without realizing he did it, holding it there over his pounding heart. "I need to lance the wound, cauterize it. I'm sorry, but it's the only way to save your leg. I think the bullet hit the radio, but even if it didn't, I can't raise anyone in this weather. The second wave of the storm is hitting now and there were three strong weather fronts coming back to back."

Rachael continued to smile at him. "I don't know why you're looking so worried. They haven't found us and I don't think they can."

Rio closed his eyes briefly, fighting for air. He wished her smile were for him, not some unknown man named Elijah. This was going to be hell, and she was so doped up he couldn't prepare her for what was to come. He had performed the procedure once before and even then it had been unpleasant. He pushed back the hair from her forehead. She was looking at him with far too much trust. "I'm just going to do what has to be done. I'm apologizing ahead of time."

She could see the reluctance and distaste in his eyes. "It's all right, Rio, I understand. I do. It had to happen sooner or later. I'm sorry he asked you to take care of it. I can see it bothers you."

"Take care of what?" he prompted. She was reassuring him, trying to make his job easier.

"I know Elijah wants me dead. I know he sent you. You look so tired and sad. It was wrong of him to ask you."

Rio swore softly, hunkering down beside her. Her eyes were glazed, dreamy even, but they carried intelligence. She believed he was there to kill her, yet she looked at him as if she felt sorry for him. "Why does Elijah want you dead?"

She blinked, her breath catching in her throat on a wave of pain. "Does it matter? Just get it over with."

"You're just going to let me kill you?" For some reason her apathy made him furious. She was going to lie there and encourage him to take her life? He wanted to shake her.

That same little smile tugged at her mouth. She seemed far away again, slowly turning her head away from him. "Even if you handed me a very large stick I wouldn't be able to lift it. I'll have to pass on being that take-forty-seven-kicks-in-the-ribs-and-keep-on-going heroine. I don't think I can lift my head."

He leaned closer. "Rachael? You're with me again." She sounded like the woman who had bashed him in the head.

"Was I gone?" She closed her eyes. "I wish I hadn't come back. What's wrong with me? Where did I go?"

"You've been rambling. I have no choice, I have to work on your leg."

"Then get to it. You're so tired you're going to fall on your face if you don't get it done." She made an effort to lift her lashes and study his face beneath heavy lids. "I'm not going to blame you if it hurts." Her eyes were clear and in that moment lucid. "I don't want to lose my leg, so by all means, do whatever is necessary to save it."

Rio wasn't going to talk about it any longer. Distaste for the ugly task glimmered in his eyes as he bent over her leg. The wound had to be lanced, thoroughly washed, cauterized and packed with more antibiotics. He had performed the surgery once out in the field when a friend had been shot and was bleeding profusely and the chopper couldn't pick them up immediately. Small beads of sweat dotted his body, then ran into his eyes to blur his vision as he placed the blade of his knife in the flames.

Opening the wound to allow the infection to run out set his stomach churning. She screamed when he poured the burning antiseptic, nearly coming up off the bed. He hesitated only a moment, leaning his weight across her thighs, and taking a deep breath laid the blade of the knife against her flesh. The odor was sickening. He didn't hurry, not wanting to make any mistakes, careful to cleanse and repair, before splinting her leg to hold it immobile in order to give it a better chance to heal.

He couldn't look at her as he cleaned the bedding and packed blankets around her leg to hold her still. She hadn't moved in a long time, her breathing shallow, her skin clammy. Definitely in shock, Rachael was trembling in reaction. Rio cursed softly. He eased down beside her, stretching out along the bed, drawing her close to him, unable to think of anything else to do.

"Rio?" Rachael didn't pull away from him, instead burrowed against him like a kitten for comfort. "Thank you for trying to save my leg. I know it was difficult for you." Her voice was thin. He barely caught the words.

Rio nuzzled the top of her head with his chin, blew at strands of hair caught in the stubble of several days growth. "Try to relax, I can't give you any more painkiller for a while. Just let me hold you." His arms tightened with possession. At the same time something was squeezing his heart like a vise. "I'll tell you a story."

Her body belonged with his—fit. He curved around her, thigh to thigh, her buttocks pressed against his groin, her head tucked safely against his throat, and she just fit there as if made for him. Her breasts were full and soft and pushed into his arms comfortably. He had lain with her before. Not once, but many times. The memory of her body was etched in his brain, in his nerves and flesh and bone.

He rubbed his cheek in the mass of silky hair. It wasn't

all physical. He *felt* something for her. Came alive around her. "That's not necessarily a good thing," he said aloud. "You know that, don't you?"

Rachael closed her eyes, willing her body to stop shaking, wanting the pain to recede if only for a brief space of time to give her a moment to breathe normally. Rio was an anchor she clung to, the one bit of reality she had. When she closed her eyes, she saw men contorting, fur rippling over their bodies, eyes glowing a fierce yellow-green. In that nightmare world the sound of guns erupted and she felt the shock of a bullet. She looked into those same intelligent eyes and saw pain and madness. And she heard his voice screaming *no*. That was all. Simply *no*.

"I need to hear your voice." Because it drove demons away. It drove the scent of gunpowder and blood from her mind, and she loved the deep caressing timbre of it.

"I don't know a lot of stories, Rachael. I never had someone telling me bedtime tales." He winced at the gruffness in his voice. It was just that she turned his insides to mush and made it difficult to remember she could have been sent to kill him. He believed in logic, and the way she affected him wasn't logical.

"I'll tell you one when I feel better," she offered.

He closed his eyes. She was like a gift, handed to him. Sent to him in his unrelenting world of violence and mistrust. "All right," he conceded to please her. "But try to go to sleep. The more you sleep the faster your leg is going to heal."

Rachael was afraid to go to sleep. Afraid of teeth and claws and the all-encompassing pain. She was afraid she would lose her tenuous hold on reality. As it was, she kept forgetting who Rio was. He felt familiar. She recognized his voice, but she couldn't remember their life together. When he talked to her, she floated on the sound of his voice. When his hands slid over her hot skin, she felt safe and cherished.

Rio told her some absurd tale of monkeys and sun bears

he made up off the top of his head. It made no sense; in fact, it was fairly awful and showed he had no imagination, but she was quiet, slipping into a fitful sleep, and that was all that mattered to him. If the woman wanted storytelling on a nightly basis, he was going to have to hastily hone some nonexistent skills and learn to make up interesting tales.

He sighed, his breath stirring tendrils of her hair. What was he thinking, wanting to be able to tell her bedtime stories? He couldn't imagine such a ridiculous thing, couldn't imagine what he was yearning for. A woman of his own? Why? To share a home deep in the forest? To share a life of death and violence? He didn't know the first thing about women. He needed to get her out of his life as quickly as possible.

Rachael murmured softly in her sleep, restless, fitful. A soft protest against nightmares creeping into her sleep. Rio soothed her with some muttered nonsense, ignoring the ache she brought to his heart. Ignoring the strange memories in his head and the hardening of his muscles. Although his body was exhausted, his brain was alive with activity. Even the normal sounds of the forest didn't soothe him.

Rio lay listening to her, fear swamping him in waves at the thought of her succumbing to blood poisoning. Her skin burned against his. He bathed her with cooling water, kept the door open with the mosquito net hanging down both at the door and around the bed. The lantern was extinguished to keep the bugs from entering.

The rain persisted, a steady rhythm until the next storm hit about an hour later. It raged with enough force to blow rain through the heavy canopy. Rio slid out of bed, padded across the room to close the door. He stood for a long time staring out into the darkness, breathing in the scent of the rain, the call of the jungle. The chorus of male frogs sang off-key, joyfully hunting mates, adding to the lure of the forest. For a moment the wildness was upon him, beating in him with the need to shift, to escape. But the call of the woman was stronger. He sighed and closed the door firmly, shutting out the wind and rain. Shutting out the heady sounds of his world. He crawled back into bed, pulling the light cover over both of them, wrapping his arms around her and welding his body to hers. He was exhausted, but it took time for his body to relax, for his mind to let go. He fell asleep with a knife under his pillow and a woman in his arms.

4

THERE were nightmares. One simply ran into the next. Rachael felt she lived in a sea of pain and darkness where nothing made sense but a male voice pitched low as it murmured soothingly to her. The voice was a lifeline, pulling her from the darkness where teeth and claws savaged her body, where bullets whistled by and thudded into bodies and blood flowed and hideous creatures lay in wait to attack her.

Shadows moved in the room. The humidity was oppressive. A cat made a chuffing noise. Another answered with a gruntlike cough. The sounds were close, within a few feet of her. Every muscle in her body reacted, tightening in terror, increasing the pain in her leg. She couldn't move her body and when she turned her head, she couldn't see enough of the room to locate the source of those wild, cat sounds.

Sometimes the wind blew a cooling wave through the room and over her. Always the rain fell. A continual, steady rhythm that both soothed and irritated her. She felt trapped and claustrophobic, confined as she was to the bed.

It was humiliating to have a man see to her every need, especially when most of the time she wasn't certain who he really was. Sometimes she thought she might be insane as the nightmare images of a man shifting into the form of a leopard replayed over and over in her head. There were moments she knew the man, where she was overwhelmed with love and tenderness, and moments when she stared into a stranger's catlike, frightening gaze and her heart pounded with terror. Time passage was impossible to know. Sometimes it was daylight, other times, night, but the one thing she counted on was the voice to steer her through nightmares and help her find her way back to reality.

She stared sightlessly at the ceiling, trying not to be alarmed at the sounds of wildcats so close to her when she couldn't see them. A shadow moved again, across the window, outside on the verandah. Her heart accelerated. The floor creaked.

Rio caught movement out of the corner of his eye and turned as Rachael attempted to slip over the side of the bed. He leapt for her, his hands stilling her struggles. "What do you think you're doing?" Fear made his voice harsh.

She looked directly into his eyes, her fingers clutching at his arms. "They're here. He's sent them to kill me. I have to get out of here." She turned her head away from him to stare eerily into the corner. "They're over there."

Whatever she saw was real to her. She was so intent, it sent a chill shivering down his spine. "Look at me, Rachael." He framed her face with his hands, forced her attention back to him. "I'm not going to let anything hurt you. It's the fever. You see things because of the fever."

She blinked rapidly, her bright eyes beginning to focus on him. "I saw them."

"Saw who? Who wants to kill you?" He'd asked her a dozen times but she never answered him. She tried to turn her head away from him and remain silent. This time he had her face in his hands, holding her still, locking her gaze to his.

"You have the most beautiful eyes I've ever seen. Your eyelashes are long. Why do men always get beautiful eyelashes?"

She had a way of throwing him off balance, disturbing his tranquility. He found it so exasperating he wanted to shake her. "Do you know how stupid that sounds?" he demanded. "Look at me, woman. I have scars all over me. My nose has been broken twice. I look like a damned murderer, not some pretty boy." The minute the words left his mouth, he regretted them. *Damned murderer* hung in the air between them. His teeth snapped together and he turned his head away from her enormous eyes, swearing silently over and over.

"Rio?" Her voice was soft. "I can see the pain in your eyes. Did I do that? Did I hurt you in some way? I don't like hurting anyone, least of all you. What did I say?"

He raked his fingers through his shaggy hair. "Of course you have to be perfectly lucid right at this moment. Why is that, Rachael? Two seconds ago you were so far out of it you didn't know your own name."

He looked so tortured her heart turned over. "Did someone accuse you of murder?"

Her gaze moved over his face, examining every inch— all-seeing eyes. He was certain she could see into his soul. Fierce anger smoldered, held deep where it couldn't be seen, burst free, a raging holocaust he couldn't prevent. She should have been afraid. He was afraid. He knew what he could do with that kind of rage, but her expression was compassionate, almost loving. Her uninjured hand went to his face, fingertips trailing over his lips, sliding around his neck so that she was cradling his head, offering, what? He didn't know. Sympathy? Love? Her body? Tenderness?

He ignored his first impulse to slap her hand away from him. He couldn't take her looking at him like that. He caught her fingers instead, pulling her palm to his bare chest, over his wildly beating heart. "You don't know the first thing about me, Rachael. You shouldn't look at me like that." He didn't know what he felt, a mixture of anger and pain and ferocious longing. Damn it all, he was over that. Over wanting. Over needing.

"You don't make sense to me." His voice deepened, sounded almost ragged. "Nothing about you makes sense. Why aren't you afraid of me?"

She blinked. Those huge chocolate eyes, so dark they were nearly black, eyes a man could get lost in. "I am afraid of you."

"Now you're humoring me."

"No, really, I'm afraid of you." Her eyes widened in earnest honesty.

"Well, damn it all, why would you be afraid of me when I've taken care of you and given up my bed for you?"

"You didn't give up your bed. You still sleep in it," she pointed out.

"There isn't anywhere else to sleep," he said.

"There's the floor."

"You want me to sleep on the floor? Do you have any idea how uncomfortable the floor would be?"

"What a baby. I thought you were a he-man." She smirked at him. "Be careful of losing your bad-boy image."

"And what about insects and snakes?"

"Snakes?" She looked around her cautiously. "What kind of snakes? You have kitty cats for friends. I'm hoping you say friendly snakes."

His mouth softened but he kept from smiling with a small effort. "I haven't known too many friendly snakes."

"Where did your kitties come from? And how come they aren't trained to meet guests properly?"

"I trained them to run off the neighbors. I hate it when they drop in unannounced."

A lock of midnight black hair fell across his forehead. Without thinking, Rachael brushed it back with her fingertips. "You need someone to look after you." The moment the words were out of her mouth she was mortified. She couldn't seem to censor her tongue with him. Every random thought just popped out, no matter how personal.

"Are you applying for the job?" His voice was harsh again, emotions welling up to choke him. It was happening again, that strange time distortion. He felt her hand in his and looked down. His hand enveloped hers, the pads of his fingers rubbing back and forth over her soft skin and he knew every indentation. The very shape of her bones was familiar. There was even a memory of doing the same thing, of her teasing voice skittering down his spine like a caress.

Rachael closed her eyes, but he thought he saw the glimmer of tears before she turned her head away. "Tell me why those cats stay here all the time. They are wild, aren't they? Clouded leopards?"

Rio looked across the room to see the two cats tumbling around in a mock fight. Each weighed in at fifty pounds, so when they banged against a chair or table, they made a ruckus.

"Are they pets?"

"I don't keep pets," he said gruffly. "I found them. The mother had been killed and skinned. I backtracked her and found them. They were very young, still needing milk."

She turned her head back toward him, lifting her lashes so her gaze nearly devoured his face. The smile lighting up her pale face nearly took his breath away. "You bottle-fed them, didn't you?"

He shrugged, trying not to be affected by the way she was looking at him. There was that dazzling admiration, a look he didn't deserve. No one ever looked at him, saw him, in the same way she did. It was disconcerting, yet gave him a rush. He spent a great deal of time trying not to allow his body to react, or his heart. He dropped her hand as if it burned him, stepping away from the bed quickly.

She laughed at him, a soft inviting sound that felt like fingers playing over his skin. He was beginning to feel desperate. She lay in his bed, her body lush and tempting, her silky hair spilling around her head like a halo. He wished it were just the allure of her body. That would at least make sense to him. He hadn't been with a woman in a long time. Womanly curves, soft flesh, heat and the fragrance of the forest were a heady combination and he could be excused for his body's fierce reaction to her. But it was far more than that. Knowledge of her body. Memories of her laughter. Whispers in the night, a secret world they shared. His mind and heart reacted to her. And damn it, if he were a man who believed in such nonsense, he would think his soul recognized hers.

"Didn't you?" Rachael persisted. "You found some baby kittens and you brought them home and bottle-fed them."

"I don't believe in skinning animals," he said tersely.

She watched the dull red creep up his neck into his face. The man wasn't in the least embarrassed about traipsing around in the nude but he turned red admitting to an act of kindness. She found that blush endearing. "Why are you always running around with no clothes on? Did I stumble into a secret nudist colony? Or do you think I enjoy staring at you in the buff?"

"You do enjoy staring at me." Rio smiled in spite of himself. She was very open about her appreciation of his body.

Rachael answered him with her usual candor. "Well, I'll admit you're beautiful to look at, but it's beginning to make me uncomfortable. Why do you do it?"

His eyebrow shot up. "It makes it so much easier to shift into leopard form and go running in the forest."

She made a face at him. "Ha ha, are you always this funny? I suppose you're never going to let me live that down. I think it's perfectly logical to have nightmares over men turning into vicious leopards after what happened."

"Vicious leopards?" He rummaged through a small wooden closet and came out with a pair of jeans. "Leopards aren't vicious. They might be natural predators, but they aren't vicious."

"Thanks for making that distinction. I had no idea there was a difference. It felt the same when they were chewing my leg off."

"That was my fault. I was focused on the idea of someone waiting to kill me."

"Why would someone want to kill you?"

He laughed softly. "Now don't you think it seems more logical for someone to want to kill a man like me than a woman like you?"

She wanted to look away from him, but she was fascinated by the play of his muscles beneath his skin. Her breath caught in her throat as she watched him step into the jeans and casually pull them up the strong column of his thighs and over his narrow hips. He carelessly buttoned a couple of buttons and left the rest undone as if it were too much of a bother.

She moistened her suddenly dry lips with the tip of her tongue before she could speak. "Rio, this is your home. I'm the intruder. If you're more comfortable without clothes, I can live with it." It touched her that he would cover up for her—and part of her didn't want him clothed. There was something primitive and sensual about the way he padded so silently through the small tree house, barefoot, in the nude.

"I don't mind, Rachael. You're stuck in bed and I know you hurt like hell. I appreciate that you don't complain." He let a heartbeat slip by. Two. "Much."

"Much!" She glared at him. "I haven't said one word about shooting your precious little kittens when I get off this bed. But I'm considering it. You spoil them rotten, by the way, and it shreds your image of a tough guy all to pieces."

The cats, in the midst of the rough-and-tumble game, slammed into the edge of the bed and all of Rachael's hard-earned bravado disappeared completely. She gasped with alarm and lunged sideways away from them. Rio, standing beside the small closet, covered the distance between them with one leap, pinning her down, his green eyes suddenly a blazing yellow-gold. His face was inches from hers. Rachael stared up at him, clutching the blanket to her bare breasts, looking frightened, trying to look brave, tempting him almost beyond his endurance.

He gathered her into his arms, careful to keep her leg from moving. "You have to keep it in your mind at all times that you cannot move. I've just about run out of antibiotics and that leg can't open up again. Give it a couple more days."

Rachael was all too aware of his naked chest pressed against her breasts, of his hands sliding up and down her back in a soothing motion. Most of all she was aware of the distance he had covered in a single leap. An impossible distance. She tilted her head to look up at him, really examine his features. He had scars, yes. His nose had been broken more than once, but she found him the most compelling man she'd ever met. His eyes were different. More like a cat's.

"You're doing it again." He lifted his chin, breaking eye contact, to rub his jaw along the top of her head. "I can see the fear on your face. Rachael, if I were going to harm you, wouldn't I have done it already?" There was exasperation in his voice.

Rachael winced at his logic. "The cats make me nervous, that's all."

His fingers went to the nape of her neck in a slow massage. "After what you went through, I don't blame you, but they won't attack you. Let me introduce them to you. That would help."

"Before you do, would you mind finding me a shirt to put on? I think I'd feel less vulnerable." And it might keep her body from reacting to his, her breasts aching with longing for his touch. Her leg was a mess, painful and swollen, fever raging, but she still seemed unable to prevent her strange attraction to him. "If your rabid pets decide to have me for dinner the least they can do is work for it by chewing through clothes." His muscles felt like steel rippling beneath very human skin. "How did you do that? How did you get across the room in one leap?" If she were losing her mind, it was better to find out immediately. "I didn't imagine it and it isn't the fever."

"No, your fever's down a bit," he conceded as he helped her ease into a fully prone position. "I live in the forest and have most of my life. I run up and down the branches and jump from one to the other all the time. I climb trees and swim rivers. It's a way of life."

She let her breath out slowly, grateful for the explanation, not wanting to examine the distance too closely. Maybe it could be done. With practice. Lots of practice. She watched him turn away from her to walk across the room back to the closet and she carefully avoided counting each step he took. He padded on bare feet, silent, not making a sound. Rachael watched him stretch, a slow, languid, sinuous catlike stretch. He stretched his hands, fingers spread wide, over his head and ran his hands down the wall. He arched his back to deepen the stretch. His fingertips traced the deep claw marks, something he'd obviously done so many times the crevices were smooth. It was a natural, uninhibited movement.

Rachael's heart slammed in her chest. Were the clouded leopards tall enough to have made those claw marks? She didn't think so. It would take a cat much larger to reach as high as the deep ruts. "How did those marks get inside the house?"

Rio dropped his arms to his sides. "It's a bad habit. I like to stretch and keep in shape." He caught up a shirt, smelled it and turned with a mischievous grin. "This one isn't too bad." He held the blue shirt up for her inspection. "What do you think?"

"Looks good to me." She started to struggle into a sitting position.

"Just wait for me." He slipped the sleeve very carefully over the makeshift splint on her wrist. "You're in such a hurry." He helped her sit, enfolding her in the shirt, his knuckles brushing soft flesh as he buttoned her into it. There was something satisfying about wrapping her in his favorite shirt, and he felt as if he'd done it a hundred times. "I think your temperature is beginning to climb again, damn it."

She pressed her fingertip over his mouth. "You swear too much."

"I do?" His eyebrow shot up. "I thought I was being very careful around you. The cats don't mind." He snapped his fingers and the two clouded leopards rushed to his side and pressed against his thigh.

Rachael forced herself to remain absolutely still. Her insides turned to jelly, but long ago she had learned the benefits of appearing composed in the face of adversity, so she kept a small smile on her face and serenity in her expression. The rain beat a steady tattoo on the roof. She was very aware of the hum of insects and the rustle of leaves and branches against the side of the house. She swallowed the little knot of fear blocking her throat and inhaled Rio's masculine scent. He smelled of danger and outdoors. "I'm certain the cats don't care, they probably have already picked up your bad habits."

Rio leaned close to her as if sensing her fear, although he rubbed the ears of the cats pressing against his legs. She could see his temple where she'd struck him, a jagged line, already healing, but looking as if it should have had stitches. Before she could stop herself, she touched it. "That's going to scar, Rio. I'm so sorry. You were so busy taking care of me, you didn't really have time to take care of yourself." She was ashamed of herself for hitting him. The details of the attack had faded in comparison to the nightmare images of men turning into leopards.

"Are you going to keep finding reasons not to touch the leopards?" He took her hand. "This one is Fritz. His ear has a little chunk missing and his spots are in a pattern much like a map." He stroked her palm over the animal's neck and back. Her skin was burning again, dry and hot to his touch. Her eyes were glazing, taking on the overbright look he had become accustomed to seeing.

Rachael made a supreme effort to keep from trembling. "Hello Fritz. If you were the one chewing off my leg the other night, please refrain from ever doing so again."

The hard line of Rio's mouth softened. "Nice greeting. I'm certain he'll remember that. This one is Franz. He has a sweet disposition most of the time, until Fritz gets a little rough with him, then he has a bit of a temper. They disappear for days on end, but most of the time they stay with me. I leave it up to them whether they want to stay or go." He pressed her hand into the cat's fur.

Rachael couldn't help the small thrill that went through her at the thought of touching such a wild, elusive creature as a clouded leopard. "Hi, Franz. Don't you know you're supposed to be afraid of humans?" She frowned. "Haven't you considered that by making them pets, you've made them more vulnerable to poachers who want their fur?"

"They aren't exactly tame, Rachael. The only reason they accept you is because my scent is all over you. We sleep together. That's why I'm reinforcing their relationship with you, so no more mistakes. They hide from humans."

"We aren't sleeping together," she objected sharply. "And I don't have a relationship with them and I can't imagine ever having one. Has it occurred to you that you're not exactly normal? This isn't the way most people prefer to live."

Rio looked around his home. "I like it."

She sighed. "I didn't mean to imply it wasn't nice." She moved again, shifting into another position in the hopes of easing the throbbing pain in her leg.

He swept her hair back from the nape of her neck. It was damp with sweat. Rachael was becoming edgy and restless, shifting her position continually in an effort to ease her discomfort. "Rachael, just relax. I'll fix a cool drink for you."

She bit her tongue as he stood up with his casual grace. He didn't mean everything to sound like an order—she was hypersensitive. Rachael tried to push at the heavy fall of hair to get it off her forehead. It was curling in every direction as it always did in high humidity. As she lay there, she swore the walls began to creep inward, boxing her in, pushing the air from the room. Everything annoyed her, from the sound of the relentless rain to the playful leopards. If she had a slipper handy she might have thrown it in a fit of petulance.

Her gaze strayed to Rio as it always did. It exasperated her that she couldn't control herself enough to stop staring at him, and that she knew exactly what he was going to do before he did it. She knew the way he moved, the graceful flow of his body as he reached into the icebox. She knew him. If she closed her eyes he would be there in her mind, talking softly to her, reaching out absently to push the hair from her face, curling his fingers around the nape of her neck.

Why did she associate every single movement, every gesture, with that of a cat? Especially his eyes. They were dilated the way a cat's eyes would be at night and yet in the daylight, the pupils were nearly invisible.

"Okay, there's no way you turned into a leopard." Rachael stared up at the ceiling and tried to work the problem out in her mind. She had to stop fantasizing about him leaping through the treetops with his little cat friends. It was idiotic and just proved she really was pushing the edges of sanity.

"What are you going on about now?" Rio stirred the contents of the glass with a long-handled spoon. "Half the time you don't make much sense."

"I'm not responsible for what I say when I'm running a fever." Rachael winced a little at her tone. She sounded snippy. She was tired. And tired of being tired. Tired of feeling out of sorts and grumpy and sick of trying to figure out what was real and what had taken place in her fevered imagination.

"You could try not saying anything," he suggested.

Rachael winced again. She always talked too much when she was nervous. "I suppose you're right. I could be a stone-faced mute staring at the walls the way you do. We'd probably get along better." Most of all she was ashamed for sniping at him, but it was that or start screaming.

His gaze shifted to her face. She was very flushed, her fingers plucking at the thin blanket with restless pinches. Each time he looked at her, he felt that strange shifting deep inside his body where a part of him still felt emotions. "We get along," he said gruffly. "It isn't you. I'm not used to having people around."

Rachael sighed. "I'm sorry." Why did he have to be so blasted nice when she wanted a rip-roaring fight? It would have been nice to take her frustration out on him and pretend justification. She heaved a long-suffering sigh. "I'm feeling sorry for myself, that's all. I honestly don't know what's going on half the time. It makes me feel stupid." And helpless. She felt so helpless she wanted to scream. She did not want to be trapped in a house with a total stranger who looked every bit as dangerous as he obviously was. "You are a stranger to me, aren't you?" She could feel the heat of his gaze right down to her toes. Why didn't he feel like a stranger? When he touched her, why was it so familiar to her?

His eyebrow shot up. "You're in my bed. I've been taking care of you night and day for a couple of days. You'd better hope I'm not a stranger."

Rachael thumped her head against the pillow in sheer frustration. "See what you do? What kind of answer is that? Did you grow up in a monastery where they taught you to speak in riddles? Because if that's what you're trying to do, believe me it sounds more annoying and idiotic than mysterious and prophetic." She blew upward at her bangs. "My hair is driving me crazy, do you have scissors?"

"Why is it you're always asking me for sharp instruments?"

She burst out laughing. The sound filled the room and

startled several birds perched on the railing of the verandah. They took flight with a noisy flutter of wings and a
scolding trill. "I feel like I have to apologize to you every
other sentence. I broke into your home, used your shower,
slept in your bed, bashed you in the head and forced you to
take care of me while I'm all out of it and grumpy. Now
I'm threatening you with sharp instruments."

"Threatening to cut your hair might hurt as much." He
moved across the distance separating them and bent down
to look into her eyes, his fingers curling in her hair. "No
one can force me to do anything I don't want to do." The
one exception might be the intriguing woman lying in his
bed, but he wasn't going to admit that to her . . . or to himself. "Your hair is short enough. You don't need to cut more
off." He rubbed the ragged edges of her hair between the
pads of her fingers.

"It used to be much longer. But it's so thick, with the
humidity it's very hot."

"I'll find something to put it up and get it off your neck."

"Don't bother, Rio, I'm just edgy." His kindness made
her ashamed.

"I found wet clothes smelling of river water that night.
Were you in the river?"

She nodded, making every effort to rally. "Bandits
attacked us. They came out of the jungle shooting guns. I
think Simon was hit. I went overboard and the river swept
me away."

His muscles clenched in reaction. "You could have been
killed."

"I was lucky. My shirt snagged on a branch below the
waterline and I managed to crawl onto a fallen tree. I made
my way here. The house was a surprise. I almost didn't see it
but the wind was blowing so hard, it took away some of the
cover. I was afraid I wouldn't find it again if I went explor-
ing so I tied a rope between two trees to show me the way. I
thought it was a native's hut, one they use when they travel
from place to place."

"And I thought you were a bandit who had circled around and managed to get in front of me and was lying in wait. I should have known better, but I was exhausted and I hurt like hell. Who is Simon?" He had waited an appropriate amount of time. Carried on a conversation like a rational human being. He could feel the intensity of his suppressed emotions eating away at his gut. He knew better than to let her inside. He knew better, but she was already there. He didn't know how it happened and worse, he didn't know how to get her out.

"Simon is one of the men in our church medical relief group."

"So he's a stranger. None of you knew one another before this trip." The relief sweeping through him irritated the hell out of him.

She nodded. "We all volunteered from various parts of the country and came together to bring the supplies."

"Who was your guide?"

"Kim Pang. He seemed very nice and I thought him very competent."

Her hand was on his thigh where he hunkered down close to the bed and she felt him stiffen. His eyes glittered with sudden menace, sending a chill through her body. "Did you see what happened to him?"

She shook her head. "The last I saw of him, he was trying frantically to cut the rope to allow the launch to get away. Is he a friend of yours?" She wanted Kim Pang to be safe. She wanted all of the others to be safe, but it would be dangerous if the guide and Rio were friends.

"Yes, I know Kim. He's a very good man." He wiped his hand over his face. "I have to go out and see if any of them are still alive, see if I can pick up any tracks."

"In this weather? And it's getting dark now. It isn't safe, Rio. They were taken on the other side of the river." She would have to leave immediately. Rachael detested how selfish it made her feel. Of course Rio needed to help the others if he could, although she didn't see how he could accomplish anything against a group of armed bandits.

In a sudden fit of temper at herself, or the situation, she flung off the thin cover. "I need to get out of this bed, this room, before I go completely mad."

"Slow down, lady." Rio caught at her, preventing movement. "Just sit still and let me see what I can do." There was a flicker of knowledge in his eyes, as if he could read her mind and knew her selfish thoughts.

Rachael watched Rio stalk outside and disappear from sight. She could hear him making noise on the verandah, unusual when he was usually so silent. The wind helped to dispel the oppressive heat and claustrophobia, but she wanted to cry, stuck in the bed, unable to get across the small distance to the open doorway. The mosquito net fluttered in the breeze. As always, Rio hadn't lit the light; he seemed to be able to see in the dark and preferred it.

The thought triggered a long-forgotten memory. Laughter, soft and contagious, the two of them whispering together in the rain. Rio swinging her into his arms and spinning in a circle while drops fell on her upturned face. Her breath caught in her throat. It never happened. She would know if she had been with him. Rio was not a man a woman would ever forget or want to give up.

"Come on, I'm going to take you outside. It's raining, but the roof over the verandah has no leaks so you can sit in the open for a while. I know what it's like to feel caged. Let me do the work," he said. He slipped his arms under her legs. "Put your arms around my neck."

"I weigh a lot," she cautioned, obediently linking her fingers behind his neck. Joy was blossoming inside her, a deep glowing warmth bubbling over at the prospect of getting out of the bed, and of looking at open sky.

"I think I can manage," he said dryly. "Be prepared when I lift you, it's going to hurt."

It did, so much so that she buried her face against the warmth of his neck, choking off a startled cry. Pain radiated up her leg, hit the pit of her stomach and exploded

throughout her body. Her fingernails dug into his skin and
she bit down hard on her thumb.

"I'm sorry, Rachael, I know it hurts," he said softly.

He moved smoothly, almost gliding so there was no jarring to her swollen leg. As he stepped through the door, the
natural hum of the forest greeted her. Insects and frogs, the
chatter of animals, the flutter of wings and the constant
sound of the rain all blended together.

Rio had pulled a soft, overstuffed chair outside, his one
prized possession. He placed her carefully in it, propping
her leg on a pillow on a kitchen chair. Rachael leaned her
head back and took in the high feathery canopy through the
fine mosquito netting. The entire verandah was enclosed.
The railings were made from tree branches, gnarled and
polished, blending in with the surrounding trees so that she
couldn't tell where the forest began and the railings left off.

Rio sank onto the chair beside her, holding out the glass
of cool liquid. "Drink this, Rachael, it might help to cool
you down. In another hour or so, I can give you more meds
to help bring down your fever."

She was sweating from the pain more than the fever, but
she didn't want to tell him that, not after he'd gone to such
trouble. The wind was cooler on her face, tugging at the
wild curls in her hopeless mass of hair. She ran her fingers
through it before taking the glass from him. Her hand was
trembling enough that some of the cool liquid splashed
over the rim of the glass. "Rio, tell me the truth." She
stared carefully out into the tree trunks and limbs heavily
laden with wild orchids of every color. "Am I going to lose
my leg?" Everything in her was still, waiting for his
answer, telling herself she could handle the truth. "I'd
much rather know now."

Rio shook his head. "I can't make promises, Rachael,
but the swelling is less. Your fever comes and goes instead
of raging all the time. There aren't any more streaks going
up your leg so I think we've avoided blood poisoning. As
soon as we can, I'll get you to a medic and have them

take a look at it. The river goes down fairly quickly."

"I can't go to a doctor," she admitted reluctantly. "No one can know I'm still alive. If they find out, I'm dead anyway."

He watched her lips touch the glass, the contents of the glass tilt, her throat work as she swallowed. He stretched his legs out in front of him, sprawling out as if totally relaxed when he was anything but. "Who wants you dead, Rachael?"

"It isn't really pertinent, is it? I had the presence of mind to shed my shoes in the water. They might be found when they look for me. And believe me, they'll look. They'll hire the best trackers they can find."

"Then they'll come looking for me. Tracking is what I do when I'm not rousting bandits."

Rachael swallowed the sudden fear welling up. "Great. It isn't like I can run from you either. They'll offer you a lot of money to turn me over to them." She shrugged, trying to be casual when she wanted to throw herself off the verandah and run. "Or maybe they'll just ask you to kill me for them. Less trouble that way."

His hand settled on her head. "Lucky for you, I'm not particularly interested in getting rich. I don't need a lot of money living here. The fruit's plentiful and I can easily hunt and trade for the things I need." He rubbed strands of her wavy hair between the pads of his fingers. "I think I have a lazy streak." He grinned at her. "Besides, you swing a mean stick. I don't think I want to mess with you."

"When they ask you, are you going to tell them where I am?"

"Why would I do that when I can keep you all to myself?"

Rachael tipped the rest of the juice down her throat. It was cooling and sweet. She rested her head on Rio's shoulder and allowed herself to relax. The night was incredibly beautiful with so many different types of foliage and trees bowing gently in the wind. The rain played a melody in the background, almost soothing now that she was outside with the breeze blowing. She could see movement in the branches as gliders flitted from one tree to another.

"Are you going to let me guess, or are you just going to keep me in suspense? Why would someone be so intent on killing you?"

5

YOU know how to wreck a perfectly good evening, don't you?" Rachael didn't lift her head from the comfort of his shoulder, but stared out into the forest. Shadows moved from canopy to floor. A symphony of music made up of every kind of rustle, croak and insect sound accompanied the wind. "I always thought it would be quiet. The edges of the forest are so active, around the swamps. Fish jumping, and insects always busy, but for some reason I thought when I reached the interior it would be peaceful."

"Think of it as songs of the forest. I've always loved the way the insects and birds sound against the leaves in the wind. It's all music if you love it, Rachael."

"I suppose it is. Why can't people just leave us alone, Rio? Yes, I ran away. Does it really matter so much why I ran? Who I ran away from? What difference does it make all the way out here, in the middle of a forest?"

Rio tried not to hear the wistful note in her voice. More, tried not to react to it. "It's perfectly reasonable of me to want and need to know why someone would want to kill you. Do you have a husband you ran away from? Someone rich and powerful enough to track you even here? Why wouldn't he just let you go?" He felt her beside him, fitting into the lines of his body. Heard her breathing softly. Her skin was hot, but soft and inviting. Even more than the physical temptation was her courage and sense of humor. She was occupying his thoughts, invading his blood. Rio reached over her to pull her broken wrist across her lap, positioning it for maximum comfort. "I guess that was a silly question. I might not have let you go myself."

Rachael lifted her head to look at him. A faint smile curved her mouth. "Rio, that was a nice thing to say to me. Thank you."

He looked harassed instead of grateful for her appreciation. "You have to tell me why, Rachael. If someone is going to come looking, I have to be prepared."

"There is no way to prepare. As soon as I'm able, I'll keep going. There has to be a place where they can't find me. I'm hoping they believe I'm dead."

"If Kim is alive, he'll know you survived. He's one of the best trackers around. And he'll go looking for you because you were in his care. The government is going to be up in arms, having a church group bringing medical supplies taken by bandits. They'll be looking for the entire group. The countries need the aid and the last thing they want is for it to get out that it's dangerous to travel along the rivers or near the forest, two major tourist draws. And if you have someone else, an outside source, pushing the government to go after the bandits, they'll search the river thoroughly."

"People drown all the time and their bodies are never found. Is Kim Pang a friend of yours? If he comes looking could you persuade him to say I drowned?"

"Kim won't lie. If he's still alive, and as soon as possible I'm going to find out, I'll ask him to disappear so he can't be questioned. He has a certain reputation, well deserved. He shouldn't lose it over this."

Rachael turned her face away from him. "I liked him. I liked him more than I liked the others. I don't think those bandits were there to kidnap us for ransom. I think they were paid a great deal of money to find me."

Rio shook his head. "I can't see anyone hating you so much."

"I didn't say he hated me."

He felt the blow in his gut, the dark spread of jealousy, the dangerous traits of his animal side. He wasn't going to let passion rule him, it was far too risky. He had a life now, one he enjoyed. One he could live with. Rachael was not going to ruin it for him.

The wind shifted, touching their faces with droplets of water. Rio immediately leaned over her, protecting her from the rain until the wind settled again. "Bandits are common in these parts. All up and down the river. Not just here but nearly all the countries where the forest and river make it easier to disappear. Indochina, Malaysia, the Philippines, Thailand, all of them. This isn't a unique situation, or even unexpected. Didn't they warn you there was danger?" He kept his voice low, even. Nothing would betray the smoldering anger stirring in his belly. She didn't belong to him. And she was never going to belong to him.

"The odds seemed in our favor."

"I see it all the time. You should have stayed home, Rachael. You should have gone to the police."

"Not everyone has options, Rio. I did the best I could in the circumstances. I won't stay here, just long enough to heal my leg."

"Do you think it's going to happen overnight?"

His voice was low, almost sensual it was so velvet soft, but she had to blink back tears. She brought danger with her whether he wanted to believe it or not. She wanted to think she could walk away, keep him safe, but she knew he was right. She didn't want the reality of her life anymore. If she were desperate enough to dare the raging river, surely he could see she needed a space of time where she could pretend she was safe.

The forest called to her, a dark sanctuary capable of

hiding all kinds of secrets. Why not her? The foliage and
creeper vines hid his entire home, cradled high in the
branches of a tree. There had to be a way to disappear in
the rain forest. "Rio, I know you're here because you're
hiding from the world. Can't you teach me how to live
here? There has to be a place for me."

"I was born here. The forest is my home and it always
will be. I can't breathe in the city. I have no desire to live
and work there. I don't want television or movies. I go in,
get my books and I'm a happy man. A woman like you
can't live here."

"Like me?" She turned the full power of her dark eyes
on him. "A woman like me? What kind of woman am I,
Rio? I'd like to hear your analysis because you use that
term a lot. A woman like me."

Rio turned his head, amusement and even admiration
welling up out of nowhere. There was a bite to her voice, a
distinctly feminine challenge. She was sitting on his front
porch wrapped in his shirt, her bare thigh pressed against
his leg, an infection ravaging her body and the jungle
creeping close, and she could still manage to act perfectly
at home and even annoyed with him.

At home with him. At ease, as if they had known one
another for all time.

A bird screeched a warning, high up in the canopy. Monkeys sounded a call for complete vigilance. Movement in
the forest ceased. There was a sudden, unnatural silence.
Only the rain fell steadily. Rio was on his feet instantly,
moving back into the shadows, lifting his face to the wind,
sniffing the air as if scenting for enemies. He snapped his
fingers, crouching low as the two clouded leopards padded
silently onto the verandah, coming quickly from the house
as if summoned. One lifted its lip, bared its teeth in a silent
snarl. Rio hunkered down, his movement slow and careful
so as not to draw attention, circled both cat's necks with his
arms, his fingers massaging the fur as he whispered to

them. When he stepped away, the two small leopards took to the trees.

Rio lifted Rachael into his arms. Again his movements were unhurried, very slow. "Don't make a sound. Not a sound, Rachael." His lips were pressed against her ear, sending a small shiver down her spine. He moved with ease inside to place her back on the bed. Pressed as close as she was to his body, she felt him trembling, something moving against his skin, pushing against hers. It made her itch for a moment. His hands were gentle as he pulled the cover around her but she felt the tug of something sharp along her skin, as if something scratched her.

Catching her face in his hands he stared into her eyes. "I need to know you know what you're doing right now. I'm better out there," he waved toward the open door. "I'm of more use to us out there. You can't have a light, Rachael, it will just give away your position. You'll have to make do in the dark and I'll give you a gun, but you have to stay alert. Can you do that?"

Rio's voice was a mere thread of sound. Rachael stared up at him, trapped in the ferocity of his gaze. His eyes were different, more yellow than green, pupils dilated and staring. A haunting, eerie, never-to-be-forgotten stare of a wild animal on the hunt. Her heart began to pound. "Rachael, answer me. I need to know." A flicker of worry crept into the wildness in his eyes. His expression was grim. "Someone's here."

There was something entirely different about his eyes. She wasn't mistaken. His eyes were enormous, wide, staring, an eerie calm about them, a dangerous intensity. His pupils, very round, were nearly three times as large as she thought a human eye would open, allowing him to see in the dark night. She moistened her dry lips with the tip of her tongue. Rio never blinked. Never moved his gaze from her face. His eyes looked like marble or glass, all-seeing, all-knowing, a strange haunting, yet beautiful glow to them. "You must have excellent night vision." The words squeaked out. Silly.

Rachael felt like a frightened child. She had a real enemy. She didn't need to be making up supernatural beings and scaring herself. She straightened her shoulders, determined to recover. "I think they've found me, Rio. They'll hurt you if you're with me, it won't matter that you don't know anything."

"It could be anything, but we definitely have an intruder. I need to know you're all right, Rachael. I don't want to come back in here and find you shot yourself by accident. And I don't want you trying to shoot me."

"Go, I'm fine. I'm not having any trouble seeing." And she wasn't. She had never had particularly great night vision, yet she seemed to be able to see much more clearly than before. Or maybe she was just getting used to the dim lighting in the forest. She only had one good hand and it was trembling badly, so she thrust it beneath the covers. Rachael wasn't about to whine about feeling sick to her stomach from the wrenching pain of movement, not when he was going out alone to face an intruder.

He checked the gun, put it on the bed beside her. His palm slipped across her forehead. Her skin was hot to the touch. "Stay focused, Rachael."

Rio was reluctant to leave her. Something told him he was replaying an old scene. He had a memory of touching her, her hair sliding through his fingers as he went into the night to hunt for an enemy. And when he returned . . . Something gripped his heart in a vise. "Rachael, be here when I get back. Stay alive for me." He had no idea why he said it. He had no idea why he felt it, but it was an overwhelming need to warn her. Something terrible had happened, or maybe was about to happen, nothing really made sense to him anymore. There seemed to be memories in his head of Rachael that shouldn't be there.

"Good hunting, Rio. May all the magic of the forest be with you and may fortune be your companion as you travel." The words came out of her mouth, were said in her voice, but Rachael had no real idea where they came from.

She knew instinctively she was reciting formal ritual words, but she didn't know what ritual or how she knew the words, only that she'd said them before.

Rachael wiped a hand over her face in an effort to wipe away things she didn't understand. "I'll be fine. I can handle a gun, I have before. Just be careful."

Rio stared into her eyes for a long moment, afraid to take his gaze from her, afraid when he returned she'd be gone . . . or he'd find her dead, her body desperately attempting to protect their son. . . . He jerked his head back, a ferocious rage and a terrible sorrow blending together into a roiling ball of emotions impossible to understand. "Stay alive, Rachael," he repeated abruptly. A command. A plea. He forced himself to turn away from her and slip outside.

The change was already taking place in his heart and mind, the dangerous animal in him bursting free, fur rippling along his arms and legs, his body bending, contorting, muscles stretching and lengthening. He embraced the change, his chosen way of life, accepting the power and strength of the leopard in him, allowing it free rein there in the security of his territory. Rio stretched his arms, fingers splayed wide as his knuckles curved and claws scraped the floor of the verandah, then retracted.

The leopard was large. It sat in absolute stillness, head lifted to scent the wind. The many whiskers acted like radar, picking up every detail of the world around him. Ropes of muscle rippled with power and strength as the animal crouched and leapt for a large branch that curved upward and away from the house. The animal moved with the wind, high under cover of the canopy. Once the leopard looked back toward the house, noted the many streamers of creeper vines and the large lacy foliage that shielded the house from prying eyes. In the darkness, it would be nearly impossible to spot unless one knew of its existence.

The forest was alive with information, from the hum of insects and the warning cry of a bird. Rio moved quickly and silently along the wide branches, staying low, claws digging into wood as he climbed, retracting as he padded through foliage, careful not to disturb the leaves. The smaller of the two clouded leopards emerged from the heavy mist, lips drawn back in a snarl. Rio went perfectly still, crouching low, his head lifted to scent the wind.

The intruder was not human. At once the fierce temper of the leopard rose and spread with the violence of a volcano. Rio accepted the rage and ferocity, channeled it deep in the heart of the beast. He moved with greater caution, knowing he was being stalked, knowing one of his own kind had chosen to betray him. His lip lifted in a silent snarl, revealing large canines. Ears flat, the leopard began a slow freeze-frame stalk through the lush vegetation high above the forest floor. The wind carried the scent of his treacherous rival, pinpointing the location only yards from Rio.

Rio crept across a large branch far above the spotted leopard. It was male and large. The animal swung its head alertly, looking suspiciously into the tree where Rio crouched motionless. At once, Franz, concealed some distance away in heavy shrubbery, deliberately stepped on a small twig, snapping it in half. The sound was loud in the silence of the forest.

The spotted leopard stilled, sank down, staring alertly in the direction of the smaller clouded leopard. Rio took the opportunity to move closer, a silent, stealthy approach. Franz had risked his life. The larger leopard would kill him easily should it find the clouded leopard. And the larger, spotted leopard was definitely in hunting mode.

Rio moved like fluid over the tree branch, sprang silently to the branch below him, froze when the spotted leopard lifted its head to scent the wind. Fritz, several hundred yards farther from Franz, let out a low moaning cry that was carried on the wind through the interior of the forest. The spotted leopard crouched low, drawing back its lips, ears flat and tail low, in position for an attack, staring intently toward the sound.

Rio launched himself, springing agilely from above. The spotted leopard twisted at the last moment, sideswiping with a huge claw, raking Rio's side but not entirely avoiding the deadly puncture of canines as Rio went for his throat.

Immediately the forest came alive with the sounds of battle, monkeys shrieking, birds taking to the air, flying fox leaping from tree to tree as the two large cats erupted into teeth and claws, rolling and ripping on the forest floor. Where there had been silence, there was now chaos, animals screaming warnings to one another as the deadly battle raged on. An orangutan, nestled for the night in his bed in the tree branches, threw a handful of leaves in disgust at the two cats as they snarled and fought in a dangerous ballet of sharpened claws and piercing teeth.

The leopards used their weight, contorting in nearly impossible positions, bending spines and whirling around, springing into the air and lunging for throats. The battle was brief, but fierce, the snarling, ferocious roars and grunts reverberating through the trees, straight up the canopy to the ominous rain clouds overhead. The clouds answered, pouring rain down. Although the drops barely made it through the thick canopy, it was enough to quiet the shrieking monkeys and settle the birds back under cover.

The spotted leopard rolled to break Rio's hold, racing away, taking to the branches and moving quickly along the overhead highway to escape. Deliberately the angry cat went toward the last location of the smaller, clouded leopard. Rio gave chase, sending out a warning cough, but the spotted leopard was on Fritz, grabbing for the neck with wicked teeth, shaking the smaller cat viciously. He dropped it onto the ground below and took off just as Rio launched another attack. Claws raked the spotted leopard's hindquarters. His yowl of pain sent the birds skittering again, but he kept going, digging into the branches with his claws to pull away.

Rio dropped quickly to the ground to assess the damage

to Fritz. The larger spotted leopard had delivered a grave injury, but left the smaller cat alive. Rio hissed an angry warning. He had to fight his own nature, the need to go after fleeing prey. Fight back the temper smoldering in his gut, red-hot and demanding revenge.

There was no doubt in his mind he had faced one of his own kind, a cunning, intelligent mixture of leopard and man. This one had come to kill him. Rio knew most of his people; there were few left in the forest. Many were scattered in other countries and some chose to live as humans in the cities, but most were known to one another. Rio did not recognize the scent of his stalker, but he recognized the intelligence of the decision not to kill the clouded leopard in a fit of temper. The attack had been cold-blooded and well thought out in the short time available. The spotted leopard knew Rio would never leave the dangerously injured cat to track him. And that told Rio something else. His stalker knew he traveled with the two clouded leopards.

He looked cautiously around, making certain to scent the wind. His cough was a demand to the tree dwellers for information. The cry came from the troupe of monkeys overhead. Rio reached for his human form, allowed the pain to engulf him as ropes of muscle and sinew contorted, contracted and stretched. He crouched beside the clouded leopard, assessing the damage to the animal. The puncture wounds were deep. He clamped his hand over the holes and applied pressure, murmuring reassurances as he did so, ignoring the deep claw marks on his own skin.

"Franz, stay alert," he ordered as he gathered Fritz into his arms. Rio had to keep pressure on the two puncture wounds as he raced through the forest, weaving his way between the trees, leaping over fallen logs, splashing through two small swollen streams, covering the uneven terrain as fast as he could. He was built much like a leopard with muscles meant for carrying large prey. He didn't feel the burden of the clouded leopard, but in his human form, his skin was not nearly as tough as in his animal form and the forest tore up his flesh as he rushed through it.

Rio leapt upon the wide low-hanging branch leading to his home with the ease of long practice and, balancing carefully, made his way along the maze of branches until he gained the verandah. He called out to warn Rachael, hoping she wouldn't shoot him as he shoved open the door with his hip. Fritz, nestled so close to him, turned his head to look up at him in silent fear. The small leopard's sides were heaving, straining for air, too much blood matting his fur.

Rachael gasped, thrusting the gun beneath the pillow. "What happened? What can I do?" Rio's face was a dangerous mask, fierce, warriorlike, his eyes alive with anger. He turned the full power of his unblinking stare on her, assessing her condition. Rachael met his piercing gaze steadily. "Really, Rio, let me help you."

He immediately switched directions, bringing the injured animal to the bed. "Can you sit up all the way by yourself?"

Rachael didn't bother with speech. She simply showed him, making certain to keep her expression serene when her heart was pounding and pain made her sick. She'd had enough practice hiding fear. The cat was badly injured and therefore far more dangerous than in its normal state. Her mouth went dry as he placed the animal in her lap and guided, first one hand, then the other to the puncture wounds. Rachael found herself with a fifty-pound leopard in her lap and her hands pressing into its neck covered in blood.

Rio lit the lamp and brought his surgical supplies to the bed, kneeling down close to the animal's head. "Be still, Fritz," he murmured, "I know it hurts, but we'll get you fixed up." He didn't look at Rachael, but worked on the animal, his hands gentle, steady and very sure.

His head was bent, dark hair spilling around his face. There was sweat and blood on his skin, and he smelled wild and of wet fur. His face could have been carved from stone as he worked to save the cat. "These are deep puncture wounds, much like your leg. I sutured the lacerations on your leg but left the punctures to drain. I'll have to do the same with Fritz. The best I can do is clean the wounds thoroughly, give him antibiotics and hope they don't abscess. If they do, I'll have to put in drains."

As Rio worked on cleansing the puncture site, Fritz opened his mouth, exposing his long, wicked canines, and yowled horribly. Rachael took a deep breath and kept her gaze locked on Rio, on his face rather than on his hands, afraid if she looked at the cat's teeth she would do a little screaming herself.

Franz answered Fritz, pacing anxiously back and forth in agitation. Without warning, he suddenly leapt onto the bed, nearly crushing Rachael's legs. Pain rushed through her body, took her breath and forced a small, strangled cry from her throat. For a moment the room spun, tilted, went black.

"Rachael!" Rio's voice was sharp, compelling, calling her back. Rio's arm swept Franz from the bed. "Stay the hell down," he snarled, his voice rumbling with menace.

To Rachael's surprise, her hands were still in Fritz's fur. She applied more pressure as she shook her head. "I'm sorry, I wasn't expecting him to do that."

"You're doing fine," he said. "Can you go on?"

"If you can, I can," she answered.

He looked at her then with his vivid green eyes, something she couldn't quite name swirling in the darker depths. His gaze drifted over her face, almost as if he were drawing strength from just looking at her. He turned his attention back to the cat.

Rachael let out her breath slowly, fighting down the bile rising in her throat from the throbbing pain in her leg. She would do anything to see that look on his face. A sharing. A connection. She listened to the sound of his voice as he talked softly to the cat, reassuring it as he stitched the deep wound. She found herself stroking the fur with her free hand as the animal trembled, but stayed still for Rio's ministrations.

Rachael waited until Rio was working on the second puncture wound. "How did this happen?"

"There was a big, spotted leopard, a male, in the forest. He attacked Fritz. Fortunately he dropped him without crushing the windpipe."

She looked at the deep angry scratches on Rio's body. "You went up against a leopard trying to kill your pet?"

Swift impatience crossed his face. "I told you, Fritz and Franz are not pets. They're my friends. I didn't save Fritz, he was trying to protect me and he put himself in harm's way."

Rachael bent over the animal in her lap, examining the chunk missing from the ear. "So this one is Fritz?"

He nodded as he peered closely at his work. "This puncture wound is not as deep as the other one. I'm going to give him something for the infection. The leopard did this deliberately."

"Why?" She didn't look at him when she asked. Rio had bitten the words out between his strong teeth, almost as if he said them without thought, angry at the leopard for hurting the smaller cat. She sensed that Rio was on the verge of telling her something very important.

Rio glanced at her. "I think he was hunting for one of us. I just am not certain which. At first I thought it was me, but now I'm not so sure."

She heard the thud of her heart and counted the beats. It was a trick she often used when she was in a dangerous situation and wanted to appear calm or when she needed more information and didn't want to react too fast. Something inside her went very still when he turned his direct, piercing gaze on her. There was something there she couldn't quite read. A swirling dangerous mixture of beast and man. Rachael knew cats' eyes contained a layer of reflective tissue behind each retina which allowed them to concentrate all possible light during the darkest nights, or in the darkest forest. Called the *tapetum lucidum,* the membrane acted like a mirror, allowing the light to bounce back

through the retina a second time for maximum ability to
see. The membrane also reflected light back in iridescent
colors of yellow-green and red, both of which Rachael had
observed in Rio and in the clouded leopards.

"Why would a leopard be hunting one or the other of us,
Rio?" she prompted. It didn't make sense that the large cat
would care which of them he killed and ate.

There was a long silence broken only by the sounds of
the moaning wind, the steady fall of rain, Franz pacing
back and forth in agitation. Rachael was certain Rio could
hear the pounding of her heart.

"I don't think he was a leopard as you know a leopard. I
think he was a different species altogether." Rio's voice
blended into the night, held secrets and shadows she didn't
want to examine.

Rachael didn't voice the protest welling up in her. She
was certain Rio wasn't being melodramatic. She didn't
think he was capable of drama for drama's sake. "I'm
sorry, I'm not certain exactly what you're saying? A new
species of leopard here in the rain forest that hasn't been
discovered? Or a genetically engineered species?"

"A species that's been around for thousands of years."

She rubbed the clouded leopard's ears. "How are they
different?"

He looked at her then, turning the full focus of his
strange eyes on her. "They are not animal, yet not human.
They're both, yet neither."

Rachael went very still, pulled her gaze from the power
of his, her mind racing with possibilities. "A long time ago,
when I was a little girl, my mother told me a story about a
species of leopards. Well, not leopards, they were a species
able to shift into the form of a leopard, or large cat. They
had some of the attributes of the leopard, but also attributes
of humans and of their own species, sort of a three-way
mixture. I've never heard anyone else ever mention them
until now. Is that what you mean?"

Few things shocked Rio anymore, but his hands stopped

in midair and he stared at her. "How would your mother have heard of the leopard people? Few people, outside the species, know of their existence."

"Do you realize what you're saying, Rio? That there is such a species? I thought it was simply a story my mother liked to tell me at night when we were alone together. She always told me tales of the leopard people when I went to bed." She frowned, trying to remember the old stories from her childhood. "She didn't call them leopard people, there was another name."

Rio stiffened, his brilliant gaze slashing at her face. "What did she call them?"

The name eluded her as hard as she tried to remember. "I was a child, Rio. I was only a young girl when she died and we went to live with . . ." She trailed off, shrugging her shoulders. "It doesn't matter. Are you saying there's a possibility that the species exists? And if it does, why would one of them want to harm you? Or me for that matter?"

"I'm on a hit list, Rachael. I've stirred up the bandits a few times, taking back what doesn't belong to them and costing them a lot of money. They don't like it and they want me dead." He shrugged his shoulders and patted the cat, straightening tiredly. "Hold him a couple more minutes while I fix a bed for him."

"And I've made it worse for you by coming here, haven't I?"

"A hit list is a hit list, Rachael. I don't think anything makes it worse, I'm already on it. If they track you to me, we'll move. They aren't going to best me here in the forest. They prefer the river, not the interior. And I have a few people who will help out if needed. I know all the local tribesmen and they know me. I'll hear if they enter the forest." He doused the light, plunging the room back into darkness.

"But not if one of these leopard people is working with them," she guessed, blinking rapidly to adjust to the change in lighting. The moon was trying valiantly to shed light in spite of the clouds and the heavy canopy of foliage, but it was a mere sliver and far away. "And if the species does exist, why haven't they been discovered yet? They'd have to be highly intelligent."

"And cool under fire—cunning, careful. Burn their dead in the hottest fires possible. Find remains of any who died by accident. Ban together to retrieve a body if one is taken by a hunter. The society would have to be a superior one, dependent on one another and highly skilled and secretive."

"Like you." She couldn't get the picture of his face changing, rushing at her with the muzzle and teeth of a fully grown male leopard out of her head.

He returned to the bed, towering over her, his vivid green eyes moving over her face. "Like me," he agreed. Rio bent and scooped up the fifty-pound clouded leopard, cradling it close to his chest.

Rachael's fingers curled in the bedcover. Was it possible? Was it her fevered imagination or was Rio able to shift into the form of a leopard? She looked at him crouched down beside the cat, streaks of blood on his back and sides, down the columns of his thighs, and a tear up near his neck. She didn't care what he was. It didn't matter to her, not when he was petting the injured cat and murmuring soft nonsense to it.

Rachael swallowed the tight knot of fear blocking her throat. "You're bleeding, Rio. Come here to me. How badly are you hurt?"

Rio stood up and turned around to look at her. There was genuine concern in her voice, in the dark depths of her eyes. Her compassion touched him somewhere deep inside, somewhere he wanted to forget existed. She shook his control, and that was more dangerous than she could possibly understand. Rio shrugged his shoulders. "It's no big deal, a few scratches."

Rachael studied him as he padded across the floor on bare feet. There was a slight stiffness to his normal

graceful, sinuous walk. The scratches looked deep and
ugly and she thought there was more than one puncture
wound. "You always take care of everything and every-
body before you take care of yourself. You fought that
leopard, didn't you? You didn't have a gun with you. I
doubt you had a knife. What did you do? Fight it with
your bare hands?"

Rio dragged out the medical kit and began dousing the
angry looking wounds with burning liquid. Rachael sighed
softly, feeling helpless. He looked tired and out of sorts
and she knew the gashes had to hurt. He didn't respond to
her comments, but she was certain she was right. He had to
have been involved in a vicious fight with a cat of some
kind without a weapon. And it couldn't have been a small
cat. She bit down on her lip to keep her mouth closed,
determined not to aggravate him with questions.

He bent to duck his head over the tub he used as a sink
and poured water over his hair. He was breathtaking, there
in the dark with just the sliver of moonlight falling across
him. His hair gleamed liked silken webs. Shadows from
the heavy foliage stirred by the wind threw the broad outline of his back and buttocks into sharp relief and then just
as quickly covered him from her sight as he washed himself. As he straightened and half turned toward her, his
eyes caught the reflection of light from the moon and
glowed an eerie red. The eyes of a predator. The eyes of a
leopard.

Rachael held her breath and made every effort to keep
the wild pounding of her heart under control. It wasn't just
his strange eyes that could frighten her; he always carried a
dangerous, untamed look about him. She was certain she
was right about his eyes being different, more like a cat's.
He took a step toward the bed and she could see him more
clearly, see the weariness and pain etched into his face.
Immediately fear was swept aside in her concern for him.

"Rio, come to bed."

He studied her expression. Soft. Inviting. Temptation.
Her mouth was sinful. He had more than his share of fantasies about her mouth. Her lush body, so soft and warm
and perfect for his, was an invitation he couldn't ignore
much longer. The longer she stayed in his home, the more
she belonged there. "Damn it, Rachael, I'm not a saint."
His voice was harsh, deliberately challenging. He was so
edgy and moody he wanted a fight with her. He wanted to
go back into the jungle and sulk far away from her. If his
obsession with her continued to grow, he didn't know what
he was going to do.

Rachael did the unexpected like she always did. She
burst out laughing, the sound carefree, not in the least bit
frightened. "You have no worries, Rio, I am not about to
mistake you for one."

"Well why the hell are you looking at me like that then?
Don't you have any idea how vulnerable you are right
now?"

"I think you're the one who's vulnerable, Rio, not me.
Come to bed and stop acting so macho. You can put on
your he-man face in the morning and I'll do my best to act
afraid if that's what you need, but right now, you need
sleep. Not sex, sleep."

"You think I need sleep," he groused, but obediently
slid into the bed beside her. She was warm and soft and
everything he knew she'd be. Rio wrapped his arms around
her, fit his body around hers, snuggling his heavy erection
tightly against the cradle of her hips, his head against the
soft swell of her breast.

"I know you need sleep. Just lay it down for a while. If
you're worried about someone sneaking up on you, I'll
watch over you." She could feel the silk of his hair, damp
from washing, teasing her nipple. Rachael wrapped her
arms around his head, cradled him to her, her fingers
woven in the thick mass of hair.

"I should check your leg after that idiot cat jumped
on it."

His breath was warm against her breast. She felt desire pierce her like a sword. "Go to sleep, Rio, we can check it in the morning." For the rest of the night, she would pretend he belonged to her. Her own gentle warrior, fresh from battle, a mixture of danger and tenderness she found impossible to resist.

6

RIO woke before dawn. It was his favorite time of day. He loved to bury his face against Rachael's warm breasts and just listen to the soft cries of the early morning birds and the continual symphony of the forest while he held her to him. He felt more alive, more complete in those moments just before dawn, before the household stirred to life and the day's demands were on him. Rachael breathed so softly, in and out, warm and welcoming, her flesh a lush invitation to paradise. He knew every line, every hollow. Her body was etched deeply into his memory. He knew her form better than she knew it, and he knew every way to please her.

Rio smiled and buried his face in the valley between her breasts just to inhale her scent. She always seemed to smell of flowers. He was certain it was the soaps and shampoo she made from the petals and herbs in the forest. His tongue swirled over her nipple, a lazy, leisurely movement. Life was perfect at dawn. He breathed her in. His Rachael. His world. There in their secret world with the light filtering in through the high canopy, Rio found strength and passion and everything he would ever need to exist and live.

He nuzzled her breast, swirled his tongue over her tempting nipple a second time and drew soft flesh into his mouth, suckling gently. Rachael stirred, shifted to bring her body more aligned with his, to arch her back a little more to offer her breasts while her arms crept around his head to cradle him close. He loved her reaction, that first drowsy offering of her body to him. He knew when he plunged his finger deep inside her to test her readiness, she would already be hot and wet and welcoming.

Making love to Rachael was always an adventure. They would be so tender together it would bring tears to his eyes, or they would be rough and wild and totally uninhibited. Rachael would rake his back, dig her nails into his flesh or ride him with wild abandon. Sometimes he spent an hour just loving on her, feasting on her. Her body was so familiar to him, yet he was full and hard and bursting to be inside her, so eager his body was painful. Like the first time. Like each and every time he touched her.

His hands moved over her body, warm, soft flesh, tantalizing, tempting, a delight he could hardly believe was his. He lifted his face to hers, fastened his mouth on hers, a hard, possessive kiss that took their breath so that they had to exchange air while the world rocked around them. Her mouth was hot and sweet and achingly familiar.

For just a moment, there in the dawn when it didn't matter, when he didn't have to have a veneer of civilization, he always allowed his wild nature to rise. Possession, jealousy, a dark predatory need to claim Rachael for his own rose up as it always did. The beast, always so close to the surface, rose with him, untamed and roaring for her, wanting her with every fiber of his being. His skin itched as he tasted her acceptance of him, ropes of muscles contracting as he dragged her closer, his thigh moving over hers to pin her beneath him. It never bothered her when the beast was so close to the surface, even if she felt the brush of fur on her sensitized skin. She always accepted him, always wanted him, always welcomed him.

She laughed softly into his mouth as he devoured her, fed on her, kissing her over and over without restraint. He wanted her so much, wanted to be buried deep inside her where he belonged, where the world was always right. He wrapped his arms around her while her hands explored the muscles over his chest. There was possession in her touch as she skimmed his belly and found the hard length of his erection. She closed her fist over him tightly and he gasped with the pleasure and the pain of it.

"I want to taste you this morning," he whispered. "I can't wait to feel you squirming the way you do, your fist yanking at my hair, telling me to hurry, hurry, hurry." He kissed her chin, her throat, the soft swell of her breast.

"Oh really." Her voice was a teasing lilt. "And here I thought I was going to drive you out of your mind this morning. Can't you just imagine being in my mouth? I think it's my turn, we were rudely interrupted last time."

Her fingers danced over him, the way only Rachael could do, teasing and stroking, small caresses designed to drive him mad. If she took him in her mouth he was going to explode, a heady, wild eruption that would make her laugh and demand satisfaction. He knew her so well, yet not at all. Rachael—his lady, his reason for existing.

He shifted his weight and dragged her body beneath his, his knee sliding between her legs with expert precision, opening her beckoning heat to him. He settled over her, into her, pressing against her tight opening, already anticipating the pleasure he would give her. He moved away from the temptation, sliding down, his tongue swirling in her sexy belly button, his teeth nipping at her flat stomach. His thigh pressed against hers in demand, shifting her leg to the side.

Rachael screamed, a cry of terrible unrelenting pain, curling up in the fetal position, curling away from him. Her cry set the monkeys in the trees chattering and the birds scolding. She choked off the sound quickly, breathing deeply to regain control.

Rio's perfect world shattered. "What the hell am I doing? Damn it, just damn it." Groaning, he rolled off her onto his back, both hands covering his face. "I'm sorry, Rachael, damn it, I'm really sorry. I don't know what happened. I swear, for a minute, I was someone else. Or you were someone else, or we were the same but different. Hell! I don't know what I'm saying." He pulled his hands from his face and looked at her, his expression grim. "Are you all right?"

To his shock, Rachael turned back, gingerly, carefully, and tunneled her fingers in his hair. "I don't break, Rio. I could have said no to you. For a moment there, I was someone else too. I knew you intimately, belonged with you and had for a long time. I was so comfortable, so complete. I think I would have been very happy to be that other person, but my leg changed my mind for me. I'm the one who's sorry."

"I frightened you."

She tugged at his hair and the gesture was strangely familiar. "Did I seem frightened to you? I thought I was very cooperative. My leg hurts when I move, otherwise, I would have been all over you."

He rolled onto his side, propping his head up with his hand. "Why, Rachael? Are you afraid to say no to me?" He couldn't quite get his breathing under control and his body was hard and painful and aching. More than anything he wanted to kiss her again, wanted her body to belong to him. Wanted her to belong to him. "I know you must feel vulnerable alone with me like this, especially injured, but I swear, I don't force myself on women."

"Rio, you're being silly. We're physically attracted to each other. I've been staring at your body for days now. How could I not be attracted? If you tried to force yourself on me and I wasn't in the least receptive, I would have hit you over the head with something." She grinned at him. "And you already know I'm perfectly capable of it. At the moment my leg is injured and you can't tell, but I have had a bit of self-defense training. You were very vulnerable there for a time in your . . . er . . . aroused state. Bad leg or no, I could have managed to injure you."

"When I'm with you. . ." Rio struggled to find the right words. "It's as if I've always been with you, as if I've always known you, as if I've always made love to you. I swear sometimes it's difficult for me to tell the difference between what's real and my imagination. It's crazy."

He leaned into her, close, so that the tips of her breasts pushed against his chest. Immediately the feeling was familiar, perfect—a coming home. He sighed. "I'm not used to being around people for any length of time, it makes me uncomfortable, but with you, I can't imagine you not being with me." His hands framed her face. "I want you so bad I can taste you in my mouth. I know exactly what you're going to feel like when I'm inside you." His fingertips slipped down her neck, over her shoulders to trace the swell of her breasts. "I know your shape, every curve, as if I have a map in my mind."

Rachael knew she was no thinking person when his hands were on her body, shaping her breasts, his thumbs sliding over her taut nipples sending bolts of lightning through her bloodstream. She wasn't an ordinary woman with a chance at love. She could have a brief affair, but she would have to move on, leave him behind. Every moment she was with him endangered him.

Her lashes hid the expression in her eyes from him, careful not to let him see the heat and fire his touch awakened in her. "I feel different. I have since I first came to the rain forest. I feel fully alive, as if something inside of me is trying to break free." And she felt highly sexual. Ever since she had come to this house, this place, was near this man, in spite of the fever or maybe because of the fever, she was in a continual state of arousal. She burned for him, thought of him night and day, dreamed of him.

"Rachael, you know the birthmark low on your hip?

I knew it was there before I ever saw it. I know exactly how you like to be touched." He sat up, pushed his hand through his hair in agitation, leaving it tousled and wild, as untamed as he. "How can I know those things?"

She knew his likes and dislikes intimately too. Sometimes her fingers itched to stroke his chest, to run her fingertips down his flat belly. Teasing and caressing, her tongue swirling in the wake of her fingers until he cried out for mercy. She knew the exact note that would be in his voice, the husky ache in his tone. Just thinking of the need and hunger in his voice sent ripples of fire racing through her body.

Rio sighed. "Let me take a look at your leg. Between the cat jumping on it and me hurting you, it probably needs a repair or two." He looked at her, dark curly hair spilling around her face, lips slightly parted, almost in invitation. Her long lashes lifted and he was staring into her eyes, seeing her need. Seeing the same smoldering heat in her that burned so hotly in him. He swore under his breath and reached beneath the cover for her ankle, guiding her leg into the open.

Rachael felt his fingers on her skin. There was a proprietary feeling to his grip. The pad of his thumb swept back and forth over her ankle in a small caress, each stroke sending flames dancing up her leg to the junction of her thighs. His hand slipped lower, over her foot, began a slow, heart-stopping massage.

"It looks far better this morning, Rachael. No red streaks at all. It's still very swollen and the two puncture sites are draining again. I'm going to take the dressing off and leave them open to drain."

She made a face. "How lovely. The sheet is going to be a mess."

"I have a couple of towels I can put under it." His fingers tightened around her foot. "Rachael, I think we're out of the woods and we've saved the leg, but it's going to scar. I tried to repair the damage, but. . ." He trailed off, the pressure of his grip hard enough to reveal his distress at his inadequacy without actual words.

Rachael shrugged. "I wasn't worried about scars, Rio. Thank you for what you did. It doesn't matter to me."

"Not right now, but when you're back in your world, dancing in a slinky dress, it may make a difference." He forced himself to say it, to think it. At once the beast rose up, fighting for control, fur threatening to burst through his skin. Wickedly sharp teeth pushing at his jaw to make room. Even his fingers curved, the stiletto-sharp claws threatening to burst out the ends.

"I can't ever go back, Rio," Rachael said firmly. "I don't want to go back. There's nothing but death there for me. I was never happy in that world. I'd like to try here, where I feel alive, where I feel close to my mother again. It was her stories that made me come to this place. When she spoke of the rain forest, she made me feel as if I were in it, sensing its sounds and smells and beauty. I felt as if I'd walked in it, long before I ever came here."

"This isn't a lark for some rich woman's fantasy," he said, abruptly standing. With the same casual immodesty he pulled on a pair of jeans. "There aren't stores here, Rachael. There are cobras and wild animals that will hunt and eat you."

"Someone managed to put a cobra in my locked room before we traveled on the river," she said. It was hard not to stare at him, not to see the play of his muscles beneath his skin. She could see the scars covering his body. Many of them were obviously from large cats. But there were scars from knives and bullets and other weapons she couldn't hope to identify.

His head snapped around, his hands stilled on the buttons of his jeans. "Are you certain the thing didn't get into your room on its own, Rachael?"

She shook her head. "No, the room was locked up tight. I made sure of it. I really prepared for this trip, Rio. I knew about the snakes and other unpleasant and poisonous crawly things. I took precautions."

Rio reached for her. "Let me help you to the bathroom."

"I think I can make it on my own," Rachael said.

He paid no attention to her protest, simply reached down and scooped her into his arms, striding into the tiny closet-sized room used for privacy. It was a primitive method, but at least Rachael had privacy. He left her alone while he went about heating water for coffee.

Rachael leaned against the wall, holding on to keep from falling on her face. She was surprised how weak she was. The infection left her shaky. She wasn't certain she could hop her way across the floor back to the bed, let alone make it outside to the verandah as she had planned. She needed a respite from Rio's untamed masculine allure. She had no way to combat his magnetic sorcery when she was so close to him. She couldn't stop staring at him, the fluid way he walked, the way his roped muscles rippled so obviously, the temptation of his mouth, the brilliance of his vivid gaze, so often hot with hunger and need when it rested on her.

She sighed as she drew aside the curtain and found him waiting. She should have known he would be right there when she needed him. No matter what he was doing he always heard everything, saw everything, was aware of everything.

When he leaned down to lift her into his arms, his face brushed against her mop of unruly curls. She felt the warmth of his breath, the heat of his skin, the faintest touch of his lips skimming her temple. Rachael closed her eyes against the rush of desire. "You can't do that, Rio. I'm not that strong."

"I can't help myself, Rachael." He cradled her against his bare chest, rubbing his chin on the top of her head. "When I'm this close to you, my body and my heart tell me you're mine. I think my brain just shuts down."

She circled his neck with her arms, thinking her brain might be shutting down too. "I guess that's a good enough excuse. I'm willing to use it if you are." She lifted her mouth to his, the aggressor this time, biting down on his lower lip, tugging until he opened his mouth to her. Her tongue tangled with his, danced and teased, stroked and caressed. A perfect match.

The world dropped away until there was only the silken heat of his mouth, the strength of his arms, the feel of his bare chest pressed against her. She buried her hands in his hair, held the back of his head tightly to prevent him from pulling away. They fed off each other, kiss after kiss, so hungry for one another they couldn't stop.

Franz yowled. Just once, but it was enough. Rio stiffened, lifted his head, listening to the sounds of the forest. He swore softly and pressed his forehead against hers, breathing deeply to regain control.

Rachael's fingers twisted deeper into his hair. "What is it? What do you hear?" She didn't care about her breathing. She didn't want to stop kissing him, not now, not ever. Her body was already in meltdown and she wanted relief.

"Listen. Do you hear them talking? The birds? The monkeys? Even the insects are warning us."

Rachael tried to still her pounding heart, tried to control her wild breathing to listen. It took a few minutes to separate the sounds. Strangely, she could hear individual notes, could tell there was a whisper of information. "What does it mean?"

"Someone is headed our way."

"The leopard?" Her mouth went dry. Rio was serious. She listened again, much more closely this time. To her astonishment, she could hear the difference in the notes the birds sang, in the way the insects carried on—more hurried in their melodies. And the monkeys shrieked to one another. It took her a moment or two to realize the monkeys were also shrieking to Rio. "They're deliberately warning you."

He set her in the overstuffed chair away from the door. "I do them favors, they do me favors. It's not a leopard, someone human. Someone they're familiar with, they've seen before." His hands lingered on her shoulders, the nape of her neck, massaging the tension out of her rather absently.

Rachael pulled the edges of the shirt she was wearing together, noticing for the first time that the buttons were completely undone. She was becoming as bad as Rio at being immodest. She allowed her head to fall back against the chair, arching her back like a lazy cat, shifting a little to ease the steady pressure building in the core of her body. Exposed in the early morning air, her skin itched. She looked down and thought, for just one second, something ran beneath the surface, raising her skin slightly, just enough to be noticeable. Then it was gone, leaving her wondering if she were so in need of a man that she was having hallucinations.

"Rachael, how did your mother come to hear of the leopard people and this place?" Reluctantly Rio allowed his hand to drop away from her neck as he went to the window and pushed aside the blanket to peer out.

"I don't know. To me her stories were just that, stories. I don't even know if I have the stories right, Rio. I probably filled in the blanks with my own versions. Does it matter? Do you really think there's truth in the stories? In the light of day it seems a little silly to think a man could be a leopard as well as a man. Or a mixture of both. What, the head and torso of a man and the body of a leopard?" She couldn't look at him without having the impression of a dangerous cat. Without thinking of the way his face had changed from a human warrior to that of a dangerous animal.

"Does it? Here in the forest, it seems anything is possible. You have to have an open mind if you're going to make your home here." He stood with his back to her and wondered how he was going to let her go.

A soft one-two note, much like a songbird, reached his ears. He turned back to her. "Rachael, Kim Pang is approaching the house."

"That's not possible, he was on the other side of the

river. It was already raging, and with the storms and so
much rain, it can't have gone down this fast." Just like that
her world was shattered, gone, and the running started
again. The lies. She turned her face away from him, not
wanting him to see the sheen of tears burning in her eyes.
She knew the day would come eventually. It made her
angry that she never wanted to accept it, that she pretended
she would find a home.

"Kim is capable of getting across the river in the same
manner I use." He searched for the right words to make her
understand. "He's the closest thing I have to a friend outside my unit."

Rachael shrugged. "It doesn't matter. Give me time to
get dressed and get out of here. Go meet him before he gets
here."

Something dangerous shifted inside him. "I don't think
so, Rachael. You can't even walk on that leg. If you try
running around the forest with those puncture wounds,
believe me, you'll pick up another infection fast. Just sit
there and let me work this out."

Rio's eyes had narrowed into that glassy, focused stare
she associated with predatory hunting. There was a soft
underlying growl to his voice that sent a chill down her spine
and the hair on the back of her neck rising. Rachael turned
her face away from him, biting down hard to keep from lash-
ing out at him. She was good at keeping her expression
serene, even in the worst of times, but she still had trouble
controlling her runaway tongue. She didn't need nor want
him to work her problems out. People stepping into her life
tended to die way too young. She didn't want to carry the
guilt of another death around, thank you very much. Rachael
smoldered with a mixture of anger and fear, feeling vulnerable and helpless with the injury to her leg.

She was surprised at the intensity of her emotions. Her
fingers even curled as if she wanted to rake and claw and
scratch something. Or someone. The need burned in her, a
startling discovery she wasn't very proud of. What was

happening to her? Sometimes when she lay in bed with her
leg throbbing, there was something stirring inside of her, a
heat and need she put down to her admiration of Rio's
anatomy.

Rachael swept a hand through her hair. She had a normal, healthy sex drive, but ever since she'd arrived, in spite
of the terrible injury she suffered, need crawled through
her body, an ever-present unrelenting ache that refused to
go away. In the middle of pain and a life or death struggle,
it seemed demeaning to her that she couldn't control such
an urge. Worse than that was the edgy, violent mood
swings, going from wanting to lash out at Rio to wanting to
tear his clothes off.

"Rachael? Where did you go?"

"Obviously nowhere."

"I'm going to call Kim in."

"What does that mean?"

"He's a tribesman, Rachael. He knows I'm on the bandits' hit list. He signaled to me who he was and he's waiting for an all-clear signal before he comes on in."

"Do you have to give it to him?"

"He'll come in fighting if I don't. I told you, he's a
friend."

"In case you haven't noticed, I need clothes. I don't
want to sit around in your shirt and nothing else in front of
your friends." She was hastily buttoning up the front of the
shirt, hiding her generous breasts from his view.

Rio didn't comment on the quarrelsome note in her
voice. He simply pulled the blanket from the bed and
tucked it around her. "Kim's father is a medicine man,
very good with herbs. He taught me quite a bit, but Kim
knows far more than I. Hopefully he can help both you
and Fritz."

When she didn't look up, Rio hunkered down beside
her. "Rachael, look at me." When she didn't respond he
caught her chin and forced her head up. The last thing
he expected to see was heat and fire glittering in her dark

eyes. Raw hunger stared back at him with an intensity that made him groan, push his brow into hers. "Don't. I mean it, Rachael. You can't look at me like that and expect me to function properly."

She had the craziest desire, no need, to squirm and rub herself all over him, much like a feline. It was a heat wave rolling through her that shook her confidence. "If I could help it, do you think I'd be making such a fool out of myself?" Scratching his eyes out seemed a better alternative than rubbing her body against his at that moment. She let him see that too.

His face was inches from hers. He was catching fire from touching her skin, feeling the crackle of electricity arcing between them. Her eyes held a challenge he couldn't resist. Rio caught the nape of her neck, cupped the back of her head and dragged her mouth to his. There was no resistance at all. She fused with him instantly. Hot. Electric. Wild for him. Climbing into his skin, wrapping herself around his heart so tightly he felt it like a vise. Devouring him just as eagerly as he was devouring her.

It was only because they had to come up for air that he found the strength to lift his head. Rachael buried her face against his throat. "This time it was my fault." Her lips moved against his neck. Rio closed his eyes against the shimmering fire the brushing of her soft mouth sent through his body in strong waves. He had to find a way just to breathe. He doubted if air was going to get his brain functioning again.

The soft one-two note was closer this time. "You just drove Kim right out of my head, Rachael." He rubbed his face in the mass of thick curly hair.

"It's shocking how well you know how to kiss."

He couldn't stop the silly grin that spread across his face. "Isn't it though? I shocked myself." The smile faded and he caught her chin again. "I'm not giving you up or betraying you, Rachael. I know Kim. He won't endanger your life, not for any reason."

"Money talks, Rio. Almost everyone has a price."

"Kim lives simply, but more than that, he has a code of honor."

Rachael nodded. There wasn't much else she could do. Rio was right in that she couldn't very well run away with her leg torn up. "Answer him then."

Rio didn't look away from her, but let out a singsong note that sounded to her exactly like the birds calling to one another just outside the walls of his home. She tucked his wild, shaggy hair behind his ear, allowing her fingertips to trail over his jaw, rub over his mouth. "I'm afraid."

"I know. I can hear your heart beating." He circled her wrist, his thumb sliding over her pulse. "There's no need to be."

"It's a great deal of money he'll pay to get me back."

"Your husband?"

She shook her head. "My brother."

His hand went to his heart, as if she'd stabbed him. Almost at once his face closed down. He drew air into his lungs, let it out. There was a watchfulness in his eyes, a suspicion that hadn't been there before. "Your brother."

"You don't have to believe me." Rachael pulled away from him, leaned back in the chair and pulled the cover closer around her. The humidity was high, even with the wind blowing. Where Rio had pulled the covering away from the window, she could see thick mist curling around the foliage and creepers surrounding the house. "I shouldn't have told you."

"Why would your brother want to have you killed, Rachael?"

"You make me tired. It does happen, Rio. Maybe not in your world, but certainly in mine."

Rio studied her averted face, trying to see past the mask she wore to what was going on in her mind, his brain racing with the possibilities. Had she found his home by accident, or had she been sent to assassinate him? She'd had a couple of opportunities. He'd given her a gun. It was still there, beneath her pillow. Maybe she hadn't taken care of it because she needed him while her leg was healing.

He straightened slowly and walked over to the stash of weapons hanging on the wall. He strapped a sheath to his leg and pulled the leg of his pants over it. A second knife was positioned between his shoulder blades. He pulled his shirt on and tucked a gun into his waistband.

"Are you expecting trouble? I thought you said Kim Pang was your friend."

"It's always better to be prepared. I don't like surprises."

"I noticed," she answered dryly, prepared to be angry with him over his boorish reaction to her admission. He may as well have slapped her. She had revealed something to him she had never admitted to another soul and he didn't believe her. She could tell by his immediate withdrawal.

Rio crouched beside the injured cat, his hands incredibly gentle as he examined the leopard. Her heart nearly turned over in her chest. His head was bent toward Fritz, his expression almost tender as he murmured softly to the cat. She had a sudden vision of him cradling his child, looking down lovingly, his thumb in the baby's tiny hand. He suddenly lifted his head and looked at her and smiled.

If it were possible to melt, Rachael was certain she did. His eyebrow arched. "What? Why are you looking at me like that?"

"I'm trying to figure out what it is about you," Rachael answered honestly. His face was no boy's face. His features were tough and hard-edged. His eyes could be ice-cold, frightening even, yet sometimes when she looked at him, Rachael couldn't breathe with wanting him.

Rio's hand stilled on the small leopard. She could shake him with just a simple sentence. It was terrifying to think of the hold she already had on him, especially since he had long ago accepted he would live alone. His life was here, in the rain forest. It was where he belonged, where he understood the rules and lived by them. He studied her face. A mystery woman with a silly made-up name.

The beast roared and Rio embraced the rising temper. He didn't want to see the expression on her face, her gaze drifting over his face with a mixture of emotions, feminine and confused, a tenderness he couldn't afford. "The rules are different here in the rain forest, Rachael. Be very careful."

As always she surprised him, her laughter invading his senses and squeezing his heart. "If you're trying to scare me, Rio, there's nothing you can do I haven't already seen. I'm not easily shocked or easily frightened. I knew the day my mother died, back when I was nine years old, that the world wasn't a safe place and there were bad people in it." She waved a dismissing hand, princess to the peasant. "Save your scare tactics for Kim Pang, or whoever else you want to impress."

Rio gave the small leopard one last pat, reached out casually to scratch Franz's ears before straightening to his full height, towering over her, filling the room with his extraordinary presence. He looked very uncivilized, completely untamed and at home in the wilds of the forest. When he moved, there was a fluid grace she'd only seen in predatory animals. When he ceased all movement, he was utterly, completely still. It was intimidating, but Rachael would never admit it.

"You'd be surprised at what I can do." He said it quietly, and there was a soft, underlying menace to his tone.

Rachael's heart skipped a beat, but she kept her expression serene and merely lifted her eyebrow in response, a gesture she'd worked hard to perfect. "You know what I think, Rio? I think you're the one who's afraid of me. I think you don't quite know what to do with me."

"I know what I'd like to do." This time he sounded gruff.

"What did I say that upset you?"

Rio stood in front of her feeling like he'd been felled by

a huge tree. He had closed that door so long ago, his emotions raw and bruised and bleeding, and he wasn't about to open the door for her or anyone else. He couldn't believe it still shook him, those occasional glimpses into a past he didn't want to remember. A different life. A different person.

Rachael watched his hands curl into fists, the only sign of his agitation. She had inadvertently touched a nerve and had no idea what it was that had done it. She shrugged. "I have a past, you have a past, we're both looking for a different life. Does it matter? You don't have to tell me, Rio. I like who you are now."

"Is that your way of subtly asking me to stay out of your business?"

She tugged at the hair at the back of her neck, obviously used to it being much longer. "I was saying it doesn't matter. No, I don't want you prying into my past. I shouldn't have told you as much as I did." She smiled at him because she couldn't help herself. She was acting out of character, telling things best left unsaid. She shouldn't have hurt feelings because he didn't want to spill his life's story to her. She doubted he would have been hiding out in the rain forest unless something traumatic had happened in his life. He made her want to tell him everything. "I'm sorry I made you uncomfortable, Rio. I won't do it again."

"Damn it, Rachael. How do you manage to do that?" One minute he could work up anger and the next she disarmed him completely. "And, by the way, how is it that you escape the mosquitoes? I only use the netting because they annoy me buzzing around, but I thought you would be covered in bites."

"Mosquitoes don't find me quite as charming as you do. I noticed all the others in my group were having to use repellent all the time. I don't think mosquitoes like the way I taste. Does it bother you that they leave me alone?"

He nodded. "It's a rare phenomenon. The mosquitoes don't bother the tribespeople. Your mother knows the stories of the leopard people. Were you born here? Is your mother from here?"

Rachael laughed again. "I thought we just agreed not to pry into one another's business and you can't let three seconds go by without asking questions. I'm beginning to think you have a double standard, Rio."

A slow, answering smile curved his mouth. "You could be right. I never thought of it that way."

"And all this time I thought you were a modern sensitive New Age man," she teased.

Franz growled, coming to his feet. At the same time, Rio leapt to one side of the door in the nearly impossible way he had of covering long distances. He signaled the cat to silence, drew his gun and simply waited.

7

THE whistle came again, a soft one-two note. The gun never moved at all, remaining steady and aimed at the entrance. Rio answered, using a different combination of sounds, but he stayed motionless, simply waiting.

"Put the gun away," Kim Pang said and pushed open the door. He stepped into the house, his clothes torn, damp and bloody, his tough features a mask of weariness. He had obviously been traveling fast and light. There was no pack and no weapon that Rachael could see.

Still, Rio remained in the shadows, to one side of the door. "I don't think so, Kim," Rio said softly, "you didn't come alone. Who's with you?"

"My brother, Tama, and Drake Donovan have come as well. You were slow in answering and Drake is scouting while Tama covers me." Kim remained very still. His gaze shifted to take in Rachael, but he gave no acknowledgment that he recognized her.

"Tama isn't doing a very good job, Kim," Rio said, but Rachael could see him visibly relax, although he did not put away the gun. "Signal him to come in." He lifted his head and coughed, a peculiar grunting cough that sounded much like that of animals Rachael had heard in the distance when she was trekking through the forest.

Kim called out loudly in another dialect, his voice raised and harsh, but when he turned back, he was smiling at Rachael. "Miss Wilson, it is good to see that you made it out of the river alive. Your apparent demise caused quite an uproar."

Rachael glanced guiltily at Rio. She'd forgotten she had come to the rain forest as Rachael Wilson. Rio grinned at her, taunting male amusement that gave her the urge to do violence.

"How nice to meet you, Miss Rachael Los Smith-Wilson," Rio said with a slight bow. "How fortunate that Kim remembered your name for you."

"Oh shut up," Rachael replied rudely. "Kim, you're hurt. If you bring Rio's medical kit over here, I'll see if I can clean those lacerations."

"You just sit there and don't move, Miss Wilson," Rio said. "Kim can stay where he is, and when Tama and Drake come in, I'll fix him up. He doesn't need a woman fussing over him." He was ashamed of the tightness in his gut, the knots lying heavy in his belly. The black jealousy the males of his kind could experience. He fought down the natural inclination but couldn't help the small, involuntary move that flushed him out of the advantage of the shadows and into the open as he placed himself slightly in front of Rachael.

Kim spread his fingers wide as if to show he held no weapons. His brother came into the room grinning sheepishly. "Sorry, Kim, I slipped on the wet branch and nearly fell. I was so busy saving my own life, I couldn't very well save yours." He glanced at Rachael and then at Rio, then looked down at the gun in Rio's hand. "Getting a little overprotective, aren't you?"

"Getting a little old to be slipping off a perfectly wide branch, aren't you?" Rio countered, but he was clearly listening for something outside the house.

With the door open, Rachael could easily hear the sudden change in the rhythm of the forest. Where there had been warning shrieks and calls and cries, now the forest once more vibrated with its natural sounds. The barking of deer, the croaking of frogs, the humming and twittering of insects and cicadas. There was always the continual call of birds, different notes, different songs, but all in harmony with the flutter of the wind and muffled and continual patter of rain.

Franz stood up and stretched, flattened his ears and hissed, facing toward the door. Rio coughed again, the sound slightly different. "Tama, toss a pair of pants to Drake. He doesn't need to come in and scare the hell out of Miss Wilson."

"Stop calling me that," Rachael snapped. "And why didn't Drake, whoever he is, wear clothes?"

"He didn't know he'd be in the company of a woman," Rio answered, as if that somehow cleared up the question.

Drake Donovan was tall and blond and swaggered in, dressed in a pair of Rio's pants and nothing else but a grin. His chest was heavily muscled, his arms thick and roped and powerful, built much like Rio. His grin widened when he saw Rachael. "No wonder you weren't answering your radio, Rio. Introduce us."

Rachael was suddenly conscious of her appearance, her uncombed unruly mop of hair and no makeup, with the four men staring at her. She lifted one hand to tidy her hair. Rio caught her wrist and pulled her hand to his hip. "You look fine, Rachael." His voice was gruff. He glared at Drake as if he had accused Rachael of looking bad.

"Hey," Drake spread his hands out in front of him with innocence. "I think she looks great. Especially for a dead woman. Kim thought you might have drowned in the river, but I see you were rescued by our resident jungle man."

"Quit trying to be charming," Rio said. "It doesn't suit you."

Rachael smiled at the blond. "I think it suits you very well."

Rio pressed her hand tightly against his hip, as if he were holding her to him. "What happened, Kim?"

"We were taken prisoner by Tomas Vien and his people. They were not after the medical supplies or even the ransom as we first thought." Kim looked at Rachael. "They were looking for Miss Wilson. They had pictures of her."

When Rachael stirred, Rio squeezed her hand, signaling her to stay silent. "How is it you managed to get away from them?"

Drake looked at Rio sharply, his strange eyes narrowing, but he said nothing.

Kim glanced at his brother. "I didn't make the meeting with my father. It was for a special ceremony my family knew I wouldn't miss unless something happened."

Tama nodded. "My father was very worried. There had been talk all up and down the river about the bandits and how they were looking for someone and if anyone harbored her they would be killed. Our people were warned. When Kim didn't return, my father sent me looking for him. I sent out a call and Drake was close, so he came along to help me track Kim."

"I called you on the radio." Drake picked up the story. "I knew you'd want to know Kim was missing and help us track him, but you didn't answer, so I was worried about you. Obviously unnecessarily."

"My radio is out of commission," Rio said tersely. "It took a bullet."

"Fritz is injured." Drake moved toward the small cat, but Franz paced back and forth in front of the wounded leopard and showed his saber-like teeth in warning.

Drake made a face at the clouded leopard but moved away from the agitated cat. "So you ran into trouble."

Rio shrugged. "Nothing I couldn't handle. You helped Tama pull Kim out of the bandit's camp?" He glanced toward the snarling cat. "Franz, settle down or go outside."

Franz hissed in warning but curled up around Fritz, eyes staring at the intruders.

Drake nodded, all the while keeping a wary eye on the clouded leopard. "Kim was in bad shape. They didn't believe him that she'd gone overboard into the river. He was beaten."

Rachael made a small, strangled sound. Rio slid his thumb over the back of her hand in a soothing gesture.

"They beat everyone, even the woman," Kim reported grimly. He looked at Rachael. "They aren't going to give up looking for you unless they find your body. Someone offered a million-dollar reward for you."

Rachael closed her eyes against the sudden despair sweeping through her. She hadn't considered that much money. People killed for far less. What would a million dollars mean to the men facing her?

"That explains a lot," Rio said. He sighed softly. "Drake, my medical supplies are running a little low, but I've got enough to clean up Kim and pack his wounds."

"I'll get the plants we need," Tama said. "We didn't stop for anything, we hurried to check on you." He left the house abruptly.

"I appreciate that," Rio answered. He sank into the chair beside Rachael, casually shifting her, careful of her leg beneath the blanket, settling her partially onto his thigh, arranging her leg and the blanket to his satisfaction. He waved at the others to find seats.

"What is it?" Drake asked as he rummaged through the medical bag. "What does a million dollars explain?"

"I had a visitor last night. One of ours, one I didn't recognize. A traitor, Drake. I couldn't imagine what would induce one of ours to turn traitor, but a million dollars can go to a man's head."

Rachael stayed very quiet, aware the information being passed back and forth was important to her. She hoped they forgot about her presence and would speak more openly.

"How could he have been one of ours if you didn't

recognize his scent, Rio?" Drake didn't look up from where he was washing Kim's wounds.

Rachael couldn't bear to look at Kim's swollen, bruised face. He was stoic as Drake cleansed the lacerations, but as he shrugged out of his torn shirt, she saw him wince. He turned slightly and she gasped. "What did they do to you?"

Rio slipped his arm around her. "Those marks are made from caning. The bandits are known for using a cane on their victims. Tomas is notorious for it. I don't think we've brought out a single kidnap victim without evidence and tales of caning."

Rachael turned her face into Rio's shoulder. "I'm sorry, Kim, I didn't want anyone hurt. I thought if I slipped into the river, they'd think I drowned."

"They would have found another reason to cane him," Rio said, his fingers massaging the nape of her neck. "Tomas is sick. He enjoys other people's pain."

"What he says is the truth, Miss Wilson," Kim agreed.

"Rachael. Call me Rachael, please."

"She has trouble with her last name," Rio offered.

Rachael glared at him. "You're just so funny. You should be a stand-up comedian."

"I didn't even know Rio had a sense of humor," Drake said, tossing a boyish grin over his shoulder at Rio.

"I don't," Rio answered ominously.

Tama hurried in, carrying several plants and roots. "These will heal you fast, Kim, and perhaps the cat too."

"Did you send word to your father that you found Kim alive?" Rio asked.

"Right away. The wind carried the news. He will see the vision in his dreams and know Kim is well," Tama answered, busily tearing strips off one of the plants and throwing shredded green stems into a pot.

Rachael frowned as Rio nodded. "Is he saying Kim's father will dream he's alive and know it's true?"

"Their father is powerful medicine man. The real thing. I believe he knows more about the plants in the forest, poisons, and visions than any man alive. If they sent him the news, he'll pick it up in a vision, or dream, if you prefer to call it that," Rio explained.

Rio didn't sound as if he were teasing her, but she found the idea of sending news via visions a bit difficult to believe. "You don't really think they can do that, do you?"

"I know they can do it. I've seen it done. I'm not good at sending visions, but I've been on the receiving end. It's better than the mail here in the forest," Rio said.

Drake nodded in agreement. "Visions are dicey things, Rachael. You have to be adept at interpreting them."

"Rachael?" Rio arched his eyebrow at Drake in warning.

"She asked to be called Rachael," Drake pointed out, looking innocent. "I was being polite."

A strange odor rose from the pot where Tama pressed leaves, petals, stems and roots from various plants into a thick paste. It wasn't unpleasant, but smelled of mint and flowers, orange and spice. Fascinated, Rachael watched carefully, ignoring the exchange between the men. "What is that?"

Tama smiled at her. "This will prevent infection." He tilted the pot so she could see the brownish-green paste.

"Will it work on Fritz?" Rachael asked. "His wounds are draining and Rio's been worried about him."

"The leopard attacked him, nearly killed him," Rio supplied. "He knew enough about me to know I'd choose to save Fritz and try to track him later."

"So he's familiar with the way you hunt." Drake sounded worried. "Not too many people know the clouded leopards go along with you when we're pulling a victim out of the bandits' camps."

Kim looked up from where his brother was applying a thick poultice to the worst of the lacerations on his chest. "Only your unit and a couple of my people, Rio."

"No one in our unit would betray Rio," Drake said. "We've been doing this together for years. We all depend on one another. I know if I'm wounded Rio's going to pull

my butt out of there. And if I'm captured, no one's going to
rest until they get me free. That's the way it is, Kim."

"And we do not sell out our friends for any amount of
money," Kim said quietly, with great dignity.

"No, your people would never consider money over
friendship, Kim," Rio agreed. "I don't know where this
traitor came from, or how he knows of me, but he is definitely one of ours, not one of yours."

"He is of the forest then," Tama said.

Drake scowled when Rio nodded. "It would be unlikely
that you wouldn't recognize the scent."

"The stench is still on Fritz," Rio challenged, "see if
you can tell me who it was."

"Send Franz out," Drake said. "He looks hungry."

"Be careful," Rachael warned, "he attacked me. Viciously,
I might add."

Drake's scowl deepened. "He attacked you?"

Rachael nodded. "And he bit me, so just be careful
around him. He has teeth like a saber-toothed tiger."

"It wasn't Franz," Rio pointed out, "it was Fritz that
actually bit you."

"Does it matter?" Drake burst out. "The animal really
attacked you? You're lucky to be alive."

"I want Tama to take a look at her leg after he finishes
with Kim," Rio said. He peered at Rachael's face closely.
"You're breaking out in a sweat. Are you getting too tired,
because I'll put you back in bed. She hasn't been up at all
yet and I don't want her to overdo."

"Let me see," Tama said, looking up from where he was
smearing paste over his brother's bare back.

It was Rio who pulled the blanket away from Rachael's
leg, revealing the swollen mass of punctures and lacerations. The two puncture wounds drained continually and it
wasn't a pretty sight. Rachael was embarrassed.

Drake winced visibly. "My God, Rio, that must hurt like
hell. Does she have an infection? We have to take her to a
hospital."

Rachael shook her head, shrinking back into the protection of Rio's larger body. "No, I told you, Rio, I can't go to a hospital."

Kim and Tama examined her leg carefully. "She's right, Rio. If you take her to a hospital, even under a false name, one of Tomas's spies will hear of it and let him know. Some are paid, some fear him, some just want the association, but they will give her up to him. You cannot protect her in that environment."

"I don't want anyone to risk their life by trying to protect me," Rachael protested. "My leg is healing fine. I'm way better than I was a few days ago, ask Rio. As soon as I can travel, I'll be on my way. I won't have anyone risking their life for me."

Rio reached across her to lace his fingers through hers. "Rachael, no one is going to turn you over to Tomas, and you're not just going to walk into the forest alone. It doesn't work that way."

Rachael wanted to argue with him that it was *exactly* that way, but she wouldn't do it in front of the others. For all his relaxed appearance, Rachael felt the tension coiled tightly in Rio. She knew him, inside and out. He was a stranger, yet all too familiar. He was uncomfortable in such close proximity to the others, although she could tell he felt a camaraderie for them. Without conscious thought she moved closer to him, shifting her weight until she was nestled beneath his shoulder, fitting into his frame as if she were born there. It was a movement of protection and he felt it.

Rio looked down at the top of her curly head. So much hair. Thick and black like a raven's wing. Curls rioting in all directions. His fingers slipped into the thick mass, rubbed and caressed the curls, watched as they coiled around his thumb. The gesture was completely familiar, was something he did automatically for comfort, for a connection between them. He would never get used to being around people, not even those he called friend, but Rachael was different, was a part of him. Belonged with him.

"Is your wrist broken?" Tama asked her, obviously concerned. "How did that happen? In the river?"

Rachael looked at the makeshift splint. Her leg always hurt so much, she almost never remembered her wrist. "Rio thinks it's broken. He splinted it, and to be honest, I hardly notice it."

Emotion welled up, nearly choking Rio. It took him a few moments to realize it was happiness. The warmth of joy spread through his body. It had been such a long while since he'd experienced the feeling he barely recognized it for what it was. Rachael didn't want to tell the others that he had been responsible for her injury. It shouldn't have mattered to him, but it did.

"Rio." Drake said his name sharply. "This traitor, the one you say was here last night, he had to be looking for her."

"I thought he'd been sent to assassinate me, that he'd joined with the bandits for the reward, but with a million dollars at stake, I doubt if they gave me a thought," Rio said wryly. He leaned over Rachael, a smile tugging at his mouth. "I guess you're worth a lot more than I am."

"She's prettier too," Drake teased.

"Well you don't need to be looking."

Kim and Tama sank down onto the floor beside the chair, pushing the blanket from Rachael's leg to examine the wounds up close. Rachael could see the terrible marks crisscrossing Kim's back. "It makes me sick to know they did that because of me. I know you don't think it's my fault, but it feels that way."

Kim smiled up at her. "All of us have things we are responsible for. There is little value in taking on what you can't control. Let it go."

Rachael wished it was that easy. She looked away from him to stare out the window into the wild green foliage. The leaves appeared feathery, the creepers wild and twisted green ropes while orchids vied with brilliantly colored fungi for space among the other flowers growing on the thick tree trunks and branches. It was beautiful and primitive and called to something inside of her. She longed to disappear into the deepest forest, simply become something else, something untouchable and wild and free.

She felt it first in her chest, a tightness making it nearly impossible to breathe. Then it was a fire in her stomach, muscles contracting and stretching. Heat seared her flesh, her bones, sizzled in every organ. She itched, a wave of it rushing over her so that she looked down and saw something move beneath her skin as if alive. Her hands curled involuntarily, fingers curving, and her fingertips ached and stung. She gasped and drew back from the edge of a great precipice, her heart pounding in her chest and her lungs fighting for air.

"I can't breathe, Rio." It took forever to get the words out. "I need to be outside where I can breathe."

Rio didn't ask questions or waste time on arguing, but lifted her immediately against his chest, rising with her as if she were a mere child instead of a fully grown woman in his arms. He stepped carefully around Kim and Tama and the pot of brown-green paste. Rachael caught a glimpse of Drake's face, his eyes wide and shocked with a knowledge she didn't possess before he managed to wipe the expression from his face.

Rachael buried her face in Rio's neck, inhaling his comforting scent, giving herself up to the strength in his arms.

"You're all right, Rachael," Rio soothed, one hand stroking her hair as he sat on the small sofa on the verandah. "Listen to the forest, to the monkeys and birds. They make life seem in balance again. Listen to the rain. It has a soothing harmony."

"What's happening to me? Do you know what happened? I swear I saw something moving beneath my skin, like a parasite or something." The humidity created the illusion of a sauna. The sound of the rain was dulled and muted by the heavy canopy overhead. Her breath was coming in ragged gasps, as if she'd run a long race. Her wounded leg was throbbing and burning, her pulse pounding there in a frantic rhythm. "I don't have panic attacks, I don't. I'm not hysterical, Rio."

"I know, Rachael. No one thinks you're hysterical. Just stay calm and when we're alone, we'll talk about this." His heart was pounding as frantically as hers. The possibilities were incredible, almost unbelievable to him. He wanted time to think about it, to do a little research before he provided answers. "Just one thing, Rachael. Have you ever heard the words Han Vol Dan before? Did your mother ever say those words to you or mention them in her stories?" He held his breath, waiting for her answer, feeling as if his world teetered on the edge of an abyss.

Rachael turned the words over in her mind. They weren't entirely unfamiliar, but she had no idea what they meant and she was fairly certain her mother had never included them in her wild rain forest adventures of the leopard people. "I don't know. My mother never said those words to me, but . . ." she trailed off in confusion.

"It doesn't matter," he said.

"What does that mean? Han Vol Dan? The words flow like music."

"It's all right, don't think about it right now," Rio reiterated. "I hope you really aren't blaming yourself for what happened to Kim. I've been rescuing kidnap victims for some time all along this river and in three countries. My unit is hired to go in and bring victims out. Sometimes the government contacts us because it's a politically sensitive situation and other times it's the family asking us to get them out. And still other times we deliver the ransom and make certain nothing goes wrong so we can return the victim to his home. In nearly every incident where Tomas and his group are involved, the victims have suffered beatings. He's one of the bloodiest of the bandit leaders. Most consider themselves businessmen. If the money is paid, they deliver the people they've taken in good health."

Rachael shook her head. "It's just a way of life to them? Kidnapping people? How do their families feel about what they do?"

"Most likely they're grateful for the money coming in. Some do it for political reasons, and those situations are much more explosive and much more dangerous to my team. And anytime we're going after someone Tomas has kidnapped, we know it's dangerous both to them and to us. Tomas has killed hostages even after the ransom's been paid. His word means nothing at all, to him or to anyone else."

"Have you met him?"

He nodded. "A few times. He's crazy and a bit drunk on his own power. He's been known to kill his own men for a perceived slight. He's death on women. I think he likes to hurt people."

"I knew someone like that. He could smile and pretend to be your best friend even as he plotted to murder your family. People like that are so twisted." Already Rachael was beginning to feel better. The strange malady that had gripped her earlier was gone, leaving her trying to remember what it felt like. She just remembered being afraid. The unexplained episode made her feel slightly ridiculous, the epitome of the hysterical woman. It was no wonder Rio didn't think she belonged in the forest. "Rio, I'm sorry for acting like such a fool in front of your friends."

"You didn't, Rachael. If you're feeling better, we'll go back inside and see if Tama and Kim can fix your leg. They're much more adept at healing than I am. Their father worked a bit with me, but they have had the benefit of his tutelage since they were little."

She circled his neck with her arms, linking her fingers at the nape of her neck. "I think I'm becoming used to you hauling me around," she teased.

"Well tuck that blanket around you. I don't mind you going without underwear in front of me, but I draw the line at parading around in the nude in front of my friends. You'll give Drake a heart attack."

"I must be picking up your bad habits," Rachael said, tugging at the blanket until it covered her bare thighs. She snuggled against his chest and wrapped her arms around his neck again, turning her head to look into his vivid green eyes.

They both smiled. It made no sense, but neither cared. They simply melted into one another. She had no idea if she moved first or if he had, but their mouths fused together and joy burst through them. The earth shifted and rocked. Monkeys chattered noisily and a bird shrieked in delight. Prisms of color radiated through the droplets of water on the leaves and moss. Petals from blossoms overhead rained down on them as the wind shifted slightly, but neither noticed. For that moment there was only the two of them, locked in their own world of pure feeling.

It was Rachael who pulled back first, smiling because she couldn't help herself. "You have an amazing mouth."

He had heard those words before uttered in that same voice, that same teasing, slightly awed tone. He had felt her fingertip tracing the outline of his lips before. He clearly remembered sweeping away the dishes and laying her on the table, wild with need, wanting her so badly he couldn't wait long enough to get her to the bedroom.

Rachael's fingers tangled in his hair, a gesture that always turned his heart over. Sometimes he felt as if he lived for her smile. For her kiss. For the sound of her laughter. He leaned close until his lips were pressed against her ear. "I wish we were alone right now." His tongue made a small foray, delving into shadows, his teeth nipping gently. Her breasts pushed against his chest, soft tempting mounds, her nipples taut peaks. He had known her body would react to that small tease of his tongue.

"It's just as well we aren't," Rachael pointed out, trying to keep her brain from melting along with the rest of her body. It had to be the humidity. She could testify she'd never quite felt so sexy and so wanting to entice and tempt a man as she did Rio. She stared into his eyes, his strange, beguiling eyes, and felt as if she were falling into him.

A leopard growled a warning, then gave a soft grunting cough from inside the house. Rachael and Rio blinked, trying to shake off the enthrallment they seemed to be under.

"Rio, you'd better tell your little friend to back off, or he's going to get a surprise," Drake called.

Rachael was shocked at the gravelly menace in Drake's voice. Rio stiffened, snapped out an instant command to Franz and the clouded leopard burst from the house. He raised his lip at Rio, his ears flat, his teeth exposed, tail switching back and forth.

"He looks really angry." Rachael couldn't quite suppress the note of fear in her voice. "It's amazing how big he looks, and his teeth are downright scary."

Rio stepped back to give the cat room. "All leopards have tempers, Rachael. They can be very moody and edgy, even the smallest brother. Franz is naturally upset and he doesn't tolerate company very well."

"He should be used to me," Drake snapped. "The little runt threatened me. If he managed to bite me, I'd stretch his hide between two trees." He stood in the doorway glaring at the clouded leopard. His eyes were brilliant and focused, almost glassy. There was an aura of danger emanating from him. His hands gripped the railing of the verandah, fingers curled tightly around the wood.

Rio slowly set Rachael onto the overstuffed sofa, never taking his eyes from Drake. There was sudden tension in Rio's body, although he appeared as relaxed as ever. His smile didn't quite reach his eyes. Rachael could see he was just as focused on Drake as Drake was on the cat. Neither man moved a muscle, so still they seemed to become part of the forest, blending into the shadows. Clouds moved overhead, darkening the skies. As the wind blew and foliage and creepers feathered back and forth the shadows grew and lengthened. A few raindrops managed to penetrate the heavy canopy and splashed on the railing of the verandah.

The sound of wood tearing was loud and unnerving. Long splinters of wood fell to the floor of the porch to lie in curls. Rachael stared at them in surprise. Franz hissed and, facing Drake, backed away as he slowly slunk toward the largest tree branch. As if his back legs were springs, the clouded leopard launched himself into the canopy and disappeared.

Drake remained motionless, watching the leaves quivering, and then he took a deep breath, let it out and glanced at Rio. "Back off, man, the little runt deserved to be kicked."

"Fritz was attacked by a leopard, Drake. Franz is a little on edge. You could have given him a break."

"I don't understand," Rachael interrupted. "I thought you two were friends."

Rio immediately dropped his hand onto her shoulder. "Drake and I understand each other, Rachael."

"Well I don't understand either of you."

Rio laughed softly. "It has something to do with bad-tempered cats. Come on, let's get that leg taken care of."

"You mean put that homemade brownish paste on it?" Rachael sounded horrified. "I don't think so. I'll take my chances with the care you gave me." She stared at the railing behind Drake. There were fresh claw marks in the wood and she couldn't remember them being there earlier.

"Surely you aren't going to be a coward," Rio teased, picking her up as if nothing had happened. He didn't glance at the claw marks or seem to notice them. All the tension was gone as if it had never been.

"Maybe we could mix a few more petals in with it and change the color," Drake suggested, preceding Rio into the house. "Tama, she doesn't want your healing concoction. Can you change the color to princess pink?"

Rachael made a face at Drake. "I'll go without it, regardless of color."

Kim smiled at her. "It works, Miss Wilson."

"Rachael," she corrected, trying to look dignified when Rio placed her on the bed. She was already tired and wanted to just lie down and sleep for a while. "How fast does it work? And does it hurt?"

"Your leg already hurts," Rio pointed out. "It won't make the pain worse."

Rachael curled up, drawing her leg up as best she could to protect it from any voodoo concoction Tama had whipped up. "I'm a modern sort of woman. The kind that goes with modern medicine."

"Haven't you ever heard the phrase, 'when in Rome . . . '?" Rio teased.

"Yes, well, we're not in Rome and I doubt if their medicine is that particular shade of green." Rachael glared at him, slapping his hand away as Rio tried to pull her leg out for inspection. "Back off if you don't want to lose that hand!"

"Is she always like this?" Drake asked.

"She gets worse. Don't put a gun in her hand."

"That was an accident. I had a high fever." She shoved Rio's hand away again. "I'm not getting near that stuff. You sure turn bossy when your friends are around."

"Stop squirming around. I want Kim and Tama to see what they can do." Rio sat on the edge of the bed, casually leaning his weight across her hips so she couldn't sit up. "Just do it, Tama, don't pay any attention to her."

"What did she shoot?" Drake asked.

"The radio."

Drake laughed. "Fortunately I brought mine. You can have it and I'll pick up another. We're going to have to go after Kim's do-gooders and get them out of Tomas's camp. That was the real reason we came, you know, not to rescue you, Rio."

"Kim's do-gooders?" Rachael echoed, feigning outrage. "When I'm feeling better, you'll be taking that back."

Rio tried to ignore the black jealousy swirling in his gut. He might come from a primitive species but he didn't have to act like it. He could be civilized. It shouldn't matter that Rachael smiled at Drake. And maybe it didn't. But it did matter that she teased him. He wanted that particular note in her voice to be reserved exclusively for him. He

reached inward, searching for a calm center, a place he
often went to conquer the part of him that lived by forest
rules. Air moved through his lungs. He breathed in and out,
determined not to sway from his chosen path. It was all
important for him to be in control.

He felt the touch of her fingers. Feather-light. Barely
there, the smallest of connections. Her fingers twisted in
the waistband of his pants, knuckles pressing against his
bare skin creating instant heat. It was a small gesture, but
he recognized her need for comfort, for reassurance. And
that brought him instant relief.

"Rio, are you going to go after Don Gregson and the
others?" Rachael had planned her escape so carefully. She
had planned to live her life alone. She hadn't even been
that afraid, yet now everything seemed different. She
didn't want Rio to leave her.

8

WE can't leave any of those people with Tomas," Rio answered with a heavy sigh. "I don't think we have a choice in the matter."

"This isn't going to be like the other times," Drake cautioned. "We've always done the smash-and-grab and gotten them out of the country while we scatter into the forest. The reward money changes everything."

Rachael could feel four pair of eyes on her. She kept her face averted. She should have known the reward would be too large to ignore, especially in countries where people had very little. "Money talks. That's the motto in my family. *El dinero pavimenta la manera.*"

"Money paves the way," Rio translated. He had heard the phrase before, but the origin eluded him. He glanced at Drake, arched an eyebrow in inquiry. "Interesting motto for a family."

Drake shrugged and shook his head. He thought he'd read the motto before, perhaps in the papers, but he couldn't remember anything about it.

"Yes, well, I have an interesting family. Sooner or later,

they'll send a representative to bribe your government officials if they haven't already. I'll have to leave the country fast." She tightened her fingers around the waistband of Rio's pants. If he was going to lie across her and hold her down while Tama smeared his foul-looking concoction over her leg, he may as well be of use. Deliberately she brushed her fingertips over his skin, hoping it was a punishment.

"You can't leave the country now, Missy." Tama shook his head. "Tell her Rio. The bandits will close the borders. They have spies all up and down the river, along the borders, everywhere. Most of the people are afraid and just want the bandits to leave them alone. With the reward so high, they'll have more help than usual. It will be better to just hole up and wait until the storm blows over."

Kim nodded his agreement. "My brother speaks the truth, Miss Rachael. There are good people up and down the river, but that much money would bring prosperity to an entire village. It would be easy to justify such a small thing as passing information along. Better you stay unseen in the forest and wait until it is believed you perished in the river."

Rachael went very still beneath Rio. She studied the four men carefully. "I suppose you're right, Kim. It would bring prosperity to an entire village. The government would want the money. Any of you could probably use it too."

Rio's hand went to the nape of her neck, his fingers beginning a slow massage as if to comfort her when they both knew there could be no comfort. Not with the kind of money being offered to betray her.

"You have nothing to fear from my people, Miss Rachael," Kim said.

She smiled at him without really looking at him. "Keep telling yourself that, Kim, and sooner or later you'll be disappointed. People who love you will betray you for less. Money buys everything from food, medicine and education to freedom and power. People kill each other for fifty dollars. Even less than that. Anyone in this room might want that money, and who could blame them? I'm a stranger to all of you."

Rio sat up, adjusting her pillows into a more comfortable position. "No one in this room will betray you, Rachael. Drake and I have prices on our heads. If we tried to betray you to any of the bandits, they would kill us on sight. Kim and Tama have no need of money."

Rachael's dark eyes met Rio's gaze in challenge. "I'd be willing to bet you wouldn't have to deal with any of the bandits. If you give me up to a government official, you'd most likely get your reward."

Rio wasn't going to continue to argue with her. And he wasn't going to admit, even to himself, that her suspicion bothered him. He met her eyes steadily. "I'm sure you're right, Rachael, but for all you know I'm wanted by the government too. You said yourself I was running away from something or I wouldn't be here."

Rachael couldn't pull her gaze away from Rio's stare. He was always direct and focused. Always intense. She felt as if she were falling into the depths of his brilliant green eyes. He was sheer black magic, a product of voodoo and love potions. She was a grown woman with a price on her head. She didn't have flights of fancy and she didn't fall head over heels just because a man had a killer body.

Rio unexpectedly leaned very close to her, his lips against her ear. "You're doing it again. You can't look at me like that. It's going to get you into trouble someday."

Drake cleared his throat. "Why in the world would someone put up a million dollars to get you back?"

Rachael continued to look at Rio. She saw only Rio. His weathered face, the lines etched there from too many missions, too many decisions he didn't want to make. Eyes that held so much focused intensity. Eyes that could be as cold as ice or burning with such heat she caught fire. Eyes that were a vivid green instead of the yellow-green she'd seen so often.

"Well, that is the question, isn't it?" Rachael murmured. "What have I done? What did I steal? Because no one would put up that kind of money without a just cause."

"You forgot the most important question. What do you know?" Rio amended.

Rachael took a deep breath, turned away from his all-seeing stare. "I thought you all had to go rescue the others."

"It isn't that easy. Tomas moves his camp and moves his prisoners all the time. They have tunnels in the fields they drop down into. The cane fields can cover a maze of tunnels that go for miles," Rio explained.

"Rat holes," Drake said. "They have so many bolt-holes it takes time to find them and pinpoint their location."

"And just about the time we have a fix on them, the prisoners are moved again," Rio added. "We have to move carefully, especially with Tomas. Drake and Tama were able to get Kim out because no one expected a rescue so soon. This series of storms are some of the worst we've experienced in years. The last thing anyone would think was that Kim's family would know something happened and go after him using one of our people to aid him."

Rachael was too exhausted to do anything but lie back on the pillows and think. She hated to admit it, but the strangely colored concoction Kim and Tama had smeared on her leg had definitely taken away much of the pain. She glanced down at her leg and nearly laughed. Her calf and ankle were still swollen nearly double the normal size and now appeared as if she were wearing a brownish-green sock. The two puncture wounds continually drained, which added to the entire effect. "Lovely," she murmured.

"I think so," Drake said, grinning at her with boyish charm.

Rio waited for the sudden surge of black jealousy that seemed to be a curse hanging over his species, but surprisingly it didn't come. He could feel the brush of Rachael's fingers along his back, the way she tugged absently on the waistband of his pants. It was such a small thing, but it was

familiar and comforting. He felt confident and secure in his
relationship. Rio smiled and shook his head. He had to
keep reminding himself he didn't have a relationship with
her. He reached behind him to capture her hand. "I swear,
Rachael, I have flashbacks around you."

They stared at one another, completely in tune at that
moment. Their smiles were slow and genuine, smiles of
complete understanding, spreading warmth through them
both.

Drake cleared his throat to draw Rio's attention. "And
you always thought it was a myth. Rachael, my dear, I
don't think you have to worry about anyone turning you in
for money or for anything else. You've come home where
you belong."

"Do you have any idea what he's talking about?"
Rachael asked. But she could see it on Rio's face. He knew
exactly what Drake was talking about. And she saw something else. Just for the briefest of moments she saw hope
and happiness in Rio's eyes. It flickered there and was
quickly covered up. "You do know."

"Drake has a thing about old legends. He believes in
fairy tales. I don't," Rio answered gruffly.

Drake nudged him. "But you're beginning to. What
about Maggie and Brandt? Are they a myth? You just don't
want to admit when you're wrong." He turned his attention
to Rachael. "Rio's stubborn. No one's ever been able to do
a thing with him. Good luck is all I'm going to say."

Rio groaned. "Don't believe him, Rachael. He always
has more to say. If we were lucky he'd shut up now, but it
isn't going to happen."

Kim and Tama nodded in agreement, laughing aloud as
they did so.

Rachael was very aware of Rio's thumb sliding intimately back and forth over her wrist. "Is that true, Drake?"

"Lies, all lies," he denied, clutching his heart. "And they
call themselves my friends. I risk my life for them and this
is how they repay me."

"Poor thing," she commiserated, trying not to laugh. Drake and Rio were such powerful, dominant-looking males, yet at that moment they looked like two boys laughing over a silly joke together. Rachael had all kinds of questions, but she put them aside until she could be alone with Rio.

"Rachael's tired," Rio said. "We should let her rest while we decide what we're going to do about finding this lost group of do-gooders." He saw her swift frown and hastily retracted. "Kidnap victims."

Drake laughed again. "I always wondered what could make you politically correct. It isn't a what, it's a who."

Rachael watched the four men go out onto the verandah, leaving her with Fritz. They closed the door, but she could hear the low sound of their voices. Somehow it was reassuring to hear them as she drifted between waking and sleeping. Rain was intermittent. There would be the murmur of the wind in the trees, the flutter of leaves and the continual sound of insects and birds, of troupes of monkeys chattering back and forth as they moved through branches. The sounds crept into her dreams, familiar and soothing. The humidity was never oppressive, but rather heightened her senses, making her aware of the curves of her body, of her nerve endings, of her sexuality. She felt drops of sweat running down the valley between her breasts.

Rachael closed her eyes and Rio was there, bending his dark head toward her body, his tongue swirling over the swell of her breast, sending a shiver down her spine. Her body tightened in anticipation. He looked at her and her breath caught in her throat. There was so much love there. So much devotion. She felt tears welling up. She knew him so well, every expression, every line. When he was tired or happy or angry. She wrapped her arms around him, held him to her while they listened to the wind and rain beating softly at the window.

Rio tapped at the window, wishing he'd thought to pull the blanket aside so he could see Rachael. He was certain she would fall asleep fast. Her leg was healing, but very slowly. He counted them lucky that she hadn't lost it. "Tama, thank you for mixing up the herbs to heal Rachael's leg. I was worried I might not be able to save it. She was pretty sick for a while."

"You know most of the healing plants," Tama replied. "This is a mixture my father uses when we must heal quickly without much pain while traveling through the forest and rivers. The river can be dangerous to open wounds. This puts a sealant over it to prevent parasites or bacteria from getting under the skin."

"Don't worry, Rio, I made certain I left the puncture wounds open to drain," Kim added. "Are you going to tell us how that happened?"

"Not to mention, you look a little worse for wear yourself," Drake pointed out.

Rio put his hand on the window, spread his fingers as if he could touch her. He felt her calling to him. There was no sound, but he knew she was there in his mind, maybe in his skin, reaching for him, separated only by the thin walls. "I took a couple of minor hits, nothing big, getting our last vic out. And I had the little run-in with the leopard. If you come across anyone with damage from a big cat, let me know. He's got to go for treatment somewhere."

"You think he was after you or after the woman?"

"I thought he was sent after me at first. He was definitely tracking, but now I think maybe it was Rachael all along."

"The reward?"

Rio's fingertips drummed on the window. "I don't think he meant to take her out of here. I think he was going to kill her."

Drake winced visibly. "One of ours? We don't kill women, Rio, especially one of our women and she is. You know she is."

"I don't know anything at this point." Rio leaned against the railing and looked at his friends. "Since she's been around I'm in a perpetual state of confusion." He grinned a little sheepishly.

"Who is she Rio? Where'd she come from?" Drake asked.

Rio shrugged. "I don't know. She doesn't talk about herself very much." He rubbed his hands together and looked out into the darkened interior of the forest. "I remember her. I remember everything about her. Sometimes when I'm with her, I can't tell the difference between the past and the present."

"Does she remember you?"

"I think she does sometimes. I see it in her eyes. And she admits to being just as confused as I am." Rio shoved both hands through his hair. "What have you heard, Kim? Did anyone in the camp give you any information on her?"

"I'm sorry, Rio. They want that money and they'll turn the forest inside out to get it. Whoever is offering the reward wants her badly."

"She said they wanted her dead," Rio admitted, "but nothing else. She didn't say why and she obviously believes they'll keep coming."

"Anyone offering a million dollars is serious," Drake concluded.

Kim shook his head. "Not dead, Rio. They are not to kill her. If she is harmed in any way, the reward will not be paid. I heard Tomas talking to his men. He repeated it several times. They are not to harm her."

The wind blew steadily through the leaves, turning them from dark to silver as the rays of diffused sunlight burst through the canopy. Rio straightened from where he was leaning against the railing, paced restlessly the length of the verandah before returning to stand in front of Kim. "You're certain of this?"

Kim nodded. "Tomas said she was not to be harmed or they wouldn't get the money. He was adamant."

"Rachael said they were trying to kill her. Could she be wrong? She said a cobra was put into her room right before they went upriver. And she left the States under false papers in order to disappear because someone wanted her dead."

"Do you think she's lying to you?" Drake asked.

Rio paced a second time, turning the idea over in his mind. Finally he shook his head. "I think she believes someone is trying to kill her. And she doesn't panic easily, so it isn't hysteria. If Rachael says someone wants her dead, I have to believe her. It's possible we're dealing with two separate factions. Someone is willing to pay a great deal of money to keep her alive. They're making a big fuss openly, going to the government demanding they find her, and someone else. Someone much quieter who is working to keep her silent. That person is hiring assassins to make certain she doesn't talk."

"That's a jump, Rio," Drake said.

"I know it is, but it's possible. I believe her when she says someone is trying to kill her. Why would a woman like Rachael try to disappear into the rain forest?"

"She's close to the Han Vol Dan, Rio. You felt it just as strongly as I did. She's very close. Maybe it draws our people back to the forest."

"Maybe. I asked her if she heard those words before and she couldn't remember. She said they weren't unfamiliar, yet she had no real knowledge of them."

"It complicates things," Drake said. "It's a dangerous time for everyone. I'm leaving here tonight. I don't dare stay around when she's so close."

"Did you feel it, Kim? Tama?" Rio asked curiously. "You've been around our people many years. I practically grew up with you."

"I've never been close to anyone during the time of the Han Vol Dan," Kim admitted. "I've heard of it, of course. Our elders speak of such things, but to my knowledge, no one other than your people have witnessed such an event." He looked to his brother for confirmation.

"I know of no one," Tama said. "But I did feel the pull of the woman. I thought it was the close proximity. She is very sensual."

Rio winced, but he was used to the open, direct nature of his friends. He felt the churning in his stomach, a sure sign of danger. "Yes she is, at least I find her so. It is best if you all leave until this time passes. Drake is right. It's dangerous to all of us."

"I'll leave the radio, Rio. We can scout around, pick up the trail, and when we have something, we'll let you know. You won't be able to leave her unless this time passes."

"We run the mission the way we always run it," Rio objected. "If we start changing things, someone is going to get killed. Let me know as soon as you have something and I'll be there."

Kim and Tama rose together as if in silent communication. Drake stepped off the verandah to the wide branch.

"Give my regards to your father, Kim," Rio said. "May all the magic of the forest be with you and may fortune be your companion as you travel."

"Good hunting to you always," Tama replied.

"Stay alert, Rio," Drake added as the two tribesmen descended carefully to the forest floor. "I'll put out the word about the leopard, but you know he'll be back if he took a contract. It is ingrained in us to never stop. You'll have to kill him."

"Damn it, Drake, don't you think I know that?"

"I know how you are. I just want you to watch your back."

Rio nodded. "You don't have to worry about me. Say hello to the others."

"You going to bring Rachael to meet everyone soon?"

"I want to give her time to adjust. Time for us to adjust." Rio hesitated. "I haven't been around anyone for more than a couple of hours at a time. Even within the unit, I work alone. I don't know if I can fit someone into my life and make it work."

Drake grinned, but there was no humor touching his eyes. "I'd be the last man to tell you how it's done, but I wish you the best of luck." He started down the tree branch, then turned back. "Don't throw it away, Rio. Not when it's handed to you like this. Most of us will never have the opportunity."

Rio nodded and watched the three men disappear into the shadows of the forest. He stood for a long while breathing in the crisp, clean air, the fragrance of flowers and rain. From habit he raised his head and sniffed the air, scenting the wind. He relied on his own resources to give him advanced warnings of impending danger, but the animals in his territory always aided him.

He coughed, a series of grunts, sending out the word to be carried near and far, from the smallest creature on the forest floor to the honeybees building their giant combs high in the canopy. Wings fluttered overhead, an orangutan moved slowly through the branches looking for better-flavored leaves and butterflies swarmed over the masses of flowers on the tree trunks. Everyone went about their business, unafraid when there were no intruders in their realm.

Rio opened the door. At once the wind rushed into his house, swirling around, sending the mosquito netting dancing. Rachael lay asleep, her black hair spilling across the pillow. The wind tugged and teased at the silky strands so that her hair moved, beckoning to him. He pulled the door closed and resisted the temptation of lying down beside her. If he were going into action again so soon, he would have to clean all his weapons and make certain he had emergency kits stashed along every escape route.

RACHAEL ate very little and stayed quiet, stroking Fritz's fur while she watched Rio work. He had more guns and more knives than anyone she'd ever met, and she was familiar with weapons. He used the same care cleaning as he did fixing up wounds, meticulous and steady, not missing a single detail. She watched as he took several sets of clothes and small medical kits along with some of the guns and put them in weatherproof packs.

"What are you doing with those?" Curiosity finally got the better of her. Rachael was comfortable with silences

and with being alone, but not like Rio. He seemed perfectly
fine going hours without saying a single word.

Rio glanced up and blinked, as if he'd just noticed her.
In truth he'd been aware of her every move. He was nearly
hypnotized by the sight of her fingers stroking the cat's fur.
"I stash the packs along my escape routes in case I'm out
of ammo, weapons or need medical supplies. It can be very
useful."

"And the clothes?"

"Comes in handy if I need a change," he answered glibly.

"I see. Are you going to tell me why your friend Drake
acted so strangely around the cats and why it didn't bother
you? I expected, just for a moment there, for him to suddenly erupt into violence. I think you expected it too."

"Drake has lived in the forest for most of his entire life.
We're very primitive here. We react to things in nature. It
sounds a little strange, but if you're here a long time, you'll
understand." His hands stilled on the knife he was sharpening. "I want you to stay a long time, Rachael."

His gaze was direct as always. Rachael couldn't have
looked away if her life depended on it. His voice was so
low she almost didn't hear him. For a moment she couldn't
breathe, her chest so tight from a mixture of hope and fear.
She almost blurted out her first thought. She wanted to
stay—needed to stay. Had never wanted a man the way she
wanted him. But death was poised over her head and it
didn't care who happened to be in the same vicinity.

"With me, Rachael. I want you to stay here with me."

"You know I can't, Rio. You know why." Her fingers
curled so tightly in the clouded leopard's fur, Fritz lifted
his head and looked at her with his lip curled.

"Then at least want to stay with me. If you could, would
you want to be with me?" She belonged with him. He
knew it with every breath he took. Knew it with every fiber
of his being. How could she not know? Not feel it? It was
so clear to him.

Rachael pulled her hand away from the cat and dragged the cover to her chin. A small protection, but it made her feel in control. Rio stood up in his lazy, languorous way, the one that always reminded her of a feline. Without hesitation he lay down beside her, fitting his body around hers, careful to keep from touching her leg.

The blanket was between them, but Rachael felt his body right through the thin weave. When she took a breath, she took him into her lungs. "You don't know me any more than I know you. We can't just pretend we don't have pasts, Rio, as much as we'd like. I'm not the woman you seem to remember in your dreams, and you can't be the man I remember. Things like that aren't real."

His fingers tangled in her hair. "How do you know they aren't real? How do you know we weren't together in a past life? Your hair felt just like this, but it was long, to your waist. When you braided it, the braid was nearly as thick as my forearm. I know the sound of your laughter, Rachael, but more importantly, I know what makes you laugh. I know what makes you sad. I know that you have an aversion to monkeys. How would I know that?" He wrapped her curls around his fingers and buried his face against the silken mass.

"I must have said something, maybe when I had such a high fever. I was probably rambling like crazy."

"Just the opposite. You were so closemouthed most of the time, it scared me. Sometimes you were barely breathing."

She laughed softly. "I was afraid you were giving me truth serum."

"So I could conduct my interrogation." He lifted his head, his green eyes blazing at her. "Are you afraid of me, Rachael? Are you afraid I'll betray you for the money?"

She studied his face feature by feature and found she was shaking her head before she could stop herself. "No, I'm not afraid of that."

"Then talk to me. Tell me who you are."

She lifted her hand to his face, traced the tiny lines

around his mouth. "You tell me who you are, Rio. Let me know you before you ask questions of me. I see suffering in your face. You've seen betrayal, you know what it is. And you came here for a reason. Tell me what it is. Why do you have to live in this place?"

"I choose to live here, Rachael, I don't have to live here. There is a difference."

"You've been here for some time. Do Kim and Tama live far away from other people? Does Drake?"

"No, Kim and Tama live in the village. Most of the time if their people move, the entire village moves. They still have longhouses when they're traveling. Drake lives near a village for our people."

"Who are your people, Rio? Why don't you want to be close to them?"

"I've always been happier on my own. I don't mind a solitary life."

Rachael smiled and snuggled deeper into her pillow. "You aren't willing to tell me anything at all about yourself. Even in friendship there has to be give-and-take, trust between two people. We don't have that between us."

"Then what do we have?" Rio knew she was right, but he didn't want to hear her say it. He wanted things to be different, but if he told her the things she wanted to know there was no chance for them.

"I'm so tired, Rio," Rachael said softly. "Can we do this tomorrow? I can't seem to stay awake no matter how hard I try. I think you keep putting something into that drink you're always telling me is so healthy."

She wanted to drop it. He recognized the signs. He was adept at avoiding topics he didn't want to discuss. And what was the point?

Rio lay listening to her breathing, his body so hard he felt that just one more brush against her skin might be the last straw. He would shatter into a million pieces. Sleeping on the floor away from her wouldn't stop it. Cold showers didn't help. The house was too small for the two of them to share unless they were together, and sleeping in the bed next to her and not touching her was just plain impossible.

Intellectually he knew it was because she was close to the Han Vol Dan and she was affecting him with her ripe scent. He wanted to blame it on that, the age-old call of female to male, but in truth, he wanted her in so many other ways. She made him happy and he didn't even know why. He didn't care why. He wanted her in his home. At his side. With him. It was fairly simple as he saw it.

Women. They always managed to complicate the simplest issue. He sat up, careful not to disturb her. He would get no sleep if he didn't slip out into the night and run. The farther and faster the better.

Rachael hoped she was dreaming. It wasn't a frightening nightmare, but it was disturbing. Not so much the images, but the idea of it all. She could see herself, stretching her body, arching her back, in the throes of sexual need. Not just a wanting—a craving, an obsession. The need was so strong she could think of nothing but finding Rio. Being with Rio. Rio's hands touching her, stroking her body, driving into her with wild abandon. There was heat and fire and still she wasn't satisfied. She could see her body rippling with pleasure, her body sleek and moist. Rio rolled over, pulling her on top of him, and Rachael threw back her head, thrust her breasts in invitation as she rode him frantically. She turned her head to look back at the sleeping Rachael, her face contorting as fur rippled over her body.

Rachael shook her head, stirred drowsily, wriggled a little to find the warmth and reassurance of Rio's body. He wasn't there. She turned over, careful of her injured leg. She was definitely alone in the bed. The house was dark, not unusual, Rio never lit a lamp, preferring to pad around the house barefoot, in the nude. He seemed to have such an affinity with the night, preferring that time to any other. Nothing in the shadows affected him or frightened him. He never really seemed to sleep deeply. The few times she

woke in the dark, he was already alert, the change in her
breathing enough to awaken him.

She lifted her head and studied the room. The mosquito
net hanging over the door swayed like a dancing ghost in
the wind. The door was open. Rio had gone on one of his
many midnight adventures. He always came back more
relaxed, the tension gone from his body. He was usually
covered in sweat and would walk softly over to the basin to
wash. Rachael loved watching him. She should have felt
guilty, a voyeur, but she didn't. She simply feasted her eyes
on his body, watched the ripple of his roped muscles and
appreciated the fact that he was so intensely male.

Something shoved at the mosquito netting. A large dark
head thrust its way into the house. Rachael froze, her heart in
her mouth. Fritz snarled, hissed and rose to back unsteadily
toward Rachael. She reached out her hand to the little
clouded leopard, touched the fur as he slunk beneath the bed,
still hissing. Rachael didn't take her gaze from the huge,
heavily muscled animal pushing his way through the flimsy
mosquito net into the house.

The leopard was the largest wild animal she'd ever
encountered. It was a male, weighing close to two hundred
pounds, pure muscle, exotic black fur from its head to the
tip of its tail, its eyes a vivid yellow-green. The leopard
swung its head this way and that, peering around the room,
ignoring the small snarling cat as if it was beneath its dignity. It stepped fully into the house, the tail switching from
side to side. It rubbed its shoulder against the chair and
sink, all the while staring at Rachael with far too much
intelligence in its eyes.

She moved her hand very slowly, bringing it into the
bed, sliding it under the pillow to find the reassuring metal
of the gun. Curling her fingers around the grip she pulled it
in slow motion toward her. Beneath the bed, Fritz snarled
loudly. "Hush," she whispered, trying to keep her voice
low so she didn't trigger the leopard into an attack.

To her amazement, the little cat went silent. The black

leopard continued rubbing its body along the furniture, all
the while staring at her. She lay still, unable to look away.
As the animal approached her, Rachael forgot to bring the
weapon up to aim. The animal didn't use a slow stalk, it
simply padded over to her, rubbing the length of its body
along the bed. It rubbed its head along her arm, the fur soft
and unbelievably luxurious. Her breath caught in her
throat. She had to fight an impulse to bury her fingers
in the fur, to rub her face in the neck and shoulder of the
animal.

The leopard began a slow systematic rub of her body
with its head, chin and cheeks, rubbing down her shoulder
and across her breasts. It stretched across the bed to rub her
stomach and the junction between her legs, took its time
rubbing over her good leg and, after sniffing her wounded
leg, was careful as it rubbed its way back up her leg to her
head.

The leopard's breath was warm against her skin as it
nudged her shoulder, giving her the impression the animal wanted her to scratch it. The gun slipped from her
hand to rest on the blanket and she sank her fingers into
the thick fur. It was daring and nearly overwhelming, a
wild and crazy impulse she couldn't control. She traced
the darker shadow of rosettes buried in the dense black
fur with her fingertips. Tentatively, she began to scratch
the leopard's ears and neck, became bold enough to
scratch along its broad chest. She could see several scars
in the fur, indicating the cat had been in more than one
fight, but the animal was a magnificent specimen of its
kind. Muscles ran like steel beneath the fur, wrapped
around the body in every direction. She should have been
terrified at being in such close proximity, but the night
took on a surreal quality.

Up so close she could see the whiskers were very long,
and were on the upper lips, cheeks, chin, over the eyes and
even on the inside of the leopard's forelegs. The hairs were
embedded in the tissue with nerve endings that transmitted

continual tangible information much like a radar system. During an attack, the leopard could extend the whiskers much like a net in front of the mouth to help it assess the prey's body position in order to administer a lethal bite. Rachael hoped the continual rubbing against her was a signal for her to scratch harder and not that the animal was becoming aggressive.

Fritz stuck his nose out from under the bed and her heart pounded in fear for the small wounded cat. The larger leopard merely touched noses, rubbed the top of the clouded leopard's head with his own. Then it stretched languidly, scraped the floor around the bed and repeated its rubbing over Rachael's body with its head before padding across the room to the kitchen area. It stood on its hind feet and raked its claws continually down the wall, leaving long, deep grooves in the wood. Exactly like the other grooves. It dropped back to the floor, turned its head to look at her once more with its focused stare, then, unhurried, padded out of the house into the darkness.

9

RACHAEL wiped the sweat from her eyes and stared at the claw marks on the wall. She hadn't been dreaming. A huge leopard had been in the house, walking around as if it owned the place. It had looked at her with its eerie stare. The animal had rubbed up against the bed, against her skin, against her entire body, not once, but twice, against the furniture and had just stretched full length to rake its enormous claws down the kitchen wall, leaving behind telltale grooves embedded deep in the wood. She couldn't have imagined such a beast any more than she could imagine the claw marks.

"Just when you think it's safe to go back into the jungle," she whispered aloud, afraid if she spoke too loudly the cat would return. "Rio? Rio, where are you?"

The door was open to the night, the mosquito net blowing gently in the mild breeze. The rain was a soft fall in the distance. Rachael sat up, taking care not to jar her leg. She had more strength, but her leg was swollen and painful even with slight movement. Dragging on Rio's shirt, muttering as it snagged on her broken wrist, she threw back the cover. The gun fell to the floor with a clatter, the noise loud in the stillness of the night.

With a little sigh, Rachael fished around for it, reaching with her fingertips, trying to spare her leg until she was forced to move. There was no sound, but she felt the impact of his eyes. At once she could breathe easier. Rachael looked up to find Rio's wide shoulders filling the doorway. She was used to the fact that he rarely wore clothes in the house. That his body was as hard as a rock. That there was something dangerous and different about him she couldn't quite put her finger on. But she would never get over the sure power of his eyes.

"Aside from the fact that you left the door open and a leopard decided to visit, you have to stop taking these midnight strolls. Hasn't anyone ever told you the forest can be dangerous at night?" Rachael curled her fingers into the blanket, making a fist, wishing she could jam it in her mouth and shut up for a change. Could she sound any more ridiculous lecturing him about the dangers of the forest when he knew far better than she? It was just that she'd been so afraid and the relief of having him back safe and unharmed was overpowering.

Rio sauntered fully into the room, totally nude but as confident as if he were wearing a three-piece suit. "I'm not about to let anything happen to you, Rachael. I should have closed the door when you were alone in the house, but I was right outside." His gaze moved over her face, a moody, edgy examination. "Were you trying to get out of bed?"

She forced a soft laugh. "Rachael to the rescue. I was going to put the leopard in a choke hold if it attacked you."

He stared at her for a long moment before a slow smile spread across his face. Her heart did a funny little flip.

"What a thought, Rachael. I have this visual of you wrestling with a leopard and it's enough to turn my hair gray."

She loved his hair. Shaggy and untamed but shiny clean,

like silk. "Rio, put some clothes on. Honestly, you're making life very difficult for me."

"Because I'm always in a state of arousal around you?" His words were low, velvet soft. The impact was physical. Her body simply dissolved into liquid heat.

She couldn't help but see him—unashamed, natural, alone. He looked so alone standing there like a Greek god, a statue of the perfect male, with roped muscles and penetrating eyes and a sinful mouth. She wanted to be feeling absolute lust. Nothing else, just good old-fashioned lust. A fling that would burn hot and burn out leaving only ashes and good wishes and freedom behind. It didn't help that she'd been dreaming strange, passionate dreams about making wild love with him.

How did she know she could drive him mad by simply running her fingertips up his thigh? How did she know his eyes would change, gleam like bright emeralds, hot and bright, consuming her with desire? She had seen tears in his eyes. She had heard his voice husky with passion. She shook her head to clear her thoughts, to free herself from the strange memories that were hers . . . yet not hers.

"While I'll admit you're more than tempting, and distracting, I'm not in shape to feel very sexy, Rio." It was a blatant lie. Rachael had never felt sexier in her life. She sighed heavily. "It scares me when you go off like that. I'm really afraid something might happen to you. It's not like I'm in any shape to go charging to the rescue."

Rio could only stare in silence. Her admission made him feel helpless and vulnerable. No one worried about him. No one cared that much if he made it back to his house at night. He fully expected to die in a fight someday and he doubted if more than a handful of men would mourn his passing, and that would be a brief salute to his marksman abilities. Rachael looked at him with the world shining in her eyes. A gift. A treasure. And he was certain she was completely unaware of it.

"I'm sorry I frightened you, Rachael," he murmured

softly and shut the door on the night—closed the door on his freedom. "I had some things to think about. I went for a run."

"Yes, well, while you were gone, we had a little visit from your friendly neighborhood leopard. Fortunately it was on its best behavior so I didn't shoot it. You may notice I'm choosing humor and bravado rather than classic hysteria. Although I thought long and hard about the hysteria."

He could feel the grin forming. It started in his gut and spread warmth through his body. "I appreciate the sacrifice. I'm not certain what I'd do with hysteria. It may be beyond my coping abilities."

"I seriously doubt anything is beyond your coping abilities. Did I upset you earlier? Is that why you couldn't sleep?"

Rio crossed to the basin as he always did after his nightly disappearances, his muscles flowing like water as he moved through the house without a whisper of sound. He remembered to light a candle, knowing she liked the scent of it. The flame flickered and set shadows dancing on the wall. "I thought a lot about what you said, that I wasn't willing to tell you about myself. Maybe you were right. I love the way you look at me. I haven't ever had anyone look at me the way that you do. It's hard to think of giving that up, or taking a chance of never seeing it again because you won't look at me the same way after I talk to you about who and what I really am."

She always did the unexpected. Rachael laughed softly. "And you must have forgotten who you're talking to, Rio. The woman with the million-dollar price on her head. Has it occurred to you, I'm a pariah in society?"

"I know exactly whom I'm talking to," he said.

Rachael stretched her leg out in front of her, careful not to jar it. She had to use both hands, even the broken one, in order to ease her leg fully off the bed. Blood rushed, causing pins and needles to add to the throbbing pain. That immediately drew his attention. Rio half turned, a small frown on his face. "Are you going somewhere?"

"Just stretching. I thought you could make me one of those drinks. I'm getting addicted to them. What do you put in them, anyway? Just for future reference, you understand." She straightened her shirt, pulled at the tails to try to cover her bare thighs. The edges were gaping open over her breasts and she awkwardly tried to button it with one hand.

Rio dragged on a pair of jeans before crossing over to the bed. "The drink is made from fruit nectar and whatever fruit I happen to harvest that morning." He hunkered down beside her and reached for the edges of the shirt—his shirt. It looked completely different on her. His knuckles brushed her full breasts. He could feel warmth and velvet-soft flesh. His knuckles lingered, deliberately rubbed gently. He hadn't planned to take advantage, it just happened. He couldn't resist the temptation. He looked up at her face, his fingers curled around the edges of his shirt.

Rachael was instantly trapped in the vivid intensity of his gaze. She fell, tumbled, dropped into his gaze. Leaned into him in invitation. His mouth took possession of hers, a fusing together, wild and tumultuous, neither quite in control. His fingers moved between her breasts, sliding the button aside to allow his hands to cup the soft weight. She gasped, arched into his palm, pushed closer, her body every bit as sensitive as in her catlike dream. She needed his touch, ached for it, dreamed of it. Was familiar with it. His mouth was pure male, driving every thought from her head so that she simply wound her arms around his neck and held him to her.

His lips blazed a trail of fire from her mouth to her chin. His teeth nibbled, moved lower to her throat, his tongue swirling along her skin just to taste her. Rachael cried out when his mouth settled over her breast, when his fingers tangled in her hair, when he spread a blazing fire through her body.

"Why did you have to put your jeans on this one time?"

Rachael complained, her voice breathless. "Just this once, wouldn't it be all right to forget everything and just be together?" The ache and the need were raw. She heard it and knew he did too.

"Damn it, Rachael." His tongue swirled over her taut nipple. He rested his forehead against her sternum, his breath warm on her breasts. "Did you have to make me think? If I take advantage of you while you're injured and you can't walk away, how are you going to feel tomorrow when you have to hear everything I have to say?"

His hands cupped her breasts, thumbs stroking, his mouth hot and moist and filled with passion as he suckled, just one more time. His body was so full and painful he moaned, an involuntary protest against the tight material covering his erection.

Rachael tugged at his zipper, thankful he wasn't wearing his button-fly jeans. "Take them off, Rio."

He reluctantly left the haven of her breasts to stand so he could drag off the jeans and kick them aside. He was standing between her legs, and Rachael simply leaned into him, her hands cupping his testicles and her mouth sliding over his erection. Hot silk surrounded him, gripped him, her tongue dancing and teasing. The rush hit him like a fireball, nearly blew out the top of his head. She was doing something with her fingertips, stroking and caressing until he thought he'd go out of his mind. He heard a sound escaping his throat, something between a growl and a groan, but he couldn't stop it.

"Rachael, *sestrilla*, you're killing me." He didn't want her to stop, but if she didn't he was going to disgrace himself. There would be no chance to satisfy her. He put his hands on her shoulders to press her back. "If we're going to do this, we're going to do it right." Even as he said it, even as he meant it, her tongue was doing a dancing foray over the head of his penis, teasing and driving him out of his skull. The breath slammed out of his lungs and he fisted his hands in her hair, his hips thrusting helplessly.

That was Rachael. Teasing and laughing, her breath hot
with passion as she drove him out of his mind. She loved
their sex life, was every bit as adventurous as he. Just looking at her could make him crazy and when she was like
this . . . Rio groaned again and shook his head to clear it of
memories. He wanted this to be here and now. This Rachael,
this Rio—not the ones from another time and place.

He tugged at her hair and she lifted her head, her dark
chocolate eyes laughing joyfully. His heart performed a
series of somersaults. He pushed her back on the bed, lifted
her leg carefully, dragging blankets, shirts and everything
else he could find to prop it up for her. The shirt fell open
to allow him to see her luscious body. Her skin was a miracle, soft and inviting.

"You're sure, Rachael. Be sure, *sestrilla,* there is no
going back once we do this." His heated gaze drifted possessively over her body, drinking her in, even when he
wanted her to be certain of what she was doing. Whatever
past life they had together was urging a passionate and
heated union. "I want this to be us. You and me and no one
else. Not past or future, but the two of us in the present."

She reached her arms up for him, locked her hands
behind his neck as he carefully lowered himself into the
cradle of her hips. Her body was as welcoming as the look
on her face. As the wonder and joy in her eyes. Rio buried
his face in the warmth of her throat, closing his eyes to
absorb the feel and texture of her skin. Of her heat.

"I know what *sestrilla* means, Rio. You are calling me
beloved one. I have no idea of the language. But I know the
word." She held his head to her, feeling the trembling in his
body. He was enormously strong, with roped muscles, yet
he trembled in her arms. It amazed and humbled her. She
swept her hands over his back, careful to keep the
makeshift splint from rubbing against his skin. She knew
the exact line of his back, but the scars were unfamiliar.
She traced each one, committing them to memory.

His full erection was heavy and thick, pressing against

her moist entrance, but he simply lay in her arms, holding
her to him while she explored his body. She felt his mouth
move against her throat and her heart began to pound in
anticipation. She couldn't stop moving as flames licked at
her body in the wake of his tongue. He worshipped her,
taking his time when they both were already on the edge of
insanity. His hands and mouth touching and tasting until
she had tears in her eyes and lifted her hips in urgent need.
He was incredibly gentle, tender even, so careful of her
injured leg, yet there wasn't a spot he missed on her body,
leisurely feasting on her as if they had all the time in the
world. His breath was warm on her stomach as he gave a
series of little nips down to the tangle of dark curls.

"Rio, it's too much."

"It's never too much." He breathed the words against
her, his finger pushing deep into her so that her muscles
clenched around him and she cried out with pleasure. "This
is the two of us, Rachael. The way we're meant to be." He
bent his head and replaced his finger with his tongue.

She clutched the sheets for an anchor. Her body
exploded, rippling with life, with pleasure, nearly sending
her off the bed. Then his mouth was fastened to hers and he
was lifting her hips, surging into her. He was thick and full
and thrust through her orgasm, sending shock waves of fire
through her body.

"More, Rachael, take me deeper, take all of me." His
voice was hoarse and he tilted her hips as he thrust deeper,
wanting to bury himself inside her body, inside her sanctuary. He wanted to share her skin, her heart, her very soul.
"That's right, *sestrilla,* more, take all of me." He could
have wept tears of joy. Everything in him remembered,
knew he had come home. He felt her shift, just that tiny bit,
felt her take him deeper into her tight sheath. Her muscles
gripped and clung and performed an amazing tango of heat
and fire on his body. He found a perfect rhythm, surging
deep, thrusting hard, immersing, losing himself in a paradise he thought lost to him.

He knew instinctively, or maybe it was a past life together, exactly how to please her. He knew what she wanted, what made her gasp and moan and cling to him. He wanted their first time together to be a memory for both of them. He forced his body under a semblance of control to give her complete satisfaction, driving her up and over the edge again and again until she cried out for mercy. He wanted to give her the perfect joy she gave to him.

Rachael dug her fingernails into Rio's back, desperate to hold on, to take him with her when she was flying so high. Lights burst behind her eyes. Her body shuddered with pleasure. She felt him swelling even more, growing larger, harder, exploding with life and joy, his growl of sheer pleasure mingling with her own cry.

They lay in the heat of the night, their scents mingling, their hearts racing. Rachael traced one long scar just over his left shoulder with her fingertip while wave after wave rocked her. "How did you get this one?"

He couldn't move, sweat beading his body. He settled into her, shifting slightly to take some of his weight off of her. "That one was a knife. I was pulling a sixteen-year-old boy out of Tomas's camp and the kid panicked and ran from me before I could stop him. A guard nabbed him and swung a machete at him." He nestled his face closer to the warmth of her breast. "That's where this scar came from." He showed her his arm and the deep scar running along his forearm. "I was able to save the kid, but a second guard knifed me from behind during the fight. That wasn't my most shining moment."

Rachael lifted her head enough to press her mouth to his forearm, her tongue swirling over the long scar. He tasted as if they'd just made love. "And this one?" She reached lower, deliberately sliding her fingertips over his firm buttocks to rest in the small white concave over his left hip. "How did you get this one?"

"A bullet." He grinned, his breath teasing her nipple into a hard peak. "Obviously I was running."

"Well at least you were showing good sense."

"There were more of them then there was of me. I walked into a hornet's nest that time. I was only scouting, looking for signs, and walked right into them. It seemed the right thing to do was to leave since I didn't have an invitation." He leaned into her breast and suckled, just for a moment because she wasn't opposed to the idea. His laughter was muffled. "I've improved my running times since then."

Just the pull of his mouth on her sensitized breast sent her body into another orgasm. He was still locked deep inside her and velvet-soft muscles gripped and clenched tightly, adding to his own pleasure.

Her fingertips avoided the raw wound on his hip and went to the myriad of deep slashes on his back. "And these?"

Rio went absolutely still. Even his breath caught in his lungs. He waited a heartbeat, listened to the air moving in and out of her lungs. Slowly he lifted his head to look down at her. "Those scars came from a few fights I had with a big cat."

Her dark eyes moved over his face. He could see her taking it in, accepting it. "A cat like the other night. A big leopard. Not Fritz or Franz."

"Not Fritz or Franz," he confirmed. Very gently he separated from her, easing his body from hers, rolling over to take his weight completely from her. He lay staring up at the ceiling. "A very large, fully grown male leopard."

Rachael could feel the stillness in him. The waiting. There was something he needed to tell her, but he was extremely reluctant. She reached for his hand, laced their fingers together. "Have you ever noticed how much easier it is to say things you need to say, but don't want to say, in the dark?" Her fingers tightened around his. "You know you're going to tell me, so just say it." She waited, her heart accelerating. She had a flashback of his face changing, of fur and teeth and eerie glowing eyes. The longer she lay in the dark waiting, the more she was afraid.

"I murdered a man." Rio said it softly, his voice so low it was barely audible. She heard pain, stark and raw in the ugly confession.

For a moment she couldn't breathe. It was the last thing she expected him to say. The last thing she expected of a man like Rio. It didn't fit with the man who cared for his leopards first. It didn't fit with the way he always put her first. "Rio, defending yourself or having to defend others by taking them back from a man like Tomas is not murder."

"It wasn't self-defense. He didn't have a chance against my skills. I hunted him down and I executed him. It was not government sanctioned and the laws of my people didn't sanction such an act. I wish I could tell you I was sorry he's dead, but I'm not." He turned his head to look at her. "Maybe that's why I can't forgive myself. And it's why I live apart from the others of my kind."

A weight seemed to be crushing her chest. "Were you arrested and charged?"

"I presented myself before the council of elders for judgment, yes. We have our own laws and courts. I was charged with murder. I didn't deny it. How could I?"

Rachael closed her eyes, tried to block out his words. *Murder. Murder. Hunted him down and executed him.* The words echoed through her mind. Flashed at her like a neon sign. "But it doesn't make sense," she murmured aloud. "Murder doesn't fit with your personality. It doesn't, Rio."

"No?" There was amusement in his voice, a twisted, humorless, sarcastic mocking that made her flinch. "You'd be surprised at what I'm capable of doing, Rachael."

"Did you go to jail?"

"In a way. I was banished. I am not allowed to live among my people. I do not have the benefit of the elders' wisdom. I am alone, yet not alone. I am close to them, yet always apart. My people cannot survive in jail. There is only death or banishment for a crime as grave as mine. I was banished. My people do not see me, or acknowledge my existence. Well, other than the unit I run with."

She listened to his voice. There was no note of self-pity. No plea for compassion. Rio stated a fact. He had committed a crime and he accepted the punishment that went along with it. She let out her breath slowly, struggling not to judge too quickly. It still didn't make sense to her.

"Are you going to tell me why you killed him?"

"Whatever my reasons are, they weren't good enough to take the life of another. Revenge is wrong, Rachael. I know that. I was taught that. I knew it when I hunted him. I didn't even give him the chance to draw a weapon so I could claim self-defense. It was an execution, pure and simple."

"Is that what you were thinking when you killed him?"

There was a silence. Rio's thumb slid over the back of her hand. "No one ever asked me that. No, of course not. I didn't look at it that way, but I did know the council would either decide to put me to death or banish me when I returned and told them what I'd done."

Rachael shook her head, more confused than ever. "You hunted this man down, killed him and then returned to your people and confessed you'd done it?"

"Of course. I wouldn't try to hide something like that."

"Why didn't you keep going, head for another country?"

"I've lived apart from the forest, apart from my people, I never want to do it again. I chose this life. It's where I belong. I knew I would have to go before the council when I chose my path, yet I stayed on it. I couldn't stop myself. I still cannot mourn his passing."

"What did he do to you?"

"He killed my mother." His voice roughened. He cleared his throat. "She was running, much like I do at night, and he stalked her and killed her. I heard the shot and I knew. I was some distance away, and by the time I reached her it was too late." Abruptly he released her hand and was on his feet, pacing across the room to the kitchen as if movement was the only thing that could keep him from exploding. "I'm not making excuses, I knew better than to take his life."

"For heaven's sake, Rio, he *killed* your mother. You must have been crazy with grief."

He turned around to face her, leaned one hip against the sink. "There's more to the story, of course there always is. You've never asked me about my people. You've never once asked why our laws are different than the human laws."

Rachael sat up slowly, pulled the edges of her shirt together and began awkwardly to button it. She suddenly felt vulnerable lying on his bed with barely any clothes and his scent permeating her body. "I am fairly certain Tama and Kim answer to the laws of their tribe. We're all subject to whatever laws govern our country, but out here, I doubt the government knows exactly what goes on. The tribes probably deal with most of their own troubles." She kept her voice very calm, her expression serene. It wouldn't help either of them to show she was suddenly very afraid.

Rio moved. It was a small, subtle movement, but distinctly feline. A supple shifting of his body so that he seemed to flow like water, then become perfectly still. His eyes dilated wide, the color changing from vivid green to a yellow-green. At once his gaze was marblelike, glassy, an eerie, focused, unblinking stare. A reddish cast gave his eyes an evil, animalistic quality. He turned his head as if listening. "I can hear your heart beating too rapidly, Rachael. You can't hide fear. There is a sound to it. A smell to it. It's in every breath you take. Every beat of your heart."

And it was killing him. He'd allowed her to get under his skin. He'd known all along he would have to tell her the truth. Rachael had been traumatized by something in her life. She'd seen and lived with violence and he suspected she had tried to escape. He had to tell her the truth, show her the truth—he couldn't live with himself if he didn't. But his heart was being ripped out of his chest and the rage that was never far from the surface welled up to choke him.

It had taken him time to realize she made him laugh, made him cry, made him *feel*. She brought life to him.

Almost from the beginning she made him feel alive again.
He couldn't imagine going back to an empty house. He
forced himself to tell her the truth, although it was terrifying. Rio had never been truly afraid in his life, yet now he
stood to lose something he never thought to have. Fear fed
the anger swirling in his belly so that he wanted to rage at
her.

Rachael nodded, swallowed the tight knot of fear threatening to suffocate her. "That's true, Rio. But you mistake
what I'm afraid of. It isn't you. It isn't what you say. Do
you think it's all new to me? That I'm so shocked by your
confession? I'm not afraid of you. You've had every opportunity to take advantage of me. To kill me, or rape me, or
use me in some way. You could have easily taken me to the
authorities for the reward money. I'm not afraid of you.
Not Rio the man."

He came closer, filling the room with dangerous power.
It emanated from every pore. There was no whisper of
sound when he walked toward her. He moved with the flowing grace of a large jungle animal. Ropes of muscle rippled
beneath his skin. He leaned closer to her. She could hear the
breath in his lungs, the low, threatening growl rumbling in
his throat. Rachael refused to be intimidated, refused to
look away. She stared at him with one eyebrow raised, daring him.

Muscles contorted, knotted, his large frame bent and he
dropped to the floor on all fours, still watching her, never
blinking, never once looking away, holding her gaze captured in the blazing intensity of his. She saw his skin lift as
if something alive ran beneath it.

"And what if Rio isn't a man?" His voice was distorted,
rough. He coughed, a strange grunt she'd heard before.

A chill ran down her spine. She stared in horrified fascination as his body stretched and lengthened, as fur rippled
over his skin, as his jaw lengthened into a muzzle and teeth
erupted in his mouth. The leopard was black with whorls
of darkened rosettes buried deep in the luxurious fur. It

wasn't the first time she found herself face-to-face with the beast.

Rachael recognized the fact that she was breathing far too fast. The leopard was inches from her, his yellow-green gaze holding hers. Waiting. There was a nobility, a dignity about the animal as he waited. Her hand shook as she reached out to touch the fur. The animal snarled, exposed the wicked canines, but she touched him. Connected to him. It was instinctive and the only thing she could think to do under the circumstances. "Fainting is out of the question," she murmured softly. "I've tried it and it just doesn't work for me. I've never figured out how other women manage it. If you were trying to shock me, believe me, you've succeeded beyond your wildest dreams."

Even as she uttered the words, she wasn't altogether certain they were the truth. There had been signs. She hadn't wanted to believe them. It seemed too far-fetched. Surely scientists would have discovered them by now, yet he stood there, staring at her with his wild eyes, his hot breath in her face. He was unmistakably a leopard. A shapeshifter. The thing of myth and legend.

"Why do you want me to be afraid of you, Rio?" She bent her head toward his, ignoring his snarl of warning. She rubbed her face over the dark fur. "You're the only person who ever looked at me for myself. You gave me acceptance even when I didn't deserve it. What is so terrible about what you are? I know people far more terrible." Tears burned behind her eyelids. It wasn't as if she could stay with him. "I guess this answers the question why you run around naked in the forest. You like to go out at night as a leopard, don't you?"

It was useless to hide from her in animal form. When he looked into her eyes there was no horror at his revelations. He could read sadness there. Rio shifted back to his human form and sat on the floor beside the bed. "I'm neither human nor animal, but a mixture of both. We have traits of both species and some of our own."

"Can you assume another form?"

He shook his head. "We are both leopard and human at the same time and only take one form or the other. This is who I am, Rachael. I'm not ashamed of what I am. My people are few, but we play an important role here in the rain forest. We have honor and commitment, and our elders are wise in things beyond modern science. While it's true we have to be careful to remain undiscovered for obvious reasons, we contribute to society in many ways."

There was pride in his voice, but she could see wariness in his eyes. "Tell me what happened to your mother, Rio." She could live with, be friends with and be the lover of a shape-shifter, but she could not live with a man who murdered people. She'd done that, and she would never do so again under any circumstances.

He raked his fingers through his hair, wreaking havoc so that his shaggy hair was more tousled then ever. Locks fell persistently over his forehead, drawing attention to the brilliance of his eyes. "I thought you'd run the minute you knew what I was."

Her smile was slow and more sensual than she knew. It nearly stopped his heart. "Well, I might have, but I can't exactly win any races at the moment."

Her smile was contagious, even then, when she could rip the heart out of his chest and change his life forever. He found an answering smile tugging at his mouth. "I'll admit I thought of that when I decided I'd better tell you. It stacked the odds just a bit in my favor."

"Smart man." Rachael stroked back the strands of hair falling across his forehead. "Tell me about it, Rio. Tell it to me the way it happened, not how other people saw it."

Rio felt the familiar pain, the anguish rising the way it always did when he thought of that day. He rubbed his suddenly pounding temples. "She loved the night. We all do. It's beautiful, the way the moon plays over the trees and the water. We're so much more alive. All the cares of the day disappear when we take the form of the leopard. I suppose

it's a form of escape, running along the branches and playing in the river. Our people love the water and we're all
good swimmers. She went out alone that night because I
was working on the house."

"Where was your father?"

"He died years earlier. It was just the two of us. She was
used to being alone. I'd been gone on and off for a few
years getting an education, so neither of us gave it much
thought. I heard the warning first, the animals, the wind.
You've heard it, you know what I'm talking about. I knew
immediately it was an intruder. Human—not one of our
people. Few people come this far into the interior unless
it's a tribesman and I could feel from the animals it was
someone different, someone dangerous to us."

Rachael eased her leg onto the floor, needing to stretch
out. Immediately Rio helped her, his hands gentle as he
took her foot carefully from the bed. To Rachael's astonishment, his hands were shaking. "Thank you, that feels
better. I'm sorry, please keep going."

Rio shrugged. "I raced after her, but it was too late. I
heard the shot. Sound travels a great distance at night.
When I reached her, she was dead and already skinned.
He'd taken her pelt and left her like so much garbage on
the ground." He closed his eyes but the memory was there.
Already the insects and carrion were moving in. He would
never forget the sight as long as he lived. "We can't take
chances with the bodies. We burn them and scatter the
remains over distances. I did what I had to do and all
the while I could feel the black rage in me turning ice cold.
I knew what I was going to do. I planned it carefully while
I took care of her. I couldn't bear to think about what I was
doing, the burning of her body, so I planned out each step
as I worked."

"Rio, she was your mother, what did you expect to
feel?" Rachael asked gently.

"Grief. Not madness. He didn't kill a woman, he killed
an animal. It's acceptable in society. It isn't legal, but it's

still acceptable. He didn't deliberately kill a human being—and in a sense, he didn't. We're taught that mistakes can occur and we have to be prepared for them. Each time we take our alternate form, we are taking a chance by running free. Poachers often enter our realm, I knew that. I was taught that. So was my mother. She took the chance just as I do nearly every night. It was her decision and her risk. That's what we're taught by the elders, and they're right. We aren't supposed to look upon it as murder. We're taught to view it as an accident."

"I'm not certain that's entirely possible, Rio. Admirable maybe, but not very likely when it comes to one's family."

He touched her mouth. That tempting, beautiful mouth so ready to defend him. There had been no one to defend him all those years ago. He'd been a hothead, rage riding him hard. Defiance his only weapon. "I don't believe in an eye for an eye." He looked down at his hands. "I didn't even back then. I know my killing him didn't accomplish anything. It didn't bring her back. It didn't make me feel better. It certainly changed my life, yet I still can't bring myself to be sorry that he's dead. Do I wish I hadn't done it? Yes. Would I do it again? I don't know. Probably. It was like a sickness inside of me, Rachael, a hole burning in my gut. I tracked him and found his hunting camp. Her pelt was hanging on the wall to dry. There was blood, her blood, on his clothes. I learned how to hate. I swear, I'd never even felt such an emotion before. He was drinking, celebrating. I didn't even give him a chance. I didn't say anything at all to him, I didn't even tell him why." He looked up to meet her eyes, wanting her to know the truth about what he was. What he'd done.

"I think I was afraid to tell him, afraid I'd see remorse or regret. I wanted him dead and I simply ripped out his throat. Her pelt was hanging on the wall behind him."

Bile rose in his throat, just as it had all those years ago. He had been physically ill, over and over, yet he had dragged the pelt from the wall and burned it as he was taught before returning to the elders to tell them what he'd done.

"You condemn yourself for going after the man who killed your mother, yet you make your living pulling people out of dangerous situations, using your skills as a marksman to free them."

"It isn't the same thing as defending my life or the life of someone else, Rachael," he said. "If I'm sent out to bring someone home, back to their family, I believe anyone in the scope of my rifle put themselves there by kidnapping and threatening the life of another. It isn't the same thing at all."

Rachael shifted her weight, bent forward to circle his neck with her arms in an effort to comfort him. Something whizzed past her ear so fast it hummed, thudding into the wall sending splinters in all directions.

10

RIO reacted instantly, wrapping his arms around her and dragging her to the floor, his body covering hers. The movement jarred her leg, sent pain radiating up her thigh and through her stomach so that she wanted to scream. It was only then that she heard the boom of the distant rifle reaching them. At once a series of spits peppered the room, tearing up the wall and showering the room with splinters of wood. Rachael jammed her good hand into her mouth to keep from crying. Her leg burned and throbbed. It felt as if it might have burst open but she couldn't move with Rio's weight on top of her.

"Stay down," he hissed. "I mean it, completely flat on the floor, Rachael. Don't you move, not for any reason." His hands were moving over her, inspecting her for damage. "You aren't hit are you? Tell me." He was shaking with rage. It welled up like a funnel cloud, dark and twisted and ferocious. The bullets hadn't been aimed at him, the marksman had gone after Rachael. There were no lights on in the house and the blanket was over the window. The flickering candle was the only light and it had been enough for the marksman to take his shot. It told Rio they were dealing with a professional.

"It's just my leg, Rio." Rachael did her best to be calm. Screaming wasn't going to help the pain and Rio's weight had her flattened like a pancake on the floor. "I can't breathe very well like this."

Fritz had been under the bed. With the bullets whining so close he emerged, snarling and spitting. Rachael risked her skin by catching the cat to prevent it from exposing itself to the gunfire. The cat's head spun around, saberlike teeth rushing toward her. Rio was quicker, pinning the animal and hissing a command. Fritz grew quiet and lay beside Rachael.

"Ungrateful wretch," she said pleasantly.

Rio ignored her comment, sliding his hand over the bed until he found the gun. It was automatic to check the load. "The clip is full and one's in the chamber." He thrust the weapon into her hand. "Stay down and behind the bed." He rolled over, found his jeans and dragged them on.

Rio propelled his body forward using his elbows, staying on his belly as he made his way across the room to his guns. Carefully he inched his hand up to drag the cache of weapons to him. Almost immediately bullets spit into the wall above him. He rolled over, strapping a knife to his leg. "I have to go out there, Rachael." His next stop was the sink where the candle was. Any professional would know he would want to douse that small light. He used a water bottle from his pack on the floor, taking aim carefully and spraying the candle until the flame went out leaving behind a small trail of smoke. Another spray of bullets peppered the wall and sink.

"I know. Is there another way out besides the door?"

"Yes, I have several. I'll use the one toward the back, farthest from his line of vision. Don't move around. He's probably got night vision glasses and he knows the layout of the house."

"How could he know that?"

Rio didn't know the answer to her question. At the moment it didn't matter. He scooted back to Rachael and laid one of his knives on the floor beside her fingertips. "You're going to have to use that if he gets close to you."

"Do you want me to shoot at him and distract him so you can get out without him seeing you?" Rachael offered.

Her voice trembled and he could hear the note of pain she was trying so hard to hide from him. With his acute sense of smell he picked up the scent of blood. The crash to the floor had caused some damage to her leg and he knew it must hurt. He leaned into her, caught her chin and brought his mouth to hers. He put everything he had into that kiss. His anger and fear, but most of all his passion and hope. He didn't want to admit to love, he barely knew her, but there was tenderness and something that tasted of love. "Don't try to help me, Rachael. This is what I do and I'm better working alone. I want you safe, here on the floor when I get back. If he comes in, use the gun. Keep firing even if he goes down. And if he keeps coming and you run out of ammo, use the knife. Keep it low, in close to your body, and thrust upward to the soft parts of his body when he's close."

She kissed him back. "I appreciate Lesson 101 in weapons training. Come back to me, Rio. I'll be very upset with you if you don't." In spite of the fact that she was terrified and trembling uncontrollably, she forced a smile. "I'll be right here, on the floor, clutching the gun in my hand, so whistle to let me know it's you coming through the door."

He kissed her again. Slower. Thoroughly. Savoring the taste of her, appreciative that he had her. "May the fortunes be with you, Rachael." He began to crawl, staying on his belly, rolling the last few feet. The pantry wall seemed solid enough, but a small section, no more than a crawl space, low to the floor was removable. He pried the boards loose and slipped through, taking the time to replace the section of wall in case his enemy shifted form.

The night was warm. The rain had momentarily stopped,

leaving the trees dripping and intensely green, even in the darkness. He slipped into the foliage, ignored a large python coiled around a thick branch only feet from his home, and moved quickly along the network of branches high above the forest floor. Often he was forced to allow the leopard form to emerge partially, so his feet could grip the slick wood and he could leap from branch to branch easily.

He knew the general direction of his enemy, but it was a big area. In human form he didn't have quite as many receptors to allow him to locate the enemy precisely, but his leopard form was highly vulnerable to the long-distance rifle. Rio was certain the intruder would be expecting the leopard. He had the advantage of knowing every branch, every tree. The animals were used to his presence and would never give away his position as they would that of the intruder. The wind didn't betray him, carrying the scent of his enemy to him, taking his scent and drawing it away.

He recognized the smell of the assassin. It didn't matter that he had taken human form, there was no doubt in Rio's mind the attacker was the same one who had hurt Fritz. He had obviously trained as a sniper and was good at guessing where his target would be. Rio slowed his progress, sacrificing speed for stealth.

The foliage just down and to his left swayed slightly against the wind. His enemy was moving in closer to the house, changing position on the chance Rio had a bead on his line of fire. Rio paced along above him, high in the branches, waiting patiently for a glimpse of the man. He eased his rifle into position, peering through the scope. His adversary never exposed so much as a part of his arm, staying in heavy flora, allowing the shrubs and flowers and leaves to keep him invisible.

Several trees to the right of the house, Rio caught sight of a pair of eyes glowing through the foliage. He knew immediately that Franz had been drawn back to the area by the gunfire. The small clouded leopard was making his way home along the upper highway made of a network of

branches. The leaves swayed. Rio swore eloquently, lifting
the rifle to his shoulder and squeezing off several rounds
into the heavy shrubbery where he was certain the intruder
had settled in for his next chance at a shot. Rio coughed
loudly, a grunting cough of warning, pinning the intruder
down with a multitude of bullets to keep him from getting
off a shot at Franz.

The small cat leapt back, disappeared completely, fading away as their kind could so easily into the thick fauna.
Rio shouldered his rifle and took off through the trees,
changing directions quickly, going up and into higher
foliage, careful to keep from shaking the brush.

He'd given away the fact that he was outside the house,
taking away any advantage he would have had. It was a
game of cat and mouse now, unless he had scored a hit on
a target he couldn't see and he very much doubted if that
had happened. Rio stayed absolutely still, lying prone in
the tree, his eyes sweeping the area continually. The
intruder had to have moved. No one could have stayed in
the spot without taking a hit, but he was a professional and
he hadn't given away his direction.

Rio worried about Rachael, all alone in the house with
the injured clouded leopard. He had no idea if she had the
patience it took for the kind of waiting a sniper often had to
contend with. It could take hours to flush out their intruder.
He should have checked her leg before he left her. He had
visions of her bleeding to death there on the floor waiting
for him to return.

His eyes never stopped moving restlessly, sweeping the
forest in a continual pattern. Nothing moved. Even the
wind seemed to die down. The rain began, a soft patter
falling on the dense canopy overhead. Minutes went by. A
half an hour. A snake crawled lazily along a branch several
feet from him, drawing his attention. Several leaves fell
from the nest of an orangutan as it shifted its weight to nes-
tle deeper into the branches of a tree. The movement, several yards from him, drew his attention.

Almost immediately Rio noticed the branches of a small shrub, just below the tree where the orangutan nested, started to quiver. It was low on the ground, an unusual choice for one of his kind. Rio watched carefully and saw the bushes move a second time, just a slight shiver, as if the wind passed by. He eased his rifle into position, careful not to make the same mistake. Back farther into the ferns and shrubs, he could make out the bruised and torn petals of an orchid scattered on top of a fallen and rotten trunk.

Rio remained unmoving, watching the area closely. Time passed. The rain fell in a steady rhythm. There was no more movement in the thick shrubbery, but he was certain the sniper lay in wait there. Several nocturnal flying squirrels leapt into the air, fleeing a tree directly across from Rio. They chattered and scolded to one another as they landed, clinging to the branches in a neighboring tree. Twigs and petals cascaded in a small shower onto the rotten log and shrubbery below. Rio smiled. "Good Franz," he whispered to himself. "Good hunting, boy." His eyes never left the forest floor.

A boot heel dug a short groove in the vegetation as the sniper shifted to get a glimpse of the treetops over his head. Rio squeezed off three shots in rapid succession, spacing each bullet up the line of the body just as the intruder realized he was exposed. The sniper screamed as he rolled over a small embankment, then abruptly was silent.

Rio was already running along the branch highway, changing position, closing in on his target. He coughed twice, dropping flat both times to distort the sound, signaling to Franz to circle around and stay under shelter, then he was up and running again, covering as much ground as possible before the sniper could possibly recover.

Rio was far more comfortable stalking prey from the treetops, but he began to make the descent to the lower reaches, using thick branches to move quickly from tree to tree, careful to keep to cover as he did so. He dropped to the forest floor, landing in a crouch and going completely motionless, blending into the deeper shadows of the forest.

He was silent, scenting the wind. Blood was a distinctive odor, unmistakable in the air. Drops of rain penetrated the canopy and splattered onto the rotting vegetation. A bright green lizard raced up the trunk of the tree, the motion drawing his attention. A red splotch smeared a lacy fern embedded in the bark. Rio remained still, his gaze relentlessly sweeping the terrain searching for any movement, any sign of the intruder.

Several short barking calls signaled a herd of adult barking deer nearby. Something had disturbed them enough to cause them to sound the alarm. Rio leapt onto a low-hanging branch and gave the grunting cough of his kind to alert Franz. The enemy was wounded and on the run. There was more blood in the thick needles and leaves on the ground where the sniper had rolled, but it wasn't arterial blood.

Rio made another careful sweep of the branches above and around him. He sighed as he bent and picked up a boot. The man had taken just enough time to wrap the wound to staunch the flow of blood, drop his rifle and clothes and had taken to the trees, using his leopard form to escape. It was much faster and more efficient to rush through the branches than to try to run wounded, weighed down with clothes, weapons and ammunition. Running down a wounded leopard at night was madness. Especially one of his own kind who had all the cunning and intelligence along with special training.

Rio scouted thoroughly, knowing leopards often backtrack and stalk their prey. Once he found blood smeared along a tree branch, and another time it was a bruised and twisted leaf, the only two signs marking the passing of the large cat. Franz joined him, scenting the air, snarling, eager to give chase. Rio was much more cautious. They were chasing a professional, a man capable of changing form. Like Rio, he would have planned several escape routes. He would have stashed weapons and clothes along the routes and he would have set traps ahead of time for the possibility of pursuit.

Rio wanted to make certain the sniper hadn't doubled back, but he didn't want to leave Rachael for too long when he didn't know the extent of damage to her leg. He dropped a hand to the top of Franz's head, a gesture of restraint. "I know. He's come at us twice now. We'll hunt him later. We've got to move our wounded, boy." He scratched behind the upright ears and resolutely turned back to gather the clothes and weapons the sniper had left behind. He doubted if he would find an identity, but he could learn something from them.

He made his way back toward the house, Franz beside him, taking his time to make a more thorough inspection of the floor and trees in his realm. He found the blind where the sniper laid waiting for just such an opportunity as Rio lighting a candle might give him. The shifting of shadows against the thin woven blanket was enough to give a marksman a chance of hitting a target. He stopped just a few steps from the verandah, breathing deeply, allowing the knowledge that Rachael could have been killed to wash over him.

He felt sick, his stomach churning. The sweat that broke out on his body had nothing to do with the heat. The wind rarely touched the forest floor. It was always uncannily still there, the dense canopy shielding it, yet high in the trees, the wind whispered and played and danced through the leaves. The sound was soothing to him, the rhythm of nature.

He could understand the laws in the forest. He could even understand the necessity for violence in his world, but he couldn't imagine what Rachael had done to deserve a death sentence. If one of his people had contracted to kill a woman in cold blood, he knew the assassin would never stop until the deed was accomplished. His kind was single-minded, and the ego of the male would now be bruised. The slow, smoldering anger would flair into a dark, twisted hatred that would spread until it became a disease. The male had missed twice and both times Rio and his clouded leopards, two lesser beings, had interfered. It would be personal now.

He stepped onto the verandah. "Rachael, I'm coming in." He waited for a sound. For a sign. He didn't realize he was holding his breath until he heard her voice. Tense. Frightened. Determined. So Rachael. She was alive.

Rachael was still in exactly the same position on the floor as when he had left. The fact that she trusted his expertise lifted his spirits even more. She looked up at him, sprawled out, his shirt barely covering her bottom, her legs splayed half under the bed, her hair tousled and wild, spilling around her face, and she grinned at him. "Nice of you to drop in. I took a little nap but was getting hungry." Her gaze moved over him anxiously, obviously inspecting for damage. Her grin widened. "And thirsty. I could use one of those drinks you're so fond of making."

"And maybe a little help in getting up?" He found his voice was husky, almost hoarse, emotion catching him off guard. Fritz lay curled up at her side and the gun and knife were on the floor beside her hand.

"That too. I heard shots." There was a little catch in her voice, but she managed to keep the smile on her face.

He knew he loved her. It was the undaunted smile. The joy in her eyes. The anxiety for his safety. He would never forget that moment. How she looked lying on the floor, blood seeping out of her leg, his shirt twisted around her waist exposing her luscious bare rump and her smile. She was so beautiful it took his breath away.

Rio hunkered down beside her, carefully inspected the damage to her leg. "We got lucky this time, Rachael. I know it hurts, but it isn't that bad. I'm going to lift you up and it's going to jar you some. Let me do the work."

She was always surprised at his enormous strength. Even after the revelation of what he was, she was shocked at how easily he lifted her and set her back on the bed. She couldn't help herself. She had to touch him, map his face, run her fingertips over his chest just to feel for herself he was alive. "I heard shots," she repeated, demanding an explanation.

"I winged him. He's one of my people, but I don't recognize his scent at all. I've never met him. We aren't the only ones. Some of us live in Africa, others South America. Someone could have imported a . . ." he trailed off.

"A hit man?" She supplied.

"I was going to say sniper, but that works. It's possible. We hire out to take back kidnap victims. We make it a policy not to mix in politics if it's at all possible, but sometimes it's inevitable. Our laws are fairly strict; they have to be. Our temperaments are not suited to everything and we have to keep that in mind always. Control is everything to our species. We have intellect and cunning, but not always the control needed to govern those things."

"He was after me, wasn't he?" Rachael asked.

Rio nodded. "Kim left the medicine for your leg and I'm going to reapply it. We have to leave here. I'm going to take you to the elders. They'll protect you there better than I can here."

"No." Rachael said it decisively. "I won't go there, Rio. I mean it. I won't go—ever. Not for any reason."

"Rachael, don't go stubborn on me. This man is a professional and he knows where you are. He probably knows you've been injured. He came far too close to killing you for my peace of mind."

"I'll leave if you want me to, but I'm not going to your elders." For the first time he heard a bite in her voice. It wasn't edgy or moody, it was sheer temper. Her dark eyes flashed fire, nearly throwing sparks.

"Rachael." He sat on the edge of the bed and pushed back the mop of curls falling in all directions. "I'm not abandoning you. It's safer for you. He's going to come back."

"Yes, I know he will. And you'll be here, won't you. Alone. By yourself. Because your idiot elders are happy enough to take the money you earn risking your life to do whatever it is you do with your little unit. You give it to them, don't you?" She glared at him. "I've seen how you live, and I can't see you having a huge bank account stashed somewhere. You give it to the others, don't you?"

Rio shrugged. She was furious. Anger was radiating from her. Her body shook with it. His fingers tunneled in her thick mass of hair. He didn't know why, maybe to hold her in place when she looked capable of flying at the elders. "Some of it. I don't need it. The money is used to help protect our environment. Our people need it, I don't. I live simply, Rachael, and I like my life. What I keep I use for weapons or food or medicine. I just don't have that many needs."

"I don't care, Rio. They're hypocrites. They banished you. You aren't good enough to live near them, but they'll take your money and they'll let you risk your life to protect their other men while they do their jobs. It stinks and I want no part of them. And if you need another reason, I'll just be followed there and bring more trouble to them. I'm not going. I'll leave and the hit man will follow me, and you'll be safe."

Laughter welled up out of nowhere. He simply leaned forward and took possession of her mouth. Her beautiful, perfect, sinfully delicious mouth. She sank into him, melted, her body pressing against his, robbing his mind of actual thought. Rio wrapped her up in his arms, hungrily devouring her, kissing her over and over because she was alive and she looked at him with that look. Because it angered her that the elders had banished him and she was so ready to defend him even when he didn't need defending. Because she made his blood sing and his body as hard as a rock.

Bolts of lightning ripped through his bloodstream. Flames danced over his skin. There was a roaring in his head and he knew he was wholly alive again. It didn't matter that he didn't know her past. He knew what she was made of, the strength of her, the fierce protective nature. Her courage and fire mattered to him. She had given him acceptance, when his own people couldn't accept what he had done.

Her hand crept around his neck. She lifted her head and looked at him. "I can't stay with you, Rio, and it breaks my heart. Why did I have to find someone who is so kind and gentle?"

"Only you would describe me as kind and gentle, Rachael." He kissed her again. "And we can work things out."

"You mean you can hunt this hit man down and kill him." She shook her head. "I'm not going to let you do that. You hate what you did, killing the man who took your mother's life. You think it's so wrong of you because you can't be sorry he's dead. Rio, you're sorry you killed him. I know you are. You may not be sorry that he's dead, but you regret the way his life was taken. You aren't going to do it all over again for me."

"It isn't for you."

She smiled at him and pushed back the hair tumbling onto his forehead. "Yes it is. It won't matter what excuse you come up with for both of us, I'll always know it was because of me and you'll always know it too. My troubles have nothing to do with you and you shouldn't ever have been made a part of them."

"I bested him twice. He was forced to run and he was wounded. He'll have to come after me. Whether you're here or not, he'll have to come after me."

"He isn't paid to come after you. Hit men work for money. They don't have very much in the way of feelings, Rio, at least not that I've ever seen. If you pay them, they do the job. It's simply business to them."

"You're talking about human beings," he pointed out. "I'll make you something to eat while we discuss this. I'm serious, Rachael, he'll come here to take me out before he ever makes another attempt on you."

Rachael watched him cross to the cupboards. There was total conviction in his voice. "I wasn't going to bring up the differences between us, but now that you mention it,

I've considered one of two problems a relationship might encounter. There's the whole crossing species thing. You didn't ask me if I was using birth control, Rio. Did it occur to you that if I became pregnant there might be a problem?"

Intent on making soup, he didn't turn around. "There wouldn't be a problem, but I knew you couldn't conceive. Not the way we made love."

"Really? Why is that?"

"Because you're one of us."

Rachael lifted an eyebrow and regarded the broad expanse of his back. "How intriguing. Why didn't I know this? You'd think my parents would have given me the information. Not that I'd mind running free in the forest though, that would be fun."

He did turn around then and there was no answering amusement on his face. His expression was grim. "No, you won't go running in the forest, Rachael. Not now, not ever." The smoldering anger was back, a fierce black roiling that swept through him like a dark tornado.

Rachael's eyebrow shot higher. "Nice to know ahead of time there seems to be a double standard in your society for women. I already come from one of those societies, Rio, where women are second-class citizens, and I didn't particularly enjoy it. I don't intend to join another one."

"My mother wasn't second-class, Rachael. She was a miracle to anyone lucky enough to know her. And running free in the forest cost her her life."

"It was a risk she took, Rio. You take it all the time. I took a risk when I let go of the boat and slipped into the rising river. It was my risk to take. In any case there's no point in arguing, I've never shifted into any other shape but this one. Well, sometimes my weight goes up and down a bit and as I get older I think it's redistributing and maybe changing my shape, but that's not what you mean."

"You're one of us, Rachael. Drake knew it and so did Kim and Tama. You're close to the Han Vol Dan. It's why you get edgy and moody."

"Edgy? Moody? I beg your pardon! I do *not* get edgy and moody. And if I do, it's only because I'm stuck in this bed."

"Maybe that wasn't such a good description. I'm trying to be discreet."

"Well forget discreet and just say it."

"All right. But don't get mad at me. You're close to the change and with it you're experiencing a powerful sexual drive, much like a female cat going into heat."

She threw the pillow at him. "I hardly think I'm acting like a cat in heat. I didn't go after every male in the room."

"No, but they wanted to go after you. It can be a dangerous time. You're putting out signals, both scent and body signals."

"You are crazy." Rachael glared at him. "Are you trying to tell me you made love to me because I was putting out some kind of scent?" His back was to her again but she saw his shoulders shake. "If you dare laugh, I'm going to let you know exactly what a woman getting hot entails."

"I wouldn't think of laughing." Sometimes lying was the better part of valor and the only way to save a man's butt. "I made love to you because every time I look at you I want you. Hell, I want you now. I can't think straight when I'm around you, but you already know that."

Rachael tried not to be mollified by what he said, but it was impossible not to be pleased. She rather liked the idea he couldn't think straight around her. "Seriously, Rio, why would you even consider I'm any other species other than human?"

"I'm being serious. I'm certain your parents were exactly as I am. I think the stories your mother told you were all the stories told to our children to teach them their heritage. You must have heard your father call your mother *sestrilla* and that's how you knew the meaning of the word. The language is ancient and used only by our people, but it is universal to all of us no matter what part of the world we reside in. So even if your parents were born and raised in

South America as I suspect, your father would have called your mother that at some time."

"I can't remember my father. I was very young when he died."

"Do you have memories of the rain forest?"

"Dreams, not memories."

"The humidity doesn't bother you and the mosquitoes don't go near you. You aren't afraid in the silences or the stillness. Hell, Rachael, I walked in here as the leopard and you didn't even flinch."

"I flinched. There was definite flinching. You're darned lucky I didn't die of sheer fright."

"You were petting the leopard. You couldn't have been that afraid."

"The soup is beginning to boil." She made a face at his back. Maybe she hadn't been as afraid of the leopard as she should have been. "Who wouldn't pet a leopard given the chance? It was a perfectly natural thing to do. I considered fainting, but I'm not very good at it so I thought I'd make the most of the opportunity. *And,*" she continued before he could interrupt, "you have two leopards for pets, who knows if the big guy was part of the family. He walked in like he owned the place."

He grinned at her. "I do."

"Well, I'm not in heat." She tried not to smile back at him. It was difficult when he was standing there, leaning one hip lazily against the sink and looking incredibly sexy.

"A man can always hope."

She managed an elegant sniff of indignation, taking the mug of soup he handed to her. "How long before the hit man comes back?" It was a much safer subject.

"He could be holed up a couple of miles from here. It depends on how badly injured he was. He was moving fast and thinking the entire time."

"Which means it wasn't that bad."

"That would be my guess. Franz is scouting and I've sent out a couple of other friends, not human in case you were wondering. They'll raise the alarm if he shows himself within a couple of mile radius. If he's smart, he's laying low waiting for us to settle down."

Rachael's heart jumped. "You mean you think he'll be coming back tonight? Why aren't we getting ready to get out of here? I can make it. It's silly to just sit here and wait for him to shoot at us."

"We're not just waiting for him, Rachael. We're fortifying ourselves and preparing for battle."

"I don't want to battle anyone. You know the old fight-or-flee adage? I believe fleeing is the smart thing to do. There must be one of the native huts I read about where we can go."

"He's a walking radar system, Rachael. He can track us, no matter where we go. If you don't want to shelter with the elders in the village then we have to face him."

Rachael shook her head sadly. "Everywhere I go, I bring death." She looked away from the door. "I'm sorry, Rio. I really am, that I brought this man into your life. I thought I could escape."

"It was his choice to take this job. Eat your soup."

Rachael sipped at the broth cautiously. It was very hot but she found she was suddenly hungry. "I'm still trying to get used to the idea that leopard men actually are real, not a myth, and you want me to believe I'm a leopard woman." She laughed softly. "It can't be real, but I saw it with my own eyes."

"I'll be happy to demonstrate for you." He wanted to get her to his safe house as quickly as possible. She wouldn't be happy with the move, and he was certain it would hurt her leg, but he felt they had no choice. The sniper wouldn't wait long. If Rio had been the hunter, he would have already been making his way slowly, patiently, back into position for the kill.

Rio dragged his large pack out. He kept it filled with necessary items for a quick getaway. He added extra shirts for Rachael. He cut the seam of a pair of his old jeans up to the knee. "I'm going to have you put these on."

"Lovely. I like the look. Are we going walking in the moonlight?" She set the soup on the small end table and held out her hand for the jeans. Her gaze met his steadily, but he saw her swallow hard. The prospect of trying to walk with the injury she'd sustained was daunting.

"Yes. Let me help you." He eased the material over her swollen ankle and calf. Her courage shook him. He expected a protest but as usual, Rachael was game.

She broke out into a sweat while dressing. "I'm out of shape."

"We're not going to talk about shapes again, are we?" He teased, needing to find a way to take the pain from her eyes. He ran his fingers through her hair. The silken strands were damp. "Are you going to be able to do this?"

"Of course. I can do anything." Rachael had no idea how she was going to stand up and actually put weight on her leg. Even with Kim and Tama's green-brown brew smeared in globs over her calf, her leg was throbbing. She was certain when she looked down to inspect the damage she would see arrows piercing her flesh. She handed him the soup mug. "I'm as ready as I'm ever going to be."

He handed her a sheathed knife and the small gun. "The safety's on." He shouldered the pack, reached down for the fifty-pound clouded leopard. "We can't leave you behind, Fritz. I have a feeling our friend is going to be feeling vindictive. You'll have to stay out of the house."

The cat yawned but stayed on his feet when Rio set him on the verandah. "Go, little one, find a place to hide until I return." He watched the small leopard limp onto a branch and disappear into the foliage. Rio looked back to see Rachael struggling to her feet. "What in the hell do you think you're doing, woman?"

"I think it's called standing but I seem to have forgotten how," she answered, sitting on the edge of the bed. "It's the green gunk you put on my leg. It's weighing me down."

"Rachael, I'm going to carry you. I don't expect you to walk."

"That's silly. I'm weak more than anything else. It isn't that painful. Well, it's painful because the swelling hasn't gone down yet."

He gathered her into his arms. "I spent all these years alone. No one ever argued with me."

"And now you have me," she said with evident satisfaction, settling into his body. "Do you have any idea where we're going? I thought you said he could track us."

"I did say that, didn't I?" He was already moving through the network of branches, far faster than Rachael considered safe.

Despite the heavy pack and her additional weight, Rio wasn't even breathing hard as he landed on the ground and began to jog, weaving through the trees back toward the river. She buried her face against his neck, trying not to cry out with each jarring step.

The roar started softly, a muffled, distant sound that quickly began to gain in strength. Rachael lifted her head in alarm, suddenly afraid of where he meant to take her.

11

THE forest appeared stately, the majestic trees rising like great cathedral pillars all around them. Smaller trees were scattered everywhere, creating a patchwork effect of silvery leaves, explosions of color and dark patches of bark. Staghorn ferns hung from trees, the vivid green prongs rustling in the slight wind as they hurried by. Moonlight filtered through the chinks in the canopy, casting flecks of light here and there on the wet forest floor. Rachael caught glimpses of leaves in every shade of red, iridescent greens and blues, anything to increase the refraction and absorption of light into the leaf pigment.

Rachael clung to Rio as he jogged through the forest. The dark never seemed to bother him. He moved at a sure, steady pace. She heard deer bark the alert signal of predators in the area as they passed, causing Rio to swear under his breath. Two very tiny deer burst out of the bushes ahead of them and raced into the undergrowth.

The roar of the river grew. The continuous croaking of frogs added to the din. Rachael's stomach lurched crazily.

"Rio, we have to stop, just for a minute. I'm going to be sick if we keep going."

"We can't, *sestrilla,* we have to reach the river. He can't track our scent in water." Rio continued moving over the thick, wet vegetation on the forest floor. It was dark and damp with small pools of water here and there. These and forest wallows didn't slow him down. He avoided the unnatural pile of leaves and twigs signaling the nest of the resident bearded pig. Ticks carrying anything from tick fever to scrub typhus were often abundant in the nests and Rio took care to stay away from them.

Rachael concentrated on the forest rather than her discomfort. Twice she caught glimpses of large deer with thick horns, the samba deer, largest in the forest. It was dizzying to be rushed through the forest at night. There was an eerie feel to the way the canopy swayed above them, continually changing the patterns of light through the trees. Plants and fungi covered tree trunks so that plants appeared to piggyback on top of one another, creating a lush environment. Every now and then Rio gave a soft, grunting cough, alerting the animals to his presence in the hopes the nightjars wouldn't raise an alarm as they darted overhead catching insects on the wing.

The roar became louder. Rachael realized they'd been traveling at an angle upriver to meet the flooded banks. She put her mouth to Rio's ear. "You're not taking me to your elders, are you?"

He heard the little catch in her voice. "I want the sniper to think I am."

Rachael didn't answer, comforted that he wasn't abandoning her. They were slogging through the swamps, climbing carefully over the myriad of tree roots extending out from the base of the trunk creating little mini cages. Water lapped at Rio's knees. The look of the forest changed as they neared the river's edge. More light was able to penetrate the canopy, and many of the trees were

smaller with crooked trunks and branches that draped low
to hang over the water.

"Aren't there alligators and other reptilian things here?"
Rachael asked. The roar of the river was deafening. The
moist heat curled her hair even more, creating a mass of
springy whorls and spirals. She had avoided the mangroves
and swamps as much as possible along with all the other
members of the group bringing medical aid. The edges of
the river could be as dangerous as they were beautiful.

Rio waded out in the fast-moving water. "We're going
to swim, Rachael. Hopefully Tama's potion will protect
your leg from any further infection. I'm going to tie you to
me, in case you get swept away by the current."

"Are you crazy? We can't swim in this." She was horrified. In the dark, the river appeared swifter and more
frightening than it had during the day. Or maybe without
bandits rushing out of the forest it seemed more dangerous.

"We have no choice if we're going to get you to safety,
Rachael. As long as he knows where you are, we're handi-
capped. He's mobile and we aren't. I swear, I won't let
anything happen to you."

She stared into his face. Into his eyes. Studied his firm
jaw, the tiny lines etched into his rough features. Rachael
lifted her hand and traced one small scar down low near his
chin. "Lucky for you, I'm a heck of a swimmer." She
smiled at him, trusting him when she hadn't trusted anyone
for as long as she could remember. "My name is Rachael
Lospostos, Rio. It isn't really Smith."

"Somehow I knew that already." He kissed her upturned
mouth gently. "Thank you. I know that wasn't easy for
you."

"It's the least I could do when I got you into this mess."
Her dark eyes glinted with amusement. "You can kiss me
again though. If I drown, I want to take the taste of your
perfectly lovely mouth with me."

"You know you're distracting me. If we get eaten by an
alligator, it's your fault."

"I heard they don't like fast-moving water," she said and fastened her mouth to his. They merged instantly the way they always did, sinking into one another and spinning away from the world.

Rio struggled to remember where they were and the danger they were in. She had a way of sweeping away sane thoughts and replacing them instantly with urgent hunger and need. Very carefully he lowered her feet into the rushing water, reluctantly lifting his head as he did so. It was the only way to breathe and keep his sanity and wits.

"I've got you, Rachael." His arm around her waist steadied her as he looped a rope around her and secured it around his own waist. "I'm not about to lose you. We're going to wade out where the water is moving faster, lift our feet and travel downstream with the current. We don't want anything to let him know what direction we're going. A leaf, the bottom of the river near the banks disturbed, anything at all can be a clue. We'll travel downriver for some time."

"Let's do it then." She didn't want to lose her nerve. She grinned at him. "At least I know you're not attracted to me because I look great." She swept a hand through her hair and took the first step. Her injured leg, even with the support of the water, didn't want to take her weight so she stretched out full length and began to swim.

Rio went after her, pride welling up at her courage. The moonlight fell across her face as she swam, and he watched the beads of water pour off of her. She used sure, strong strokes, cut cleanly through the water, almost as silent as he was. There it was again, that strange disorienting feeling of familiarity. He had been swimming with her before. He had seen an exact image, he knew the moment she would turn her head and take a breath of air.

The current was stronger in the center of the river and took them both with little effort, carrying them downstream. Rio caught her hand and held tight as they both bent knees and lifted feet to avoid rocks and snags as they

were swept along. It was a dizzying experience, looking up
at the night sky after so many days seeing nothing but
canopy overhead. Stars, scattered across the dark back-
drop, glittered like gems in spite of the clouds. The rain fell
lightly, a fine mist, more than an actual shower so that
Rachael turned up her face to feel the spray.

The river wasn't nearly as ferocious as when it was
raging in the storm. There were no dragging undercurrents
trying to pull her down. Rachael found she rather enjoyed
the experience after lying in bed for so long. Rio stayed
very close to her, hovering protectively, which made her
feel cherished, something she'd never experienced. It was
like a dream. Neither spoke as sound traveled great distances at night on the river.

They were swept around a bend and down a mini waterfall. Abruptly, Rio caught her around the waist and put his
feet down. He struggled against the current, walking in the
waist-deep water, dragging her with him. Rachael couldn't
help him, other than to try to stroke strongly in the direction he wanted to go. Even with Rio's incredible strength,
it was a battle to reach the small waterfall. He put his
mouth against her ear. "Wait just a moment, I'm going
under."

She held her breath as he disappeared. She felt the tug
of the rope around her waist, but she was able to hold
against the pull of the water. It seemed minutes before he
rose up out of the water. She sighed with relief and flung
her arms around him.

Again he put his mouth against her ear. "You'll have to
hold your breath and duck underwater, we're going to
swim through a tube."

She nodded to show she understood and went with him,
allowing the swirling water to close over the top of her head.
It was impossible to see anything and she didn't even try,
hanging on to Rio with all her strength. He pulled her
through a small channel, a tube beneath the water. She felt
the walls brushing against her shoulders and when she

reached above her she could feel the roof inches from her head. She fought back claustrophobia, concentrating on the unexpected feelings she had for Rio to get her through. She detested small enclosed places, and swimming in the dark waters through a tunnel she'd never seen was a true test of her trust in Rio.

How had she come to feel such faith in him in such a short time? It didn't feel like a short time. She felt the tug on her body indicating she could stand. Rio wrapped his arm around her waist to help her out of the water. Her head broke the surface and she opened her eyes. It was pitch-black. The waterfall was a loud echo matching the continual sound of running water.

"Where are we?"

"It's a cave. You have to wade through water and keep your head low for a short distance and then we'll get you settled. I made the tube and hollowed out most of the entrance to the chamber. The chamber was a great find. It seemed a good place to escape to if I was seriously wounded."

She caught the small bit of pride in his tone and smiled. "It sounds lovely. I've always thought being a troll's lover was incredibly romantic."

There was a small silence and then he laughed softly. "I've been called many things in my life, but troll is a new one." He swung her into his arms. "I'm going to carry you across the threshold."

"Lovers don't get carried," Rachael reminded. His ear was close to her face so she leaned forward and nibbled. "Only brides do."

"Well then, consider yourself married. And stop doing that thing with your teeth because I'm having one hell of a reaction to it."

"That sounds like it has possibilities. But I've been thinking. Why wouldn't some horrible reptile have discovered your handiwork and made a little nest inside your cave? If I were an alligator I'd be happy to use your hideaway. And if you came to visit, all to the good. Meals are hard to come by sometimes."

He laughed. "You have no faith, woman. I put in a plug to keep the creatures out. I unfastened the locks and opened the door, that's why we were in the tube so long."

"You didn't close the door."

"I'm taking you to high ground first. That's the gentleman in me."

She nuzzled his neck. "I do appreciate it, Rio, I really do, but in this one instance, I'll be happy to sort of stand here while you go back and secure the tube. I'm not ready for visitors yet, especially reptilian ones."

Rio caught the little tremor in her voice. "I'll do that immediately, Rachael. We're already in the cavern. Fortunately we're back far enough and the cave opens up into a wide chamber here so we can light a lamp. I brought several with me over a period of time." He set her down on a flat surface.

Rachael waited anxiously while he lit one of the lamps and hooked it above their heads for maximum coverage. She looked around her. The chamber was fairly large. Roots protruded and water dripped continually from several walls. There was no sign of alligators. Rio had quite a supply of items in the cave.

There was a large plastic container she assumed was waterproof inside a cage of roots. She could see there were several blankets and one of his many medical kits inside. She was sitting on a flat slab of stone. It was the only rock she could see in the entire cave. The floor around the walls was damp, but most of the water ran back toward the river. Rio had hollowed out a ditch to keep the water from dampening the floor of the cave.

"So what do you think?" Rio returned, soaking wet, sweeping his hair back with careless fingers. "Not too bad."

"I think it's wonderful," Rachael said. She was soaked and uncomfortable. She looked down at the shirt and realized it didn't do her much good. As wet as her shirt was, it was nearly transparent. "If you don't mind, I'd like to get out of these clothes. You should too, Rio."

"I've got a few things packed in waterproof bags for us," he said. He opened the container and rummaged through the supplies until he found a towel.

Rio knelt beside her and unbuttoned the shirt, dragging it off her wet skin and tossing it aside. "Come on, *sestrilla,* stand up so I can get rid of these jeans."

His voice was gentle, tender even. Rachael allowed him to help her up, leaning into his body as he peeled the material from her hips. He wrapped the towel around her and began rubbing the drops of water from her skin. She swayed with weariness and it embarrassed her. He was the one who had jogged through miles of forest with her in his arms. He had been the one to use his strength to keep them from being swept apart in the river. And he was as soaked as she was.

"I've never met anyone like you," Rachael said. "Sometimes I'm not certain you're real."

Rio wrapped her in a dry shirt. "I have my good side," he teased. "Unfortunately, it just doesn't come out that often." He laid a mat on the slab of rock and covered it with a thick sleeping bag before helping her to sit down. Rubbing the thick mass of curls, he studied her leg. "The green gunk held up. We want to get that off the puncture wounds in case they still need to drain."

"It does feel better," Rachael said. "I'll have to remember to tell Tama he's a miracle worker."

Rio made certain she was comfortable before he peeled off his own clothes and rubbed the towel over his body.

"How long do you think we'll have to stay here?" Rachael asked.

"I'm going to use the rest of the night to hunt the shooter. He's leaving his own trail and he was injured. It will be easier for me to find him. I'll know you're safe and won't worry about him circling back and finding you alone in the house. Franz is already scouting for me. He'll pick up the trail, and he knows how to stay out of sight."

Rachael's eyes widened in shock. "You can't do that, Rio. Not after what you told me."

"He's hunting us. The only way to stop him is to go after him. Did you think we were going to live in a cave for the rest of our lives?"

"No." Rachael wanted to pull the covers over her head. There was no way to shield Rio from her past. "But before you go out and risk your life maybe you'd better find out who you're risking your life for."

"I know who you are."

"No you don't. You have no idea who my family is."

"I don't need to know about your family, Rachael. We'll talk about it when I get back. Wait here for at least forty-eight hours. If something goes wrong, head upriver toward Kim and Tama's village. Ask them to take you to the elders. The Han Vol Dan is your first changing. You can't allow it to happen until your leg is strong enough to stand up to the change. You'll have problems with sexual feelings. Emotions will continue to heighten, the heat, the need, the edgy, moody feelings you can barely control. You have to stay in control, especially if you haven't gone through the Han Vol Dan. The combination of the two passages can be explosive."

"Do you know how completely ridiculous that sounds? If I was watching a movie, I'd burst out laughing."

"Except you know what I'm saying is true. You've felt the animal roaring to get out. I've seen you come close to the change."

"Why wouldn't my mother tell me? In all the stories she told me, she never once mentioned I could assume another form."

"I don't know, Rachael, but I'm certain you're one of us."

"And if I'm not?" Her dark eyes moved over his face. "If you're wrong, would that mean that we can't be together? Are you allowed to be with someone that isn't a part of your people?"

His palm cupped her face, his thumb sliding over her skin. "I've been banished, *sestrilla,* no one can tell me what I can or cannot do." He leaned down to kiss her. "I'm coming back for you."

"You'd better come back for me. I don't want to wrestle alligators by myself." She tried not to cling to him, although she wanted to hold him to her. There was nothing she could say or do to stop him. Rachael knew how stubborn he could be. It was impossible to argue with him when he made up his mind to do something. She shook her head to clear her thoughts. Whatever past they may have had seemed to intrude at the worst times. She knew him. She knew what he was like. "Just go, now, while it's dark. Remember, if you're right and he followed us, he could already be searching the riverbanks to see where we came out."

"You're upset."

"Of course I'm upset. I'm stuck here with this stupid leg and you're going to risk your life to stop this hit man." She shoved her hand through her hair, angry and near tears. "Don't you realize he'll send another? And one after that? And another and another? He'll never stop."

Rio nodded. "I figured as much. It doesn't matter, Rachael. We'll take them one at time and if necessary, I'll have a little talk with him."

Her face drained of all color. "No. No, promise me, Rio. You can't ever try to get near him. Not for any reason. You can't hurt him. And you can't try to see him."

The anxiety on Rachael's face twisted at his insides. "Rachael, I'm coming back."

"I know you will." He had to. She couldn't stay in a cave beneath the riverbank forever—unless he was with her. She might be able to live anywhere with him. The thought was frightening. She'd never considered that she might want to spend her life with someone. A lifetime seemed a long time to want to be with someone, yet, if she could have him, she would want more than one lifetime with Rio.

Rio forced himself to turn away from her, from the look

on her face, so lonely, so vulnerable, so much pain in her eyes. He didn't dare gather her to him, he'd never let her go. He waded away from her.

"May all the magic of the forest be with you and may good fortune be your companion as you travel." Her voice was rough with raw pain. "Good hunting, Rio."

He stopped, keeping his back to her. He had glimpsed pain in her before. Knew the signs of trauma and betrayal. Was familiar with rage born of helplessness. The anguish went deep and left scars. He couldn't look at her. Her suffering was harder to bear than his own. "I don't know anything about love, Rachael. Meeting you was unexpected, but everything about you makes me happy. I'm coming back for you."

He continued to wade out into the water. She was crying. Her tears would be the end of him. He'd rather face the entire bandit camp than face her tears. There was no way to change what he had to do. He couldn't comfort her. There had been violence in her life. He recognized the signs. He could only hope that by doing what was necessary he didn't lose his chance with her.

Rio went under the water, swimming through the narrow tunnel he had painstakingly scooped out and shored up with an artificial tube. It had taken several years to find the chamber and secure an entrance. He had several places scattered around the river and forest he could use if necessary. His people were a secretive, cautious species and he had learned over the years the value of preparation.

Once under the small falls, he swam underwater to the center of the river and allowed it to sweep him farther downstream. He didn't want to leave tracks or scent for the hunter after he'd taken such careful precautions to keep Rachael safe. It was a risk leaving her in the chamber injured as she was. She had the weapons and light and food for several days, but still she could easily panic being underground. They were arboreal, preferring the high branches of the trees to the ground.

Rio spent many hours lying perfectly still, backup for his men. The others entered the camps to retrieve the victims. He remained outside from some vantage point, a marksman few could surpass, the last line of defense for his unit. He was used to the solitary life, living alone the way he did and carrying out his job, but unlike the leopard, his species were not meant to be alone. They mated for life and beyond. Rachael was certain to have a difficult time alone.

He exited the water a mile downstream from the waterfall, shifting into his animal form, happy to feel the full strength and power of his kind. He lifted his muzzle and scented the wind. At once he was flooded with information. He stretched languidly before springing easily over a fallen trunk. Dawn was beginning to break in the forest.

The thick, haunting mist shrouding the forest began to lift, slowly evaporating as the warmth of the sun penetrated the clouds. A chorus of birds began, each trying to outdo the other as the strange music rang through the trees. The range went from melodious to harsh, even tuneless, as they all called to one another flitting from branch to branch. A burst of colors as birds took to wing signaled morning in the forest. Gibbons joined in, claiming territory with gurgling cries and whooping yells.

The leopard ignored the noisy flapping and whooshing of birds with great wings as he leapt into the lower branches of a nearby tree to make use of the overhead highway. The forest had stirred to life and Rio utilized the noisy chatter, hurrying through the trees back toward his home in the hopes of picking up the scent of the hunter. Rio made his way quickly back upriver, listening for calls of warning or sudden silences that would indicate an intruder was stalking through the territory of the pigtailed macaque. Timid and shy, the macaque would often leap to the forest floor and run when disturbed, another sign of trouble.

It was the barking of the deer that alerted him first. The short, harsh calls were used to warn members of the herd

among the trees as tail flipping couldn't be seen through
the heavy shrubbery and thick tree trunks. Rio snarled and
sank low on the branch, going completely motionless in
the way of his kind. The hunter had just become the
hunted.

Because he wasn't high up in the canopy, the leaves of
the tree he was crouched in remained still, unaffected by
the wind. The sunlight filtered through the breaks of
foliage overhead to dapple the leaves and forest floor
below. That provided more concealment for him, a natural
camouflage. Insects buzzed around him; a green fence
lizard shifted its color from bright green to dark brown as it
settled against a branch just a few feet from him.

A bearded pig grunted and crashed through the shrubbery beneath his tree, startled by something. Spring-loaded
muscles bunched in anticipation. The tip of his tail occasionally switched, the only thing to move. Piercing yellow-
green eyes smoldered with fire and intelligence. The leopard
waited, frozen in place. The spotted leopard, a fully grown
male, emerged cautiously, pushing its head through a multitude of ferns. The animal limped as it padded across the
forest floor, snarling at the troupe of gibbons screaming
foul things at him from the safety of the canopy. Twigs and
leaves rained down as the monkeys threw things in defiance. The spotted leopard maintained his dignity for a few
moments, then in the mercurial way of their kind leapt into
the lower branches with flattened ears and exposed teeth.
The gibbons erupted into a wild, terrified frenzy, rushing
through the trees in every direction in an effort to get away.

Rio never moved, not even when the evil eyes, two spots
lost in a pattern of spots, appeared to be staring right at him.
Rio locked in on his prey. His yellow-green stare became
focused, all tension gathered in his eyes. With great
patience, he waited and watched, completely motionless.
The intruder leapt back to the forest floor, a silent lift of his
lip indicating his contempt for the gibbons. Cushioned feet
allowed him to move in silence over the thick vegetation.

Rio stretched out on the branch, a slow belly-to-branch stalk, using incredible muscle control. He crawled forward a few inches, froze and repeated the crawl, going from cover to cover—gaining inches, then feet, pacing above the spotted leopard. He reached the end of the branch. The spotted leopard moved silently just below him, unaware of Rio stalking him from above.

The intruder took one step. Another. Hesitated, opening his mouth wide. Rio sprang from above, hitting him hard, sinking canines deep, puncturing the fur-covered throat, while razor-sharp claws dug deep in an effort to rip and tear. Rio wanted the battle over as fast as possible. Fights between leopards were extraordinarily dangerous.

The spotted leopard was game, twisting with its flexible backbone, raking with extended claws, bucking hard to try to throw the larger cat off. Rio held on grimly, determined to end it. The roars and grunts echoed through the forest, a vicious battle between two dangerous foes. Overhead the birds took flight, calling warnings in every language they could. Squirrels and lemurs chattered and scolded. Monkeys screamed in panic. Flying fox took to the air along with the birds so that the sky seemed alive with wings.

The spotted leopard shook and twisted and snarled, raking at Rio, trying to eviscerate or cripple him. He couldn't shake the black leopard off; the canines remained buried in the nape of his neck, the jaw pressure enough to snap bone. It was over quickly, the surprise attack giving Rio the edge he needed in the fight. The spotted leopard gasped, suffocating, the throat crushed. The black leopard held him longer, making certain it was really over before dropping the cat on the ground.

Rio shifted into his human form, staring at the leopard regretfully. They needed every member of their species alive. Each leopard they lost was a blow to their survival. There had been no labels in the clothing the sniper had left behind, no means of identification. Rio had no idea which country his enemy had come from, or why one of his kind would choose to betray his people with such an act, but he was certain this one had not been born anywhere near his village.

Did that mean that Rachael's people knew what she was and that she was under a death sentence? They had strict rules they all lived under. The laws of the forest were for the common good of their species. If she had committed some crime against her people, it was possible they would send hunters after her.

Rio rubbed his hand over his face. If that were the case, her elders could appeal to the elders of his village to carry out the sentence for them. Rio was already under banishment. He doubted if the elders would stick up for his mate, especially if she wasn't known to them and under a legitimate sentence of death. He swore as he shifted back into the shape of a leopard to drag the carcass up into the high branches of a tree. He had no choice but to burn the leopard to preserve the secrets of their species. He had to find his nearest stash of supplies fast. Leaving the body of a leopard was extremely dangerous so he had no choice but to cache the body until he returned.

His mind raced with the possibility of Rachael's people condemning her. She admitted her own brother had taken out a contract on her life. It made sense, although he couldn't imagine what Rachael could have done to warrant a death sentence. He moved swiftly through the forest, ignoring the warning cries of the gibbons, still panic-stricken from the fierce fight that had ensued. Birds fluttered overhead, darting in and out of the trees. Deer crashed ahead of him, scattering as he leapt from branch to branch, occasionally taking to the forest floor and leaping over rotting tree trunks.

The wind shifted slightly, a tiny breeze where ordinarily the uncanny stillness in the air gave nothing away. Rio came to an abrupt halt. There was another in the forest close by. He recognized the scent of the leopard. The birds and gibbons and even the deer had been warning him, but he'd been so distressed over the thought of Rachael being under a death sentence, he hadn't picked up on it.

Fortunately, he was close to his pack. The box was buried nearby, in the cage created by the buttress roots of a large dipterocarp tree. He had marked the fruit-bearing tree with a small symbol. Using his claws, he dug up the box quickly, listening now to the news of the forest. The second leopard was approaching quickly, obviously catching his scent.

Rio shifted to human form, strapping on weapons as fast as possible, his expression grim. Only after his guns were checked and his knives concealed did he drag on the clothes and attach the small medical kit to his belt. Feeling the impact of the leopard's focused stare, he whipped around, rifle up and ready, finger on the trigger.

"You're up early, Drake." His voice was pleasant, relaxed, casual even, but the barrel never wavered from dead center on the cat's brain and he didn't take his finger from the trigger.

They stared at one another for a long moment. Drake's form contorted, lengthened, muscles reshaping to form the man. He glared at Rio. "You want to tell me why you're still pointing that thing at me?"

"You want to tell me what you're doing here?"

"I spent most of the night tracking you and that rogue leopard. You, I lost, he wasn't as good. You wounded him and that made it easier for me to track him."

"Why?"

Drake frowned. "You tick-ridden son of a bearded pig. I decided to go back to guard your butt out of concern for your well-being. By the time I got back to your place, you and Rachael were gone and I had to track you through the forest. It was slow going when I realized the sniper was tracking you as well. He lost you a few times and I stayed behind him, wanting to see what he did." Abruptly he stopped and glared. "Damn it, Rio, put the rifle down. It's not only insulting, it's annoying."

Rio slung the rifle over his shoulder. He kept his hand free, ready to go for his knife even while he grinned at Drake. "I am not tick-ridden."

"That depends on who you ask. Where's Rachael?"

The smile faded from Rio's face. "Did the elders send you, Drake?"

"What is wrong with you? Why would the elders send me to protect your sorry butt, Rio?"

Rio didn't smile. His eyes gleamed with piercing intelligence, smoldered with danger. "Did they send you after Rachael?"

Drake frowned. "I never made it back to the village. I went with Kim and Tama upriver toward their village, but changed my mind and doubled back. As far as I know, the elders have never heard of Rachael. And if they have, they certainly don't know she's with you. Tama and Kim would never say anything. You know them. You know they could be tortured and they'd never say anything. What's this all about?"

Rio shrugged. "He was one of us. Not our village, I doubt if he was born in this country, but he was one of us. Why would he hire out to kill one of his own kind? A woman at that?"

"We aren't a perfect species, Rio, you should know that." The moment the words escaped, Drake shook his head. "I'm sorry, I didn't mean it that way. There have been a few rumors over the years. A few going after money, women, power. We aren't immune to those things, you know."

"I guess not. I appreciate you watching my back, Drake. Sorry for the reception."

"The pitiful reception. I trust you got him."

"He's dead. He left his clothes behind last night and there was nothing in them, not even a label. I needed matches."

"You haven't told me where Rachael is. You didn't leave her alone, did you?" Drake sounded anxious.

"She's fine. She has a couple of guns and a few knives. She's handy with a stick too. I'll tell her you were expressing your concern."

A slow grin spread over Drake's face. "You're jealous, Rio. You've been bitten by the green-eyed monster. I never thought it would happen, but you fell like a tree in the forest."

"I'm cautious, Drake. There's a difference."

"I think you just tried to insult me, but I'm laughing too damned hard to care. Where is this mystery man? You go get your lady and I'll take care of the mop-up. I'm heading back to the village to call up the unit. We're going in after that church group."

"Who's guarding your worthless butts, Drake?"

Drake shrugged. "Conner is a crack marksman. He isn't you, but he'll handle it." He held out his hand for the matches.

"I don't like it, Drake. Breaking up the unit is a bad idea."

"What's the alternative? You can't leave Rachael alone. Unless you bring her to the village. You know that would be risky. You two belong together. I don't know how well that's going to sit with them."

Rio handed him the matches. "I'm heading home, Drake, call me on the radio when you're going in."

12

RACHAEL leaned against the cavern wall for support as she put weight on her injured leg. Surprisingly, the pain she expected didn't flood her entire body. The puncture wounds had stopped draining. She felt strange, itchy. Something crawled under her skin. Her body seemed foreign to her—sexual, intensely feminine. She could barely stand the feel of the shirt against her skin and slipped the buttons open, wanting to be free of the slight weight of it. She would have torn it off of her but it retained Rio's scent.

She inhaled sharply, drew him into her lungs, into her body, and held him there. Her breasts ached unexpectedly, nipples tightened and her feminine sheath wept for him. She burned. There was no other way she could describe what was happening, her skin burning with need, her body unable to stay still. She turned to the cavern wall and placed her hands high over her head, curled her fingers into the dirt wall and raked downward, leaving behind deep grooves.

Rachael felt his breath on the back of her neck and she stiffened, but didn't turn around. His arms slipped around her body, his hands cupping the soft weight of her breasts, thumbs sliding over her aching nipples. His body, wet and naked, pressed against hers. She recognized the feel of him instantly, the hard frame, the thick, rigid erection pressing against her bare buttocks. Rachael closed her eyes and breathed his name with relief. "Rio." She rubbed her bottom back and forth against him, nearly purring like a contented cat. "I'm so glad you're safe."

Rio kissed the nape of her neck, his teeth nipping her skin, teasing her senses. His hands stroked and caressed her breasts, while his mouth nudged the collar of the shirt aside. She allowed the shirt to slip from her arms, arcing into him, bending forward to push tightly against him. His hands left her breasts to explore her body and she almost sobbed with the intensity of pleasure. A single sound tore from her throat when his hand teased the curls at the junction of her legs, pressed into her heat.

There was a strange roaring in her ears, anxiety, hunger and need. His finger slipped inside her and at once her muscles clenched and gripped. She couldn't help pushing back, riding his hand on the edge of control. She wanted him inside her, wanted him deep, thrusting with hard urgent strokes.

He pressed her forward to rest her hands against a shelf. She could barely breathe with wanting him, *needing* him inside of her. He pressed tightly against her entrance, his hands on her hips. Rachael couldn't wait, wanting to take him deep, thrusting back as he surged forward. Her joyous cry of relief and welcome echoed through the cavern.

Rio tightened his hold on her, throwing his head back, desperate to hold on to control. She was hot velvet, gripping him as tightly as a fist, the friction fiery, sending flames along his nerve endings. The tango was wild and fast, a coming together so fast and hard it was feral, a ferocious joining neither could stop.

Rachael pushed back again and again, wanting more, always more, ravenously hungry for his body, a voracious sexual appetite that could only be assuaged by his deep, hard thrusts, creating fire. Creating heaven. She wept with the beauty of it, with the absolute perfection of their joining. He filled her as no other could, his body completing hers. Sharing hers. He rode her hard, thrusting deeper and deeper, but she still wanted more. Craved more. She felt her body tightening, heat rushing, gathering into a terrible force. He seemed to swell inside of her, thickening until she was exploding, imploding, fragmenting into a million pieces, and her body rippled with waves of pleasure. She heard her voice, his voice, husky growls of ecstasy ripping through a throat in a tone that was not hers, could never be hers, yet wasn't his either. They blended together, united.

Rio bit her shoulder, a teasing bite he couldn't help, kissing her skin, the line of her back. Anything he could reach. He wrapped her up in his arms, just held her while he tried to recover his ability to breathe. Every moment that he was with her made him feel more alive. He thought running in the forest was the most freeing feeling, but being with Rachael gave him something else, something he couldn't quite put a name to, but he never wanted to do without. Slowly, reluctantly, he eased his body from the haven of hers, a wide smile on his face.

Rachael sagged to the floor of the cavern as if her legs simply collapsed. Rio eased her down onto the sleeping bag. To his horror she burst into tears and covered her face with her hands. He stared down at her helplessly, astonished that she would be sobbing as if he'd broken her heart.

"Rachael. Damn it. You didn't even cry when Fritz nearly tore your leg off. What's wrong with you?" He sat down beside her and clumsily put his arm around her shaking shoulders. "Tell me."

It was the first awkward movement Rachael had ever seen him make and it comforted her when she thought there could be no comfort. "I don't know myself like this. It frightens me, the way I feel for you. The way I think about you. I don't even know my own body anymore. I like sex, Rio, but I'm not driven by sex. I'm a thinking person. I like to think about things from every angle. When I'm with you, like this, I disappear completely and there's only how it feels. How you feel."

He pulled her to him, pillowing her head on his shoulder when she wanted to hold herself stiffly away. "How we feel *together,* Rachael. It's being one person, in the same skin, our minds in the same place. It's how we are together. Why would you be afraid of that?"

"I can't fall in love with you, Rio, and you can't love me. If we just wanted to have sex and it was pleasant or even fireworks, it would be fine, but this is different. It's so much more. It's like an addiction. Not to the sex, that's only a small part of it. I feel like I have to be with you. That you're in some way essential to my life, to my reason for existing." She shoved her hand through her hair, lifted her head from his shoulder and glared at him. "I wish it was a past life that makes me want you so much, but I can't even blame it on that. Love shouldn't be so all-consuming. I'm not an all-consuming person. I'm not."

"Are you trying to convince me or yourself? I never thought about loving someone, Rachael. I wish I could tell you how I know we're destined to be together, it sounds so stupid even when I say it to myself, but I know we're meant to be man and wife. I can't imagine waking up in the morning and not having you beside me. Hell, I don't even have all that much to offer you. I have a risky job, a people who won't welcome me into their village, let alone their lives, and that would certainly spill over to you and our children, but it doesn't matter. I know I have to find a way to make it worth it to you to stay with me."

"Are you even listening to me? Does any of this make sense to you? Because it doesn't make a bit of sense to me. What do you know about me other than I have a million-dollar price on my head? And some leopard man is running around trying to kill me. And I may or may not be part of a species I didn't know existed until a couple of days ago. That's it. That's what you know, yet you're ready to spend your life with me. Is that normal, Rio? Do you think people really react that way?"

"What's normal, *sestrilla,* and why does there even have to be a normal for us? If you aren't one of my people I still want to share your life." He touched her tear-wet face. "This should never happen, not because you think you're falling in love with me."

"Don't sound happy about it, Rio. Do you think it's going to end happily? How can it? They won't stop with one killer. They'll send another and another until one of them kills you or me or both of us."

He kissed her. It was the only thing he could think to do, tasting her tears, feeling her terror. Not for herself but for him. She melted into him the way he was coming to know, every bit as hungry as he was. Feeding on his mouth. Committing to him with her body when she wasn't ready to do so with words. And that was all right with him. He tasted her complete acceptance of him. Felt it in her response. She simply surrendered everything she was into his keeping and just as wholly made her own demands.

Rachael leaned her head against his chest with a small sigh. "I'm not going to think about it anymore, Rio. Let's just see where it all takes us." She rubbed his jaw with the heel of her hand. "Did you find him?"

"He was not from our area. I'm guessing South America. He was definitely one of our species. Have you ever been to South America, Rachael?"

"You're not very good at sounding casual when you really want to know something, Rio," she reprimanded. "I was born in South America. I spent the first four years of my life there. We immigrated to the United States. My father, well, he's really not my birth father but to me he was my father, was born in South America and lived there most of his life, just as my mother had, but he had a lot of family in the United States."

"You have a stepfather?"

"Had. He's dead. He and my mother were murdered. And he was my father as far as I'm concerned. I loved him very much and he treated me as if I were his own flesh and blood. My brother too. He couldn't have been better to us."

There was defiance in her voice. She stirred as if she wanted to get away from him. Rio began to repack the boxes carefully, trying not to look at her so it would be easier when he asked her questions. "Rachael, is it possible you did something to anger the elders of your people? Maybe inadvertently committed a crime against your people that might earn you banishment or the death penalty?"

She looked up sharply, eyes flashing fire, but Rio only glanced at her and then away, deliberately not engaging in a staring match. "I don't have people. I'm not a different species."

"How do you explain your ability to see in the dark? The fact that mosquitoes avoid you? Your heightened sexual awareness and the different emotions you've been experiencing?" he asked gently as he snapped the lid on the box and replaced it in the cage of roots.

"There are perfectly acceptable explanations. My good eating habits could account for great eyesight and lack of mosquito bites. And you're responsible for my heightened sexual awareness and my moods. You parade around naked half the time, what do you expect?"

He grinned at her. "Getting a little moody on me now, aren't you?" He held out his hand. "Let's get out of here."

"Where are we going?"

"Home. We're going home. I'm going to teach you how to live here, Rachael, and whatever happens, we'll just deal with it."

She took his hand, weaving her fingers through his. "You do realize I haven't got a stitch on."

He leaned forward to press his lips against her breast, his tongue teasing her nipple. "I did notice, yes. I've got

clothes in a waterproof bag so we can get out of the river
and be dry."

"Isn't it daylight? Someone might see us."

"Most people along the river aren't going to care
whether we have clothes on or not." He drew her breast
into the warmth of his mouth, his hands moving over her
body with possession, with desire. He pressed a kiss
against her throat, her chin, the corner of her mouth. "Let's
get you home. I have a bathtub." He turned off the lamp,
plunging the cave into darkness.

"No, you don't. I looked for a bathtub." She found his
hand. "You're trying to bribe me and it isn't going to work."

"You didn't look in the right places. I have a tub I fill
with hot water when I want to soak an injury. Most of the
time I use the cold shower, but I've got a tub."

The water swirled around her ankles, rose to her calf.
"My brother did things, bad things, Rio." There in the
blackness, underground where no one could overhear
them, she confessed. "I can't go to the police because
they'd arrest him. I'd never do that to him. I love him. So I
had no choice but to leave."

He recognized the enormity of her confidence in him.
He slipped his arm around her waist. "What kinds of bad
things, Rachael?"

She shook her head, the silken curls brushing against his
bare skin. "Don't ask me anything more about him. If it
wasn't for him, I would have been dead a long time ago. I
owe him so much. You have no idea what we went through.
I'm not going to betray him. I can't." She took a breath.
"I'm not lying about the elders, Rio. I don't have any elders
that I know of, alive or dead, to issue a death sentence for an
imaginary indiscretion. I would tell you if there were."

"I believe you, *sestrilla*." He touched her to let her
know they had to go under the water and swim through the
narrow tube. He went first, trying to figure out what she
could have done to make her brother want her dead. Especially when she obviously loved him. He heard it in her

voice. The smoldering anger of his kind, always so dangerous and unpredictable, swirled in his belly as he swam. It
didn't make sense that the man didn't love her back. Who
wouldn't love Rachael?

They broke the surface together, just under the falls,
hoping the water would screen them from sight should
anyone be close by. Rio went back under to secure the
heavy mesh over the tube. Rachael waited, staring at the
opposite bank through the pouring water of the falls, sub-
consciously counting to herself until Rio emerged beside
her. She put her arms around his neck and pressed her body
close to his. "I should never have told you."

"You can tell me anything. I told you about my mother."

She kissed his throat, trailed little kisses up his jaw.
"And I still think your elders stink. They didn't recognize
how courageous you were in going to them and admitting
what you'd done."

"It wasn't courage. It was what she taught me. I chose
to do something and I had to take the consequences. It was
her rule and one I respected." The joy burst through him
like a rainbow of colors. Rachael had a way of making him
feel worthwhile. Feel like someone special and amazing.
He tied the rope around her waist and waded out into the
fast-moving current. "We have to swim to shore. The current will take us a bit downstream but we have to angle for
the other side of the river."

She nodded to show him she understood. This time when
she put her foot down in the water, she could rest her weight
briefly on it. It was a good sign that she was finally healing.
She had taken a close look at it in the cave and there would
definitely be scarring, but at least she had the leg.

They were swept downriver even as they swam strongly
toward shore. Rio reeled her in close to him and fought his
way to the shore, dragging her along. He managed to catch
a low-hanging branch and easily pulled himself up onto it,
lifting her out of the water with his incredible strength.

Rachael clung to the tree branch, her feet still dangling

in the water. The bark was rough on her bare skin and for
some reason she was suddenly self-conscious of her
nakedness. She looked around and saw only monkeys staring at her.

"If I get a leech on me, even one, I'm going to be
upset," she promised. "And make those monkeys stop staring. They're making me feel naked."

"You are naked." He laughed as he pulled her completely from the water, holding her close to his body, her
breasts mashed against his chest. "And you're ruining the
romantic ambience."

Her eyebrow nearly reached her hairline. "Romantic
ambience? What are you going on about?"

"I hardly think leeches should enter into a romantic
walk through the forest, especially when your body is
incredible sexy and bare at the moment." He cradled her in
his arms and leapt to the ground, landing softly.

She circled his neck with her arms and looked up into
the trees. It seemed as if a thousand eyes were staring at
them. "Rio. The monkeys really are staring."

On the riverbank they were much more exposed. She
had spent the last two weeks in a small house in the forest,
beneath a heavy canopy. Her only relief had been an
underground cavern. The rain began, a soft steady drizzle
that washed the river water from their skin as he carried her
through the bogs and swamp to the edge of the forest. The
wind touched their faces, flitted playfully through the
leaves in the trees. All the while the gibbons, macaques, an
orangutan and various species of birds watched them.

"I'm not making it up. They're staring."

"They should be staring. I'm about to show them how
good certain things in life are." There was wicked amusement in his voice. And something else—a note that rasped
over her skin and sent heat spiraling through her body.

"I don't think so, you pervert. We are not putting on a
show for those voyeurs." Just his voice could melt her
body. The look in his eyes was her undoing. His eyes

burned with desire, hunger, even as she could see the teasing challenge in his expression.

"Next you're going to be telling me some strange story about how you go into heat and need a female."

He shifted her, sliding her legs around his waist so that her wet channel was positioned over the head of his penis. "Not any female, Rachael, you."

She tightened her hold around his neck, lifted her body so he could suckle her breast. Just that easy she was hot and wet and needful. He did things with his tongue, stroking and dancing and teasing until she couldn't stand it and she began to slowly settle over his thick erection.

"Oh, yeah, that's what I want," he said, his breath hissing out of his lungs. "Arch back and ride me, nice and slow, take your time."

She leaned back, turning her face to the sky, to the warm rain and slowly slid her body up and down his. The rain fell on her face, droplets trickled between her breasts, down her stomach to sizzle in the heat of their joining. She smiled up at their audience, wishing them all the pleasure in the world. Wishing them the joy and freedom of a sensual relationship.

"You're so beautiful," he gasped the words, shocked at how the light fell across her face, revealing the intensity of her pleasure. It heightened her natural beauty. She was so uninhibited with him. So uncaring that he could see how much she wanted him, how much she enjoyed his body.

She laughed softly. "I'm only beautiful because you make me feel that way." Lightning sizzled in her veins. Fire raced over her skin. She controlled the pace, deliberately moving slow, taking him deep, gripping tight with her muscles.

Rachael had no idea how Rio managed to make the world a place of sunlight and paradise when she'd lived in the shadows for so long. The rain fell softly, enhancing brilliant color in every direction, scattering rainbow prisms across the sky. Or maybe it was behind her eyes. It didn't matter. There was only Rio in her world and he was all that mattered.

She felt his body gathering power and strength, she felt her own tightening in anticipation. Then they were spinning out of control on a dizzying ride, clinging to one another for safety. The leaves overhead whirled in a kaleidoscope of colors and shapes. Patterns of light and dark flecked the ground. It was necessary to share breathing as they kissed, hands moving over sensitized skin in a kind of worship.

Rachael laid her head on his shoulder, holding him close to her. Their hearts beat out a wild, frantic tattoo even as the rain continued to fall softly. "I love it here, Rio," she murmured, her lips against his throat. "I love everything about this place."

"You came home," he answered, slowly lowering her feet to the forest floor.

The pack was stashed high up in the tree in case of flooding. Rio went up the trunk quickly and tossed her clothes, shoes and a towel. Rachael found herself laughing. "This is a crazy way to live. Have you ever had the monkeys steal your pack?"

"Not yet. They are very respectful of my things." He glanced upward at the animals as the gibbons moved through the trees foraging for food before he dropped down beside her.

Rachael dressed quickly in the shelter of a large tree. "It's so much quieter."

"The birds are busy looking for food. Fruit, nectar, insects, they don't have much time to call back and forth, although you'll hear them occasionally. During midday, there's often a bit of a lull in the chatter." He buttoned his jeans and reached over to straighten the tails of her shirt. "You always look so cute in my clothes."

Her eyebrow shot up. "I've never been called cute. Elegant, but not cute."

"That's right. You're a rich lady. You wear designer clothes."

"How did you know they were designer clothes, jungle boy?"

He grinned at her. "I get around. You'd be surprised where this jungle boy has been." He leered deliberately.

Rachael laughed, then sobered, her gaze drifting over his face. "Nothing about you would surprise me, Rio."

Just like that she managed to put a lump in his throat. "Come here and let me carry you." He held out his hand.

"I'd like to try to walk, even for a short distance. It feels so good to be managing a bit on my own." Her fingers found his and clung.

Rio brought her hand to the warmth of his mouth, pressed a kiss into her palm. "Just a short distance. You haven't been able to bear any weight on the leg and I don't want you to overdue it. Tama's potion will only help so much."

"I know." Her ankle and calf were throbbing, but she was never going to admit that to him, not if she wanted to walk on her own. He had a stubborn jaw, and his eyes could go from shimmering fire to ice cold in a heartbeat. Rio was a man who could get bossy very quickly given the right circumstances. She smiled to herself and took the first step, tugging at his hand. "I can't wait for a hot bath, come on."

He frowned but he went with her, keeping a watchful eye on how she walked. "Out here, Rachael, you always have to be alert to your surroundings. The birds are going to sound a warning and you have to notice, you have to hear the different notes. They'll call to you, and depending on what frightens them, you can pick up what's intruding into our neighborhood."

"I've caught it a couple of times." She tried not to limp. Walking on her own seemed a miracle to her. She looked around at the trees laden with fruit. Everywhere she looked color exploded. The massive tree trunks came in all colors and were covered by life-forms. Lichen, fungi, fern and orchids grew on the trunks. Creeper vines hung down everywhere. At first there was quite a bit of light, the shorter trees along the river allowing the sun to blaze down, but as they went deeper into the interior, the taller trees sheltered them with denser canopy.

"Look at these tracks, Rachael." Rio crouched down to study the myriad of tracks near a shallow pool. He touched a larger paw print with four distinct toes. "This is clouded leopard. Probably Franz watching our backtrail. They started following me when I went to work, even when I crossed borders, so it was safer to train them. I couldn't stop the silly things from following me everywhere."

"Are you worried about Fritz?"

"No, he's had wounds before. He knows how to hole up in the forest. He'll come back when it's safe. I didn't want him at the house alone. If the spotted leopard found him, it would have killed him just out of sheer meanness. Look at this one." He pointed to a very small track much like the clouded leopard track. "This is a leopard cat. They're about the size of a domestic cat, usually reddish or yellowish coats with black rosettes. This was a busy place this morning."

"What's that strange track? It looks like it has webbing on the feet."

"That's a masked civet. They're nocturnal." He looked up at her. "Are you ready for me to carry you?" He straightened slowly. "Or do I have to pull rank and give you an order? You're limping."

"I didn't realize we were in the military."

"Anytime we're under a death threat, we're under military rules."

Her laughter rose to the forest canopy, blended with the continuous call of the barbet, a bird that seemed to love the sound of its own voice. "Are you making up rules as we go along?"

"It was quick thinking on my part. Aren't you impressed?" He swung her into his arms. "I want to know a little more about your mother's family. Did you meet your grandparents?"

"I don't remember hearing of my mother's parents at all. My brother spoke of our birth father's parents. He said we went to visit them in deep jungle once. They gave him treats and my grandmother rocked me. But they died around the same time as my father. He was on a trip and he never came back."

"And then your mother took you away?"

"I don't honestly remember, I was so young. Most of what I know is what my brother told me. After my father died, my mother took us to another small village on the edge of the forest. She met my stepfather. His family was very wealthy and they had a lot of land, a lot of power where we lived. We were there for some time and then he moved us to the United States."

Rachael looked around her, drinking in the scents and sights of the rain forest. It was truly beautiful with thousands of varieties of plant life in every color. Butterflies were in abundance, sometimes covering trunks of flowering fruit trees, adding to the explosion of color everywhere she looked. The forest seemed alive, leaves swaying, lizards and insects continually on the move, birds flitting from tree to tree. It was teaming with life. Termites and ants vied for territory near a large fallen tree.

"We lived in Florida on a huge estate. It was such beautiful and wild country in the mangroves and swamp. We had humidity and lots of alligators." She brushed back his hair. "No one turned into leopards."

"There were no big cats in the area? No signs of big cats?"

Rachael frowned. "Well of course there were rumors of panthers, the Florida panther in the swamps, but I never saw one. There are rumors of Bigfoot in the Cascades but no one actually has proof of Bigfoot. There aren't any cats in my family."

"Did your brother spend a lot of time in the swamp?"

Rachael stiffened. It was more a shift of her body, but Rio was so in tune with her he felt her slight withdrawal.

She averted her face and looked upward at the feathery foliage, the bright red fungi and fruit draping heavily on the tree. Antlerlike fungi and cups of brilliant color covered the trunks. Large mushrooms grew around the bases and made fields of large caps inside the buttress roots.

"The humidity in Florida isn't as intense, but it can be oppressive to some people. It doesn't rain nearly as much either."

"Did he go into the swamp, Rachael?" He kept his tone low, gentle even. Rachael wasn't a woman to be pushed. She trusted him with her life, but she didn't trust him with her brother's life. He couldn't push her too hard. She'd walk away first.

"My brother is a long way away from here, Rio. I don't want any part of him here, not even his spirit. Don't bring him into this place."

Temper rode him hard and he was silent as he walked quickly through the patches of light and dark, heading deeper into the forest. It took him a few minutes to work it out. "You don't want him in our place. My place. You don't want him anywhere near me."

"He doesn't belong here, Rio. Not at all, not with us." Rachael looked down at the splint on her wrist. She probably didn't belong with Rio either. She'd been lucky enough to meet him, but she didn't want him in danger.

"Sometimes, *sestrilla* I feel like I'm trying to hold water in my hand. You flow right through my fingers."

Rachael looked at him with her dark, liquid eyes. Sad eyes. "I can't give you what it is you want."

"Before my father died, Rachael, he asked my mother to promise him that she'd take me and leave the village. He wanted her to find another man so she wouldn't have to raise me alone. A man or woman who lost their mate would never choose another husband or wife from our people. My father talked to my mother more than once but she didn't want to live with another man. She stayed near the village."

"Why wouldn't the others want to take care of her and you too? If there aren't very many of you, surely they would want to make certain you were well taken care of?" She sounded outraged all over again. "I don't think I like your elders very much."

"The elders would want to care for widows and children, but there would be problems. Most leave if they want to find a companion to spend their life with. We can live and love outside of the rain forest, and many do. It's possible your father asked your mother to take you and your brother and find another man to fill his shoes."

"How did your father die?"

"He went in with a team to pull a diplomat from a rebel force. He was shot. It happens."

Rachael rested her head against his shoulder. "I'm sorry. It must have been so difficult for your mother to know that you chose to carry on your father's work."

"She didn't like it. My mother didn't do what my father wanted her to do. She stayed in the rain forest on the edge of the village. It caused some problems occasionally. She was a beautiful woman and it was easy enough to fall in love with her. Do you look like your mother?"

She smiled and relaxed in his arms, sinking into him without being aware of it. "I do look somewhat like her pictures. We have the same eyes, and my face is shaped like hers. And I have her smile. She wasn't as tall or as heavy."

Rio stopped right there under a tall tree with silvery bark and hundreds of orchids cascading down the trunk. "Heavy? You have curves, Rachael. I'm very fond of your curves." He bent his head to her throat, his breath whispering fire against her skin. "Don't say anything bad about yourself or I might be forced to prove you wrong."

Rachael laughed happily. He made her feel bright and alive when she had been so close to gloom. "I don't think that's much of a threat, Rio. And thank you for bringing up my mother. It's been a while since I had such a mental picture of her. When you asked me about her, I began to think of all the little details and I can see her again so clearly. She had thick hair. Very curly." She touched her hair. "I always kept my hair long because she wore hers that way. When I wanted to disappear, I cut my hair to my shoulders because I thought having it reach to my rear end was too conspicuous. I cried myself to sleep every night for a week."

"Wear your hair any way you want to wear it, Rachael. They've already found you here." He began walking again, picking up the pace, wanting to get back to the house and get her settled again. She was obviously growing tired and attempting to hide it from him.

"But they don't know I'm still alive. We might be able to make them think I drowned in the river. I threw my shoes in so something would turn up if they were really looking."

"Rachael, the only way we're going to be able to live a normal life is to remove the threat completely. We don't want to be looking over our shoulders the rest of our lives."

Rachael was silent, turning his words over and over in her mind. Rio was thinking along the lines of a permanent relationship, she was still taking it one day at a time. She looked closely at his face. The right thing to do would be to leave him as quickly as possible, remove all threats to him. She took a deep breath and let it out slowly. "I'm just realizing I have an incredible selfish streak. I always thought I was unselfish, but I don't want to give you up. It isn't the greatest moment in one's life to find out how completely self-centered you really are."

"It might be my greatest moment, to find out you want to keep me."

"Tell me that in a couple of weeks and I might believe you. This is all so unexpected. And as for normal, is how you live here in the rainforest your definition of normal?"

"I've rarely lived any other way." The smile faded from his face. "I doubt if they'll allow us to live in the village. I can shop there, although I don't much. It's uncomfortable for some of the people. As I'm supposed to be dead to them, shopping is difficult. They look through me, I can't ask questions, I leave money on the counter."

Her dark eyes flashed. "I know what I'd like to say to them. I don't want to live in the village. Not now. Not ever. And I'll have to think about shopping there. I wouldn't mind making everyone uncomfortable, but on the other hand, I would hate to help them out by supporting them."

Rio made an effort to keep from laughing. Rachael didn't need to be encouraged in her defense of him, but he couldn't help secretly loving it. "You might want the protection of the village when we have children."

"Are we going to have children?"

"Don't look so shocked. I like children—I think." He frowned. "I haven't actually been around any children, but I think I'd like them."

Rachael threw back her head and laughed more, hugging him to her as they drew closer to the house.

13

THE bath was heaven. Rachael slipped beneath the water to soak her entire head. She hadn't felt clean in weeks. Days of taking sponge baths didn't work for her, especially when an infection ravaged through her body the way it had. She came up and looked at Rio, trying not to let the happiness in her burst out. He'd been through such an ordeal, fighting the leopard, and he hadn't talked much about it. He looked older, the lines in his face deeper, shadows lurking in his eyes.

He rubbed shampoo into her hair. "You look happy."

"I never thought a bath would feel so good. Whatever Tama used on my leg is a miracle product. I couldn't believe the difference in the swelling and I'm certain it helped heal the puncture wounds. They'd been draining all the time, but now it's stopped. I feel so much better."

"Good." His fingertips rubbed her head in a slow massage. "Fritz is back. He snuck in when I was heating the water. I saw him go under the bed."

"What about Franz?" She wanted to moan with ecstasy. His fingers massaging her head were magical. "I'm worried that we haven't seen him."

"He followed us through the forest. He was in the canopy. He'll come in when he's ready."

"You should have pointed him out to me. I have to be more alert." She smiled up at him through the shampoo. "See, if I were a leopard, I would have noticed."

"I expected him, and we travel together all the time. I know his patterns. Leopards will even cache food in the same place repeatedly, making it easy for poachers to destroy them. We have to fight to keep from setting patterns. We all have that tendency and in a business like ours, it can get a person killed. I try never to use the same path twice. I never use the same escape route twice. I don't come to the house the same way. I have to make certain I always think about it."

Rachael ducked under the water to rinse out her hair. She didn't feel feline right then, she loved water, the hotter the better. She wanted to stay in the bath for as long as possible. She was beginning to realize bathing was a luxury. When she came up, wiping her eyes, she heard the radio crackling.

"I thought that was broken. Didn't I shoot it?"

"Drake left his for me." He picked up the small hand-held radio and listened to the warble of distorted voices. "They think they've found the right camp. They're going in soon, probably after midnight."

She read the anxiety in his voice. "You stayed behind because of me, didn't you? Rio, if you need to be with them, go. I'm perfectly fine by myself. I've got weapons here. You know I can use them."

"There's more to it than that, Rachael. You always take on responsibilities that aren't yours. I make my own choices, the same as you. I wanted to stay with you."

"Because you didn't altogether trust them."

He shrugged. "Maybe I don't right now, not where you're concerned. If the elders of your village contacted the elders in mine and asked them to aid in carrying out a death sentence, it's possible the elders here would agree.

They don't know you and our laws are very strict. Some might think harsh."

"You really think I'm some sort of a shape-shifter, don't you? I can't change my form. I've thought about it and tried, just to see if you're right, but nothing happens. I'm still me."

"Just hear me out for a moment, Rachael. Suppose your mother took you and your brother away from her village. She didn't want to upset the balance in the village but she decided she was too young to live the rest of her life alone so she chose to give up her heritage and live entirely with her human side."

Rachael rested her head against the back of the small tub he had carried up from a locked shed nearby and painstakingly filled with water he had heated. Darkness was slowly falling in the forest. The night creatures were stirring to life. "I suppose she might have thought that way."

"She met your stepfather."

"Antonio."

"She met Antonio. He was handsome, wealthy and very nice. He courted her, she fell in love with him and married him. His estate was on the edge of the forest. Every night it called to her. Night after night. The Han Vol Dan, the way of the change, whispered and tempted. Finally she began to steal away and run free in the forest in the way our kind is meant to do. Antonio wakes up night after night and his woman is gone. He's alone in his bed. What do you suppose this good man thinks?" Rio helped her stand and wrapped a towel around her. Lifting her from the tub he leaned into her, catching a bead of water that was running down her neck, lapping with his tongue. "He would think what any man would think. His beautiful wife was stepping out on him. And he would follow her."

Rachael shivered at the tone of his voice. "Okay, you don't have to add any drama in. You're a very scary man when you want to be."

"I was just thinking how I'd feel if I thought you were sneaking out of our bed to go meet with another man."

"Well quit thinking about it. You obviously have a very vivid imagination, and in case you haven't noticed, your claws are bursting through your fingertips."

He looked down with some surprise to find she was right. His hands were curled and stiletto switchblades—thick, curved and dangerous—had emerged with his rising temper. His claws could be rapidly extended through muscles, ligaments and tendons when needed or retracted when not in use. His frown gave way to a wry grin. "I'm not too civilized, am I?"

"I guess we can't take the jungle out of the man."

"But you weren't afraid of me, *sestrilla,* that should tell you something right there. Any normal woman would be terrified to see claws on a man."

She sat on the edge of bed, laughter in her eyes. "Are you saying I'm not normal? I think you've managed to mention that a couple of times now. It's rather like the old saying, 'the pot calling the kettle black'. In comparison, I'm *perfectly* normal."

"I think being what I am is perfectly normal, Rachael, and I'm more and more convinced that you're like me. I think your stepfather saw your mother shift shape. He loved her and it didn't matter. He may have even thought it was extraordinary. But if the elders in her village found out that he knew, that a human knew, they might banish her or worse, sentence him to death."

"Kim and Tama know."

"They're tribesmen. They live in the forest and have a deep respect of nature and other species. Not all men do."

"So my stepfather moves us in the dead of night into the city and we immigrate to the United States."

She obviously didn't realize how much that single sentence told him. Her stepfather had been afraid for his family, moving them at night to the States. "Where he has family and an estate in Florida on the edge of the Everglades. Where your mother can continue her nightly runs without fear of reprisals. I think he moved to protect your family." He watched her closely, with sharp, piercing intelligence shining in his eyes.

She averted her face, tossed off the towel and reached for a shirt. "Well he didn't do a very good job of protecting us. Or himself. His own family isn't so very hot. Not in the rain forest and not in the States. They're probably every bit as rigid or worse than your elders. You're on the wrong track, Rio."

"Maybe. It's possible. Didn't his family accept you and your brother?"

She shrugged casually —too casually. "At first they pretended they did."

"He came from money," Rio guessed.

"He had money. A lot of it. At least his family did."

"What family? Did he own the estate near the forest outright, or did it belong to his family?"

"His brother owned it with him." Her voice was without any inflection whatsoever, but he felt the distaste. Revulsion even. It was almost tangible in the room between them. "They shared all the homes, even the ones in the States."

Rio's radar went off immediately. "So they are very wealthy. They really can afford the million-dollar reward. Rachael, has it occurred to you that the reward is only to be paid if you're returned alive? The sniper wanted you dead. Could there be two factions at work here?"

She swung her head around to look at him, some emotion flickering in the depths of her eyes. "I didn't think of that."

"So it's possible."

Rachael nodded reluctantly. "Yes. And both sides have a great deal of money. My brother and I inherited my stepfather's share of the estates and his part of the businesses."

"How did your stepfather and your mother die?"

"They were executed. The official police report said they were murdered."

"Then there were autopsies performed."

She shook her head. "The bodies disappeared out of the morgue. They were stolen. It was a big scandal. I was still young and it was a terrifying time."

"So where did you and your brother go after your parents died?"

Her shoulders were rigid. "To our uncle, my step-father's brother. He shared the estates and businesses and took us in."

"So it's your uncle who is either paying to keep you alive or wants you dead."

"He would never pay to keep me alive." She struggled to keep bitterness from stealing into her voice. "Why are we talking about this, Rio? Just the thought of him makes my skin crawl. I left that place. I left those people. I don't want them here in this house with us."

"Your brother is a part of you, Rachael. I can tell you love him. It's in your voice when you talk about him. Sooner or later this has to be resolved."

"You obviously care about the elders in your village, but they banished you. I can love my brother and know I'm a liability to him and that it's better for him if I'm not around. Better for both of us."

He tapped his finger on the wall. "Why? What have you done that makes him better off without you?"

Her gaze was suddenly cool as it swept over him. "I don't talk about my brother with anyone, Rio. It isn't safe for you, for me or for him. If you can't accept that . . ."

"Don't go getting all edgy on me again. I asked a perfectly reasonable question."

She watched the heat shimmer in his eyes. "I don't think anyone with a temper like yours should ever call me edgy. I'm hungry, not edgy."

His eyebrow shot up. "Do you know how to cook?"

She glared at him. "I'm a perfectly good cook. I've been polite not wanting to get in your way. I've noticed you have a tendency to be territorial."

Before he could reply, the radio crackled again. Rio spun around and rushed across the room to snatch it up. There was a moment of silence. "It's a go. We've got a go." There was more static and words Rachael couldn't catch.

"What are they saying?"

"I'm listening to them talking to one another. They're going in to get out the victims. They'll have to go in like ghosts. With one, it's more a grab and get out, but you're talking several victims. There's bound to be one that panics and that's what makes it so dangerous."

"What happens if someone panics?" She could feel the tension in the room rising. Rio paced back and forth with quick restless steps. She watched him from the safety of the bed. He seemed to flow across the floor, every bit as graceful and fluid as a jungle cat. And just as caged there in the house with her.

Rio paused beside his rifle, slid his hand over the barrel. "This is where it could get bad. Conner better be watching out for them," he said in a low tone, almost to himself.

"This Conner is doing your job, is that it? What exactly do you usually do?"

"I protect them. I can hit a bird on a wing in a high wind. So I lay up above them where I can sight the entire camp and I keep the bandits off of them. I provide cover fire and lay it down thick when they retreat. We scatter, each man assigned a job, taking the victims into the forest. Drake usually gets them to the helicopter while the rest of the team goes in every direction. I draw the bandits after me. I provide heavy fire and keep them busy and following me until I hear from each team member they are safe and we can stand down."

"The bandits chase you through the forest."

He grinned at her, a small, mischievous little boy grin. "Several forests. There aren't any such things as borders or rivers or places we can't go. We do have to be a little careful in their territory. They're like rats, they go underground in their maze of tunnels in the fields. That's why we lead them into the forest. We scatter, the men change form and I'm the bandit's only hope of retribution."

She was furious all over again at the elders. So much so that she balled the pillow into her hand and threw it against the wall in a small fit of temper. "They take advantage of you, Rio. You're risking your life to help them get away."

"*Sestrilla,* it isn't like that. The others risk their lives going into the camp while I'm safe a mile away. We all take risks. We're at risk when the poachers enter our territory and try to kill the endangered animals. It's what we do, who we are. I want to do what I do."

"And the elders sit back and count the money you all bring them. I'll bet there's no risk at all to them. They just send you out, filling your head full of good deeds and necessity and count themselves lucky you're willing to risk your life for the cause."

"You're really angry." She was. He could see her body was trembling. More than that, she was close again. He could feel the sudden tension, the wild power in the room, caged but seeking freedom. She exuded a strong sensual pull.

"I detest people like that. They make the rules for everyone else and then sit back nice and safe calling the shots, making life-and-death decisions for people and reaping the monetary rewards."

She wasn't talking about the elders in his village. Rio remained silent, waiting to see if she would continue, but she pushed off the bed and went to the door, flinging it open to stare outside at the beckoning forest.

All the talk of the mythical Han Vol Dan, of her mother running free, made her yearn for the same freedom. Just for a few minutes to be something else, something different, with more control, more freedom. The ability to run along the branches of the tree. She held up her arms to embrace the idea. Deep within her she felt the stirring of power. Something untamed. Wild. Something desiring to be free. Fire raced through her bloodstream and something alive moved beneath her skin. Her fingers curved. Her face ached. Bones cracked and snapped.

"No!" Rio said it sharply, caught her shoulder and jerked her away from the door, back into the safety of his house. He wrapped his arm around her waist as if that would anchor her to him. "What did you think you were doing?"

"I don't know." She didn't look at him. She could only look at the temptation of the trees, the swaying foliage and thick canopy. Even the rain seemed to call her with its steady rhythm. "What am I doing, Rio?"

"Your leg isn't healed enough for that. It would never survive the change without further injury. You can't give in to it yet."

"Is it possible to stop? If it's in me, won't it come out as it does with you?" She was outwardly calm, but inside a mixture of excitement and fear were beginning to blend. She scented the wind and understood the messages it carried. She heard the notes overhead in the canopy and knew the song. She saw small lizards, insects, a preying mantis, hidden among the leaves of the trees as if they stood out in bright images.

The radio in Rio's hand crackled. A burst of static followed. "We're in. We're in." The voice was a mere whisper.

Rachael knew the radio was important. She could hear the tension in the voice. She could feel it in Rio, but the wildness in her was blossoming, spreading like a savage heat through her body. With it came sight as she'd never known it. Thermal images rippled in reds and yellows as she stared out into the darkness. Night had fallen completely and the ghostly mist once more shrouded the canopy. White tails drifted in and out of the trees. They looked like white lace. She inhaled sharply and drew the night into her lungs.

"Damn it, Rachael, I'm closing the door." Rio bent down to peer at her face. "Your eyes are changing, your pupils dilating. You have to fight it."

Rachael blinked up at him. Rio sounded urgent, worried. She smiled at him to reassure him she wasn't afraid. Well, maybe a little, but it was a good kind of fear. She wanted to reach for that other side of herself. She felt it strong now, purposeful, growing inside of her. She could shake off the anguish and pain and feel the sheer joy of living free. No responsibilities. No ties. There would be nothing but being alive to the sounds and scents of nature.

The temptation was so strong she pushed away from Rio, back toward the door. Rio's hands nearly crushed her shoulders. "Rachael, look at me." He dragged her into his arms, held her tightly against his chest. He could feel the wildness rising in her, see it as she looked at him with eyes no longer entirely human. "Fight it. Stay with me, now. You can't risk the change with your leg in such bad shape. Not the first time."

He kissed her. It was the only thing he could think to do when she was slipping away from him. When she looked so alluring, a temptress of the rain forest. The moment his mouth fastened onto hers, she circled his neck with her arms, pressed her body into his so that they simply melted together. In the heat of the forest her skin felt like hot velvet, sliding and rubbing against his so that the friction brought its own heat and excitement. His fingers tunneled in her hair, fisted there to hold her to him while he kissed her voraciously. Ravenously. Forgetting everything but the feel and taste of her.

Rachael felt she'd gone from one dream to another. The wildness subsided into her to be replaced by another kind. Untamed, unbridled passion welled up and spilled over for this one man. The only man. She had thought to let him go. She thought to protect him and leave him behind. It would never happen. He was as much a part of her as her own head was. When they were together there was magic, laughter— love. It was a silly, simplistic ideal, but it worked with Rio.

Rachael lifted her head to look at him, to take in his face, feature by feature. Tears swam in her eyes and she had to blink them away. "You're so beautiful, Rio." Her throat ached and her eyes burned with love welling up like a fountain.

"You always tell me I'm beautiful. Men aren't supposed to be beautiful."

"Maybe you aren't supposed to be, but you are. I've never been around a man like you before." Her fingertips traced the lines in his face, smoothed over his mouth. She looked into his eyes, and smiled. "It isn't just your body that's so perfect, Rio, you're such a good man."

How could a woman tear a man up with a few simple words? Maybe it was the honesty in her expression, the love in her eyes. "Rachael." Her name came out in a husky whisper. He couldn't control his own voice.

The radio crackled to life. The sound of gunfire could be heard in short bursts. Someone screamed. Pandemonium rang out. "Joshua's hit. Conner's trying to cover Drake and the vics. Damn it. Damn it." More static.

Rachael was watching Rio's face carefully. His expression disappeared and he wore a grim mask. "How far away are they? How many miles away?"

He looked down at her, blinked, kissed her mouth hard and turned to catch up his rifle. Rachael handed him the two knives lying side by side on the counter.

"Rachael." He hesitated at the door, radio in hand.

"Just go. Hurry. It's what you do. I'll be fine here with Fritz."

Rio turned and was gone. She didn't hear him on the verandah. She didn't hear anything at all. He was as silent in human form as he was in the form of a cat. Rachael limped over to the small counter. Fritz stuck his head out from under the bed to watch her. She smiled at the little leopard. "I may as well see how all this works."

Rio could hear Rachael murmuring softly to the cat. He shrugged into the harnesses and positioned the weapons for easy access before leaping to the next tree branch. He used creeper vines to swing to some of the closer branches, and hit the forest floor running. He ran through streams and small creek beds, pulled himself up the embankments using the vines and once more took to the trees.

"Coming in from the south," he reported into the radio.

"Go for Joshua, he's running hurt, leaving a trail. Conner's guarding the vics. Team is spreading out to leave tracks." Drake's voice came in a stream of static and heavy breathing.

"I'll intercept. Who's on Josh?"

"He's on his own. Hurry, Rio."

"Tell him to come to me. I'll meet him."

They kept the transmissions brief and spoke in their own dialect, which would be nearly impossible for anyone overhearing to translate. Only members of their species spoke the guttural mixture of tones and words. It was one of their greatest strengths when working.

Rio covered several miles in record time, using Drake's short bursts of static for direction. He had to get to Joshua before Tomas or one of his men did. Joshua was in trouble, wounded and on his own. The other team members were needed to bring out the many victims and get them to safety.

He heard the sound of a gunshot echoing through the trees. White mist shrouded the canopy as he flung himself through the branches. He was forced to slow down to cross the river, using a precarious route, two low-hanging branches and a creeper vine. He nearly lost his footing, leapt to the next tree, his hands shifting to claws to cling to the bark. The trunk was wide with a multitude of plants growing up it, covering the bark. The branches raised toward the sky, seeking light, but the heavy foliage from the taller trees around it blocked it from the precious source causing the tree's limbs to curl and the leaves to feather. He flattened himself against the trunk, hooked claws clinging precariously as two bandits consulted in loud whispers beneath him.

The two men were out of breath having run ahead of the melee in the hopes of setting up an ambush. They consulted in their native tongue, gesturing wildly, all the while staring back toward the sounds of gunfire.

Rio's breath hissed out slowly as he felt for the closest branch with his foot. He willed them not to look up. As high up as he was, the wind fingered his face, but below, on the forest floor, the air was completely still and sound carried easily. His toes managed to find footing and he eased down, keeping his claws hooked as an anchor as he gained more solid territory. When he was on the branch, he leaned against the trunk and slid his rifle into position, careful not to rustle the leaves. And then he froze, every muscle locked into a ready position as only his kind could do. Waiting. Watching. Marking his prey.

The bandits were oblivious to his presence. They separated, moving off the trail, one bandit crouched low in the leafy foliage of the shrubbery. Impatiently the man flicked a caterpillar from a leaf onto the faint trail. Rio didn't follow the path of the caterpillar. He never took his gaze from his prey. One hand slipped up to his neck to pull the long knife from its sheath. The rifle remained rock steady, the barrel aimed squarely on target, finger on the trigger. Rio pulled the knife free. Careful to keep the first man in sight, he followed the progress of the second, who had moved ahead and off the trail to climb into the low-hanging branches of a fruit tree. As he climbed, his boot scraped lichen from the trunk and his weight, as he pulled himself up, sent fruit tumbling to the ground.

The wind shifted slightly, playing through the leaves. The rain began again, a steady fall that had both bandits cursing as the drops soaked their clothing. Rio remained still, high in the branches above them. He caught the scent of fresh blood. He heard the whisper of clothing against a bush. That told him, more than anything else, that Joshua was badly injured. He would have shifted shape if he could and used the strength and speed of the leopard to get him home. Instead, he was dragging himself through the forest, using the easiest and most open trails.

Rio didn't wait to see Joshua's approach. He kept his eyes on the two bandits hiding in ambush. The one below him put down his rifle twice. Tied his boot. Fidgeted. The one in the tree held his gun and watched the trail. Rio kept his rifle aimed at the bandit in the tree. The moment he saw the man raise the gun to his shoulder, he fired.

Rio didn't wait to see the results of his marksmanship; he threw the knife at the man below him. The gurgling sound was ugly, but it told him what he needed to know as he changed position, leaping to another branch and sighting the first bandit a second time.

"He's down," Joshua said. He leaned against a tree trunk tiredly. Blood soaked his right side. "Thanks, Rio. You're a welcome sight. They would have killed me. I don't have much fight left in me." He slid down the tree and sank to the forest floor, his legs going out from under him.

Rio dropped to the ground and inspected the two bandits before going to Joshua. The man had lost too much blood. "You should have put a field bandage on this."

"I tried. No time. They were everywhere. We pulled everyone out that was there. One of the men had gone missing and no one knows what happened to him. The team scattered, each taking a vic, and Conner had to cover them." He looked up at Rio. "Drake took a hit. I don't know how bad."

Rio stiffened, forced himself to be gentle as he worked quickly on the wound. "He sent me to you."

"I know, I heard on the radio. That's like him. Three reported in clear. You had your radio off, I tried to let you know." Joshua began to slump to one side.

"Damn it, Josh, don't you die on me. I'll be pissed off if you do." Rio swore under his breath as he quickly worked on the wound to stem the flow of blood. The entrance hole was small and neat but the exit was a mangled, bloody mess.

The wind tapped him on the shoulder, brought him the scent of the hunters. A pack of them, out for blood, hot on

Joshua's trail. They'd be furious when they found their dead lying in the midst of the shrubs.

"Josh, I have to take you up into the trees. I have no choice. I don't want to give you morphine, you're already in shock."

"Do what you have to do," Joshua muttered. His lids fluttered, but he was unable to find the energy to open his eyes. "If you have to leave me, Rio, give me a gun. I don't want Tomas to get his hands on me."

"Shut up," Rio said rudely. He retrieved his knife, cleaning the blade in the leaves before returning it to its sheath. "Let's go, the hounds are getting close."

Joshua made no sound as Rio slung him over his shoulder in a dead man's carry. Rio hoped he'd lost consciousness. The steel muscles running beneath his skin would be needed, the enormous strength of his kind. He went up the tree, higher than he'd like but where there was more cover. He wouldn't have the necessary speed for traveling along the branches carrying Joshua's weight, so he'd need stealth and cover.

The continual rain added to the complications, making the branches slick. Several times he disturbed birds and gliding lemurs. Squirrels scolded him and a thick snake uncoiled when he accidentally gripped it for an anchor as he made his way along the branch highway with Joshua.

He was nearing the river when, without warning, the birds took to the sky. Joshua stirred, but Rio's soft command stopped him from moving. Rio cached Joshua in the crotch of a thick branch, much like a leopard might with his dinner. It was the only tree with enough foliage to hide them. He had hoped to be on the other side of the river before the bandits caught up with them. His pulley and sling was stashed and would be useful, but he'd have to leave Joshua to set it up. He checked to make certain no blood dripped to give away their position. The roar of the river drowned most of the noise, but couldn't take away the other signs of approach. "Tomas and his crew are coming, Josh.

You'll have to be quiet and stay right there, no moving."

Joshua nodded his understanding. "I think I can hold a gun."

Rio shook his head. "No need." He crouched down beside Joshua, felt for his pulse. The man needed medical attention as quickly as possible. Rain-soaked, clothes clung to their bodies, boots rubbed blisters into skin. The conditions were miserable, but Rio had been in worse. "We'll get you home," he assured Joshua.

Rio didn't waste time hesitating. Leaving the rifle behind, he went through the trees as quickly as he could, rushing to beat the arrival of the bandits. He dropped into the open onto a low-hanging branch and dove into the river. His arms cut strong, clean strokes, taking him across the river even as the current pulled him downstream. On the other side, he dragged himself up the embankment, rolled beneath a tangle of buttress roots and caught up the pack stashed in the hole in the trunk.

The bandits had broken out of the forest on the other side. They spread out, examining the ground for tracks. One was too close to the tree where he had cached Joshua. Josh was barely conscious and one wrong move would instantly bring him to the bandits' attention. Rio slowly and carefully pulled the rifle from the cover of the trunk and laid it over a root to steady his hand. He was in a bog and leeches would be swarming to his body heat if he didn't move immediately.

He squeezed off three shots in rapid succession, looking to wound his targets rather than kill them. Tomas would be forced to carry his men to safety rather than keep up the chase. Rio scooted backward on his belly, seeking the heavier cover of brush, trying to keep larger trees between him and the river.

The bandits returned fire, a rapid burst of bullets that chewed the bark from the trees and spit leaves and needles close to him. He stayed very still, not giving away his position as he marked new targets.

Tomas was no fool. He knew whom he faced. He'd run up against Rio's marksmanship many times and he didn't want to lose any more men. He signaled them back into the timberline. They melted away, carrying their wounded. Several discharged their guns in a last show of anger, but they moved off rather than try to cross the river in the open to track him. They might try it further upriver, but by that time, Rio hoped to have Joshua deep inside the forest and in the hands of his people.

Worried that they may have left a sniper behind, Rio took his time coming out of the bog. He felt the sting of a couple of leeches as he crawled into deeper forest. It took several minutes to remove the creatures with his knife. As he retrieved the pulley and sling from his pack and rose, a bullet whistled by his head. Rio threw himself to one side, eyes examining the surrounding area. He thought he'd been well hidden, but his enemy had guessed where he would go to escape the leech-infested ground.

The bullet had missed him by inches, but he had more of a problem than a few leeches. He had to hunt. The bandit would be patient, lie in wait for him, knowing he would have to move soon. The river separated them and Joshua was cached up in a tree, wounded and in dire need of medical attention.

In the shelter of several thick trees, Rio shed his clothes, folding them neatly and setting the pile on a tree branch along with his boots. He shifted into his other form, embracing the power within him. The brute strength. The perfect hunting machine. Bold and clever, highly intelligent and cunning, the leopard began his stalk. Staying in the shadows of the trees, the large cat angled downstream, padding swiftly through the vegetation. The leopard scented blood and gunpowder as it leapt onto the low-hanging branches of a tree at the edge of the river. The cat snarled as the sniper fired repeatedly, sweeping the area where Rio had been.

The leopard plunged into fast-moving water, using

powerful muscles to swim across to the other side. The cat climbed up the embankment, slinking across the open area in small stop-and-start bursts, going to ground and freezing behind the cover of the shrubbery. He gained yards, then feet, until he was a short distance from the bandit.

The man hurried quickly through the trees, intent on the other side of the river. He never saw the leopard crouched only feet from him. He never saw the rush, only felt the hit, hard like a freight train, driving him backward with powerful legs and muscles. He was hit so hard he never felt the crushing weight of the jaws that ended his life.

Rio fought the wild nature of the beast, pulled back from the heady scent of the kill and shifted shape quickly. He still had to get Joshua across the water. It would take too much time to set up the pulley and sling. He hurried back to the man, grateful to find him still alive.

"We're going into the river, Josh; I'm taking you to the village."

"You don't have to do that, Rio. Don't put yourself in that position."

Rio hoisted him onto his shoulder. "I don't give a damn what they think about me, Josh. You need help as quickly as possible."

"Did you lose your clothes?"

Rio grinned, a show of teeth. "I left them on the other side of the river in a tree."

"You've always been crazy, Rio."

Rio heard the utter weariness in the voice. Joshua hung like a dead weight, not even attempting to hold on. Worried, Rio plunged into the river, using every bit of his strength to fight the current to get them both to the other side. Then he began to jog.

It was a hellish, nightmare journey. Joshua's body slammed against Rio's. Brush tore at his skin. The rain soaked them both as the miles passed. Rio began to tire, his legs rubbery, his lungs burning for air. His feet, although tough and used to the travel, were torn and bloody. It took

several hours and he stopped three times to rest, give
Joshua water and tighten the pressure bandages over the
wounds.

Rio staggered into the village, tired and hot and soaked
from the rain just before dawn. No one came out of their
houses, although they knew he was there. Joshua's blood
soaked Rio's skin where the man was pressed tight against
him. The rain continued, a steady cascading fall that created a haze between Rio and the houses. He started toward
the house of their only medic. Movement caught his attention. The elders came onto their verandahs, watching him
through the downpour.

Rio stood for a moment, swaying with weariness, feeling anger wash over him. Shame. He was twenty-two again
and standing before the council with his mother's blood
and the blood of her murderer on his hands. He lifted his
head and set his jaw. They would never accept him. Never
want the taint of his life to touch theirs. He could protect
their people, give them his share of the money, but he
would always have blood on his hands and they would
never forgive him. His mouth hardened and he squared his
shoulders. His eyes were fiercely proud, his jaw strong and
stubborn. It didn't matter if he wasn't welcome in their village. He didn't want to be there. He refused to believe that
he could miss the interaction with others of his kind.

Inside the houses the whispers would start. It always did
if he had to make the journey and intrude on their space.
Each time he was certain it would be different, better—that
they would accept him. But their faces would be hard, or
averted or they simply looked past him as if he didn't exist.
He forced strength into his tired body and carried Joshua
straight to the house of the medic. They would never allow
him entrance, nor would they speak to him. Even if they
thought the blood on his body belonged to him, they
wouldn't ask questions or attempt to help. He was dead to
them.

Rio deliberately went up the stairs to the verandah and

placed Joshua's body onto the chair there. As he turned to
leave, Joshua caught his arm. His grip was feeble but he
hung on. Rio turned back, bent down to him. "You're home
now, you're safe."

"Thanks, Rio. Thanks for what you did."

Rio gripped the hand for a moment, covering the gesture with his body so Joshua wouldn't get reprimanded in
front of the council. "Good fortune, Josh."

He turned, ramrod straight, walked down the steps and
paused to allow his gaze to sweep with contempt, with
arrogance through the village. To take in the familiar setting. Something wrenched at his heart, something deep and
terrible. His temper was a sharp thorn, sticking in his gut
and burning there. Resolutely he turned his back on them
all and walked into the forest where he belonged. For a
moment everything blurred around him. He thought it was
the rain, but when he blinked, his vision cleared and his
eyes burned. Rio forced the air through his lungs and told
himself he was alive and on his way back to Rachael and
that was all that mattered.

14

RIO entered the house in silence, leaving the door open to catch even the slightest breeze. The rain poured down in a steady rhythm, concealing the verandah and house in heavy white mists. The mosquito net performed a ghostly dance but his gaze was riveted to Rachael's face. He didn't even remember jogging home to her. His feet hurt, his body was tired and sore and a rage burned like a firestorm deep inside of him. He had stopped to bathe before coming to her, hoping the rage and pain would lessen beneath the spray of cleansing water. It hadn't.

He loomed over her, brooding, watching her, fury riding him hard. Pain eating away at his insides. He tasted loneliness for the first time. Rachael had done that, brought him back to life. She fascinated him, tempted him. Made him happy, sad, angry—everything all at once. And he was addicted to the scent and feel of her. Lust rose, a craving as dark as the fury swirling like a black, tumultuous cloud inside of him.

Rachael lay asleep on the bed. His bed. One hand was flung across his pillow, across the empty spot where he

belonged. The thin cover was on the floor leaving her long
legs sprawled across the sheet. She wore only his shirt,
unbuttoned and open, exposing the creamy swell of her
breasts. Her hair, as black as midnight, spilled across the
white pillow in whorls and spirals, begging to be touched.
She looked young in her sleep, long lashes forming two
crescents against her skin. Her body lay open to him, soft
and warm, an offering to appease the terrible hunger burning in him.

He didn't feel gentle or loverlike. He felt wild and
inflamed, his body's urgent demands riding him hard. He
knew it was a part of his heritage, but intellect didn't count
when he stood in his home, when Rachael lay naked in his
bed, her body open and waiting for his. Rio moved closer,
laid his weapons aside, never taking his burning gaze from
her. Soft skin, lush curves, her breasts a tempting invitation.

Rio was already as hard as a rock, but looking at her
while she slept so peacefully, so unaware of her vulnerabil-
ity, he thickened and hardened more. He touched his erection, for relief, wrapped his fist around the throbbing
demand as he attempted to walk across the room to her.
Taking steps was painful with his body so full and tight.
There was a roaring in his head. His body dripped with his
lust, his belly burned with it.

Rachael shifted restlessly as if she instinctively knew
she was being stalked. She opened her eyes and saw his
face, dark with passion, etched with lust. With intent. With
something beyond mere desire. His look set her heart
pounding. Made her mouth go dry. Turned her body to a
pool of hot liquid. His gaze burned over her, hungry flames
that sent electricity sparking on her skin everywhere his
look brushed.

He struck swiftly, his fingers circling her arm, a throaty
growl sending a shiver down her spine as he yanked her up
so that his mouth melded to hers, one hand at the back of
her head holding her still for his kiss. Not a kiss, fierce possession. Heat rushed over her like molten lava, blossomed

and burst into volcanic flame. He dragged her closer, crushed
her to him, his strength enormous, wanting skin against
skin, wanting to feel her body impressed into the heat of
his. Breath slammed out of her lungs and into his. His kiss
was hungry, savage, devouring her, taking rather than asking, as if his hunger knew no boundaries.

His arms locked her to him, so tight she felt his every
muscle, every beat of his heart, every breath he took. She
tasted lust. She tasted desire. She tasted his fierce pride and
something else. Pain. She knew bone-deep anguish and she
recognized it in him. She knew what he was doing even
when he didn't. His mouth was hot velvet, his tongue duel-
ing with hers, a tango of breath and moist heat. He gave her
no chance to breathe, to do anything but accept the
firestorm in him. To let it wash over her so that she caught
flame too, was pulled into a whirling vortex, a tornado of
pure desire.

Rachael kissed him back, every bit as wild, allowing the
greedy lust to rise in her, to match the fierce inferno raging
in him. She gave herself up to him, her arms around his
neck, holding him to her. He stole the breath from her body
and used it for his own air. His teeth moved down her chin,
her throat, taking small greedy bites as if he would devour
her alive. Rachael gasped with the wash of sensation, her
nails biting deep into his arms as she arched her body.
Waiting. Aching. Wanting more.

His mouth, hot and insistent with demands, went lower
still, closed over her breast and suckled strongly. She cried
out, unable to contain the blaze sweeping through her body.
She thrust against his mouth, her fingers finding his hair,
closing in two fists, dragging him closer. She didn't want
him gentle and considerate, she wanted him exactly the way
he was, wild, untamed, driven beyond control, on fire with
urgent need and ravenous hunger. For her. For her body.

His mouth took away sanity and replaced it with feeling.
Abruptly he lifted his head, eyes glittering as he dragged
the pillows and blankets beneath her hips. She could see

his body, hard and perfect, every muscle defined as if
carved from rock. His face was etched with dark hunger.
His gaze dropped to the triangle of black tiny curls and her
heart pounded wildly. There was an unspoken command in
his look. A demand.

A wave of heat swept over her. She felt her body go liquid in her deepest core. Very slowly she obeyed that silent
command, shifting her legs, opening them for him. The air
on her slick, wet entrance inflamed her more. His fingers
circled her good ankle. He bent her leg at the knee. There
was a proprietary feel to his hand on her leg. He was much
more gentle helping her with her injured leg. His hands
went to her thighs, gripping, opening her wider, one knee
on the bed between her legs. Not once did he raise his gaze
to her face. He seemed fascinated with her glistening body.

She waited, hardly daring to breathe, her heart pounding in anticipation. She wanted to plead with him, weep
with the dark passion riding her so hard. There wasn't an
inch on her body that didn't ache for his touch. His tongue
moistened his lower lip and she writhed with pleasure. He
hadn't touched her, but the force of his gaze had. And it left
her needing—craving.

His thumbs bit into her thighs as he wedged his shoulders between her legs, opened her completely to him. She
knew what he was doing. Claiming her. Branding her.
Making her his so that no one else would ever do. He
breathed warmth into the seething pool of fire. She cried
out, would have jumped away but he held her still, without
mercy, for his invasion. His tongue stabbed deep, a weapon
of wicked pleasure, lapping and licking and stroking while
she screamed in a wild, endless orgasm.

"More," he growled ruthlessly. "I want more."

He pushed his finger deep inside of her, pressed deep
while she thrust against his palm, while her body clamped
around him, gripped in the throes of passion. He put his
finger to his mouth, surged over the top of her, bracing his
body with his arms. He ducked his head, leaned forward to

suckle at her breast. Her body nearly exploded. She clung to his arms, trying to hold on when the world seemed to be spinning out of control.

Lying as he was, her hips cradling his, the head of his penis was against her wet, throbbing entrance. She tried to take him inside of her, but he held her still, waiting, pushing up her need, the sense of urgency consuming them both. Then he thrust hard, buried himself deep, driving into her velvet sheath so that her folds parted like the soft petals of a flower and she opened to him. He tilted her hips, urging her to take all of him, every inch, welding them together in a frenzy of fury and dark passion.

He whispered to her in the ancient tongue of his people, admitting he loved her, that he needed her, but the words beat more in his head than in his throat. He drove her up higher and higher, pushing them both to their limits, a wild, tumultuous ride. He clenched his teeth against the waves of sensations, against the jackhammers tripping in his head, against the tightness sweeping through his body and the inevitable explosion that started in his toes and burst upward.

A tidal wave swept through Rachael, carried her up and up until there was no where to go and she was free-falling, imploding, fragmenting. Until there was no part of her that wasn't consumed by fiery pleasure. It licked over her skin and behind her eyelids. Flames rolled in her stomach and burned in her deepest core. Her body rocked with quakes, a riptide of sensations that went on and on. If she moved, if he moved, the rippling effect started all over again.

Rio lay over her, his head resting on hers, breathing deeply, fighting for control. Most of his fury was spent in her arms. Rachael. Only Rachael would have accepted such a joining. Only Rachael would look at him with her heart in her eyes. No matter how tight he clung to her, she never pushed him away. Never said enough. There were questions in her eyes, but she didn't ask them, not even when he separated them. She simply wrapped her arms around him, turning a bit on her side to give him room, his head against the soft pillow of her breasts.

"You need sleep, Rio. You're exhausted."

He didn't say anything, just lay next to her, taking in their combined scents, listening to the endless rain. He found it soothing. The forest had stirred to life, animals calling out, insects humming, birds singing. The background music, always present.

Rio lay awake long after Rachael had gone to sleep. Fear choked him, nearly suffocated him. When had she become so damned essential to breathing? How had she managed to invade his life and wrap herself around his heart? He couldn't imagine his life without her. She was so warm and soft and perfect. He had memories of warm and soft and perfect and those memories turned into nightmares of blood and death and rage.

He wanted this to be his life. Rachael—her laughter, her courage, her moods and shifts of temper. Lovemaking as sweet and tender as he could make it or a fierce need that could only be assuaged with a wild mating.

Her breast was a temptation he couldn't ignore. He flicked her nipple with his tongue, then sucked the creamy mound into his mouth. It seemed a miracle to be able to lie with her, suckling her breast when he wanted, sliding his hand over her body to dip his finger deep inside of her. Even in her sleep she was responsive. Clenching her muscles around him, shifting to arch into his mouth deeper. She smiled, murmured something incoherent and tunneled her fingers in his hair. She slept like that, her body wet with wanting him, his mouth on her breast and his hand cupping her tight curls possessively, while her fingers were buried in his hair.

Rio woke to the feel of Rachael's tongue lapping at his morning erection. Her mouth was hot and teasing, her tongue playing over him, her teeth sliding gently, wickedly. For a moment she sucked him deep into her throat and he groaned, lifting his hips, helpless in her thrall. His eyes weren't even open and she was cupping his balls; he was already rock hard with her ministrations. He lifted his lashes to watch her. She looked like a contented cat, pleased and stimulated, her silken hair tumbling in curls around her face. She knelt between his legs, her beautiful derrière raised and keeping time with the lapping of her tongue. Her breasts were full, nipples erect. He watched his body slide in and out of her mouth, glistening wet, growing thicker and harder as he began to thrust forward and withdraw. "You're the most beautiful thing I've ever seen." He meant to say it, but the words came out somewhere between a groan and a husky whisper. She did things with her tongue and teeth and her sinful mouth that drove him out of his mind.

She pulled her hot mouth away and replaced it with something cold and wet and sticky. Rachael smiled as she teased him with a ripe mango fruit, sliding it over and around him, thoroughly dripping the nectar over his bulging erection. He didn't think he could get any harder or thicker, but she managed it. "Good morning. I thought you could use breakfast." She handed him the fruit and went back to licking, this time teasing with her tongue as she tried to retrieve every drop of juice.

Rio stared at her dumbly, shocked to find the mango in his palm. He lay back and took a bite of the juicy exotic fruit. It ran down his chin but he was too caught up in watching Rachael enjoying herself. There couldn't be another woman like her on the face of the earth. He found everything about her sexy, especially the way she enjoyed his body. She was proprietarial about it, as if his body belonged to her and she could do whatever she wanted. And right now she wanted to sit astride him.

Rachael didn't wait. Rio had suckled her breast on and off while she dozed, had pushed his fingers deep inside of her, keeping her wet and on edge and in need. He could do something about it now that he was awake. She'd been patient enough. She knelt over him and slowly lowered herself over his burgeoning penis.

He gasped as he felt his body push its way into hers. She was tight and hot and slick all at the same time. She wanted control and he gave it to her, eating the mango she'd given him while she began a slow, sensual ride. Her breasts jiggled with invitation as she picked up her rhythm, sliding up and down him with obvious relish. He dripped some of the juice over her breast, watched it run over the swell to the tip of her nipple. He leaned forward and caught it lazily with his tongue. His body was on sweet fire, and if she wanted to play he could oblige.

She opened her mouth. Rio fed her a bite, watched her chew as her body slid over his. Rubbed his with heat and fire. She licked his finger, her tongue curling around him in a sexy, explicit manner. He closed his eyes and groaned. He couldn't take much more. She seemed in no hurry, simply pleasuring herself and him at a leisurely pace. The pressure started slow, he didn't even notice it at first, but then it began to lick at his skin, tighten his muscles and put every cell in his body on alert.

He tried to thrust upward to meet her body, but she glared at him and he stopped. A flush spread over her skin until she glowed. Her breath came in small gasps and her nipples tightened. She reached almost blindly for Rio's hands. He had enough sense to take the last bite of mango and catch her, bracing her while she rode hard, grinding against him, bringing both of their bodies to a fever pitch. He met the rhythm of her ride, thrusting into her, bringing the last exquisite peak to them. They finished together, a whirlwind of pounding blood and rockets.

Rachael laughed happily and leaned forward to lick the juice from his chin. "You're a sticky mess. Luckily we have the tub still here."

"With cold water," he felt compelled to point out.

Her smile widened into a mischievous grin. "Well, I did heat it up a bit while you slept. It wasn't that difficult."

"You heated up bathwater for me? And I slept right through it? I never do that. I wake up at the slightest sound.

You're ruining me, woman." No one had ever heated up bathwater for him. It was a tedious task. It had to be done on the gas stove if the fireplace wasn't lit. She had obviously spent a great deal of time on the task. Happiness burst through him like the sun rising.

"I hope I'm ruining you. What a marvelous concept." She collapsed, lying partially on top of him, her soft breasts mashed against his chest. He could feel her there, a part of him, taking over his heart and lungs, even his life, until he couldn't breathe without her. "Are you going to tell me what happened, Rio?" Her fingertips brushed at his hair, slid over his face, made every muscle in his stomach clench tightly. Her voice was very gentle. Her eyes too compassionate.

Rio tried a casual shrug. "It was a mission, just like every other." He didn't want to talk about it. He didn't want her to ever see him the way the elders had. Stripped naked of all pride. Vulnerable. His life in their hands. Their disgust. Their betrayal,—or maybe it was his. He honestly didn't know.

"Not like every other," Rachael persisted. "What was different about this one?"

He wanted to push her away. He wanted to shift shape and run free in the forest. The urge was on him wild and strong, a rush of fur rippling as his muscles contracted, crackled and snapped.

"Oh no you don't," Rachael flung her arms around him. "You stay with me. I'm not about to let you escape. This is too important."

It was ludicrous to think she could hold him. His strength was enormous, but she was looking at him with her large, liquid eyes and he couldn't bear to break her heart. Better his than hers. He tried to shrug casually, difficult when she was clinging like a monkey. "Joshua told me Drake was shot. I tried to get information, couldn't raise anyone on the radio. Two men tried to ambush Joshua and I had no choice other than to take them out." He looked away from her. She saw too damned much with those eyes of hers. "I killed them."

She said nothing, but her hand slipped into his.

"I had to get Joshua across the river and back to the village where there was medical help. I field dressed his wounds, but he lost too much blood and needed immediate attention."

"What happened?" She knew there was far more to the story than the bare bones he was giving her.

"Tomas and his men caught us at the river. I'd left Josh in a tree, hoping to get him across before Tomas caught up with us. I didn't want to take the chance with his open wounds in the river. If I stumbled, he could get a major infection." A ghost of a smile crossed his face. "Unfortunately, I didn't have any of Tama's famous green gunk to smear on him."

"So you left him in the tree and went to do what?"

"I have a pulley and sling I sometimes use for the cats, especially if the current is strong. I went to retrieve it, but Tomas showed up. I winged a couple of his men, forcing him to get them medical aid."

"But he left someone behind."

Rio sat up and pushed his hands through his dark hair. "A bath sounds good."

She took his hand and tugged. "Come on then. Get in and I'll wash you, like you did me. It felt delicious."

Rio stretched and padded across to the small closet that passed for the bathroom. He wasn't going to tell Rachael he preferred the jungle. After his performance at dawn, she very well might think him entirely uncivilized. Rachael was making him coffee when he returned.

"You're spoiling me."

"I hope so." She frowned at the marks on his body. "Leeches? Did those nasty little things manage to get on you again?"

"I was laying in the bog, waiting for my shot. They go for body heat."

She grinned at him and pushed him toward the tub. "Well, we both know you have plenty of heat."

He sank into the steaming water. Her hands went to his shoulders, soapy, sliding as she massaged the aches away. "Tell me what happened to upset you, Rio."

She was standing behind him, her hands wielding magic on his sore muscles. It was far easier to talk about it when he wasn't facing her. "I took him to the village. It was a long, difficult journey lugging Josh. Half the time I was afraid he was dead and the other half I knew I was hurting him. I didn't have time to change into clothes so I had to go through the shrubbery bare."

"That's where all the scratches and cuts came from. Why did you shift?" She kept her voice curious, careful not to sound judgmental or accusing.

"To get back across the river before the man left behind spotted Joshua."

Rachael kept kneading the tight muscles in his shoulders. He had made a third kill and wounded others. It had been a bad night. She remained silent, leaning down to brush a kiss on the top of his head.

"I don't know what happened, Rachael. I guess I was tired. I don't care what the elders think of me. I knowingly broke our rules. I accepted the consequences. I live with the banishment and it's never made me feel less of a human being."

Her hands stilled on his shoulders. Something frightening bubbled in the pit of her stomach. "You carried Josh home and they said something mean to you?"

"They don't speak to me. They don't look at me. I'm dead to them. If they happen to look my way, they look through me. If I spoke, if I had tried to tell them what happened to Joshua, they wouldn't have heard me."

"Those bloody bastards," she hissed.

Her swearing startled him. Not just her swearing but her choice of expletives. "That doesn't sound like South America to me." He turned his head to look at her, a small grin

on his face because she could take the sting of the elders'
rejection away with a few choice words.

"I went to school for a year in England. You'd be surprised the things you pick up," she said and rubbed shampoo into his hair with a little too much vigor. "I'd like to
have the chance to meet these wise elders of yours. Greedy
little vultures with their hands out and you doing the risky
jobs. What about the men you work with?"

If she rubbed any harder she was going to take his scalp
off. "Most of them live away from the village and of course
we talk. You saw Drake. It's better for them if they don't
advertise we're friendly because technically they're breaking the rules. I guess if the elders can't see it, they don't
mind it."

"Sanctimonious bastards."

He caught her wrist gently. "I'm going bald, *sestrilla*. I
can't afford the hair loss. I have a woman now and she's
very edgy about certain things."

She smacked the top of his head with the flat of her
hand. Soap bubbles flew everywhere, making her laugh.
"I'm not in the least edgy. It's just that these idiot
elders . . ."

"*Wise* elders," he corrected and hastily ducked under the
water before she could smack him again. He stayed low
while she massaged the soap out of his hair. When he came
up she made a sound of complete disgust.

"I don't know who gave them that title. Most likely they
did. In any case, are you telling me that you hauled that
man through miles of forest and those men didn't even say
thank you?"

"Normally it doesn't bother me. It really doesn't. But
standing there with Joshua's blood all over me and my feet
hurting like a son of a gun, I felt like a kid again. I felt
ashamed of my actions, my lack of control, the terrible
thing inside of me that won't forgive the one who killed
my mother. And I wasn't certain I could forgive them, and
still don't know if I have. Not one of them said they were

sorry for her death. I felt like I mourned her alone. I felt rage and I felt shame. Damn it, Rachael, I hated that."

"They're the ones who should be ashamed with their no forgiveness." There was a fierce, protective instinct welling up in her. "They don't know the difference between good and evil. They aren't very wise."

"And you do?" He lifted an eyebrow at her.

Outside the birds shrieked and several monkeys screamed a warning. Rio stood up, the water pouring off of him. He turned his head alertly toward the door, taking the towel she handed him. "You need clothes on, Rachael," Rio said. "Company's coming and coming fast."

"I thought you said I didn't need clothes and I had to get over my civilized inhibited ways."

Her voice teased his senses, whispered over his skin like a silken glove. She made life worth living. He caught her hair gently, tugged her head to him and fastened his mouth to hers. He was instantly, ravenously hungry all over again. "You're killing me, *sestrilla,* I'm not going to survive. I don't think I have the stamina."

She laughed softly and flung her arms around him, holding him to her as if he were the most precious thing in the world. She peppered kisses all over his face. "You do just fine. I need to start cooking for you, build up your strength."

He couldn't stop his roving hands from sliding down her back, shaping the curve of her hip, cupping her bare buttocks. Rio allowed himself the luxury of burying his face against her soft throat. Love filled him up, burst out of him, a tide he couldn't stem, but he couldn't find the words to say it without choking. He held her, feeling her alive and warm and real in his arms. "Damn it, Rachael." His voice was gruff as he pushed her way, holding her at arm's length. "You're turning me into a poodle."

Her entire face lit up, her dark eyes laughing, her mouth curved and soft and beautiful. He ached to kiss her again, but tossed her a pair of jeans instead. "Stop laughing at me and put your clothes on."

"A poodle? Have you ever seen a poodle?" She finger-combed her hair, grinning at him. "I have the hair, maybe we can make a match." The sunlight pooled around her, soft rays that barely filtered through the canopy but found her, were drawn to her in the same way he was drawn. She looked radiant, filled with joy.

He had been so filled with pain and shame and anger the night before. In a few hours of bliss, she had shaken his world, turned it so that he could only feel joy and laughter and a paradise of pleasure. "You're tempting me, woman, and I'm going to throw you back in that bed."

She arched an eyebrow at him. "I doubt if I'm in any danger when you were just complaining about stamina. Wimpy male."

He tackled her, driving her back onto the mattress, throwing his body over hers. She was laughing so hard she could barely breathe. He pressed his erection against her, rubbing back and forth to show her what stamina was all about. Rachael didn't seem very impressed, laughing until he stopped her with his kisses.

The *whoop, whoop* of warning by the birds just outside on the railing of the verandah forced him to leave the temptation of her body. She lay on the bed, laughter fading into a smile as she looked at him. Something about her mysterious, feminine smile set his heart pounding.

Deliberately she began to pull his jeans slowly up her bare legs, wiggling to bring them over her hips and bare bottom. She left them open, exposing the triangle of tiny black curls. She stood there with her bare breasts thrusting toward him invitingly. "I can't find my shirt."

His mouth was dry. "You shameless hussy. You're deliberately provoking me." His fingers crushed the material of the shirt, his gaze drinking her in.

"Is it working?"

"Damn right it is. Put the shirt on before we shock poor Kim."

Rachael looked alarmed. "Kim? The guide?" She held out her hand for the shirt.

He held the shirt to his chest. "Come and get it."

Rachael went without hesitation, one arm sliding around his neck, pressing her breasts against his chest while her other hand slipped between his legs and began to caress and dance and cup him right through the material of his jeans. Her lips were at his throat, tongue swirling in a small, deliberate caress. Rio rocked against her hand, wanting her all over again with such an urgency it was as if he'd never once made love to her. Or as if his body remembered every magical moment and was obsessed.

Franz coughed a warning. Rio groaned and dragged the shirt around her, buttoning it quickly. It was the only safe thing to do. Barefoot, he pulled her with him onto the verandah to wait for their guest.

Rachael looked down to see Kim climbing the tree. He wasn't as fast or as efficient as Rio, but he was sure and steady. He gained the lower branches and made his way up to them.

"What brings you so far from home?" Rio greeted.

"My father sent me with news and I wanted to tell you about the man from the church group who was missing." Kim smiled at Rachael. "You look so much better, Miss Rachael. How is your leg?"

"It's far better, Kim. I see you're looking good. I hate to admit this, and let's not tell your brother, but his green gunk works."

Kim nodded seriously, willing to be a conspirator. "Tama is renowned for his healing skills. It was foul-looking though, wasn't it?" He exchanged a smile of understanding with her.

"Which man got away from the bandits?" Rachael asked.

"The one called Duncan Powell."

She remembered Duncan well. He stayed to himself a lot, but was always extremely polite. "I hope he managed to get away safely."

"That is what you both need to know. The man who escaped on his own from Tomas was one of your kind, Rio. He shifted into the form of a cat and mauled a guard, escaping into the forest. None of Tomas's people spoke of it, but two of the church group saw the shadow of the leopard on the rocks. They said they saw the guard ripped up and it had to have been a large cat."

"The men are very superstitious," Rio explained to Rachael. "They believe that the bigger cats are deities. Leopards are rare in these forests, so seeing one, especially attacking a guard at night, means many things to them. Unfortunately, it will also bring poachers here. The attack will most likely be talked about and the incident will grow into multiple incidents and the gossip will be we have a man killer on our hands." Rio sighed and pushed his hand through his hair. "Damn that idiot anyway. He could have gotten out of the camp without being seen and no one would have been the wiser."

"The guard had beaten him," Kim said.

A humorless smile curved Rio's mouth. "We never forget, that's one thing about our people."

"He will most likely come here," Kim pointed out.

"He's dead," Rio said abruptly. "He tried to kill us a couple of nights ago and I took Rachael to a safe place and tracked him. He's dead. Drake destroyed the body. Have you heard anything about the raid last night? I understand Drake took a hit. I've heard nothing on the radio. How bad was it?"

"He lost a lot of blood and his leg was shattered. They've flown him to a hospital for surgery. One of your own doctors is attempting to repair the damage. He'll live, but I don't know if they can save his leg."

Rachael put her hand on Rio's shoulder when she heard him swear softly under his breath. "He's strong, Rio."

"No man wants to lose his leg."

Her fingers went to the nape of his neck in a slow massage. "No they don't. Let's hope that's not what happens."

She rubbed her face along Rio's arm, much like a cat giving affection. "Kim, Rio told me a man named Joshua was hurt last night too. Have you heard anything about him?"

"He is going to be down for a long while, but he will recover."

"Why did your father send you to us?" Rio asked abruptly.

"There's a large party moving through the forest, Rio." Kim's face was open and friendly, but there was a hint of shadow in his eyes. "A man came to our village seeking my father's counsel. He said he needed help, that he does medical research and was looking for a variety of plants for his work. He knew all of the old traditions. He was very respectful and he gifted my father with a spear."

Rio's head went up. Rachael could see his frown. "He gave your father a spear?"

"It was old, very old. And it was one of ours. He claimed that the spear was handed down two generations. That it was given to honor his grandfather for saving the life of a child, and that if it was returned, a debt of honor would be repaid."

"This man is a doctor?"

Kim shook his head. "I don't think so. I think he is not telling the truth. He asked for a guide and father sent Tama with him and then sent me to find you. My father believes this man is looking for Miss Rachael."

"Why would he think that?" Rachael asked. "Did he ask about me?"

"My father had a vision. He saw this man standing beside you with a gun in his hand. He sent me to warn Rio." Kim looked at Rachael. "I see disbelief in your eyes, Miss Rachael. Don't discount my father's visions because you have not experienced such a thing. He has kept our people from harm over many years."

"He's a powerful medicine man," Rio added. "I won't allow Rachael to take chances, Kim. Thank you for warning us. You've come a long way. Come in and have something to drink. I can fix us a meal."

Kim stepped into the house and glanced across the room toward the rumbled bed. Rachael found herself blushing. Rio laced his fingers through hers and drew her hand to his mouth, teeth nibbling gently before pressing a kiss against her knuckles. "Does this doctor have a large party with him?"

Kim nodded. "Many men. All are armed. Why would a research team need guns? Where would they get such guns just coming into the country? Money changed hands, a lot of it, for this man to have those weapons available to him. They have supplies enough for several weeks. The luggage is top of the line. Whoever it is, he has money and doesn't mind spending it. There are no women along, and that's a bad sign. All of the men in his party are warriors."

Rio brought Rachael's hand to his heart. She didn't look at him. She was staring out the door into the forest. There was regret and sadness on her face. He caught the sheen of tears in her eyes. Rio pressed her hand tighter to his chest. "It doesn't change anything, Rachael."

"It changes everything. You know it does. You know who he is. I never thought he'd go this far." Her voice was choked with tears.

"Rachael, this is my world. If I have to . . ."

"No! Don't you touch him. Don't you go near him." There was a fierce, protective note in her voice. "You have no idea what he gave up for me. What he's had to cope with all of his life. Don't you dare judge him." Rachael pulled away from him and went out the door to stand on the edge of the verandah, staring out into the forest.

15

THERE was no way to make Rio understand. There was no way for anyone to understand. Rachael wasn't certain she understood anymore. Despair hit her in waves. She had known all along she couldn't stay with Rio. She had wanted him, wanted to share her life almost from the first time he spoke to her. She hadn't intended it to happen, it just had. Through Rio, she had glimpsed what it could be like to have a real partner to go through life with. A soul mate.

She closed her eyes and stood on the edge of the verandah listening to the soothing rhythm of the rain. She inhaled the scent of the forest. It called to her. Called her with whispers of freedom. She couldn't have Rio. She accepted that. She was not about to get him killed. No one saw him for the miracle he was. A good man who cared about his people, cared about the forest, the environment where he lived. Who was kind and gentle and compassionate. He had been so unexpected, a treasure to her, here in this place of beauty.

Her only gift to him was danger. Rachael sighed and

curved her fingers around the railing wanting to weep with a terrible sorrow. She didn't dare give in to it. Once she started to cry, she would never stop.

The call came again, and something deep inside of her answered, grew in power. She didn't realize it at first, not until the wind touched her skin. The wildness swelled in strength, was without mercy, calling to her, roaring at her, insisting she listen. Her vision changed, cleared, waves of colored heat expanded her sight. Bands of red and yellow and blue. Scents burst through her like bubbles of information. She smelled individual flowers, fruits, even scented the creatures in the trees.

Rachael's skin itched, hurt with the weight of the material pressed against it. She peeled off the shirt and flung it aside. Her muscles were already stretching. Her spine cracked and she fell to the verandah floor. She found herself on her stomach staring at the wooden floor while her body took on a life of its own. The material rubbed her skin raw. Desperate, she yanked at the buttons. It took only moments to shed the jeans, to fling them away from her. The pain in her injured leg was excruciating as the muscles cramped, stretched and contorted. Ligaments popped. She could actually hear the sound of her body changing.

Grief was overwhelming. She mourned for what she couldn't have. But there was this—her other self. It fought to aid her, fought to free her, to protect her from pain in a world she couldn't control—or have. Her skin itched and her fingers curled. Fur burst through her pores, her muzzle extended to accommodate teeth. Her legs bent, stretched, her injured calf and ankle burning. Hooked nails sprang from her fingers, leaving her clawing at the wooden floor.

There should have been fear. It wasn't a pleasant sensation to jerk to the floor, every muscle and sinew popping and crackling. It didn't matter, she embraced the change, the opportunity to be something different. To have a chance at something else. The forest sprang to vivid life, a new world when she had no other. When she belonged nowhere

else. The leopard lifted its head for the first time and sur-
veyed her realm. Sounds poured in from all directions.
Information transmitted by her whiskers. Scents and
intriguing rustles. She could actually feel the distance from
one object to another. It was exciting, exhilarating even.

Rachael got unsteadily to her feet, collapsed and tried
again. She stretched languidly, feeling the enormous
strength running like steel through her body. It had taken
only a brief minute, yet it seemed a lifetime to shed her
other self. She took several cautious steps, staggered and
fell. The murmur of men's voices was loud behind her,
their scents filling her lungs. The pull to Rio was strong,
overwhelming even, so that for a moment she hesitated.
Grief welled up, sharp and black and all-consuming.
Rachael wrenched her thoughts from him. She couldn't
have him. Heart pounding, she leapt to the branch below.
Her injured leg burned but it held. She could ignore the
throbbing pain and embrace what the leopard had to offer.

Sharp claws dug into bark as she teetered precariously,
and then she felt the rhythm. The perfect rhythm of nature.
The rain. The birds. The continual rustle of the leaves. The
hum in her muscles. The beat of her heart. She felt strength
flowing through her like a gift. Joy flooded her, replacing
despair and anguish. She leapt from branch to branch, feeling the power within her growing. And then she was on the
forest floor, running for the sheer joy of it. Running to feel
her sleek muscles stretching and her legs reacting like
springs as she bounded effortlessly over fallen tree trunks.
She splashed through puddles and small streams and leapt
up embankments that would have been impossible to climb.

Sunlight dappled the floor in places and she pounced on
the ever-moving rays, slapped at leaves and pine needles,
sending them up in a shower of vegetation just because she
could. She chased deer, climbed trees and ran along the
overhead highway, disturbing birds and agitating the gibbons on purpose. Laughter bubbled up, a well of happiness.
She turned to tell him. Rio. She remembered this. She

remembered the joy of taking this other form and running with him. Sharing the forest paths with him. Of rubbing her muzzle along his great head in affection. They had shared a life together, one of intense love and compelling sexual attraction. She knew him in this form just as she knew him in their human form.

Rachael stopped suddenly, her heart pounding in terror. She was alone. Rio was not in her life and he could never be. Whatever life they may have shared in another time, another place, they couldn't have it in this one. He couldn't take this form and give up his human side as she had chosen to do. He had responsibilities. She knew him well enough to know he would never let his people down. Sorrow was a heavy burden and she felt it equally in both forms. She lay in the branches of a tall tree, far from his house, put her head on her paws and wept.

Rio listened politely to Kim, glancing every now and then toward the verandah. Rachael had moved away from the open door and he could no longer see her. She had looked so defeated, so unlike Rachael. He wanted to go to her, felt he needed to go to her, but Kim wanted to tell him of his father's vision, stressing the importance of it, warning Rio that something was not right with the party searching the forest for medicinal plants.

"He knew the names of all the plants and their properties," Kim explained, in his slow, deliberate way. "My father does not know why he had such a vision when the man clearly knows the ways of the forest."

Rio took a step toward the door, shifting slightly in an effort to try to see Rachael. "Many men come into the forest knowing its ways but not respecting them, Kim. It's possible this man is one. Could he be a poacher, after fur or the elephants?" The more information he had the better to judge if more trouble was coming their way.

Kim followed his single step. "Perhaps. He had weapons enough."

"Tama would never lead him this way, especially if the

party is a group of poachers. The debt of honor would never extend that far."

"No, but if he is more than a poacher, if his game is larger, if it is the woman or you, Tama won't know until it's too late."

"Was there anything in the vision to make your father think either of us are in danger? If there was more to it, tell me, Kim." Rio took another step toward the door. His heart was beginning to pound and his mouth went dry.

"My father was disturbed by what he saw, so much so that he sent me to you. He could not interpret the vision fully. He felt that there was much danger, but he didn't know if it was to the man, to you or to the woman. He said I must come and let you know."

"Thank you, Kim, tell your father he is much honored and I appreciate his warning and that I'll heed it."

It was far too quiet on the verandah. There was a sudden hush in the forest and then creatures began calling frantically. Rio stiffened, swore softly, eloquently, repeatedly. "She's gone." He uttered the two words to taste them. To make them real. Black anger swirled, rioted, destructive and mindless. He fought it back. "Rachael." He said her name as a talisman, to help him think, to bring back intellect when he needed a cool brain.

"What is it, Rio?" Kim asked, taking a step back, recognizing danger when he saw it. When he felt it. Rio's face was a mask, his eyes glittering, and danger emanated from every pore.

"The Han Vol Dan. Damn it all to hell, she went through the Han Vol Dan. Her leg isn't even healed yet. I told her not to do it, but, she just has to do whatever the hell she wants whether it's logical or not." He was furious. Absolutely, completely furious. It had nothing to do with fear for her, for her safety or her injured leg or that he might have lost her. Or that she might have left him. He clenched his fists hard, trying to keep the roaring from his head. "She isn't safe in the forest by herself."

Kim merely looked at him. "She has become her true self. She will know how to care for herself."

"It isn't that easy. We can't stay in the form too long." Rio stripped off the jeans he'd so hastily pulled on. "Thank you for the warning. Stay away from this man. If he's who I think he may be, he's very dangerous. Give your father my thanks. Good fortune to you, Kim." He was being impolite with a man raised on tradition, ritual and above all else politeness, but it didn't matter. Nothing else mattered except to find Rachael and bring her back safely.

"And good hunting to you." Kim looked away courteously as Rio leapt to the branches above, shifting as he did so, claws out for traction. He began to follow the sounds and silences of the forest. He knew every tree in his realm. He would find her. He had to find her. The burning black temper swirled in the leopard, making him doubly dangerous, so animals shifted out of his way, immediately sensing his mood.

He nearly flew across the trees, hurdling branches and shrubs. He stopped only to lift his face and scent the wind. There were no signs of humans in his territory, but that didn't mean they weren't coming. Tomas was bound to send a party in after him. He did it every so often, hoping to find his home. Poachers often came to the area, sweeping the forests of Malaysia, Borneo and Indochina for the sun bear, the leopards and elephants, even the rhinos, the most protected of their animals. And the research teams came, studying the rain forest. The environmentalists. The veterinarians who trailed the elephants and counted them. And the latest party of researchers who were probably not researchers at all. He moved stealthily through the forest, knowing from the chatter in the trees and sky, she wasn't that far ahead of him.

He leapt over the same fallen logs, inhaling her scent, splashed through the same streams. Saw the scratches in the leaves and needles. He knew what she felt, the indescribable joy of freedom through the senses, allowing the wild nature to escape and dominate. It was a seductive temptation to live untamed and without responsibilities. Each of them had to face the lure of the forest and choose to be what they were. Neither one nor the other, but both. A species capable of shifting from one form to the other with obligations and responsibilities.

He padded softly through the trees, knowing he was gaining on her. Her scent was heady, provocative, so Rachael. The forest grew silent as the shadows lengthened. They had slept a good portion of the day away and now dusk was falling. He wanted to find her before the seduction of the night could touch her.

Rio felt her presence long before he ever came upon her. She lay in the cradle of tree branches, looking sleek and elegant and every bit as alluring in leopard form as she did in human form. She sat silently staring down at him, her eyes lost in the sea of dots across her face, but he felt her focused stare. Her ears were upright, alert, her body tense. He widened his eyes and deliberately pressed his ears forward, arching his back as he pounced on a pile of leaves and twigs, sending them scattering in all directions. To entice her further, he curled his tail as he sidestepped toward her, rolled over and held his tail in a hook position.

A long-buried instinct remembered the playful invitation. Rachael got slowly to her feet, and, ignoring the warning throb in her leg, leapt to the ground below. At once the large male leopard nuzzled her, rubbing his head and body along hers. His tongue licked over her fur. He pawed her, even bit at her gently with his teeth. Rachael returned the signs of affection, rubbing her smaller, sleeker body along his. She touched her nose to his and licked his fur. The sensations were amazing to her, even her rough tongue provided her with information.

She turned and ran, looking over her shoulder in a blatant invitation to follow her. He was fast, a blur of motion, nearly crashing into her as he matched her pace, turning her so that she ran in a different direction. Rachael, deep inside the leopard's body, laughed and cleared a fallen tree trunk,

waited until he joined her and pounced him. They rolled
over in the soft vegetation, scrambled to their feet and raced
off again. The male shouldered her several times, knocking
into her so that she ran in the direction he chose.

They splashed through two puddles, sending up wide
sprays of water. They nuzzled each other beside a large
fruit tree with a hundred flying fox watching them from
above. The two leopards rolled in the shadow of tall trees
and chased a herd of barking deer for a few minutes.
Always he rubbed his body along hers, nuzzled and licked
her fur, urging her to keep moving when she would have
lain down.

Her leg was burning, her sides heaving from the wild,
playful fun. Twice she tried to crouch on the ground, indicating the need for rest. Both times his heavier shoulder
struck hers. She snarled at him. He snarled back and
pressed into her, nearly knocking her down. He was enormously strong. Rachael began to grow apprehensive. She
was limping, doing her best to keep weight off her injured
leg. Still he pushed her on. She looked around her and realized she recognized the area. Rio had brought her back
home.

Snarling, she whirled around, ears flat, swiping at him
with her paw. He was lightning fast, dancing away from
her, and then running flat out, knocking her off her feet so
she lay on the ground trying to regain her breath. At once
he was on her, pinning her down, his teeth driving into her
shoulder. He held her still and simply waited.

Rachael knew what he wanted. What he was demanding
of her. He wanted her back in her other form. Stubbornly
she growled at him, grimacing to show her displeasure.
The position of submission angered her, but it also left her
feeling vulnerable and afraid. She tried to wait, but she
knew he wouldn't give in. His teeth bit down harder into
her shoulder, his hot breath fanning her neck.

Furious, Rachael reached for her intellect, her human
brain, her human body. Rio might have the upper hand as a

male leopard, but he wasn't going to boss her around as a human woman. She should have seen that he was circling back to the house. She should have recognized what was in his mind and taken steps to stop him.

Already she could feel the change start. She didn't want it. Didn't want to go back to human form and face whatever was going to happen in her future, not after running free in the forest, but it was already too late. She felt it first in her head. The need for her human body. She felt the contraction of muscles, the sudden burning in her leg. She heard a cry escape her throat, half human, half animal as the pain in her shoulder increased.

Rio released her immediately but didn't make the mistake of stepping away. The huge leopard stood over her as she thrashed for a moment in the miracle of the change, then sprawled beneath him in human form. She lay on the ground, facedown, her shoulders shaking slightly, and he knew she was crying. He touched her with his muzzle, rubbing along her back to reassure her.

Rachael rolled over, punching him hard, her eyes blazing with fury. She pummeled the male leopard, uncaring that he could rip her throat out. Uncaring that leopards were notorious for their tempers. Rio leapt sideways away from her, shifting as he did so, catching her wrists when she followed him. He swept her feet out from under her, tumbling her back to the ground, going down with her so that his larger body pressed hers into the thick mat of vegetation.

"Calm down, Rachael." He bit back laughter. The last rays of the sun hit her face, the soft sheen of sweat on her body. Leaves and twigs decorated the riot of curls and she was surrounded with a bright aura. She radiated fury and sex. He couldn't help seeing her that way. She made him happy, even when she clearly wanted to scratch his eyes out. "Did you really think I was going to go crawl in a hole and live a miserable life without you? What kind of a man do you think I am?"

"You're an idiot, that's what you are," she spat back,

although his words took most of her fury. She hated that, hated that he could defuse her justified anger with a few charming words, his brilliant eyes, so intensely hungry when he looked at her, and his blazingly sinful, wicked mouth. "Damn you, Rio." She wrapped her arms around his neck and kissed him.

Lightning streaked in his veins, sizzled through his bloodstream. He was alive again, his heart beating and his lungs working. He lifted his head, his green gaze burning over her face. "Damn you back, Rachael. You left me. You made me feel and then you just left me. You didn't even have the guts to talk it over with me first. Damn you to hell for that." He caught her head, held her still and devoured her. Kiss after kiss.

She tasted his anger. It was hot and spicy and ferocious. She tasted his love. Tender and hungry and consuming. And she wanted him. Forever. For all time. As short a time or as long a time as she could have him.

Rachael lay in the pine needles staring up at his beloved face. "I'm sorry, Rio. I didn't mean to hurt you. I should have had the courage to talk it over with you. I thought I could live here in the forest, in my other form. I thought they wouldn't find me if I was a leopard. At least I could still be close to you."

He shook his head. "If you're one of us, then so is your brother. The sniper, the one they called Duncan, he had to be the one who put the cobra in your room before you went on the river. And he had to be the one who tried to kill you a couple of nights ago. He shifted into the form of a leopard. Only a few of us around the world can do that. He had to have known you're capable. They would bring in hunters. Eventually they would kill you. We can't run scared. If I've ever learned anything in this life, it's that we have to think something all the way through."

The needles poked into her bare skin. She stood up gingerly. It was far easier maneuvering through the forest in leopard form than human. "I don't want you hurt."

"And you think your brother will try to hurt me?" He took her hand, tugging until she walked with him toward the house. He pulled twigs and leaves from her hair and tossed them aside.

She flashed a small smile. "I feel a bit like Adam and Eve."

His hand tightened on hers. "You have to talk to me about him. I don't want to harm the man, but you have to give me something to work with, Rachael. You either trust me or you don't."

She stood at the bottom of the large tree, staring up into the canopy where his house was hidden. "Do you think it's a matter of trust?"

He rested his palm on her bare bottom, helping her up to the lower branches. She pulled herself up using the creepers hanging like streamers. Rio stood back watching her body, the flexing muscles, the curves and hollows. She had a beautiful butt. He grinned as he leapt up to the lower branch easily, caught the creeper, his hands above hers, his body caging hers between his and the tree trunk. He pressed against her, much in the way of a dominant cat, his teeth nipping her shoulder, his breath teasing her nape. "I know it's a matter of trust."

Instead of pulling away or stiffening as he expected, she leaned back against him, rubbing her alluring derrière against his thickening groin. "I do trust you. I trust you completely with my life. I'm here with you. I've chosen you. I've always chosen you."

And she had. She knew it. She had always chosen him. Would always choose him. "Don't you feel it, Rio? We've always been together. I know we have. Somewhere else, somewhere good."

He shook his head, urging her up to the house. "It wasn't somewhere different, Rachael. There's always been blood and bullets and things to fear. But we managed them together. That's what we do. We live our life the best that we can, together, facing whatever comes our way."

She pulled herself up to the verandah. Her clothes were

lying in a heap where she'd stripped. She picked up the shirt, held it to her. "I love him, Rio. I know he's done things, horrible, hideous things. People think he's a monster and they think I should help destroy him. But I can't. I won't. I understand how he came to be what he is." Very slowly she pulled on the shirt. Rio's shirt. It seemed everything came back to Rio. "Do you really think we were together in another time?"

His brilliant green gaze drifted over her. "Don't you?"

She leaned against the chair and smiled at him. "I think you're beautiful, Rio. I thought it then too, wherever we were. I remember that much."

He stepped very close to her, his body crowding hers. Tall, muscular, broad shoulders and incredible strength. He caught her chin firmly and tilted her face up to his. There was no laughter in his eyes. "Don't ever do that again. Don't leave me. I think you tore the heart out of my chest with your bare hands." He felt like an idiot saying it. He didn't write poetry and he didn't know the first thing about romance, but he had to find a way to make her understand the enormity of what she'd done.

She lifted her hand to map his face, her fingertips very gentle. "I won't, Rio. If you're willing to take the chance, I'll make my stand, here, with you." She stepped back when he reached for her. "I want you to know about me before you make up your mind."

"Rachael." He said her name softly, lovingly. "I have made up my mind. I would want you in my life no matter what the circumstances. I lay beside you the other night and thought about whether I would want you if we could no longer have sex. I have to tell you, sex with you is amazing. I look forward to it and I think about it a lot."

"That's a surprise." She managed a small grin.

"The point is, I would want you in my life, in my bed. I want your laughter and your temper. It's you, not your past, not even your body, amazing as that is." His hand skimmed over the swell of her breast. "Not that I want that to change."

"My brother and I inherited a drug empire."

Her gaze was fastened to his face. He felt the hit somewhere in the region of his gut, but he didn't flinch. Didn't change expressions. She was waiting for that. Waiting for rejection. For betrayal. He didn't even blink.

She waited in silence for his reaction. For his disgust. Her mouth was dry with fear of losing him but she went on. He had to know. He deserved the truth. Rachael spread her hands out in front of her. "It's actually worse than it's portrayed in the movies, Rio. There are the fields and the workers and the laboratories. There are endless supplies of cocaine. There are guns and murder and treachery. We live in a house that has everything money can buy. We wear the best clothes and have the finest jewelry. The cars are fast and powerful and the lifestyle is decadent. We can have anything we want. Especially if you overlook the bodyguards and the guards at the gates. If you can overlook the corruption of officials and police departments and the murders when some poor man tries to steal to feed his family. When you can overlook the addicts and women selling their bodies and their children, then I suppose, it would be a great life."

She turned away from him, unable to have him look at her. She couldn't look at herself. "That's my inheritance, Rio. It's what got my father and my mother killed." Rachael felt behind her for the chair. Her leg throbbed and burned from overuse, but that wasn't what made her legs shaky.

"My brother told me that our father fell in love with our mother and he wanted out of the business. Once she found out, she would have left him, so he wanted to go legitimate. I have no idea why we moved from South America, but we have estates there as well as in Florida." She sank into the chair, grateful to be off of her leg. "I think he thought it would be different in Florida, but they were still in the business there. No matter what he did, he couldn't change anything."

Rio fixed her a cool drink. He could see pain eating her from the inside out. Two small children thrown into the middle of a world of violence. He knew the strict rules of the society their mother had grown up in. She must have tried to pass her morality, her honor and integrity to her children. He handed her the drink and sat on the floor, taking her injured leg into his hands.

Rachael looked down at his face. She couldn't find evidence of a judgment. There was nothing but acceptance in his expression. There was compassion in his eyes and she had to look away from that. Tears burned too close. She didn't dare begin to cry. She was afraid if the floodgates opened, she'd never be able to close them.

She sipped at the cooling nectar, trying to think how to tell him. What to tell him. She'd never told anyone. People died over the kinds of information she carried with her. Rio's fingers were gentle on her skin as he bathed her leg, elevating it while he examined the puncture wounds. His hands were sure and steady and her heart did a funny little flip. She touched the top of his head, the thick shaggy hair. "You're a good man, Rio. Don't let your elders or anyone else tell you different."

Her heart was in her voice. Rio leaned down to press a kiss against the largest scar. "What happened to you, Rachael? What happened to your brother?"

"My uncle Armando ran the business with our father. They were twins, you know. Very close we thought. We spent so much time with him. He came to dinner all the time. He treated Elijah as his own son. He even took Elijah to ball games and into the Everglades. We thought he loved us. He certainly acted like he did. I never heard Armando and Antonio fight. Not once. They always hugged one another, and it seemed genuine."

Rio looked up when she fell silent again, frowning into her drink. He waited. Whatever trauma she'd experienced, he had the patience to wait for the telling. She was trusting him with things he was certain no other knew.

Rachael took a deep breath, glanced toward the door. The windows. "Are you certain no one is around? Could Kim be within hearing distance?" Her tone was low, a ghostlike whisper, and there was a childish quality to her voice. "In our home they sweep for electronic devices every day. Sometimes a couple of times a day. And Elijah has them sweep every car for bombs before we ever get into them."

He circled her ankle with his fingers, wanting to touch her. Wanting to be an anchor for her. "It must be a terrible way to live, always thinking someone might want you dead."

"I was nine years old when I walked into a room and saw my parents murdered. Armando was stabbing his brother over and over. Mom was already dead. He cut her throat. There wasn't a spot in the room free of blood."

Rio could see she was far away from him, was still that little girl, walking innocently into a room, perhaps coming home from school and wanting to show her parents something special. His fingers tightened, holding her to him.

"He looked up and saw me. I screamed. I remember I couldn't stop screaming. No matter how hard I tried, I couldn't make the sound go away. He came toward me with the knife. There was blood all over it, all over him and his hands. I just stood there screaming. I know he would have killed me. He couldn't do anything but kill me. I was a witness. I saw him murder them."

"Why didn't he?" It was like pulling teeth. She revealed something and then fell silent. The trauma ran deep and it would never go away. He knew her life couldn't have gotten much better in the intervening years, not with a million-dollar price on her head.

Rio lifted her, slid into the chair and cradled her on his lap. Rachael snuggled into him, wanting the comfort and safety of his arms. She turned her face into his throat. "Elijah came in. He wanted Elijah alive more than he wanted me dead. Armando had no family, no one to run his empire, no one to carry on his work. He had taken Elijah with him on small things, let him see what a big deal he was. He stood there in that room with my parents' blood pooling around his feet, holding a knife to my throat, and he told Elijah to make up his mind. To swear loyalty to him and be his son or he would kill me right there."

"And Elijah chose to keep you alive."

She couldn't look at him. "Our lives were hell, especially Elijah's life. Armando wanted Elijah to be mired in so deep, with so much blood on his hands neither of us could ever go the police." Her eyes filled with tears. "I knew Elijah did it for me, to keep me alive, but it wasn't right. It was never right. He should have let me go. I should have had the courage to save him."

"By doing what? Killing yourself?" He turned her arms over to run the pad of his thumb over the scars on her wrists, scars he'd never mentioned. "He couldn't let you do that. So he joined the man who murdered your parents."

"And he learned from him. And he grew stronger and more powerful and more cold and distant every day."

Rio felt tears, rain-wet, against his skin. Her body trembled. "It was always us against everyone else, but suddenly we began to have terrible fights. Elijah became very secretive. He wouldn't let me leave the compound. He had someone with me all the time and drove away every friend I had."

"He was splitting with your uncle. Starting a war."

"I had a friend, Tony, the brother of my girlfriend. We hardly knew each other. I met Tony at her house. He'd recently moved back to town. I had dated a couple of times and it always ended in disaster. Once it turned out to be an undercover cop, and another time I found out the man I was dating had been paid by Elijah to take me out." Utter humiliation clogged her throat. "I don't think I can remember a man having an interest in me as a woman. The police wanted information to convict Elijah, and I guess they thought they could send in an undercover man to romance me. Armando wanted a way to get close to Elijah again to be able to kill him. He was so furious, so absolutely furious with Elijah. He's done everything he can to try to kill him."

"Tell me about this man." She was avoiding it. Rio knew her now, knew her every little sign of agitation and distress. She was burrowing deeper into his body, trembling, her breath coming in hard gasps of despair.

"I didn't tell Elijah about Tony because I knew he would never allow me to go out alone with him. I couldn't go anywhere alone. He seemed a nice man. Marcia, his sister, and I were good friends. He moved in with her and when I went to visit, he was there. At first we just talked, played Scrabble, that sort of thing. I just wanted a few ordinary hours, a place I could go where I wasn't Elijah Lospostos's sister. Where no one carried a gun and plotted to kill each other."

She dragged her hands through her hair. "I wasn't in love with Tony. I wasn't sleeping with him and telling secrets. I would never sell Elijah out. I'd never give him up. I saw all those years when he was forced to do terrible things. I can't tell you how often Armando threatened me. How many times he would shove a gun in my mouth and scream at Elijah, how often I wanted him to pull the trigger just to take the pain and rage off Elijah's face. It was a hellish existence until Elijah was strong enough to move against him. But Armando got away. And then the war started, and it was hell all over again."

"Why would Elijah object to your friend's brother?"

"I don't know, but I didn't want Tony to know about that part of my life. Marcia didn't know. We met at the library one day, ended up having coffee and became good friends. She didn't know who I was and I didn't want to tell her. She was a nice woman from a nice family."

"What does she do?"

"She teaches school, for heaven's sake. She teaches sixth-grade science. I went to see her as often as I could. Her home was like a sanctuary to me. Elijah always sent someone with me but they waited outside, in the car. Marcia thought they were my chauffeurs. She joked about it a couple of times. And then her brother moved back home. I got to know him and he was just as nice. One day he asked if I wanted to go to see an opening at an art museum. He was really into art." She hung her head. "I said yes."

A chill went through Rio's body. He knew what was coming. Death had a feeling to it, a presence. It was in the room. It was in her eyes. That stricken look she carried that never quite went away. He tightened his hold on her and rocked her back and forth gently, trying to give her a sense of peace, of comfort. There was neither in betrayal. "And your brother found you."

16

RACHAEL took a deep breath and exhaled slowly. "I went to Marcia's house and had the guards stay outside. Tony and I got into Marcia's car and drove away. I bent down as if I were looking for something when we drove out so the guards wouldn't see me. For a few miles I thought it was safe. The next thing I knew, we were in a high-speed chase with cars on either side of us. They were Elijah's men, not Armando's. I knew them all. They forced the car to the side of the road. Elijah opened the door and yanked me out. There was shouting back and forth and then suddenly Elijah emptied a gun into Tony." She covered her face with her hands.

Her sobs were heart-wrenching, dragged from a woman with tremendous courage and control and all the more terrible because of it. Rio rested his head over hers as he rocked her, his mind racing, trying to figure out why her brother would want her dead after trading his honor to keep her alive.

"I couldn't believe what he'd done. It was too many deaths on my hands." She held them up. "I felt covered in blood. Everyone I touched. Everything Elijah had done was because of me. He was so angry. He shook me over and over and said he should have put the gun to my head."

So many emotions ate at him that Rio didn't know what he was feeling. Part of him wanted to weep for her. Part of him was so angry he wanted to hunt her brother and uncle down. "Rachael, *sestrilla*. It's good you came here, to me, to your home where you belong." He caught her wrists and brought the scars to his mouth. "Here, with me. Every morning the birds will sing to you. The rain has beautiful songs and it will play them for us. This is our world." He felt a damn fool for uttering the words to her, yet so humbled that she'd accepted his own violent past. That she could look on what he did and not judge him harshly after all she'd been through. He would have quoted her a poem had he known one, just to ease her suffering.

"Elijah will never stop looking for me." She caught his face in her hands. "You should have known him all those years ago. He struggled so hard to work behind Armando's back to get us free. It was such a terrible life, always poised on the brink of death. He walked that fine line every day. We whispered together, passed notes we burned so no one would know what we were planning. He stood between me and our uncle all the time."

"It must have been difficult."

"We had no life. We were still in school but we couldn't bring home friends. We couldn't have any friends. We couldn't trust anyone, only each other. There were no dates, no dances. We lived in constant fear. Sometimes, if Armando didn't think Elijah was taking care of business, he and his men would break into our rooms in the middle of the night. They'd drag me into Elijah's room and put a knife to my throat or a gun to my head. Elijah was so calm. He never wept. He never panicked. He looked at them and he looked at me and he would say to Armando, 'What do you want me to do?' That was all. And he did whatever it took to save my life."

"Why do you feel ashamed?"

"He sold drugs. I'm certain he killed people. He was so beautiful, so full of laughter. He never smiles. He has nothing in his life. All for me. All in payment for my life. He would have been better off if they had killed me too. He would have been free. He could have broken away. He has skills like a chameleon. They never would have found him if he was alone."

"He must have been extraordinary, even as a teenager. I would like to meet him. It may be that we can work something out."

"But don't you see why I don't want you near him? He's not my Elijah anymore. He's turned into someone I don't know. Someone dark and dangerous and twisted inside, I can't say he's evil. I know he was trying to get out from under the drug business and sell off the companies that weren't legitimate. He promised me he would. Both of our names are on those companies. We own everything together."

"So if you die, everything goes to him."

Rachael nodded. "He wouldn't kill me for the money, Rio, if that's what you're thinking. I know he wouldn't. I don't ever look at the books. I don't even own a car. I don't care about the money, and he knows I don't."

"Is it possible Elijah is the one putting out the reward money to keep you alive and your uncle is the one who has hired assassins to kill you? That would make more sense. You had a fight with Elijah and he said some harsh things to you, but why would your uncle suddenly want to keep you alive? You aren't worth anything to him if he can't hold you over Elijah's head."

She was silent for a long time, but he felt her relax a little. "I didn't think of that. I couldn't believe it when Elijah just shot Tony right in front of me. He was so angry. I'd never seen him like that before. He's always in control, always very cool under fire."

"So he wasn't acting in character?"

"He feels dangerous now. He really does. I can't describe it, but he never did to me before. We were so close, and then somehow he began to push me away. He didn't want to talk about the business. He wouldn't answer my questions about Armando. He insisted I stay home, indoors, away from the windows."

"Maybe he was afraid for your life."

She sighed and reached over to take the drink from the small table where she'd set it. The juice felt cool and refreshing on her sore throat. "We were always afraid for my life. We lived in fear, it was our everyday existence."

"You thought by telling me who you are, who your family is, that I'd not want to be with you? Rachael, how could you think that?" His hand cupped her face, his thumb sliding over her high cheekbone.

"If I had tried to go to the police . . ." She trailed off.

"Why didn't you?"

"Two reasons. Armando had police working for him and we didn't know who they were, and of course, Elijah was heavily involved in the business. That's how Armando thought to trap him. If he made Elijah dirty enough, he would never be able to get out and they would need one another. Armando was willing to kill his brother, but he genuinely wanted his brother's son. It made no sense to me. I've never understood it. I would never betray Elijah for any reason."

"And you think I wouldn't forgive you that? There's nothing to forgive, Rachael." Rio lifted his head from hers, drawing in his breath. "He knew. Your uncle knew about your mother being a shape-shifter, and he must have known about your brother."

"*I* don't know about my brother."

"You said they were close, Rachael. Antonio and Armando. If Antonio had discovered that his wife was a shifter and they moved the family from South America in order to protect them from the elders, then he may have confided in his brother. Why wouldn't he? Antonio would have told his twin brother why he had to move his family to Florida so quickly, especially if he needed help fast and if he was leaving the running of the plantations to Armando or hired help."

"I suppose so. But I don't know if my brother can shift shape. Why wouldn't he tell me? We talked about mom and dad a lot. Wouldn't that be a rather large piece of information to leave out?"

"Not if he was protecting you. You say your uncle took him out all the time alone. They spent a great deal of time in the Everglades. What were they doing there?"

She shrugged. "I don't honestly know. I was a little child. I thought they were fishing or scuba diving or watching alligators. He never came back upset."

"If you were a kid and you could run free in the Glades, shifting shape and becoming something as powerful as a leopard, wouldn't you do it? And if you did things for your uncle, such as pick up packages, wouldn't that be a small price to pay? Armando would have realized the potential of such a gift. He would have a trained assassin, as silent and deadly as they came and no one the wiser. We can swim great distances and get into places humans can't. Elijah would have welcomed the trips in the beginning. He would have felt the freedom of running and becoming something so powerful. Do you see that?"

Rachael thought of how it felt to be in the form of such a powerful creature. A teenager would have found the excitement of it a heady and addicting experience. Add in the thrill of secrecy and it would have been too much for a boy to pass up. "I remember him coming home and being so excited after his trips with Armando he could hardly contain himself. He'd lock his bedroom door and play wild music for hours."

"Your uncle was probably training him then, but Elijah didn't know what he was carrying, or even doing. It was all a game. He loved and trusted your uncle. Finding your parents murdered must have been a terrible shock and betrayal to him. He loved Armando and he had to have realized what his uncle was and what he'd been doing all that time. The guilt must have been unbearable."

That brought a fresh flood of tears. Rachael clung to him, weeping for her lost brother, for their childhood, for all the things they had done and couldn't change. Rio held her in his arms, offering comfort and acceptance. He rocked her gently back and forth, crooning some nonsense, anything at all to console her. It had been years since she'd allowed herself the luxury of tears. She had worked so hard to be like her brother, not giving Armando the satisfaction of seeing her fear.

She rubbed Rio's strong jaw. "Thank you for not condemning us. We probably did everything wrong, made every mistake, but I was a child and he was thirteen. We had no one to go to, no one to tell. Of course Armando had custody of us, and from the moment we went to live with him, we had nothing but each other. I don't think I could bear it if you despised him."

"Rachael, love of my life, how could you think I, of all people, would presume to judge another? All one can do in this life is to try to do their best in any given circumstances."

She lifted her head and stared into his face, his eyes. "I don't deserve you, Rio."

He fought back the strange lump in his throat. His people wouldn't see him or speak with him, yet she thought she didn't deserve him. His hand went to the nape of her neck, held her still for his kiss. He put every bit of tenderness he could find in himself in that kiss, tasting her tears, her sorrow, tasting love.

"I think you're an amazing woman," he murmured when he lifted his head.

She managed to smile at him. "It's a darned good thing because it might be difficult to get rid of me." Rachael slowly uncurled her body. She had cried so much her eyes burned and her throat ached. She was determined to pull herself together before Rio grew impatient and tossed her over the railing. "You know those little leech things you love so much? They just sink their teeth in and hold on, well that's me with you."

He made a face at her, reluctantly allowing his arms to drop away as she stretched and stood up to limp across the room to open the door.

"Isn't it strange how the house can feel so small at times?"

He smiled at her, knowing she was trying to regain some semblance of control. "Why do you think I often leave the door open?" Her body was supple and strong with generous feminine curves, a body a man could lose himself in. He liked watching her move around his home. She touched a candle, her fingers gliding gracefully over it. She picked up his clothes and tossed them in the small box he never used for dirty clothes.

"I'm messy."

A ghost of a smile curved her mouth. "You think that's news to me?"

"I was hoping you hadn't noticed."

Her smile widened. "It's impossible not to notice. You like soaking dishes in the sink. It drives me crazy. What's the point of soaking them? Why don't you just do them? You've already gone to the trouble of scraping them and rinsing, you might as well get it over with."

"There's a perfectly logical explanation," he said. "To wash the dishes in hot water, I have to actually use the gas or the wood. It's more economical to wait and wash a bunch together. Hauling gas in is a pain. I use it sparingly."

She made a face at him. "I suppose I'll have to concede the point."

He stood up, filling the room immediately with his wide shoulders and powerful presence. "Do you want to move, Rachael?" He had spent years building his house and the underground storage hidden beneath it. The water system had been difficult to hide. He had everything he wanted in that house, but they had no amenities. If she wanted all the things necessary in modern living, he would have to build a house closer to the protection of the village where they could have a generator. So far from protection, the noise and smell of a generator was too dangerous, a complete giveaway to Tomas and anyone else chasing him.

"Move?" Rachael gripped the edge of the door and turned back to look at him with her enormous eyes. "Why would you want to leave this beautiful house? The carvings are extraordinary. I love this house. I don't think there's any reason to move."

"We don't have a decent cooler most of the time. Hauling ice is nearly impossible, unless I get it from the village, and I rarely shop there."

"Your system works quite well. I don't think we'll starve."

"You might not feel that way when the kids start coming."

Rachael stepped backwards out the door, laughing at him. "Kids? They're going to start coming our way, are they?"

He stalked her, following her onto the verandah and pinning her against the rail. "I think there's bound to be lots of kids," he murmured. His hands came up to cup the soft weight of her breasts. He rubbed his shadowed jaw over her sensitive skin, gently over her peaking nipples. "Marry me, Rachael. We can't use the ritual ceremony of our people, but Kim's father can marry us."

"It isn't necessary. I know we're married already."

"I know it isn't necessary, but I want to marry you. I want to feel my child growing inside of you someday. I want it all with you." He lowered his mouth to her breasts, suckling gently, so that she arched her back and thrust into him, holding his head while he feasted on her. The rain began a slow drizzle and the wind blew endlessly but up high, in their own world, it all seemed perfect.

She lifted her face to look up at the gently falling rain while fire burst through her veins and sizzled and danced over her skin. "How many children are a lot?" Her fingers tangled in his hair. "Are you thinking two, three? Give me a number." She tried to listen to the songs of the rain the way he'd instructed. It was such a medley of sounds, never the same, ever changing, all of it seeping into her veins like a drug. Like the fire he produced with the hot silk of his mouth with the heat of the forest pressing in on them.

Rio straightened, held her in his arms. Just held her to him. "We can have a houseful, Rachael. Little girls to look like you. With your laughter and your courage."

She wrapped her arms around him, sank deep into his hard frame. "And with all those little children running around, how are we going to manage times like these?"

Living with Rio was a sensual adventure. Her body always seemed ripe and ready, never sated for long no matter how often he touched her. She wanted more. Wanted him a million times, a million ways. She wrapped her leg around his waist, pressing her hot, slick body against him suggestively. Her fingers tunneled in his hair, her teeth nibbled his ear, his shoulder, anything she could reach.

"We'll find a way. We'll find a million ways."

Rio lifted her, so that she could wrap both legs around him, so that she could settle over his body, fitting sword to sheath. He rested her against the railing and they looked at one another, locked together. Rachael leaned forward and buried her face against his neck. They clung to one another, holding tightly.

He whispered to her words of love in the language of his people. *Sestrilla.* Beloved one. *Hafelina.* Small cat. *Jue amourusestrilla.* I love you for all time. *Anwou Jue selaviena en patreJue.* In this time and in all other time.

She heard the words, recognized them although she couldn't respond in kind. The vocalization was a mixture of notes a feline used. She knew them, recognized them and found them beautiful, but she couldn't produce them exactly. Rachael lifted her head and looked at him. At his face. His eyes. His mouth. "I love you too, Rio."

As fierce as his lovemaking could be, as wild and rough
as he was at times, he was infinitely tender. Kissing her
with such tenderness tears welled up. His body moved in
hers with deep, sure strokes, striving always for her pleasure. His hands worshipped her, shaped every curve, slid
over her skin as if memorizing every detail.

He took his time, long slow strokes designed to burrow
deeper, to fill her with his love. As the fever pitch rose, as
they climbed together, the white mist swirled around them,
as if they had created steam with the intensity of their heat.
She dug her nails into his back and threw back her head,
moving her hips in an answering rhythm, a dance of love,
there on the verandah with the scent of orchids enfolding
them and the breeze touching their bodies like fingers. All
the while the rain came down, droplets of silver as the night
settled in.

Rachael gasped as she felt him swell with victory, with
the sheer pleasure of their joining, and she tightened her
muscles around him, carrying them both over the edge. His
voice blended with hers, a cry of joy in the darkness. They
clung to one another, both reluctant to let go of the other.

A small flurry of leaves and a shower of orchid petals
rained down from a branch above them and Franz tumbled
onto the verandah at their feet. They jumped apart, Rio
alert and ready, pressing her body against the rail in an
effort to protect her. The bundle of fur rolled, bouncing off
Rio's calves. The small, clouded leopard dug paws into the
floor and raked his hooked claws sharply over the wood.

"I looked for claw marks in the trees," Rachael said,
bending down to burrow her fingers in the small cat's fur.
"But I never saw any. Why do you rake claws in the house?"

"It's more than marking territory. It's the sharpening
and disposing of old sheaths. It's actually necessary, but
we've been taught not to mark our passing in the forest
because it draws poachers. Let them think we're gone, no
longer here, and hopefully they'll stop shooting us. We
choose to sharpen and mark indoors where we won't be

discovered." He grinned at her, looking suddenly boyish. "Fritz and Franz learned from me."

"That's right, you're the mommy figure."

"Hey now." He toed the cat rubbing along their legs with his bare foot. "He's lonely for Fritz. They normally go everywhere together. I was hoping they'd find mates and bring me back a kitten or two, but they don't seem interested."

"Your life is much more exciting," she pointed out. "They get to brag to all the other little cats about their adventures."

They curled up on the small sofa in each other's arms, on the verandah, passing the night away, listening to the endless rain. Watching the white mist curl around them until it felt as though they were high up in the clouds. Rio held her in his arms. "I do love you, Rachael. You brought something into my life I never want to do without."

She rested her head on his chest. "I feel the same way."

Franz jumped up onto the couch, nosing the two of them, doing his best to burrow between their bodies. Rio growled at the leopard. "You're heavy, Franz, get down. You don't need to be up here."

Rachael laughed. Rio hadn't pushed the leopard off, instead, he wrapped his arm around the small cat's neck. Almost at once, Fritz hobbled out onto the deck, yowled softly and rubbed back and forth against their legs.

"Someone's a little jealous," Rachael pointed out and moved as close as she could to Rio to give the cat room to get up with them.

"Don't encourage the little demon. Don't you remember he's the one that took a chunk out of your leg?" Rio groused.

"Poor little thing, he's just lonely and he doesn't feel very good." She helped the cat up so he was lying partially across her lap. "If we had a houseful of children, they'd be all over us too."

Rio groaned and shifted until he found a comfortable

position. "I don't want to think about it right now. Go to sleep."

"We're going to sleep out here?" The idea pleased her. The wind rustled the leaves of the trees so that they fluttered gracefully around them.

"For a little while." Rio kissed the top of her bent head, content to hold her, to sit on his porch with Rachael and the leopards close to him and the rain falling softly in the background lulling them to sleep.

He woke close to dawn, jerking awake, his mind and senses instantly alert. Somewhere, deep in the forest, a nightjar screamed. A deer barked. A chorus of gibbons gave a full-throated warning. He closed his eyes for just a moment, savoring waking up with her next to him, with the small cats cuddled close. He hated to disturb her, hated to try to prepare her for the next crisis. There always seemed to be one and Rachael had gone through enough already. He wanted to protect her, make her life smooth and happy.

Regret in every line of his body, he did what he had to do. "Wake up, *sestrilla*." He kissed her face, her eyelashes, the corners of her mouth. "The neighbors are getting noisy on us."

Rachael listened for a moment then wrapped her arms tightly around Rio's neck. "He's here." There was sheer terror in her voice.

Rio inhaled deeply. He swept back her hair, his touch lingering against her skin. "It isn't your brother." His tone was grim. He signaled the small leopard off the sofa.

"Then who?"

"Someone they know. Someone familiar to them. One of my people, yet one who doesn't travel in my realm. Not one of my unit."

Rachael reluctantly unfolded her body, stood on her own, yawning sleepily. She let her breath out slowly. "How far away?"

"A few minutes." His hand slipped over her face. She felt it tremble.

Rachael caught his hand and held it to her breast, over her heart. "We're in this together, Rio. Tell me what to do."

"We're going into the house and see to your leg. You're favoring it and I see it's swollen again from overuse. Then we'll dress and straighten up our home and wait to see what he wants." He reached past her to open the door courteously.

"Then you know who it is."

He inhaled again. "Yes, I know him. It is Peter Delgrotto. He is of the high council. And his word is law to our people."

Her dark eyes moved over his face. Saw too much. Saw into his heart. "You think he may tell me I have to go away."

Rio shrugged. "I'll hear him out before I get stirred up."

She buttoned the shirt, realizing for the first time she still wore it. "This elder is coming here? That certainly takes a lot of nerve." She snatched the jeans out of his hand and limped quickly over to the bed. "Your neighbors seem to drop in uninvited on a regular basis."

"Not much sugar in the neighborhood and I'm known for my sweetness," he quipped.

She groaned and rolled her eyes. "Your little elder friend is going to think you're the sweet one after he meets me. Why would he come here?"

"Elders do what they want and go where they will."

"Sort of like leeches. No one invited him."

There it was again—that little tug on his heart. She could make him smile in the worst of circumstances. He had no idea how he would react if the elders tried to take her from him, but he knew he wouldn't allow it. He followed her, hunkered down beside her and examined her leg. He was certain Rachael would never recognize the authority of the elders. She wasn't raised with their rules and she had already formed her allegiance with him. They might try ordering her around, but it would never work.

"You have a smug look on your face."

"Smug? I'm never smug." But he was feeling smug. The elders were going to get an earful if they tried to force Rachael to accept his banishment.

Rachael touched his dark hair, tugged at the silky strands until he looked at her. "If they think they're going to change your sentence from banishment to death, they're going to have a fight on their hands."

She looked so warriorlike he grinned as he washed her calf gently and applied more of Tama's magic healing potion. "Once a sentence is handed down, they won't change it. My skills are of value to the community, so I doubt they'd even ask me to leave this area."

His fingers were soothing on her leg but his comment set her teeth on edge. "Let them ask us to leave. They don't own the forest. Blast them anyway. I hate bullies." She yanked her jeans over her leg and began making up the bed with fast, jerky movements. She nearly kicked Fritz with her bare foot, forgetting he had taken refuge under the bed.

Rachael looked flaming mad. Even her hair crackled with electricity. He grinned to himself as he pulled on his own clothes. The house was being put back in shape in rapid order although she was limping even more.

"Sit down, *sestrilla*." He kept his voice gentle. "All that hopping around isn't doing your leg any good." He pulled out his guns and checked the chambers, setting each one carefully on the table.

"We have a tub in the middle of the floor," she pointed out, her dark eyes spitting sparks. "You could do something about it instead of idly babying your guns."

His eyebrow shot up. "Idly babying my guns?" he repeated.

"Exactly. What do you intend to do? Shoot the man? The precious, all-wise elder? Not that I mind, but at least warn me."

"You're in one of your little moods again, aren't you? I think if you had some sort of signal to give to me before you went off, it would help tremendously."

She straightened up and turned around very slowly to face him. "My little moods?"

His mouth twitched. He forced his features to remain expressionless. She looked like a volcano about to explode. His smile would definitely trigger dynamite. "I may have no choice but to shoot him. Think about it, Rachael. Why would he come here when he isn't allowed to acknowledge my existence? There's little point in it." The tub of water was bothering her, so just to keep her from pitching the wadded-up pillow at him, he scooped out a few bucketfuls of water and dumped it down the sink.

Rachael was silent for a long time watching him. She sank into a chair. "Aren't these elders the lawmakers? Are they holy people? What exactly are they? Besides imbeciles, I mean."

"You can't call them imbeciles to their faces, Rachael," he pointed out.

"If you can shoot them, I can call them names." She glared at him, daring him to contradict her. "Are elders called elders because they're old? Ancient? Full of hot air?"

"You haven't even met the man and you're already belligerent."

Her dark eyes swept over him with repressed fury. "I am never belligerent."

He picked up the tub and carried it out to the verandah. It was still fairly full and very heavy. Water sloshed as he tipped it over the railing. "I suppose there's some logic in you having permission to call them names if I can shoot them," he agreed to appease her. He didn't bother to take the tub to the small hut hidden in the trees some distance away. He set it to one side, out of the way should he need to take to the trees fast. Outside, he listened to the night creatures calling to one another, giving away the location of the intruder as he moved closer to the house.

Had he not been banished he would have gone, out of respect, to meet the man instead of making him come all the way up the tree to him. The elder was in his eighties and, although in great shape, would still feel the affects of the long distance. He ducked back inside to comb his hair into some semblance of order.

Rachael watched him, saw the small frown, the worry lines around his eyes. Most of all she saw that Rio changed his casual appearance, and that meant something. She took her cue from him, brushing the tangles from her hair, checking to see that her skin was clean and brushing her teeth. She hadn't used the small stash of beauty supplies she'd stuffed in her pack since she'd arrived, but she pulled them out.

"What is that?"

"Makeup. I thought I'd try to look presentable for your elder." She hesitated, tried again. "Wise man. Personage."

"Elder is fine." He stalked across the room and took the lip gloss from her hand. "You're beautiful, Rachael, and you damned well don't have to look perfect for him."

For the first time in a while a ghost of a smile curved her mouth. "Talk about someone who has little moods! Actually, tree dweller, I was going to look perfect for *you,* not your brainless elder." She held out her hand for the lip gloss.

He put it in her palm. "I should at least get points for the beautiful compliment."

Her smile widened. "I censored because of the beautiful compliment. It would have been a lot worse than tree dweller."

"You terrify me." Rio bent and kissed her upturned mouth. How had he managed to live so long without her and think he was alive? Had he just been walking through life all those years? Loving her terrified him. It was so strong, a tidal wave welling up inside of him, consuming him, so at times he couldn't even look at her.

"Well that's a good thing as far as I'm concerned." Rachael applied the lip gloss and a bit of mascara. She was apprehensive and struggled to hide it. She glanced at Rio from under her long lashes. He was definitely on alert in spite of the banter back and forth between them. She reached across to the table, slipped a knife from the sheath and slid it beneath the cushion of her chair. Assassins came in all shapes and sizes and genders. Age never seemed to matter either.

17

PETER Delgrotto was tall and thin, a tough, sinewy man with lines etched deeply in his face. His eyes were a strange amber, glittering with some hidden fire, a focused, haunting stare that carried a great degree of menace. Rachael had expected a wizened, elderly man staggering under the weight of his years, but Delgrotto carried power and danger in his piercing eyes. He stood straight, fully clothed. The only sign of the long, arduous trip was the sheen of sweat on his skin and the breath moving in bursts in and out of his lungs that he couldn't quite hide.

"You honor us with your presence, Wise One," Rio said formally.

Rachael made a small strangling noise in her throat and then covered her displeasure by coughing when Rio tossed a quick warning glance her way.

Rio stepped back to allow the older man entrance. "If you wish to come in, please do so." He felt awkward, uncertain what to say or how to act. By all of their laws, the elder should not come near him, acknowledge him or speak to him, let alone enter his dwelling. Rio had no idea whether he was being discourteous in inviting the man inside.

Delgrotto bowed low. "I must ask you for a glass of water. I have not traveled so fast, or so far, in years. My lungs are not what they used to be. Forgive me bothering you, when I have not properly greeted you in many years." His gaze settled on Rachael.

There was a small silence. Rio stood very still. Rachael lifted her chin, her dark eyes alive with distaste.

"This is obviously your woman. You've found her. You must introduce me."

"I'm sorry, Elder, forgive my lack of manners. I'm so surprised by your visit I've forgotten basic courtesy." Rio handed the man a glass of water. "This is Rachael. Rachael, Peter Delgrotto, an elder in our village."

Rachael managed a smile but she didn't murmur pleasantries. She was pleased that Rio thought to protect her, that he hadn't given away her infamous last name. Sensing how nervous Rio was, she stood up and casually crossed the room to stand just behind him, wanting to be close in case he needed her.

Delgrotto inclined his head, returning her smile, but it didn't quite reach his eyes. "Very nice to meet you, Rachael." He turned to look at Rio and the smile faded.

Rio felt the impact of the elder's stare. It had been many years since any other than his unit members had looked at him or spoken to him. He felt behind him for the sink, something to grip out of sight of the elder. Rachael slipped her hand into his. A show of solidarity and support. "What is it, Elder? What is so important that you would break the law of our people?" There was little point in beating around the bush.

"I have no right to come to you, Rio. Not after the sentence handed down by the council." Delgrotto met his gaze steadily. "By me. I have removed myself as a council member and am prepared to pay the consequences of my actions. I told the Seat of Power what I intended and asked they withhold sentencing until it is done. They agreed."

Rachael could see the pride on the older man's face. Rio reached out and took his arm, led him to the most comfortable chair and seated him. "What is it?" Delgrotto suddenly looked every bit of his eighty years and then some.

"My grandson lies near death No one can save him without your blood. None of us carry the rare blood you have. Without you he will die. I lost my firstborn son to poachers. He had no children. I lost my only other child and his mate to an accident. I have no other family left. I don't want to lose him. Not out of pride or stubbornness. Not for any antiquated law. I'm asking you to save him."

"Where is he?"

"He lies in the village at the small hospital there."

"I'll leave now, Elder. I can go faster alone. Will they allow my help?"

"Joshua said you would come." Delgrotto nodded his head. "They're waiting for you, keeping him alive with fluids. We used the blood you had stored for yourself." He looked down at his shaking hands, tears glittering in his eyes. "It was my decision to steal from you, no one else. Without it, he would have died. It isn't enough, only to prolong his life until you manage to arrive."

"It was not stealing, Elder, I would have given it all freely to save the life of a child." Rio caught Rachael by the shoulders. "You'll be here when I return." He made it a statement. A command.

"I'll be here." She kissed the side of his mouth, his jaw. Her lips moved gently against his ear as she whispered to him. "You're a good man, Rio."

"I'll follow as soon as I've rested," Delgrotto said.

"Sleep here, Elder. I'll return quickly," Rio said and went out to the verandah, pulling off his shirt as he did so. Rachael hobbled after him. "Do you want me to go with you?"

"No, I can travel much faster alone. I want you to stay off your leg for a couple of days and give it a rest. I'll be back as soon as possible." He tucked the shirt and then his jeans into a small pack that he secured around his neck.

"Clever." She realized they all had to travel with a small pack, the elder included. "Good fortune, Rio."

"Be safe, Rachael." He caught her head and dragged her to him, kissing her with fierce possession, with tenderness. She felt the fur rushing over his skin, felt his hands curl into huge paws and marveled at his ability to be so precise in his shifting.

She blinked and the black leopard melted into the forest. "Great. Leave me to entertain the guests." She took a deep breath and went back inside. To her relief, the old man had already sunk into a fitful sleep. She covered him with a thin blanket and went out to sit on the verandah with the small leopards.

The rhythm of the forest changed at various intervals during the day. Dawn activities were quite different from the lull in the afternoon. She read a book and listened to the continual chatter in the forest, trying hard to study which bird sang which song and what sounds emerged from the various species of monkeys.

She heard the old man stirring as the sun set, and she forced herself to go back inside to be as pleasant and accommodating as she was able. "I trust you slept well."

"Please forgive an old man's rudeness. Traveling the distance really took more strength than I realized."

"I can imagine. Rio was very tired when he arrived home the other night after packing Joshua all those miles by himself. Without food or drink or medical attention."

The elder looked at her, his expression as calm as ever. "Touché, my dear."

She pulled open the vegetable bin, slapping vegetables on the counter. "I'm not your dear. Let's just get that straight right now. Are you hungry? I haven't had dinner yet, and Rio wouldn't want me to let you starve."

"By all means, I would enjoy sharing a meal with you. You shouldn't be on your leg. I make a decent soup; why don't you let me fix it?"

Rachael hesitated, unsure if she should let him have the

run of Rio's home. The elder seemed unshakable even in the face of her distrust.

He took the decision out of her hands by going through the pantry. She retrieved the knife from the chair cushions while his back was turned and replaced it in the sheath. As casually as possible she put the weapons out of sight.

"You don't think much of me, do you?" he asked as he began chopping vegetables.

She picked up a second knife and helped. "Not much. I can't see much wisdom in your sentence of banishment. It smacks of hypocrisy if you ask me, which technically you didn't so I guess I shouldn't offer my opinion on the subject." She hacked a tomato into tiny little pieces. The sound of the blade hitting the chopping board beat out a fast tattoo of annoyance.

Delgrotto paused in the act of cutting up wild mushrooms. "You've used a knife before," he observed.

"You'd be surprised what I can do with this baby. Working in a kitchen can be damned boring, and we women just think up things to hurl the cutlery at. In South America, we pride ourselves on target practice." She gave him a chatty smirk. "Sometimes it was the chef if he was particularly obnoxious."

"I see." Delgrotto raised his eyebrow. "What might constitute being obnoxious, just so I don't make the same mistake."

"Oh, you may as well be as obnoxious as you like. You're already in my book of evil and obnoxious people. I think I even underlined your name a couple of times." She slashed an onion until it was nothing but sauce.

"I'm certainly not evil, my dear. I may have made one or two mistakes in my life, but I don't think I've ever been evil."

She shrugged. "I suppose passing that sort of judgment is all subjective. It depends on the point of view. You don't think you're evil, but someone else may very well think you're the devil incarnate."

Delgrotto paused to watch in fascination as the knife

chopped through the remainder of the vegetables so fast her movements were a blur. "I suppose that's true. If one turns the view even slightly, there is always a different slant. Where were you raised? You are obviously one of us."

Her hands stilled and she looked up at him. There was a moment of silence. Only the sound of the rain on the roof could be heard. Even the wind stilled, holding its breath. Delgrotto glimpsed the fury in her eyes. In her heart. "I am not one of you. I will never be one of you. I don't like people who play god, not in this life, and not in any other life."

"Is that what you think we did?" His voice was gentle.

Rachael dropped the knife and put distance between them, going to the door and staring out into the darkness. She didn't trust herself or her over-the-top fury with this man who had presumed to judge Rio so harshly. She would like the old man to meet her uncle, to show him what true evil was.

Rachael took a deep calming breath. Her bad temper was beginning to affect the small leopard under the bed. Fritz snarled and showed his teeth, but remained still. She looked down at the forest floor. Somewhere out there Rio ran, flat out, expending every drop of energy he had, risking his life to save the life of the child. And the child's grandfather had condemned him to a life of banishment.

"You think we take advantage of Rio." There was no inflection whatsoever in his voice, no anger, no denial. No remorse.

"Of course you take advantage of him. You're doing it now, aren't you? You came here knowing he wouldn't hesitate. Knowing he would risk everything for your grandson. You knew what his nature was when you condemned him, yet you did it anyway. You put the yoke of service around his neck and kept him chained to a society, to a people who used him, but weren't willing to associate with him or lift a finger to help him. You need him and what he's able to do, but you don't want him to taint your perfect society."

Tears burned in her eyes. She kept her back to him and her fists clenched tightly at her sides while the anger swirled in a black knot in her stomach. "He was injured often, I've seen the scars. He must have been so alone and depressed at times. You left him to live always feeling ashamed and not good enough no matter what he did. And all the time you knew what he was on the inside. You knew his true nature."

Fritz emerged from under the bed and rubbed along her leg, wrapping his tail around her. He glared at the elder, hissed and spit before slipping out into the night. Rachael caught a glimpse of Franz waiting in the shadows of the canopy.

"Yes I did know him," Delgrotto admitted.

She could hear the sounds of him dumping vegetables into the broth, but she didn't turn around, disgusted that she was in the same house with him. "Power is a strange thing. It seems so innocent on the surface, yet it twists and corrupts until the user is no longer anything but a weapon." There was a lash of contempt in her voice.

"It does seem so when viewed from a distance," Delgrotto said mildly. "Yet just as you observed, turn the view slightly and you see something else. Rio stood before the entire village. Not just the council. He was young and strong and filled with power. He was covered in the blood of the man whose life he took."

"He was covered in his mother's blood." Rachael whipped around to face him, her dark eyes flashing.

Delgrotto nodded, conceding her point. "That is true also. Rio had skills far beyond his years. He was an expert marksman even as a young boy. Few of our strongest men could defeat him in the mock battles we have. He was popular with the young crowd, everyone looked up to him. And he violated our most sacred law. We work at teaching our children that hunters did not come into our forests, our home, with the intention of committing murder. We eat meat, and we kill animals to eat it. They hunted for fur. This man did not stalk and kill Violet Santana in cold blood. He had no idea she had a human side. He would have been appalled at the idea of killing a woman."

"And because he didn't know, that lessens his crime?"

"How could it be a crime if he didn't know what he'd done?"

"He was poaching. The leopards are protected."

"It was still an animal to him, not a human. How can we teach our children otherwise, Rachael? We are a lethal species, with cunning and intelligence and gifts beyond the ordinary, but we also have the mood swings and tempera- ments of our animal cousins and that makes us far too dan- gerous without laws to guide us. What would you have us do? He was a hero to the young men. Where he went, they would follow."

"He didn't obey you, that was his crime. He stood before you with his head unbowed and his shoulders straight ready to accept responsibility for his actions."

"Without remorse."

"The man killed his mother."

"And you believe an eye for eye is logical? Is justice? Where does it stop? Do we then carry on feud after feud until we no longer exist? Rio chose his path with full knowledge of the consequences and full knowledge that he was in the wrong." Delgrotto pulled two bowls from the cupboard. "We spent a hundred years to try to convince our people we could not brand hunters and poachers as mur- derers. In one day, Rio Santana changed all that. Our peo- ple have been divided ever since."

"Because they see into his heart. They see what he does for them. For all of them. For you, for your grandson, for Joshua. Even the local tribesmen seek him out because they see into his heart and know he's worthwhile. He's extraordinary." Rachael, in her frustration, wanted to shake the calm demeanor of the elder. How could he stand there and possibly think he was fit to deliver a judgment against Rio? She seethed with frustration and anger and she didn't understand how Rio had accepted and lived with their blatantly unfair sentence.

"The young men saw Rio as a leader, as a man with skills and the ability to take charge. Some of them followed him. They separated themselves from the village, living outside the protection of the community yet stayed involved. Rio committed murder on a human being. Whatever the circumstances, whatever the reasons, he hunted the man, using his skills as one of our people, and he deliberately took that man's life. He not only put all of our lives in jeopardy from possible reprisal, from someone finding our species, but he put our very way of life in jeopardy. We have laws for reasons, Rachael. Should he have gone unpunished? Rio knew and accepted the laws of our society."

Rachael watched as the elder set the table and lit a candle as a centerpiece. She couldn't quite leave the doorway and the night. Rio was a presence everywhere, but out in the darkness, he was in his element. She knew he was far from her, yet she still felt him. All the nights she woke to find him gone, or just returning, he had been running free, running in his other form. She longed to be at his side instead of debating an issue neither could resolve.

"Come sit down and eat," Delgrotto said kindly. "You have great courage, Rachael, and you protect those you love fiercely, just as Rio does. I'm grateful he found you. You've brought him happiness."

"He would have been happy if you hadn't taken everything away from him."

"We spared his life. It was the only choice open to us. Banishment or death. No one wanted it, and no one was happy with the sentence, but we felt we had no choice. We spared his life and lived without him. We caught glimpses of his greatness, this son to our people. A born leader. We saw what it did to him. You can't see what it did to us."

"I hope you don't want me to feel sorry for you." Rachael limped across the room to the table. She left the door wide open. There would be no sleeping until Rio returned safely and the sound of the rain soothed her ragged nerves and made her feel closer to him. Rio's rain songs. The sound made him closer to her.

"Not sorry for us. Perhaps understanding. We lost him and his mother. Banishment means he is dead to us. We can't see him or speak to him, yet he gives his money to us for the preservation of the forest."

"How could you take it?"

"If we can't see him or speak to him, how could we return it?"

"So you could see the money, just not the giver."

Delgrotto smiled at her ferocity. "You must promise me you'll have many children with him. We need them."

The soup was delicious. She hated to even concede him that much and it annoyed her. A faint grin stole over her face. "I think I have a closed mind where you're concerned. I don't want to see your point of view."

"At least you can admit that." He seemed to savor the taste of the broth. "You would make a good member of the high council."

Rachael managed a rude noise around the next mouthful of soup.

Delgrotto's eyebrow shot up. "You don't think so? One has to look at a problem from every angle. Before you can do that, you have to acknowledge there is more than one angle. I didn't agree with banishment, but the alternative was beyond our capabilities to impose on him."

"Well for heaven's sake, did you consider another punishment? Something not quite so harsh? Live a little, make a few laws up, that's what every other governing body does."

He nodded his head politely, considering her suggestion. "What do you believe is a fair punishment for murder?"

"It wasn't murder."

"What was it then?"

"I don't know, but I've seen murder. I've felt the malev-
olence of a cold-blooded murderer, of someone truly evil,
and that is *not* Rio."

An owl hooted in the distance. The elder lifted his head
and stared toward the door for a long moment. "I'm sorry
you've had to be exposed to such a thing, Rachael, and, of
course, you're right. There is nothing evil about Rio." Delgrotto ate another spoonful of the soup. "We can agree he
took a life."

Somewhat mollified, Rachael nodded. "I can't very well
deny it when he told me so himself." She sighed. "He
doesn't blame you for what you did."

"No, he doesn't, because he understands the need for
laws." The owl hooted a second time. Delgrotto leaned forward and blew out the candle. "Close the door and be very
quiet."

"The birds aren't sounding off, neither are the monkeys." But Rachael obediently closed the door and dropped
the bar in place. "What's wrong?" Always before she'd
heard the clear warning of the animals as an intruder
moved through their territory. "Maybe it's Rio coming
back." But she knew it wasn't. Cold fingers touched her
spine, sent a chill of fear through her body.

"It isn't Rio. Do you know the way to the village?"

Rachael shook her head. "I've never been there."

"You might be able to follow Rio, using scent, but I
know him. He'll have tried to go to water several times to
throw anyone off. He's very careful. He must have an
escape hole other than the front door."

"Yes, but we don't even know what's out there."

"If a man was out there, the forest would have been in
an uproar. It's a leopard, and he knows the ways of the animals. He knows to soothe them as he passes by, careful not
to look as if he's hunting. And he must be hunting to want
to come to us so silently."

"I came here hoping to escape the trouble I was in,"
Rachael confessed readily. "They sent someone after me

once already. You should go, I can show you the escape door. You shouldn't be here with me."

"I may be an old man, Rachael, but I am capable of helping you protect your life. I would never slink back to Rio and tell him I left his woman alone to fend off an attacker. I could never live with myself."

She had an idea Rio might not look too kindly on him either. "Kim Pang came by earlier and told Rio his father had a vision about a party of researchers entering the forest looking for medicinal plants. Tama is guiding them, but his father was still very much worried. He didn't believe they were researchers."

"An ordinary man would not be able to keep the animals quiet. Nor would he be able to escape the eye of one of Pang's sons."

"He also said the man who approached him asking for a guide knew the traditions and honor system of the forest. I think he suspected he was of the same species as Rio." She took a deep breath. "It could be that my brother is hunting me."

"Your own kin?"

"It's a possibility. There's a price on my head. I think it best that you go while you can."

"To trade the life of my grandson for your life? I will not. I doubt it's safe in the forest. We're better off here, with Rio's weapons. If we must escape, we'll do so when we know it's our only option," Delgrotto decided.

A leopard moaned quite close. She recognized the haunting call of the clouded leopard, Fritz warning her. Somehow the small leopard's acceptance gave her hope. Rachael shoved a knife, sheathed in leather, into the waistband of her jeans. She picked up the smaller of the two handguns.

Delgrotto reached out and drew her into the center of the room, away from the windows. "Don't move."

She heard the soft thud of something heavy landing on the verandah. Something walked around the house, fur whispering along the railing, brushing against the creeper vines and sliding over the window. Shadows moved, dark enough to make her heart leap into her throat.

They waited. Rachael did what she always did when the tension was too much. She counted. It was a mindless, silly habit, but it worked to keep her brain calm, allowing her to think clearly. There was silence again. The wind sighed through the canopy and the rain poured down steadily. The tip of a knife appeared along the inside edge of the door beneath the bar. It slowly began to rise.

Rachael moved to the side of the door. "Here's the thing about night visitors." She spoke very matter-of-factly. "If they don't have manners, we figure they aren't worth keeping around so we just shoot them. Take your knife out of my door and knock like a normal person or I'm going to empty this gun into the wall."

There was a brief hesitation and the knife disappeared. Another moment of silence and the knock came on the door.

Rachael signaled to the elder to take a gun and move into the shadow of the bedroom out of sight. Only when he had merged into the gray did she reach out and lift the bar. "Only one person better step through that door and you'd better step through with your hands raised." She moved again, so they wouldn't be able to get a fix on her voice if they came in shooting.

The door swung open slowly. "I'm not armed, Rachael."

For a moment she couldn't think. Couldn't breathe. Her heart pounded like a runaway drum and her mouth went dry. She stood there, fighting for air, uncertain what she would do. Rachael cleared her throat and forced the words out. "Come in, shut the door and bar it. I want to see your hands every second."

"Damn it, Rachael. You know who I am." The door was slammed just that bit too hard. Elijah dropped the bar in place and swung his head to glare at her. Tall, muscular, broad-shouldered, his black hair fell in the same riot of waves as hers did. "What the hell were you thinking, taking off like that?"

"Why are you here?" She didn't lower the gun an inch.

"Put the damn thing down before you shoot yourself. You wouldn't shoot me, not in a million years, so quit pretending you're tough." He took a step toward her.

"She might not shoot you, but I have a very clear shot and I won't hesitate," Delgrotto said in a low, disembodied tone.

Rachael watched her brother stiffen, watched the shock spread over his face. He'd always been so careful, paid attention to every detail. "Rachael, tell him who I am."

"Elijah Lospostos. My brother. You have a lot of explaining to do Elijah." She was looking at his bare feet, jeans, and unbuttoned shirt. "You shifted into the form of a leopard, didn't you? How long have you been able to do that?"

He shrugged. "I've been traveling fast, Rachael. It wasn't easy picking up your scent, not until I found it in the leopard form. I had a hell of a time getting away from camp with that guide always watching my every move. I could use something to drink, and I wouldn't mind sitting down. And put the guns down. What kind of welcome is this? I traveled a thousand miles to save your butt."

"No one asked you to, Elijah," she said softly. "I never asked to be saved." She blinked back tears. "Do you know a man named Duncan Powell?"

Her brother went ramrod stiff. "Has he been here? He's a killer, Rachael and he's one of us, He'll be able to track you anywhere. Duncan is one of Armando's hired guns. If he's here . . ."

"He's dead," she interrupted. "He left a cobra in my bedroom and then followed me here." She lifted her chin and glared at him. "Why did you come?"

Elijah pulled out a chair from the table and sank into it. "I told you why. Why do I always come after you? You can't go running around unprotected, Rachael. If Armando gets his hands on you . . ."

"He'll have me killed? He's been trying to do that since I was nine. You should have let me disappear, Elijah. I didn't go to the police, I didn't say a word to the authorities about Tony and I wouldn't. I just want out. You should have let me go."

"You think Armando's going to believe you drowned in a river without seeing the body? Hell, Rachael, you've forgotten everything I taught you. He knows you're here. He's coming after you with everything he's got."

"And so you dropped all your business and hastily rushed off to the wilds of the rain forest to save me the way you always do."

"Rachael, what's this about? Why didn't you come to me, talk about this? Of course I followed you. I'm not going to allow him to kill you."

Rachael placed the gun on the sink and pressed her back into the wall beside it. She looked small and vulnerable instead of the woman who had been so ready to fight just minutes earlier. Tears glittered in her eyes. "No? I thought it might be a help to you. Isn't that what you said, Elijah? Didn't you hope he'd find me and take the burden off your hands once and for all? Didn't you tell me yourself your life would be so much better, so much easier if I were dead?"

He stood up so fast the chair went over backwards, taking a step toward her. The elder, deep in the shadows, stirred, reminding him to be cautious, and Elijah stopped. "Rachael. Do you honestly think I came here to kill you?"

"There's a price on my head."

"To keep you *alive*. Armando moved fast. He picked up the girl who wore your clothes and a wig. She was sent to me via messenger and it wasn't a pretty sight."

Rachael turned her face away, her hand going to her throat in a protective gesture, a sound, much like strangling, emerging.

"This gun is getting heavy, Rachael," Delgrotto said. "I

think you and your brother should be alone. I doubt if he poses much of a threat, but Rio might come back unexpectedly. I'll go onto the verandah."

"Rio couldn't possibly return before dawn."

"He travels with those small leopards. It's likely one went to warn him."

The color drained from Rachael's face. "You have to go, Elijah. Get out of here right now."

Elijah waved her words away. "Look at me, Rachael. Turn your head and look at me. I want to see your face when you tell me you believed I sent those men out to kill you. Damn it." His fist hit the tabletop. "I spent my life fighting to keep us alive."

"You said you wished I was dead."

"I *never* said that." He glanced at the elder, frustration plain on his face. Delgrotto took the hint and slipped outside to leave them alone. "All right, the truth is, I don't know what the hell I said to you that day. I was terrified for you and angry at you for not confiding in me. I had to shoot Tony right in front of you." Elijah swept a hand over his face. "I knew what that would do to you, shooting him in front of you."

Rachael faced her brother across the table. "You killed him, Elijah. You killed Tony because he was with me. You became the very thing we both abhorred."

"You aren't thinking, Rachael." He dragged his hands through his hair in agitation. "He knew about us. He knew what we were. Worse, he belonged to Armando's crew. He was feeding him information."

"You don't know that."

"Who was he Rachael? How did you meet him?"

"Marcia Tolstoy is his sister. She introduced us. We weren't dating. He was just a nice man, lonely like me."

"He wasn't a nice man, and he wasn't Marcia Tolstoy's brother. Armando paid her to tell you that, and before you say she would never do that, remember everyone has a price. Armando found hers. If you'd told me about Tony, I would have checked him out quietly and let you know to break off the friendship. By the time I found out about him, you were already in the car with him. I didn't have time to take him down easy. He was taking you to one of Armando's warehouses."

"We were going out to dinner."

"Have I ever lied to you? Never, Rachael. It's always been the two of us, ever since we were children and there was only us."

"How do I know you're telling me the truth? How do I know what's the truth and what's a lie? My uncle murdered my parents. I thought he loved us. I thought he loved Mom and Dad. Dad was his brother. What does that tell a child, Elijah? The world isn't a very safe place and you can't trust anyone. Not even family." Rachael swung around and filled a glass of water for him, needing something to do.

"I would never, under any circumstances, order your death. You're my sister, my only family, and I love you. You don't have to believe me, Rachael. I know you're hurt and angry and very mixed-up. I didn't have time to talk to you."

"You had time to pull me out of the car before you killed him. And you had time to lock me in the house afterward."

"You were hysterical. He went for his gun, Rachael. You didn't see him make his move because you were fighting me as I pulled you out of the car. You wouldn't listen to me and you were threatening to go to the police. I did my best to carry out Dad's wishes and make the business legitimate. It hasn't been easy. I know too much about Armando, just as you do. He can't allow us to live. As long as he thought I was with him, that I could control you, we both were safe. Once I made my move against him, Armando wanted to kill you not only to punish me, but to silence you. You should never have talked to Tony."

Her dark eyes flashed. "I would *never* tell an outsider our business, certainly not a man I knew nothing about. I wouldn't risk your life or his. I went out with him."

"And he never asked you questions about me?"

"He asked if you were my brother and I said yes. You are. It's common knowledge. It shouldn't have gotten him killed."

"Rachael, let's start with something we know. Tell me you know I love you. You must know everything I've done in my life I've done for you. For us. To keep us alive. I was a child too. I had no power. No one to help us. I had no choice if we were to stay alive. I had to join with Armando or he would have killed us both on the spot. I traded my soul for a chance for both of us to live."

She flung herself into his arms. "I know you did. I know you did it for me. I knew you could have gotten away if you didn't have me to try to protect."

"Does it really make sense to you that I spent all those years protecting you and now I'd suddenly want you dead?" He wrapped his arms around her, hugged her hard.

"It was so awful. I felt responsible and I didn't know why you would do such a terrible thing. Power corrupts, Elijah. I've seen you fight it. You tried to make the business legitimate, but at the same time, you had to do the things that allowed Armando to think you were a part of the business."

"I had no choice but to run the business the way Armando wanted. We inherited half of everything, Rachael. Armando wanted it all, and he wanted it to remain his. When he found out Dad wanted to get out from under it, he had them followed. He discovered Mom could shift into the form of a leopard. He found his perfect assassins. Stealthy. Cunning. Intelligent."

"So Dad took us all to Florida."

"That was because Mom was afraid her people would harm Dad. So he moved us to the Glades. Mom could still run, and he was out from under the business. But of course it didn't work that way. He owned too much and knew too much. He was slowly trying to get out from under the companies. Armando wasn't going to let that happen. All the while I was out with my wonderful uncle, doing his little tasks for him because he let me run free. I was so stupid. I told Mom and Dad that Armando knew about me shifting, that I did it all the time in front of him. Mom had been so secretive and I wanted her to know it was okay, that he didn't mind. They were both so upset, and they must have talked to him. Armando arranged to meet with Mom and Dad and he killed both of them."

"And I saw it." Rachael pulled away from him. "I'll never forget his face when he turned and saw me standing there."

"Do you think I liked doing the things I had to do? He held you hostage, Rachael. He never bothered to hide what he did from you. The more you knew, the more of a liability you were to him and the more I had to do to make it worth his while to keep you alive. He needed me. I was like Mom and a tremendous asset to him. And he knew that he couldn't kill both of us and get away with it. As soon as possible, I made certain he knew there was proof, if something happened to either of us."

"But Elijah, I saw you do things just like he did them. You're not the same. You've grown distant and colder. I tried to talk to you about it and you brushed it off."

"He was making another move against us. And I was planning to kill him. I didn't want you involved." He said it bluntly. "If you knew, you'd be as guilty as me. You couldn't know the things I had to do. One of us had to be something Mom would be proud of." He looked down at his hands. "If it makes you feel any better, I never killed an innocent. I never stooped that low."

"You ran drugs, you smuggled weapons. You trained assassins." She flung the accusations at him, stepping away, pain breathing in her lungs.

He took a step toward her, wanting to shake her. "Damn it, Rachael. If you don't want to believe me about Tony, don't, but don't look at me as if I'm some monster you don't know. Armando isn't going to let you live. He can't. You're a knife poised over his head. You're an eyewitness to murder. I have no intention of leaving here without you. Armando's men are swarming up and down the river. He imported a couple of the best trackers. Men like Duncan. You can't stay here, Rachael. Come home with me where I can keep you safe."

There was no sound other than the wind and rain. The door was partially open and the wind blew in, stirring the mosquito net, setting it dancing. Rachael felt the wind on her face. Elijah felt the blade cut into his throat. Hot breath fanned his cheek. A soft growl rumbled dangerously close to his ear. "She isn't going anywhere with you."

18

RIO pressed the blade deeper into Elijah's throat. "She isn't going anywhere with you." His voice was gravelly, a growl of sheer menace. "Not now. Not ever."

"Rio, no, you can't hurt him," Rachael protested. "This is Elijah, my brother."

Elijah didn't move a muscle. He stayed perfectly still, feeling the burning sting of the blade across his throat. Instead of loosening his grip at Rachael's command, Rio tightened his arm until it was a steel band, a vise squeezing ever tighter.

"Stay where you are, Rachael. This gentleman and I are going outside together. If you want to live, Elijah, take very small steps in exact sync with mine. One wrong move and you're a dead man."

"Rio, what are you doing?" Rachael took a step toward them.

The knife drew blood. Elijah held up his hand to his sister, halting her progress instantly. She watched with enormous eyes as the two men moved together out the door, back onto the verandah. Rachael followed at a safe distance, her heart pounding.

"I know you're armed."

"Yes."

"Where?"

"Gun at the small of my back. A second strapped to my leg. I have a knife up my sleeve and a second under my left arm."

Rachael blinked. She glanced at the elder, who remained sitting quietly on the sofa as if they were all having tea. She had no idea her brother was armed. Where had all the weapons come from?

"Tell me why I should keep you alive." The words were barely audible, a whisper of menace in the dead of the night. "Don't look to Rachael to get you out of this. She loves you. It's me you have to convince. Because I don't love you."

Rio ignored the elder sitting so quietly on the verandah. He was already banished, condemned for all time for a deed he could never take back. He might as well do something worthwhile and remove all threats to Rachael's life while he was racking up the sins.

"I love my sister," Elijah answered quietly. His voice came out in a croak. "You don't have to believe me."

"I have to believe you if you're going to live. Rachael deserves a life."

"Yes she does. I'm not her enemy." Elijah stayed very still, aware that at no time did the knife waver from his throat. He had learned patience in a hard school, knowing most of the time there would be a moment of distraction when he could make his move, but there was no give in the man behind him. The dozens of defense moves he had perfected would never work against that viselike grip. Elijah sighed. "Two reasons. I followed her here to save her life. And better than that, if you don't release me, she's going to be so pissed with you, you'll wish you'd stayed in your animal form."

Rio glanced at the open door where Rachael stood with her hand pressed to her mouth. She looked a bit shocked but it wouldn't last long. She shook her head at him in silent appeal, her eyes anxious.

Rio slowly eased the razor-sharp blade from Elijah's throat and stepped away. "Put all your weapons on the floor in front of you. Be very careful, Elijah. You know our people. We see everything in hunting mode. Right now, consider me a hunter."

Elijah, with deliberate slowness, removed the weapons and stacked them neatly on the verandah. Rachael stared in horror at the growing pile.

"Take them into the house, *sestrilla*," Rio said, keeping his voice as gentle as possible. He waited until she'd gathered up the guns and knives and disappeared into the house. "Turn around, very slowly."

Elijah turned around to face Rio for the first time. They stared at one another, two strong males with ice-cold eyes and a dangerous temperament disguised with a carefully cultivated civilized demeanor.

Rachael's brother spoke first. "I'm Elijah Lospostos, Rachael's brother."

"You're the one who put a million-dollar price on her head."

"I had to move fast. I figured between the government officials and bandits, everyone would work very hard to keep Rachael alive. Our uncle would have to use his assassins to hunt her. He wouldn't find anyone willing to give up that kind of money, not and kill her. I made it too irresistible to pass it up. No one was going to kill her." He tilted his head to one side studying Rio. "You've forgotten your clothes."

Rio shrugged, the knife never wavering. "Bad habit of mine. Have you had any coffee? I could use something to drink."

Rachael pushed past her brother to wrap her arm around Rio's waist. "You need to sit down. Did you get there in time?"

Rio kept his penetrating gaze on Elijah. "Yes. He's going to be fine, Elder."

Rachael couldn't help smiling at the older man, but he turned his face away. She caught the sheen of tears glistening in his eyes, and his hands shook as he lifted them to wipe his face. "Thank you, Rio." The voice was choked, barely audible.

"He's a good boy."

Rachael urged Rio toward the door. He was swaying with weariness. Rio bared his teeth at Elijah in a semblance of a smile and waved him toward the door first.

"Call off the others first," Elijah said without moving. "I know they're waiting."

Rachael listened. She heard the moaning of the wind, The rhythm of the rain. "Fritz and Franz," she turned her face up toward Rio. "Are they inside? Waiting for him to go in?"

Rio grinned at her. His face was pale and there was a sheen of perspiration coating his skin. "Of course. They like to hunt too."

"Very funny. Call them off."

Rio uttered a series of vocalizations. Rachael watched her brother's face. He was frowning. She dug her nails into Rio's bare skin. "What exactly did you tell them?"

"To be alert," Elijah answered for her. "What are those two little cubs doing? I've never heard of training cubs for combat."

Rachael rolled her eyes. "Don't think for one minute those little demon seeds are cubs. They're fully grown clouded leopards with bad manners, tempers and very lethal saber-toothed tiger teeth."

"I take it you had a run-in with them." Elijah hadn't budged. He stared into the darkened interior of the house, but refused to take one step into the room.

"One of them nearly took my leg off. Don't be a baby." She was trying not to notice her brother's throat was bleeding. He hadn't once touched it. She tried not to notice the knife still in Rio's hand, his gaze focused and unblinking on her brother's face. "Rio wouldn't have you go in if it wasn't safe." She tried to say the words with conviction, but her tone was more a question than reassurance.

"It might be a good way to get rid of me without guilt," Elijah said.

"I wouldn't feel guilt if I had to get rid of you," Rio answered easily. "Go in."

Elijah sighed and entered the house, obviously on the alert. He was a shifter, a very good one, fast and efficient, a killer should there be need, but his clothes would hamper him, slow him down when he might need the speed against two fifty-pound leopards. He saw the eyes gleaming at him in the darkness. The two cats had separated and were waiting patiently. One crouched on the mantle, the other was belly to the ground beside the chair. Just waiting. Ears flat, lips snarling. Eyes glowing.

Rio felt the effects of traveling so many miles in such a short time. His body burned with fatigue. He hadn't had the necessary time to recoup after donating more blood than he could afford. Franz had called him from a distance, alerting him to the danger to Rachael. Rio slugged down the orange juice and rushed out, not taking the time to rest from the dizzying blood loss. The trip back had been a nightmare, terror choking him. He pushed the swift-moving leopard to the limit, racing across the miles even when the beast burned for air.

"Rio?" Rachael's voice was a soft concern. "Come sit down. Between your arsenal and my brother's, we have enough weapons to start a war. If any other neighbor comes calling, begging for sugar, I say we should just shoot them."

"We can't do that," Rio protested. "Tama's bound to come looking for his stray researcher."

Elijah pushed his hand through his hair. "That guide is a pain in the butt. I had to have a couple of my men create a minor catastrophe in order to get his eyes off of me." He stepped cautiously around the chair and sank onto the sofa.

"The garrote." Rio ordered as he caught up a pair of jeans and stepped into them. "Take that off too."

Rachael's eyebrows flew up. "Elijah, you can't be carrying a garrote."

"I forgot about it." Elijah reached up to remove the necklace from around his throat. He handed it to his sister to be added to the growing stockpile of weapons.

Rachael heaved an exaggerated sigh. "The two of you are crazy."

"Probably," Rio conceded. He took the glass of water she gave him and tipped the entire contents down his throat. "I take it Elijah didn't try to kill you."

"Tony was working for Armando." She busied herself making coffee so she wouldn't have to look at either of them. Her hands were shaking. Her knees felt weak. She had dreaded this moment for so long and now she didn't know how to feel. She almost didn't trust the relief sweeping through her and she was afraid she might start crying all over both of them. "You had it figured out. Elijah is a shifter."

"So of course you couldn't go to the police. The first rule is we keep everything in our realm." Rio let out his breath slowly. "And Armando is using shifters as assassins."

"He bribed a couple of shifters in South America. Or maybe he blackmailed them, I don't know. He's capable of anything. He could have threatened to burn down the rain forest, or take a major hunting party in to wipe everyone out." Elijah stretched his legs out in front of him, his black eyes gleaming like obsidian in the night. "I'm not certain he's human. I went into his house one night. The leopard can go in so stealthily, I was certain I could take him." He sighed and shook his head. "He isn't a man, he's a devil. He had a double in his room and he was nowhere to be found."

"How many shifters does he have?"

"Two that I know of. I doubt if he has more. We're an elusive bunch, and he doesn't spend a great deal of time in South America. Duncan was one of them."

The elder came in and inclined his head. "I must go back to the village and care for my grandson. I thank you for what you did, Rio."

"I was happy to be of some small service, Elder," Rio replied. "I do want news of Drake should you hear. I was unable to get near Joshua and no one else volunteered the information."

Rachael's head snapped up. She glared at the old man. "Who did you say was civilized?" She asked sweetly.

"Hafelina." There was more love than reprimand in the single endearment.

Little cat. She knew it now. Knew what he called her. The long-forgotten language was one she distantly remembered from her childhood and it was beginning to come back to her.

Elijah sat up very straight, a frown on his face. He shook his head but remained silent as the older man came into the room. There was a dignity about him that demanded respect.

"Don't reprimand her for speaking her mind or defending you, Rio," the elder said. "She is a woman of courage and integrity. I am no longer a member of the council, but I am bound by our laws. I'll do my best to change what was decreed, but I face punishment for my actions. I wish that I'd taken action some time ago instead of waiting until a personal crisis happened. I'll send word of Drake's condition immediately. Don't get up, I'll shift on the verandah. My pack is out there." He smiled at Rachael. "I am blessed I had such an opportunity to meet you and exchange ideas." His gaze went to Elijah. "Your sister has taught an old man it is never too late to right a wrong. You know the right path."

Elijah gripped the arms of the chair hard, nails digging deep. "There is no redemption for what I've done."

Delgrotto smiled. "Even the sacred high council can be wrong. Who can measure the worth of a man but his own sense of honor?"

Elijah looked away from the warmth in those old eyes. "If I can't forgive myself, how would I ever accept forgiveness from others?"

"No council can turn away the request of asylum, of sanctuary. It matters little where you were born. There are few true shifters left in this world. We can't afford to lose any of them." The elder moved into the shadows of the verandah, shedding his clothes and packing them carefully in the traditional leather bag he strapped around his neck before shifting.

There was a long silence. Rachael sighed. "I really wanted to detest that man."

"He's a good man," Rio said. "He's right to believe in the laws that govern our people. We can't be judged by human standards and we can't take our problems to the police. We have to protect and patrol our own ranks."

"I see what's going on here," Elijah said. "Only a man who has found his mate refers to her as *sestrilla* or *hafelina*. You can't have Rachael. You can't possibly protect her from Armando. I didn't keep her alive this entire time to let her die out here in this jungle."

There was a whip to his voice and Rachael winced visibly. Ignoring Elijah, she took a bowl of the vegetable soup and a cup of coffee to Rio. "Eat all of it, you need it," she encouraged. "And don't give me any guff over your precious elder. He isn't a bad man, he's just not as wise as a woman."

Elijah groaned. "Don't get her started with the women being superior to men argument, we'll get nowhere with this. Rachael, you can't stay. I can tell you feel something for this man, but you can't stay."

"I'm in love with him, Elijah." Rachael said it quietly, staring into her brother's eyes as she handed him a bowl of soup.

"Damn it, Rachael."

Rachael huffed out her breath in exasperation. "Why is it men always say that to me? I seem to bring out swearing in the male species."

She curled up across from Elijah, settling on the arm of Rio's chair, her arms curving around his neck. She had to touch him, her fingers smoothing his shaggy hair. She wanted to inspect his body and make certain there were no scratches to get infected in the humidity of the forest. She had to be content with teasing the nape of his neck with her fingers.

Rio exchanged a long look of understanding with Elijah. "I understand completely, she tends to make me swear too." He followed the admission with a yelp when she tugged at his hair. "I'm Rio, by the way, Rio Santana."

"You'll have to come back where I can protect you too, then. I have soldiers. My home is a fortress. I can keep you both safe. I live near the Glades so you'll be able to run free when the need strikes." Elijah stared at Rio hard, his gaze piercing and focused, a mixture of promised retaliation and challenge.

"You may be able to protect Rachael there, but I can do just as good a job or better here," Rio replied mildly. He leaned his head back into the strong massage of her fingers. "Before you get all bent out of shape, has it occurred to you that you need to do something different? Something unexpected? Your uncle knows you. He raised you. He knows how your mind works. But he doesn't know how my mind works. He doesn't even know about me."

Rachael nuzzled the top of Rio's head with her chin. Her breasts brushed the side of his face, soft and warm and inviting when he was bone weary. "You need to sleep, Rio. I can feel how tired you are."

"Armando will not come to this place."

"Sure he will. If the stakes are high enough. If he thinks he has a chance to win the game for good. It isn't all that hard to find someone to bribe to leak vital information. He has to have someone in his pay, someone who can supply him with information. It could even be some of the bandits. They'd want to collect from both sides."

Rio drank the remainder of the soup and put the bowl on

a small end table. His hand found Rachael's. At once he brought her fingers to his mouth. All the time he watched Elijah.

Elijah regarded him through half-closed eyes. "You're thinking to feed him information on Rachael. Something that will bring him here to make certain the job is done right. He'd want to know it's finished. He'd want to know she was dead and he'd want me to know it."

Rio nodded. "There are bandits up and down the river. Some are fairly decent men, just trying to make a living. There are one or two tribes who would be willing to give us aid here and there. This is my realm, not his. He's infiltrated South America; I doubt he's had time here."

"Duncan knew the layout of the house," Rachael said. "Someone told him."

"Not necessarily. Delgrotto knew nothing of Duncan. As an elder, all information of importance is brought before the council. A member of our species unknown to us would be considered of great importance. I doubt if Duncan had any contact with anyone from my people. He was a shifter and he knew shifters populated this area. He listened to Tomas and his men, gathered information on my team and guessed we were shifters. As a leopard, he could easily find the scents and track us, where as a man, he would find it impossible. Most importantly, Duncan didn't have time to get this information to Armando. He was captured by bandits and then he came nosing around here, looking for Rachael. He found me instead."

Elijah rubbed his jaw. "So your idea is to bring Armando here."

"Rachael isn't going back. She's my woman. You know the legends, and you can call them myths if you like, but I know she's supposed to be with me and the only way you're going to take her from me is over my dead body."

Elijah shrugged his broad shoulders. "It wouldn't be the first time."

Rachael knocked a heavy book to the floor. It hit with a

thud and brought an abrupt silence. "If you both keep it up," she hissed between bared teeth, "I'm dumping the rest of the soup over your heads. Get some brain cells working here, you two. I love you both. Posturing and threatening each other isn't winning any points with me. In fact, it's downright irritating." Rachael snatched her hand back from Rio and caught up the empty soup bowl. "Elijah, you want coffee or not?"

"Are you going to dump it in my lap?"

"I'm not sure yet."

"Then I think I'll pass until you get over your little . . ." he broke off abruptly as Rio frantically signaled him to silence.

Rachael turned to glare at her brother. "I know you weren't going to accuse me of being moody—or temperamental. You deserve an entire pot of coffee in your lap. You should have talked to me. I'm a grown woman, not a child to be protected. I know exactly what Armando's capable of and I knew you had no choice but to try to get rid of him if either of us was going to have a chance at a normal life." She swung around to include Rio in her displeasure. "If you ever get a thick-headed notion to go all silent and macho on me, please just get over it fast. I'm likely to smack you with another stick if you do."

Elijah's eyebrow shot up. "She smacked you with a stick?"

"Gave me a scar," Rio said proudly and swept back his black hair to reveal the jagged white line. "Right on the temple too. She nearly took my head off."

"She knows what she's doing," Elijah confirmed. "And she hits like a man, but she can't cook very well."

"I'm a good cook," Rachael said, outraged. "I'm a very good cook. I can't help it if you don't like anything other than rice and beans. And no spices."

"There's such a thing as too much spice," Elijah said.

Rio grinned wickedly at Rachael. "Oh, I don't know, Elijah, you might be missing out. Live a little."

Rachael groaned and rinsed the dishes, but she was smiling again. The man had a sinful mouth and he had a way of putting fantasies in her head at the most inopportune times.

Rio leaned back in his chair. "The elder had a good idea. If you went to the village and asked for asylum, they'd have to give it to you. You'd be placed under the protection of our lair. It just gives us more people to count on our side."

"What exactly do you do aside from piss off the local bandits?" Elijah asked.

Rio's grin widened. "You've been talking to Tomas and his men, haven't you? Basically that's exactly what I do. That's my job."

"You do that to everyone without much effort," Rachael pointed out.

Franz leapt down from the mantel and scooted under Rio's feet, peering out at Elijah curiously. Rio stretched his legs further to accommodate the small leopard. "I lay up on a knoll, or in a tree, or wherever I can find and guard my team as they go in to bring out kidnap victims, or pay ransom. I do whatever it takes to keep them safe. Once they're out, I lay a false trail and lead the bandits away from the team and into the forest."

"I've heard the bandits have bolt-holes."

"There are mazes of tunnels in the cane fields, just about every field. You don't want to drop into one of them and try to pursue, not if you value your life. We've had to go in a couple of times when the bandits used the tunnels to hide their prisoners. We blew up the tunnels in order to discourage them from using them for that purpose. It's too dangerous to us, although we'll go in if we have to."

"So we don't want Armando to fall in with the bandits and get the idea of using the tunnels."

"If your uncle finds out she's playing house in the forest with some local yokel, don't you think he'd come with guns blazing? Especially if the information was given out to you, instead of him, for the million-dollar reward. We have to locate Armando's mole and let him overhear Rachael's been found. He'll immediately contact your uncle and Armando will come very quickly to get here before you."

"He'll send his killer after her."

Rio shrugged. "Of course he will. He'll want to confirm her presence and he'll want me out of the way. They'll expect an easy kill."

"He'll hunt you, Rio. Leopards make frightening enemies. They never turn aside and they're as cunning as hell. I ought to know."

Rio grinned at Elijah, but it was a particularly lethal smirk. "I'm very aware of what a leopard can do."

Rachael curled up in Rio's lap. Fitting herself to his body seemed perfectly natural. The night had taken on a surreal feel, a dreamlike quality. She couldn't believe Elijah was sprawled in a chair only feet away from Rio, looking relaxed and at home. How had she ever doubted him? His eyes didn't look ice-cold and merciless, although she knew they could. Right now he looked like her big brother, just lying around the house talking. She had forgotten that image of him. Elijah at rest. Elijah relaxed. Elijah with a faint smile on his face.

She buried her face against Rio's chest, confident he wouldn't say a word when he felt her hot tears against his skin. He would understand the enormity of the gift she'd been given this one night. Rio wrapped his arms around her tightly, holding her close to him, protectively, just as she knew he would. He nuzzled the top of her head with his chin, one hand tunneling in her thick mass of hair, just holding her close.

"This is my territory, Elijah. My realm. Those who enter it are subject to the laws of my people and my laws. Man or beast, it matters little. Armando may be a big deal in South America and in Florida, but he's no one here."

Elijah nodded his head. "I've been slowly cashing out

our assets and putting the money where Armando can't touch it. He doesn't know, of course. But I'm hoping to get Rachael and me free of our estate and go back to my homeland. Unfortunately, there are problems."

"You could come here, Elijah," Rachael offered. Her voice was muffled against Rio's chest and he couldn't see her face. "The elders would accept you, Delgrotto already said as much. No one knows you here. You could have a new start."

"I don't even know how anymore, Rachael." Elijah looked at his sister through long lashes. His eyes were flat and cold. "If I can't talk to you, my own sister, how do you think I could ever learn to live with others again? Thank you for the offer, but if we manage to remove the threat of Armando, the last thing I intend to do is taint your life."

Rachael stirred as if to protest, but Rio's arm tightened in warning. "Let's just take one thing at a time. Armando is first. Let's find his mole and put out the word."

"He'll know I'm here."

"All to the good. He'll want to kill Rachael right under your nose. You've already established a research camp as your cover so you look as though you're trying to appear legitimate to him while you search for her. Just search in the wrong areas so he'll be convinced you're combing the region for Rachael."

"So I'm the dope miles away when he tries to hit Rachael. I don't think so. If that man sets foot in this country, I'm not leaving Rachael's side."

Rachael sighed heavily. "Do you see where I get words like 'imbecile' and 'idiot' in my vocabulary? Elijah, just this once, please, for me, listen to what Rio has to say."

"What do you know of this man, Rachael? You're betting your life on him."

"I know that. And if you're insisting on staying, maybe both of our lives, and that ought to tell you all you need to know. I left home rather than put you in a position of having to . . ." She trailed off. Only Rio knew she jammed her

fist in her mouth to choke back the words before they could
be said.

Elijah sat up straight. "I never wanted you dead. Never,
Rachael. It was always the two of us. Hell, without you,
what did I have to fight for? Why would I bother? I would
have disappeared into the jungle and he would never have
tracked me. But I didn't think you could."

"Because I couldn't shift?" She turned her head to look
at her brother. "I didn't even know we were capable of
shifting. How did you know?"

"It just happened. When I was young, a little boy. Mom
told me not to say anything. We always spoke of it in
whispers."

Rio brought up his hand to the nape of Rachael's neck
in a slow massage. "Of course. She was still trying to hide
it from her new husband. He didn't know until later. And
then the elders of your mother's lair found out an outsider
knew. It had to have happened that way."

"Something went wrong. Mom and Dad were very nervous until we reached Florida. They were nervous for a
couple of years. Mom wouldn't allow me to shift and said
I wasn't to tell anyone." Elijah sighed. "They were trying
to protect us from our own kind. They should have been
looking toward Armando."

"He knew, though." Rio said. "He used to take you
places and let you run."

"If I had just told Mom right away—but I didn't. Just
once, if I had said something to her, they might still be
alive." Elijah fell silent, listening to the soothing rain.
"And then when I did tell her, I should have kept my
mouth shut. Armando already had made his plans and he
killed them."

"Their deaths had nothing to do with what you didn't or
did tell our parents, Elijah," Rachael denied. "You can't
take on the responsibility. You did everything you could to
keep us alive."

"I didn't kill Armando, Rachael."

"Killing him might set the two of you free, Elijah," Rio said, "but it won't bring anyone back, and it won't make you feel any better."

"I'll settle for making certain Rachael is safe. Even if we could find a way to put him in jail, he'd send someone after her and he'd never stop until she was dead. It doesn't matter if I went against the laws of our people and got a conviction, he'd find a way to kill her. I know him. Armando is vindictive and he hates me. In his mind, I betrayed him. He offered to make me his son. I was the heir to his empire and I went along with it for years. I had to make him believe it."

Elijah looked into Rio's eyes with the focused stare of his kind. "You probably can't understand that kind of twisted hatred, but he wants to kill Rachael more than he wants anything else. I chose her over him. That's the way he looks at it. She held some kind of power over me, otherwise, I would have become his son."

"But you made your move too soon and you couldn't get him. Why?" Rio returned the focused stare, every bit as unblinking and merciless.

"He came to me one night and told me it was time to clean house. He wanted Rachael dead. He said he knew I couldn't do it, so he wasn't asking me to kill her, he didn't need a sign of loyalty. He told me he was going to do it himself, that he wouldn't take the chance that any of the men would dishonor her first." Elijah drummed his fingers on the arm of the chair. "That's exactly how he put it to me. He was casually talking about killing my sister, but not to worry, none of the men would be allowed to rape her first."

"So you had to make your move."

"I had my men in place. I had a loyal following. I got Rachael to a safe house and made my move. Unfortunately, he was still too strong. He knows the way to defeat me is to get to her. She's everything I care about. You know that, don't you, Rachael? I swear I don't know what I said to you when I pulled you out of that car, but Tony was taking you to Armando, and you would have been sent back to me in pieces."

"It's all right," she said softly. "Elijah, I'm sorry I ever doubted you. Whatever was said is forgotten. Please forgive me for the terrible things I was thinking."

"Who could blame you, Rachael? We've lived with betrayal for so long it's become a way of life for the both of us." Elijah shifted in his chair. "So tell me what you want me to do, Rio. Let's see if we can manage to hash out a plan to remove the threat to Rachael."

Rio rocked Rachael gently, a soothing, comforting gesture he was barely aware of making. Her body trembled in his arms. She was overwhelmed by everything but hung on to her calm demeanor because she was Rachael and that's what she did. She had a way of moving him, turning him inside out over the simplest things. He felt the love she had for her brother and the fear for him all mixed together.

"Have Tama take you downriver, far downriver, as many miles as possible. We'll start the rumor that Rachael's shoe was found. Then let's get an informant on the river to tell a government official in front of Armando's mole that Rachael is living in the forest. Once the mole gets the information to your uncle, he'll send his leopard out to confirm first."

"Or kill her."

"Or kill her," Rio agreed. "That will be the most critical time. You'll have to put your trust in me and stay a long way away. I'll try to keep you informed, but this won't work if he even thinks you're anywhere near her. He'll sense a trap. You'll have to be downriver and on the lookout for a hit on you."

Rachael stirred restlessly, shooting an apprehensive look at her brother. "What kind of protection did you bring with you?"

"I have some of my best men. In the forest, it won't be easy to surprise me, not even for his leopard assassin.

Rachael, don't worry about me. I can take care of myself,"
Elijah reassured.

"Elijah's right, *sestrilla,*" Rio murmured softly, adding
his own reassurance. "I suspect your uncle would want him
alive, would want him to suffer with the knowledge of your
death before anything else. If we're wrong and he sends
the leopard to kill Elijah, you have to have faith in your
brother's abilities. He's stayed alive and kept you alive all
these years. He won't be taken easily. And Tama will be
with him. There isn't a better guide, or a more responsible
one, unless it's Kim."

Rachael bit at her knuckles. "I don't like this, I don't
like us separated when he comes after us."

"He won't come if he knows you're with Elijah," Rio
said patiently. "He's afraid of Elijah. Your brother is probably the only man he is afraid of. That's why he has to
destroy him before he kills him. And the only means he has
of destroying him is through you."

"I know of his leopard assassin, Rachael," Elijah added.
"I can take him if he comes at me. I can take him in either
form, human or animal." There was complete confidence
in his voice.

Rachael nodded and managed a faint smile, but Rio
could feel her body trembling. He pulled her closer, trying
to protect her from her brother's all-seeing eyes. "Once
Armando has entered the country, Kim Pang, Tama's
brother, will get word to Tama. You can head this way the
moment Armando has entered our forest. I'll have a few of
my men standing by with radios to let us know where he is.
He can't take animal form, but he'll come in with hunters,
hoping to protect himself. What do you think, Elijah?"

"I think I'm going to trust you with my sister's life."
Elijah stood up, stretched, a completely feline motion. His
eyes were hard and cold and without mercy. "Don't let me
down."

"Aren't you going to stay?" Rachael asked, looking
close to tears again.

"I have to be back in camp. You never know if he has eyes or ears planted and I don't want to blow the plan before we have a chance to see if it will even work." Elijah loomed over them, tall and dangerous and very alone. "You take care of her, Rio." He brushed Rachael's head with a gentle kiss, touched her shoulder and went out into the night.

Rachael tried to pull away from Rio to go after her brother. "Let him go. This is hard for him, to let loose of you after all these years. He needs to be alone. People like us need space, Rachael. He has to find his own way. He's spent a lifetime concentrating on keeping the both of you alive. He'll need to adjust in order to find another reason to go on. The forest is where he'll find it. He doesn't know that yet, but it will call to him."

She ran her hands over his body, inspecting him for damage after his long run. "You need rest, Rio. At least come to bed with me."

It sounded good to him. He wanted to lie down beside her, hold her in his arms and feel her warmth after the terror of thinking someone was attacking her. He lay for a long time listening to the wind moaning in the trees. Listening to the songs of the rain through the canopy. Listening to the rhythm of her breathing. Holding her soft body next to his, her hair crushed in his hands, his body wrapped protectively around hers. He remembered thinking happiness was an illusion, that life was simply to live until it was over, giving service to his people. Happiness was this woman in his arms. He allowed himself to drift off with the scent of her filling his lungs and the feel of her imprinted into his flesh and bones.

19

RACHAEL gripped the railing and leaned over to peer at the forest floor below. "I think I'm going stir crazy." She turned around to smile at Rio, half sitting on the banister. "Is that possible out here in this huge forest? And don't say I'm in one of my little moods either!"

"Sure it is. Waiting is always the most difficult part. We know the mole passed the word, so it won't be much longer. I received word that Armando and a huge party arrived and were making their way up the river. We've got people in place watching him. He brought four big-name game hunters with him, which did cause a bit of a problem as the officials don't encourage that sort of thing."

Ruchael shivered. "Knowing that man is walking in the same forest is frightening. Armando is truly evil, Rio. It won't take him long to send out his men."

"I know, but it's what we've been waiting for. This is probably our last chance for a little fun. They aren't in our area yet."

"I hate that Elijah is so close and I can't go see him. I worry about him. I've always been afraid for him."

Rio reached out to take her hand, holding her open palm over his heart. "At least this has given us some time for your leg to heal properly."

She turned her calf this way and that, frowning. "Properly? Is that what you call it? At least I have a leg. And Fritz is better too. He went out this morning around dawn to hunt food with Franz. I thought that was such a good sign."

Rio tugged on her hand until her body was tight against his. "We don't have to stay here if you'd rather go play," he invited softly.

Rachael looked up at him, his weathered, beloved face. She knew every inch of that face, by touch, by vision. There was a playful gleam in his eyes, one rarely seen by anyone other than Rachael. She loved that boyish, mischievous side of him that crept out at unexpected times. "Is it safe?"

"At the moment. I didn't expect Armando to come himself so soon, but it doesn't really change anything. I'm expecting your uncle's assassin to come checking any day now, but the forest animals will alert us. We don't have to stay here in this house if you want to stretch your legs and play a bit. I have one or two beautiful spots I haven't had a chance to show you." His fingers crushed strands of her hair, rubbed them together. "We've been putting all our energy toward rehearsals for the arrival of your uncle and we haven't managed to take a much-needed break. The temporary hut is built, we've moved you in, we have people up and down the river and in the forest keeping an eye on them. I think we can take a small break."

Rio hadn't chanced a single late night run since her brother had shown up. He didn't want to leave her alone and he felt it was better to give her leg a chance to fully heal. The lure of the forest was on him, calling continually.

Rachael's smile widened and she peeled off the shirt she was wearing, flinging it aside without hesitation. It left her standing in her silky thong and nothing else. Rio inhaled sharply, drawing the scent of her into his lungs.

Breathing Rachael in was becoming a habit. "Maybe we should just stay here," he murmured softly. Her breasts were beautiful, full and ripe and so perfect he had to touch them. His fingers whispered over her skin, tugged at her nipples just to see them peak for him.

"Maybe we shouldn't. I want to go run. You can wait here for me though." Rachael shimmied out of her thong, enjoying the way he watched her. She had never thought about being a sexual being until she was around Rio. He made her so aware of her own body, of his body. Of what they could have together. She moved enticingly, wholly feminine, catching at a branch above her head. "You can be thinking about me while I'm gone," she teased.

"You aren't going anywhere without me," he declared, hastily shedding clothes. She was already shifting, a sleek female leopard with rounded curves and a feline body built for speed and endurance. She leapt to a neighboring branch and hurried along the slanting limb to the next overlapping one.

Rio didn't take time to fold his clothes neatly. The wildness was already upon him, starting in the pit of his stomach, an uncontrollable longing for freedom. His muscles contorted and he shifted in the air, making a flying dive for the branches below him that intersected with the ones she was on.

Rachael leapt from branch to branch, fully aware that Rio was giving chase. If a leopard could have laughed aloud, she would have. She couldn't believe the turn her life had taken. She'd made one small mistake, thinking his house was a hut travelers used, and it had been the best mistake she'd ever made.

Happiness burst through her, shining bright and perfect. She made it to the forest floor and took off, leaping over fallen tree trunks and larger shrubs. Her claws dug into the vegetation to give her extra spring. Rio was coming at her fast, an enormous male with every intention of running her down.

Rachael began to play at dodging him, winding through the trees, staying on the course he obviously wanted her to take. When she went in the wrong direction, he loomed in front of her, too large to go around and too big to confront. She didn't care, the freedom of playing was wonderful. The forest was beautiful, every detail vivid and bright. She played with a toad who didn't seem too appreciative of the company and then raced ahead when Rio nosed at the little creature.

She didn't see the embankment until too late, trying to put the brakes on as she tumbled and landed in the wide blue pool. It was a natural small fall, a basin formed of solid rock. The waterfall was gentle, a long spray of white froth that fell into the clear water. Ferns sprouted everywhere, long and lacy and tall and bushy. Rachael came up for air, shifting as she did so, laughing so hard she went under twice.

Rio caught her around the waist with one strong arm, lifting her to her feet near the edge of the pool. "You reckless, crazy woman. You nearly gave me a heart attack." His voice purred rather than scolded, a wash of velvet over her skin.

Rio touched her face gently, his fingertips tracing the line of her cheek, her jaw, his touch as light as the brush of the wings of the bright butterflies that swarmed over the trees. Yet the impact was a bolt of lightning streaking through her body. His hands settled on the sides of her face, framing her with tenderness while he stared into her eyes.

There was such an intensity of love there, deep in the depths of his vivid green gaze. Desire and hunger burned in the background, but love shone like a bright light consuming her. He lowered his head slowly toward hers. That sensual movement caused her deepest core to react, an exquisite tightening of every muscle, a heat spreading through her to pool into a piercing ache at the junction of her legs.

His body bent over hers, yet his skin didn't quite touch her, a breath of air between them, a breeze fanning the heat that made up their skin. Water slapped at their bodies, frothing from the beat of the falls as millions of droplets entered the pool to swarm around them, touching skin like fingers, stroking a river of sensation over them.

His lips just brushed hers. Gently. Tenderly. The merest touch, yet flames flickered and danced. Hot need rushed through her and spread to every vein, every cell. Rachael leaned closer, lifting her mouth to his. The tips of her breasts caressed his chest lightly, spread flames across skin, a flash point neither expected. Rachael sighed against his mouth, a soft submissive sound, as she opened her mouth to his. Took him inside her. Heat and fire and silk. Something moved inside of her. Recognized him. She felt her other self—rising. Not a takeover, rather a joining.

Rio deepened the kiss, cupping her face in his hands, sliding his fingers around to cradle the back of her head as he kissed her, and his other self rose up to merge with her. Sensation increased, every touch, every taste. The mist from the waterfall on their skin was a tongue touching, licking along their bodies.

Rachael gasped as sensual pleasure infused her, took her over, robbing her of breath, of thought. She leaned into him, rubbed her skin against his skin, wanting the tactile contact. When he lifted his head to take a breath, she lapped at the mist on his chest, her tongue following tiny beads down his belly. His hands moved over her, finding every spot that could make her cry out with passion, that would inflame her more.

Rachael melted into him, skin to skin, rubbing and caressing and needing to touch him, every square inch of him. There was never enough kissing, never enough tasting, and there would never be enough time to explore him the way she wanted before her body made urgent demands.

"You're purring," he murmured softly. "I love the way you purr when I touch you." His mouth wandered down her throat, lingered in the inviting hollow there, drifted lower to taste the droplets of water running over her. His hands went lower, shaped her hips, smoothed over her buttocks to lift her off her feet.

Rachael locked her legs around him. "Do I purr? I didn't know that. I can't help myself." Her teeth nibbled over his shoulder, up his neck to the point of his chin. Her breath was warm and inviting like the soft satin of her skin. "You'd make anyone purr, Rio. Do you feel the leopard in me merging with the leopard in you? How can that happen? How can we experience what they feel when we're really one with them?"

"You're letting me all the way into your mind. All the way into your heart and body. That includes the leopard in you, and my leopard is eager for yours. We're a mated pair, Rachael. Not all of us have that in a single lifetime. I suspect we've been a mated pair in more than one lifetime. You feel so familiar to me." He lowered her body over his and closed his eyes as the incredible sensual pleasure engulfed him.

His blood ran hot through his body, burst through his veins like a wildfire out of control, raced to his head to explode in a rush of heat and flame. She was tight and hot, a velvet sheath gripping his body, surrounding him with so much pleasure it rode the edge of pain. He felt everything for her at once, wild lust, a greedy need, overwhelming love and tenderness. He wanted to take his time, surging in and out of her, rocking her while the water lapped at their bodies, but the pleasure was too intense, even with his slow thrusting. They were too hot, the heat arcing between them and rising fast no matter how hard he tried to slow them down. Her nails dug into his skin. Her head was thrown back, the line of her throat exposed.

Deep inside where it counted, they moved together, blended and merged, becoming one being in one skin. Rachael's soft cry took the last of his control. Her body tightened around his, gripped and clung and made demands.

He lifted his face to the sky, soaring there, taking her with him while the water splashed around their bodies.

"You're swearing," Rachael whispered. There was laughter in her voice. She kissed his shoulder, moved her hips in the rhythm of his, allowing the little aftershocks to ride over both of them.

"You do that to me, Rachael. I think you're going to give me a heart attack. I could make love to you a hundred times a day." He lowered her gently until she was standing waist deep in water, leaning into his body, his arms enfolding her close. "I'm losing my staying power, have you noticed?"

Her soft laughter tightened every cell in his body, washed over him like clean rain. "I thought that was me."

A crash in the bushes near the embankment alerted them that they weren't alone. Rio whirled to face the danger, putting his body between Rachael and the wildly thrashing shrubbery. Two small cats tumbled out into the open, Fritz sliding down the muddy bank and landing in the water almost at their feet. Rachael's hand, on the small of Rio's back, felt the tension drain out of him.

Fritz howled as he pulled himself out of the water, spitting and hissing at Franz. The other male cat clearly laughed, waiting beneath the ferns until Fritz shook off the wet fur. Franz pounced a second time, leaping on his brother and rolling him back down the embankment. They tumbled together in a wild frenzy of fur and claws, making more noises than Rachael had ever heard a cat make.

She burst out laughing and hugged Rio around his narrow waist. "They're like a couple of kids."

He shoved his hand through his mass of silky black hair. "I know." He sounded totally exasperated. "I can't do a thing with them."

That made her laugh all the more. "You have no idea how incredibly sexy I find you." She kissed his chin. "I'm going to swim while I still have the chance. The rain is going to start up again any minute."

"It is raining."

"That's just mist. Look at the rainbow!" She pointed overhead and dove beneath the surface, a flash of bare skin and black silky hair.

He shook his head as he watched her swim away, then turned to look at the two clouded leopards pouncing on one another like leapfrogs. There was no stopping the young cats when they wanted to play rough. He waded through the water to the flat rock where he often lay to soak up the sun. It was always humid and hot, but the spray of water from the fall misted over him, keeping him cool. His gaze strayed to Rachael as she swam in the pool, her bare skin pale in the clear blue of the water.

Rachael rose up under the waterfall, lifting her head to allow the water to cascade over her face. She pushed back the heavy fall of her hair and smiled with the sheer joy of being alive. The water was an amazing shade of blue, the white mist hovering above in the canopy like fluffy clouds. Twilight was falling, a soft gray sky that brought out the bats, wheeling and dipping as they darted for insects over the water. She glanced across the small pool toward Rio. He was stretched out full-length on a large gray slab of rock, his vivid green gaze fixed on her intently.

"I love this place, Rio. Do you come here often?"

"When I want a good long soak and a lazy swim." He didn't lift his head, just watched her standing waist deep in the water looking like a tempting water nymph. "There aren't any leeches in the water here, so it's safe to swim."

Rachael smiled at Rio and began wading toward him. Birds lifted up into the air from the branches of several trees around them, wings fluttering strongly, filling the air with a humming noise. She froze in midstride, looking up toward the airborne flock. Her heart began to pound. She looked across the water at Rio. He was no longer lying lazily but crouched on the rock, all senses alert. He signaled to her without looking at her, moving his hand in a semicircle.

Rachael glanced at the two small clouded leopards

lying partially hidden in the overgrown fern. Sleepy from their rough-and-tumble play, the two had been drowsing in the shelter of the fronds; now they were as alert as Rio, mouths open wide, ears up, scenting the air. She forced her body to move, heading in the direction Rio signaled. He wanted her out of the water and into deeper cover immediately. The forest sentinels were on the alert. A hunter had moved into their realm.

Rio's arm swept around her. "It's all right. We knew this was coming. It's important for him to spot you." He brushed a kiss across her temple. "Just not until you get clothes on. We left a fairly clear trail leading to the small hut Tama and Kim and I put up for you. You'll look like a native woman trying to make it on your own."

Rachael leaned into him for comfort. Rio's arm tightened. "We don't have to do it this way, *sestrilla*. If you're afraid, we can find another way to let him see you."

She shook her head decisively. "No. I want to be the bait. Armando has held my life over Elijah for so long, it feels good to be able to do something positive. I don't care if it is acting like a ninny in a native hut to put on a show for Armando's spy. It makes me feel empowered against that horrible monster. He destroyed Elijah, and he used me to do it."

He nuzzled her ear, all the while walking her out of the water and into the shelter of the trees. "We shift here, Rachael. Armando's spy can't see you as a leopard. We have to give him a wide berth and get you back to the hut. We don't want him coming across your scent as a leopard and identifying you as a shifter. Let him see you from a distance in human form. I'll be covering you. If he makes a wrong move, I'll kill him."

She winced over his bluntness. That was so like Rio. "You're certain he's alone, it's just the spy and not my uncle?"

"Listen to the animals. It's the leopard, and he's heading toward the hut."

She let her breath out. "What about Fritz and Franz? You'll have to make certain they stay away. I don't want them to get hurt. You know they'll follow you wherever you go."

"Don't worry, we've hunted many times together. This will work, Rachael. Your uncle has too big an ego to just let his leopard handle it. If he thinks he can kill you under Elijah's nose, that's what he'll choose to do."

"Don't worry about me. I'll admit to being afraid, but in a positive way. I finally feel useful to Elijah." She turned her face into his shoulder and rubbed affectionately in the way of the big cats. "I'll be fine."

"He may try to grab you to bring you to your uncle, but I doubt it. I'm counting on this being a scouting trip, just to confirm your presence. Be alert anyway, Rachael, just in case I'm wrong."

He stepped up onto the embankment and pulled her up with him so they were nearly hidden in the thick brush. He was already shifting, his fur brushing her bare skin as he did so. That always amazed her, the miracle of change. It seemed incredible that she could plunge her hands into the fur of a leopard, even more incredible that she could stroke its back and rub its ears. In spite of the very real danger from her uncle, Rachael smiled happily as she allowed the change to take hold of her.

The trip through the forest was much longer, slinking carefully along the path leading away from their home. A small hut had been erected in a particularly thick grove of trees. The trunks were thinner and the trees closer together. Rio wanted to make certain a marksman would have a difficult time shooting through the trees. If Armando's hit man wanted to kill Rachael, he would have to do it up close and personal. He would have to use his leopard form to attack her.

Rachael stayed close to Rio as they moved through the trees, making certain to show the gibbons and birds they weren't hunting. They didn't want the intruder alerted to their presence as they wound their way through the trees and brush to the three-sided hut. The fourth side was open and sheltered by the overhead canopy and thatched roof. It was the type of travelers' hut often used by the tribesmen as they moved from place to place.

Rachael's clothes were already stashed in the hut and she hastily shifted to pull them on. Rio remained in his leopard form, his unblinking, watchful gaze fixed on her as she tugged on her jeans and pulled on a shirt. She smiled at him, leaned down and brushed a kiss on top of the leopard's head. "Be safe, Rio. Keep Elijah safe for me." Her heart was pounding, she knew her leopard could hear it, could smell her fear, just as she could taste it in her mouth. When the big cat rubbed up against her leg she wrapped her arm around the thick neck. "Don't underestimate him. Armando Lospostos is a monster. You can't forget that, not even for a moment."

Rio wanted to shift, just for a moment and hold her in his arms to comfort and reassure her, but he didn't dare. The forest had come alive with news. Her uncle had done the unexpected, arriving with his large contingent of men along with his leopard spy. Armando was taking no chances of missing his opportunity. He sent the spy from his hunting camp already being established a few miles upriver. Rio hoped Elijah was listening to the chatter of the creatures as well as their human allies as they carried the news up and down the river and through the trees.

Rio rubbed against Rachael's body in a long caress one last time before leaping into the low-hanging branches of a tree near the open side of the hut. She looked alone and vulnerable. It was just the way she was supposed to look, but damn it all, it still twisted at his heart. He disappeared into the thick foliage, knowing she couldn't see him, hoping she would feel him close. If the spy leopard made a move against her instead of just confirming her presence, Rio had no doubt he would have to make a kill.

It took the leopard a day and night of searching to find

Rachael's little hut. She lay alone in the bed, her heart pounding, breathing deep, fighting off the wild side of her nature, trying to be a lamb to lure in the monster that had ruined their lives. She ate alone, did endless, useless chores, found busywork. She went so far as to begin a semblance of a garden, replanting herbs closer to the hut. All the while she felt Rio close to her. She never saw him, but she knew he was there and it warmed her. She was unafraid for her own safety. She trusted Rio, knew his capabilities.

Rachael was in the small garden when she heard the first whisper of unease among the birds in the canopy above her home. The flutter of wings as some took flight. The trilling of alarm as sentinels sounded a warning. She pretended not to hear, drawing on the skills she'd acquired over the years to appear calm and relaxed in the face of every crisis. The leopard spy was stalking her. The monkeys reported his movements as he neared her little hut. The animal was casting for signs of Elijah, of a trap for Armando. All he was going to find was Rachael attempting to make a home in a travelers' hut.

She stood up and smelled him. The wild, feral scent of the intruder creeping up on her. She felt the impact of his gaze as he watched her, excitement taking him. The knowledge that he could take her life, that she was alone, an easy target for a predator such as a leopard. The leopard was certain she didn't have the gift. Armando had assured him she was not a shifter, tied to the human form and not worthy of life. Although she couldn't see him, she could almost feel how his body shook with eagerness for the kill. The hair on the back of her neck stood up. Goose bumps rose on her skin. A chill slid down her spine.

Rachael hummed softly to herself, deliberately walked to the nearest tree trunk laden with perfumed orchids and cut several to place on the wooden slab that served as her table. She stayed outdoors within striking distance, knowing Rio had his rifle trained on the leopard at all times. She went inside her little hut and casually arranged the flowers. Her legs were beginning to turn to rubber so she sat on one of the stumps and stared out into the beauty of the forest, attempting to look at ease with her surroundings.

To her astonishment Tama and Kim arrived with four of their tribesmen, talking and gesturing as they asked for water. Kim winked at her. It was the only way to insure the spy leopard didn't try to grab her and carry her back to Armando's camp. He could give Armando reassurance Rachael was alone and Elijah was nowhere near her, but they would have to return to the hut a second time in order to capture her. Even so, she felt the leopard's presence for most of the night. The tribesmen settled down around her, talking long into the night, giving her the courtesy of the hut but successfully preventing the spy from making a move against her. It seemed forever before the feeling of danger passed. She remained still, waiting, wanting to curl up in a little ball and cry with relief.

Rio arrived at dawn, dragging her into his arms, raining kisses over her face. Elijah was with him, real and solid, hugging her hard, telling her how brave she was.

"Did it work? Did he go back to Armando and tell him I was living here alone and you didn't know about it?" Rachael's voice was muffled against Rio's shirt. She inhaled him, touched him, needing to feel his enormous strength when she felt so fragile.

"It worked, Rachael," Elijah assured. "He went back to Armando like the good little spy and reported everything he saw."

"I felt how eager he was to kill me," she said. "I don't know what he would have done if Kim and Tama hadn't shown up."

"I did too," Rio acknowledged. "He was in my sights the entire time. He never had a chance, *sestrilla*."

"Now what do we do?" Rachael asked.

"Tama and Kim are going to escort you to their village. You'll be safe with them. Armando will send his men back here to the hut and they'll find it empty. They'll stake it out thinking you'll come back. In the meantime, we have to get rid of his big-game hunters. It looks as if Armando instructed them to bag him a leopard. He knows he can't take Elijah at his camp with all the guards there, but he believes Elijah is shifting at night and hunting for signs of you."

Elijah grinned at her. His gaze remained flat and cold. "It's like him to bring in professional hunters. He couldn't very well tell them I'm a shifter. That would take away one of his big secrets."

"The hunters staked out a goat hoping to draw in a leopard. There aren't supposed to be any big leopards in these parts, only the clouded leopard and the smaller cats. We don't want to take the chance on any other leopard prowling around getting killed. We sent out the word, but we can't be too careful."

"Four big-game hunters?" Rachael echoed. "You mean men who hunt big cats for a living? That's like Armando. I should have guessed he'd do that."

Elijah touched her shoulder gently. "I knew he would. We're prepared for it. You'll be safe with Tama and Kim."

"Don't you think the leopard spy will come back to watch me? I should be here, where he can give his little daily reports to Armando."

"He would never be able to resist killing you," Rio said. "You felt him, his need for the kill. We can't risk it again." Rio caught her face between his hands. "I will not risk you. He's dangerous, and I have to help Elijah with the hunters. We can't afford them at our backs. In any case, Armando would send his men here to grab you. You have to go where it's safe."

At once her heart leapt. Rio could do that with a touch, with a look. Rachael forced a smile when she met his gaze. "You know what you're asking of me, don't you? I had to stand by and watch Armando ruin Elijah's life, torture and torment him over me. He used me to hurt my brother. He can't take you both from me. I would never survive it. You both have to come back to me." She didn't look at her brother, but her voice was choked with tears. "Elijah is going to try to sacrifice himself because he thinks there can be no redemption. Rio, you have to find a way to bring him safely back."

Rio brushed her mouth with his. "You promised to marry me, *sestrilla*. My beloved one. We need Elijah to give you to me in a proper ceremony. You can be very sure I'll bring him back."

"Thank you." Rachael went with the tribesmen. She only looked back once, and both Elijah and Rio were watching her until she was out of sight.

The two men looked at one another, stripped hastily, and without a word shifted into their animal forms. It was time to go hunting.

The first night Rio and Elijah took the first hunter. He was lying in the blind, his eye glued to his scope, his finger on the trigger of his rifle. Below him, on the forest floor, a small goat cried out in fear. Rio knew the spy leopard walked close, a lookout for the hunters, but they were already inside the hunter's trap, high in the canopy watching.

The second night the spy leopard was waiting in the trees above their kill. His yellow eyes glittered with menace, with a promise of retaliation. They had made him look bad, a creature who felt superior to those he worked with, and he had failed in his job. He didn't want to fail a second time. It was Elijah who made the second kill right under the spy leopard's nose, slipping down into the blind and dispatching the second hunter where he lay in wait.

The leopard discovered the kill on one of his sweeps of the area and went berserk, roaring with rage, promising retaliation. He raced through the forest in the direction of Rachael's small, deserted hut. Rio was grateful she was long gone. The leopard was in a killing mood and wanted desperately to rip something or someone to shreds. Rio followed at a much more leisurely pace, letting the intruder expend energy. He watched from a distance as the shapeshifter ripped apart the small, makeshift hut. He was so enraged, he tore furniture into small sticks and smashed the little bowl of orchids.

Rio gave him no warning, no room to fight, leaping on him from the roof above, teeth sinking deep and hanging on while the leopard rolled and clawed and raked at him. Rio spent most of his life in the forest, most of his life running through the trees both in human and in animal form. The spy leopard had left his normal life for the city and the promise of power and money. He wasn't nearly as fast or as ruthless. Rio accorded the body the respect of his kind, burning it to a fine ash and scattering the remains before joining Elijah.

The third hunter was taken at dusk on the third day, and this time they waited until the last of the professionals realized what happened and hurried away from the scene of death. Elijah padded after the lone hunter, a grim elation spreading through him. The hunter had finally conceded defeat and was stumbling back to camp, horrified at the loss of his friends. He clutched his gun to him as if that single item could save him from the terrors of the darkened forest. The man winced when he heard the low moan of the clouded leopards. He ran when he heard the grunting cough answering the smaller cousins. He burst into the heavily armed camp, clothes torn, parasites on his body and his friends' blood on his clothes.

Armando reacted in his typical fashion. Aggressive, furious that his plans were thwarted and not in the least listening to the hunter's account of his nightmare hunt. Elijah had witnessed the scene many times in the past and knew his uncle was quite capable of erupting into extreme violence. His men knew it too, looking at one another uneasily as the lone hunter tried to explain his failure. Even in the high humidity, the heat of the forest, Armando wore his usual turtleneck sweater, stretched tight over his chest. It was his trademark, that soft expensive shirt that screamed of money and power. He was sweating, but his ego would never allow him to remove it. The leopard curled its lip in a silent snarl of contempt—of hatred.

"What the hell are you talking about?" Armando snapped, fingering his gun continually as a threat. His face twisted with black anger. "I hired four big-game hunters. What's so damned hard about capturing a leopard? You're being paid enough money not to care whether I want the thing alive or dead. Throw a net on it. Wound it. I don't care how you do it. Tranquilize it. Do I have to think for you? If you fail me after the money I'm paying you, you aren't walking out of this forest alive and I can guarantee that. There are four of you and one of him. It can't be that difficult. So get the hell out of my sight and do your damned job."

The man stepped back, this time careful to keep his rifle in front of him, ready to bring it up if he were forced to defend himself. "You aren't listening to me, sir." He glanced warily at the bodyguards, all armed to the teeth. "There aren't four of us. The leopard killed Bob the first night. He just ignored the goat we staked out and went straight to the blind. We left Bob there to lure him in, all of us up in the trees with scopes. He took out Leonard the second night. Craig went last night. Whatever that thing is, he's a man killer. He's as cunning as hell. He didn't even eat them, it was as if he was playing with us all."

Armando swore as he jumped to his feet. The hunter stepped back, gave way immediately. "I don't like any of this. If Rachael isn't back at that hut tomorrow we get out of here. All of us are going to pay her a little visit." When the hunter started toward his tent, Armando caught his arm and jerked him around. "Not you. You have a job to do. You took the money, go get the leopard. Get out of here."

Elijah crouched in the tree, hidden in the foliage overlooking the camp watching the last of the professional hunters reluctantly leave the safety of the site. He waited with endless patience, knowing the rhythm of the hunting camps. Talk died down when the mosquitoes came. Men slapped at the insects, tempers rising. The rain began, a steady downpour increasing everyone's misery. They were

essentially city men, only the four hunters were professionals and now three of the four were dead. That put a pall
over the campsite. Men disappeared into tents, leaving
only the guards at the perimeters. All of them tried to shelter beneath trees. None paid attention to the branches
above them. Still he waited, patient. Leopards were always
patient. He didn't mind the insects or the rain. This was his
world and they were the intruders. He settled down to wait,
to get the rhythm of the camp and the men in it.

It was important to go in quietly, get the deed done and
get out unseen. The camp was heavily armed. Elijah didn't
want a bloodbath here in the forest. They didn't want an
investigation. This had to be a stealthy, silent assassination.
He crouched there in the bushes not ten feet from one of
the sentries and watched his uncle. The light from the lamp
illuminated the inside of the tent. One side remained open
to give Armando a wide sweep of the area with his gun.
And the gun was never more than an inch from his fingertips. One by one the lamps were turned out so that darkness settled over the camp.

The wind blew. The rain fell. Elijah waited until the
guards began to grow sleepy. The leopard suddenly came
to life. Elijah crept closer, using the freeze-frame, slow
motion stalk of the skilled leopard. His focused gaze never
left Armando moving around in his tent, gun inches from
his fingers. Demon incarnate. Murderer. Every dark deed
Armando had committed against his family raged in Elijah's soul. He slipped passed the first guard. The man
looked right at him twice and never saw the leopard slinking into the camp.

A man emerged from his tent and stumbled to a nearby
tree. He nearly stepped on the leopard, missing the creature by no more than a few inches. Elijah crept forward out
of the man's path, gaining another yard. Armando went to
the entrance and swept the area for the hundredth time,
uneasy with the way the night felt. The rifle was cradled in
his arms, snug against his chest. Elijah didn't take his eyes

off his target, lying hidden in the small shrubbery only a few yards from the tent.

Armando turned his back and the leopard crept forward in silence, moving like fluid over the uneven ground, paws cushioning the heavy body so there was no noise. Only the steady sound of the rain. Elijah paused at the entrance to the tent, careful to stay in the shadow where the light spilling from the lamp couldn't reach him. His gaze settled on his target, his muscles bunched, coiled tight until he was a living spring. He felt the power rush through him, over him.

As if sensing danger, Armando turned back, half lifting the rifle, his eyes searching the night frantically. The leopard hit him hard, driving him backward, teeth sinking into the throat. The powerful jaws crunched down hard in a crushing blow, but the teeth hit metal, not flesh. Elijah tried to power through the protective barrier, bringing up claws to rake at the exposed belly. The same coating of metal covered the soft parts of the body.

Armando had gone over backward, landing hard on the ground, dropping his rifle in the process. The jaws clamped harder, crushing his throat, cutting off all air in spite of his hidden armor. The knife, hidden up his sleeve, sprang into his hand, and he plunged it into the leopard's side repeatedly. The leopard hung on grimly, the yellow-green eyes boring into him. Armando thrashed wildly, but no sound emerged from his laboring throat.

A guard, alerted by the darker shadows, rushed to the opening of the tent, rifle to his shoulder. A second leopard dropped from the tree above, taking him to the ground in a stranglehold. It was done in absolute silence. Rio shook the man one last time to insure he couldn't possibly raise an alarm. He dragged the carcass inside the tent and doused the lamp, plunging the tent into darkness so there would be no shadows to give away the life-and-death struggle between the two combatants.

Rio partially shifted, catching Armando's wrist and

twisting to rid him of the knife. He was already dying, black venomous hatred congealed in his eyes as he stared at the face of his nephew, into the eyes of the leopard that slowly crushed his airway, cutting off precious oxygen.

Elijah lay gripping the throat, his sides heaving and slick with blood. Rio nosed him, pushed at him in an effort to get him up and moving before they were discovered. Rio shifted into his human form. "He's gone, Elijah. He's dead." Just to be certain Rio checked the man's pulse. "You're losing too much blood, come on, let's get out of here. Go for the branches just outside the tent."

Elijah couldn't believe the monster was dead. He stared dumbly at Armando, at the open, glassy eyes and knew he looked on the face of evil. There was pain, but it was distant and far away. He pawed clumsily at the shirt, ripping the material to expose the meshed braided steel plate beneath it.

"Elijah, we don't have much time." Rio caught the large male around the neck and tried to pull the head around, away from the monster lying crushed and beaten. "You're losing too much blood. You aren't going to survive if we don't get out of here now." When the leopard remained standing over Armando's body, Rio changed tactics. "Rachael's waiting, Elijah. She's afraid for us. Let's get home to her."

The leopard lifted his muzzle and looked at Rio with sad eyes. Despair was there. Confusion. A deep, deep sorrow. Rio touched the furred head again. "You're free. Both of you are free. Your life belongs to you now." Rio shifted shape, taking his animal form, leading the way out of the darkened tent. Leading the way back to Rachael. Back to life.

20

THERE was music playing. Rio hadn't heard anything other than tribal music in so long he'd forgotten how beautiful it could be. There was the powerful scent of flowers, orchid blossoms bursting out all over. All over the trees, in the hair of the women. And there were people. There seemed to be people standing everywhere he looked. He'd never been around so many people, not in years.

"You're a bit pale there, brother." Elijah stole up behind him in his silent way, still favoring his right side. It had taken Tama and Kim's father to save his life. He was still recovering from the severe wounds inflicted by Armando. "You aren't going to faint or anything, are you?"

Rio glared at him. "Who the hell are all these people? Where'd they come from? Don't they have homes or something?"

"Rachael said you were going to be a big baby over this," Elijah said. He pulled a twig from a tree and put the end in his mouth, his strong teeth chewing on the green stem.

"Your seven stab wounds aren't going to keep me from kicking your butt if you call me that again."

"Twelve," Elijah corrected. "It's true five weren't that deep, but still . . ."

Rio scowled at him. "A little bit of overkill, don't you think? Letting that son of a bitch stab you twelve times? You could have gotten the same amount of sympathy with just three or four times."

Elijah nodded, straight-faced. "True, but the story isn't as good in the retelling."

"Well, the number's probably going to grow with the retelling anyway so you could have saved yourself a bit of trouble and a hell of a lot of stitches," Rio pointed out.

"I didn't think of that."

"How are your teeth?"

"Still in my head, but they hurt like hell. Don't talk about my teeth." Elijah groaned, "I think they're still loose."

"You wouldn't be such a pretty boy without all those teeth," Rio observed. "It might not be such a loss." He slapped his palm against his leg. "Where the hell is she? I should have had Conner or Joshua stand guard and keep her from running away. Are you sure she's here?" His chest was tight and his lungs screamed for air. He ran his finger around his collar to loosen it.

"She's here. She looks beautiful."

The burning in his lungs lessened, and Rio could breathe again. "Don't look at me like that. I want to do this, it's just that all these people are a little too close."

Elijah grinned at him. "I hate to admit it, but I feel the same way and I'm always surrounded by people, by my crew." He waved his hand toward the surrounding trees, wincing as his body protested. "It's different here. I feel different here."

"This forest has a way of doing that, Elijah, although maybe with Armando finally dead, you're beginning to feel the relief."

"It hasn't begun to sink in yet. At this point I'm telling myself every few minutes I don't have to look over my shoulder. It doesn't seem real. I don't know if it ever will.

I've watched every word I've ever said and made certain I was absolutely alone so he couldn't do to anyone else what he did to Rachael. Frankly, I don't know how to act."

Rio touched the man's shoulder briefly. Elijah wasn't a man to encourage physical contact or sympathy or compassion. "It will come with time."

"I'm sure you're right."

Rio suddenly stiffened, looking past Elijah. Rachael's brother turned to see an elderly man and a young boy of about twelve walking toward them. He recognized the older man. "What's wrong, Rio?" Elijah shifted slightly to put his body between Rio and the newcomers.

"You don't have to do that, Elijah," Rio stepped in front of him. "I appreciate that your protection would extend to me, but I'm perfectly capable of defending myself. Relax, you're at a wedding. All you have to do is give me the bride."

Elijah's shrug was casual, but there was nothing casual about his eyes. Alert. Suspicious. A mixture of cold ice and hot flame. He looked every bit as ruthless and merciless as he was reputed to be. There was a sudden silence in the trees where monkeys had been chattering to one another. Several birds took flight.

Rio nudged him. "Give it a rest, Elijah, you're going to scare the guests."

"I thought you wanted less people around," Elijah murmured, but managed a small nod when the elderly man and young boy reached them.

"Elder Delgrotto, this is a surprise," Rio greeted. "You've met Elijah."

"Not formally." Peter Delgrotto bowed slightly. "This is my grandson, Paul." The older man dropped his hand on the boy's head. "He is much better thanks to you, Rio. I've come to perform the ceremony, of course. I spoke with Shaman Pang and explained it would be better if one of the high council performed the binding as it is customary in our lair."

Rio just stood there, staring blankly. "I thought you had resigned, Elder."

"It seems my resignation was not accepted."

"And the council knows you've offered to marry us? To perform the ceremony outside the circle of the lair?" Rio was shocked and it showed.

"I must perform the ceremony," Delgrotto said. "Your Rachael is one of us, and your successful mating is essential for the good of the lair. Look around you, Rio. Every member of your unit is here, with the exception of Drake, and he would be here if he could. Those with families brought them. Others have come to support you. Nearly half of the lair is here. That should tell you something."

Rio wasn't certain what the attendance record was supposed to tell him, but he wasn't going to rain on the elder's parade. He knew what it must have cost Delgrotto to go up against the council. There was always a penalty of some kind. He didn't want to throw the old man's gesture of peace back in his face. "It's an honor to have you, Elder. Tell me how Drake is doing." Rio knew Drake would have moved heaven and earth to stand up for him, but he was locked away in a hospital with one of their surgeons.

Delgrotto looked grim. "Our kind heal fast under most circumstances, but the leg was shattered, the bone in fragments. They operated of course and used steel pins and bolts to hold it all together. You know what that means to him."

Rio turned away, swore under his breath. "Is that what he wanted? Was that his choice? He could have had it removed."

Delgrotto shook his head. "Drake's a strong man. He'll find a way to get past this. Who is standing for you in his place?"

"Joshua. I'll go see Drake as soon as possible."

"That would be wise. Is Maggie with Rachael? I see that Brandt is here."

"Yes, Maggie offered to help her get ready. Maggie's the first female shifter Rachael's had the opportunity to meet, so I thought it would be good for her to make a friend on our wedding day."

"It was a good idea," Delgrotto agreed. "Everyone is assembling, Rio, you should take your place in the circle of the lair."

Elijah had slipped away to go to his sister. Rio looked around him at the large gathering of tribesmen. Tama and Kim's people. Scattered among them were his own people, drawing closer, members of his lair. He had to look away. He hadn't known they would come. He had never imagined they would share this day with him. His team would be there, men who stood with him to guard the forest and do the things needed to protect one another, but not so many of the others. He didn't know what to think or feel.

A murmur went through the circle and they opened a path. His breath stopped in his lungs. His heart ceased to beat. He could only stare at her. Rachael walking toward him on Elijah's arm. Rio's world narrowed. Everyone disappeared. There was only Rachael coming to him. She wore some lacy dress that alternately clung and flowed as if alive, enhancing every feminine curve. Her hair spilled around her face and down to her shoulders in a cascade of black silk. A crown of flowers circled her head. She looked a vision out of a fairy tale. Not for him. Never for him. For a moment his vision blurred. All for him.

She lifted her head and her gaze met his. Struck him hard. Pierced his skin and went straight to his heart. He knew they belonged, knew it with every cell in his body. Rachael could make him so angry he wanted to break off branches and throw them like the apes. Rachael could make him laugh over anything. Rachael could make his body come alive with just a look or a touch. Rachael could make him feel like a poet or a warrior, and she could steal the breath from his body at the mere thought of losing her.

Rachael wanted to weep with happiness. Rio was standing there waiting for her, looking like the god of the forest. She loved everything about him. She said his name softly to herself, amazed at how he had wound himself so tightly into her heart and mind. She had come to the forest with such a grim future, but Rio had changed all that. He had given her a gift more precious than all the money in the world. He'd given her himself.

Rio felt Elijah place her hand in his, felt his fingers close around hers. Hard. Tight. A lifeline. He drew her to him, beneath the protection of his shoulder, into the shelter of his heart. Rachael tilted her head to look up at him, her black eyes laughing, soft with love. He leaned down, his lips brushing her skin. "You did this. You gave me this. You changed my entire life, Rachael." He whispered the words, meaning them. Astonished by them. How could one person, one woman, have made such a difference?

She touched his face, her fingertips moving intimately over every feature. "And you changed mine, Rio."

Delgrotto cleared his throat to draw their attention to him. He began the ceremony of joining. "The circle of life continues. The lair grows stronger with the joining of these two. No couple stands alone. The lair protects the safety of our mated pairs so that the circle of life continues and the lair grows ever stronger . . ."

Turn the page for a preview of
Christine Feehan's
paranormal romantic thriller

MIND GAME

available now from Jove

"JUST a few more minutes," Dahlia consoled herself aloud. It didn't matter how many deep breaths she took, she was on serious overload and shards of glass seemed to be stabbing through her head. Her vision blurred so that she couldn't adequately make out the dangerous terrain. One misstep and she would sink into the bogs of the swamp. The ground beneath her feet was spongy, matted with thick grasses. The foul stench of stagnant water permeated the air.

There was no more than a sliver of moon to spill light across the swamp. In the darkness, the cypress trees looked macabre, as if they stretched long stick arms instead of branches. Grayish moss hanging like streamers looked like tattered clothes fluttering occasionally above the blackened water. The breeze barely stirred, so that the muggy air seemed barely breathable.

Dahlia pressed her fingers to her temple and paused, her body swaying, rocking back and forth to console herself. Stars exploded in front of her eyes. Her stomach lurched.

She lifted her head, suddenly wary. She should be feeling better, not worse, out in the swamp, far from the human emotions always breaching the walls of her unprotected brain. She went still, a shadow in the darkness, blurring her image further to keep prying eyes from spotting her.

There was definitely something or someone stalking her, waiting for her to come into the web. Her heart accelerated with fear for those she called family: her nurses, or guards—she had never really defined them, but they were all she'd known most of her life. Milly and Bernadette. They were mother and sister and friend and nurse to her. Women who insisted she learn to do things she always pretended to dislike. She often teased them that crochet and knitting were for old women, that the sewing they did made them squint.

No one knew about her or her home. She was human, yet not normal, so different she could never be accepted in the world. Nor could she ever fit in and live comfortably. She had a vague idea of her childhood, but mostly she remembered pain. It lived and breathed in her body as if alive. The only way to turn it off was to go to her sanctuary, her home. And someone hunted her, using her home as a trap.

The knowledge blossomed, nearly consuming her brain, a stark reality she couldn't avoid. Her mission had had unexpected complications, but she'd made it out and knew no one had followed her. Had they learned another way to find her home? Everything that could go wrong had certainly gone wrong, but she absolutely knew she hadn't been followed. Jesse Calhoun, her handler, was certain to be waiting for her. He was lethal and fast when he needed to be. Jesse interested her because he was the only other human being she knew of with capabilities close to hers. And he was also telepathic, so why wasn't he warning her of the danger?

Dahlia knew how to be patient. She pushed the pain aside and waited there in the swamp, inhaling to try to catch a scent. Listening for a sound. There was only the occasional plop of a snake dropping from overhead branches into the murky waters. Still, she waited, knowing movement drew the eye. The faint smell of smoke drifted to her on the breeze.

Her breath caught in her throat. There was only one building that could feed a fire. She *needed* her home. She couldn't survive without it. If they took her residence, they might as well put a bullet in her head. Dahlia took two steps to her right. She doubted anyone knew the way through the swamp. Anyone waiting for her would be expecting her to be coming in by boat. Most likely they would be watching the dock. She stepped carefully on the trail, knowing she could sink into the bog if she took one misstep. An alligator growled somewhere close. Dahlia merely glanced in the direction of the sound, a quick acknowledgment of the creature's presence.

She took another cautious step forward. She counted ten steps and stepped to her right again. Moving through the swamp was nearly automatic. She counted steps in her mind, but was really concentrating on the smell drifting on the slight breeze. Dahlia peered through the night, her instincts sharp and alert. Something waited for her, something terrible, and a dark dread was taking hold.

She approached her home from the north, the only real safe passage through the swamp. Twice she had to wade knee deep through the black water, using the cypress trees to guide her progress. Dahlia was careful to make no sound, blending with the night creatures, tuning to them so the insects continued in harmony and the frogs croaked with annoying repetition. The last thing she wanted was to give her position away by having the animals go abruptly silent. It took stealth and calm to move in their world and not disturb them. Dahlia could do it, but it required all of her skills when her heart was pounding in alarm.

The smell of something smoldering choked her as she approached the sanitarium. She could make out the cloud of black smoke rising and orange-red flames pouring from inside the building. The sanitarium was built on solid ground in the center of the small island. A walkway led from the dock over spongy marsh to the higher terrain where the building was located. Dahlia had taken two steps toward her home when the first wave of energy hit her so hard it drove her to her knees.

Violence. Dark. Malevolent. It poured from the building and rolled off the walls. Something terrible had happened, confirming the dread that had been growing so steadily inside of her. The energy was living, left behind by the aftermath of what had created it. Death. She smelled it. Knew it waited just inside the building.

Dahlia fought to breathe her way through the pain. She avoided violent energy whenever possible, but she could force herself to endure it if necessary. She'd done it before. She had to go inside. She had to know what had happened. And she had to get to Milly and Bernadette and maybe even Jesse. Resolutely, she drew air into her lungs and stood up. Her tongue moistened her suddenly dry lips. It was difficult to concentrate with so much pain, but she'd learned to push it to the back of her head. And she had to see what had happened. What was left. It was the only home she could remember. The only people she had contact with lived there with her. Her books, her music, her entire world was in that building.

She kept to the trees, running lightly through the tall grass, moving with the breeze rather than against it. She knew there was someone left behind. Someone waiting for her arrival. Energy flowed toward her and it confused her.

There was the violence, hot angry waves rolling in to swamp her, and a secondary source, completely different. Quiet. Calm. Centered. Patient. The contrast was shocking. She'd never experienced it before and it made her all the more wary.

As she approached her home, she could see several men dragging Jesse Calhoun down the well-worn path to the boat docks. Jesse appeared unconscious and was covered in blood. His legs dragged uselessly and she could see the damage, raw and ugly, even in the night. "Jesse." She whispered his name and switched directions, hurrying toward him, using the natural cover, uncertain how she could help him. She never carried a gun anymore. She had long ago realized she couldn't survive the deliberate taking of a life.

There were too many men slipping through the night toward the waterway. A purge. The men had come to kill her, to wipe out her existence. Why? She'd completed her mission. She tried to maneuver closer, thinking she might be able to scare them away from Jesse with heat and fire. The sound of gunfire erupted from within the building.

"Milly. Bernadette." She'd never felt so helpless or torn in her life.

Shouts broke out as Jesse woke, struggling and fighting. Dahlia immediately followed the group of men, reaching out to Jesse as she did so. She wasn't particularly telepathic, but Jesse was and he would feel her energy and know she was present. *Jesse. Tell me what to do.*

A man's voice answered in a hard, authoritative tone. . . . And it wasn't Jesse. *Don't do anything. Stay away from here.*

She froze, sinking into the tall grass. No one else had ever spoken to her like that. In her head. The world was crashing down around her and nothing made sense. The overload of violent energy made her sick, her stomach

rebelling as the waves rushed over her, wanting to con-
sume her. Her head was throbbing with pain. She kept her
eyes on Jesse, hoping he would reach out to her, tell her
what was going on. She saw one of the men deliberately
reach down and slam the butt of his gun into the raw mess
that was Jesse's leg. Jesse screamed, a terrible sound that
would echo in her dreams for a long time.

The rush of violence hit her hard, swamping her so that
she sagged backward, but she kept her gaze focused on the
man who had struck Jesse so viciously. Flames rushed up
and over him, huge leaping streaks of orange and red, as
high as a bonfire, flames she couldn't possibly control.
Chaos erupted. Several men fired shots in scattered directions, uncertain where the attack was coming from. One
man rolled his partner in a jacket to put out the flames.

A third man simply shot Jesse a second time, this time
in his other leg. Dahlia had never heard so much agony in a
scream. She was sick, over and over, the power of the violent energy swirling around her and beating at her with
more force than she'd ever endured before.

"We'll keep shooting him. You can't get all of us," the
man who had shot Jesse shouted. They kept moving, a tight
unit now, Jesse in the middle, being dragged away while
the men faced outward with their guns.

Dahlia was too sick to move, to think. She cursed her
inability to do more than sit there, hiding like a rabbit in
the grass while they tortured Jesse and took him away from
her. Jesse who had taught her to play chess and gave her
more relief than she'd ever imagined possible by just his
presence. Jesse with his easy, engaging smile. He was the
only person who ever teased her. She hadn't even known
what teasing was until Jesse had come into her life.

She should have carried a gun. She knew how to use
one. She could only watch helplessly until they were out of

sight and she heard the boat motor start up. Dahlia rushed down to the docks to see two boats disappearing down the channel. The only evidence of Jesse was the terrible blood-stain. The red puddle looked shiny black in the darkness.

Dahlia turned back toward her home. Smoke poured from the windows and doors, drifted toward the sky. She could see the flames licking at the walls. Jesse was gone. They'd taken him. *I'll find you. Stay alive, Jesse. I'll come for you.* She made it a vow. Just using telepathy without him creating the bond sent shards of glass ripping at her brain, but she was far beyond caring.

That's what they want, Dahlia. I'm the bait. Don't let them kill us both.

Jesse's voice was weak, tinged with pain. Her heart turned over. *I'll find you, Jesse.* She vowed it with determination. Dahlia knew Jesse was aware she was stubborn and would do exactly what she said. She hoped it gave him the necessary hope to stay alive in the worst of circumstances. Knowing there was nothing she could do for him, she made her way up the path to the house.

She staggered at the entrance. The energy was much stronger close to the source of the violence. Her body was rebelling and she could feel the reaction building no matter how hard she tried to keep control. She had only a few minutes to discover whether Bernadette and Milly had survived the purge.

Dahlia curled her fingers into a tight fist, nails digging into her palm. There was only one person whose energy she could feel emanating from her home. Malc. A stranger. She couldn't get a direction on him, the energy level was too low and too spread out, almost as if he could disperse it deliberately across a vast area. She gained the wide veranda, her soft soles making no noise on the wood. "Be alive." She heard the whisper of breath and knew she said it, although she didn't remember the actual thought. She already knew, her sense told her the truth, but her mind wouldn't accept it.

Smoke poured out the open door leading to the entryway and offices. No one ever manned the offices, they were there mostly for show if anyone visited. No one ever did ... until now. She glanced inside and saw the file cabinets overturned and the folders spilled onto the floor and smoldering or already succumbing to the flames. Her heart began to pound loudly. She could see a ribbon of wool, a pale blue splashed with a bright red.

Tears swam in her eyes, blurred her vision. She swallowed hard and brushed at her cheeks and lashes. There was a strange roaring in her head. She didn't want to look, the dread was there, the certain knowledge, but she couldn't prevent her terrified gaze from following the blue string to the blood-soaked ball of wool and the outstretched hand beside it.

Milly lay sprawled on the floor. Dahlia heard a noise escape her throat, a high keening sound of grief. She hurried to the older woman, stroked back her hair. She'd been shot in the forehead. Dahlia couldn't bear to have her lying on the floor with the horrible mess around her and the smell of gasoline heavy in the room. Bernadette lay only a few feet away. Dahlia sat between them, rocking back and forth, the keening sound that she was certain was not really coming from her throat sounding loud in her ears.

Dahlia could barely contain her grief. It built in her, fed by the voracious appetites of the violence embedded deep in the waves of energy rolling through her burning home. These two women were her only family. Jesse had been her only friend. She sat on the floor in the midst of blood and violence while her home burned around her. She reached out to touch Bernadette, a silent apology for being late. She stroked a caress down her arm and tried to weave her fingers through Bernadette's, needing to hold her hand. To simply have the contact. There was something in Bernadette's hand.

Dahlia leaned over her to pry the object from her fingers. It was a heart shaped of amethyst. Dahlia had brought it to her a few years earlier. Bernadette's eyes had brightened as she took it, murmuring something about a waste of money for Dahlia to buy her such trinkets. She had worn it around her neck every day since.

Grief clawed at Dahlia's insides, raked hard so that she felt raw and wounded. She took the small heart and pressed it to her face. Tears poured down her face, and her chest hurt so badly she was afraid it would explode. Heat seared the air around her, shimmering in the room. Papers ignited only a few scant inches from where she sat.

Without warning she heard a door bang in the gymnasium. Startled, she glanced at the open door to see a man sprinting toward her.

"Run!" She heard the command, a sharp imperious demand that cut through the terrible pain burning in her chest. He seemed to flow across the gym floor, a sinuous movement of muscle and power. Immediately she had the impression of a great tiger bearing down on her.

"Run. Get out of here."

As he bore down on her, she felt the first flutter of fear. It blossomed immediately into a panic attack. For the first time in her life, Dahlia was frozen, unable to move or think. She could only watch as the heavily muscled man closed the distance between them with his long strides. He reached down without missing a step and scooped her up effortlessly, as casually as he would have retrieved a ball, and continued running from the building.

Dahlia found herself upside down over his shoulder, a package much like his rifle and gear. She had never experienced grief before, not the mind-numbing kind that pervaded her body and left her pliant in a stranger's arms.

She'd never been in any man's arms. She'd never been this close to a man before in her life.

"Keep your head down. The building's rigged with explosives. When it goes off we want to be far away." Nicolas gave Dahlia the explanation, though he rarely thought it necessary to explain his actions. It was just that she was so pale and shell-shocked. He could feel her heart pounding, threatening to come right through her chest. He didn't expect her to be so fragile and to feel so feminine against his body. He didn't expect to notice her much at all, yet he was acutely aware of her, even in the life-threatening situation.

"I can't just leave them." The words slipped out, choked with grief, even though she knew it was silly to say it. To think it. Who would be stupid enough to go back into a burning building that might blow up at any moment to retrieve two dead bodies?

"You're in shock, Dahlia. Let me get us to safe ground."

There was no safe ground. He didn't understand that. No one was safe, least of all the man trying to save her life. She clung to his back, a dizzying ride as he raced across the bog to save their lives.

Nicolas counted to himself, judging the time they had, knowing it couldn't be long, but wanting to use every second to put distance between them and the blast. Dahlia was making the most heartbreaking noise he'd ever heard and it was twisting his insides and tearing at his heart, a first for him. He wanted to hold her in his arms and comfort her as he would a child. Worse, he was certain she wasn't even aware she was making the noise. Her fingers were clutched in his jacket and she didn't fight him at all. The Dahlia he had seen in the tapes had been a fighter all the way and that told him more than anything about how shocked she really was.

Well into the tree line, he dragged her from his shoulder and pushed her into the water-logged ground, following her down, pinning her there with his much-heavier body. Almost at once the ground shook and the force of the explosion rocked the entire island.

Look for the new Carpathian novel from
#1 *New York Times* bestselling author

CHRISTINE FEEHAN

the "Queen of Paranormal Romance"*

DARK PERIL

A CARPATHIAN NOVEL

Dominic, of the Dragonseeker lineage—one of the most
powerful lines of the Carpathian people—ingests vampire
blood laced with parasites in order to go the very heart of
the enemy camp and learn their plans. He hopes to get in
fast, relay the information to the leader of the Carpathians,
and fight to the end.

Solange Sangria is one of the last of the jaguar people, a
royal pureblood. She has long been alone, fighting to save
the remaining female shapeshifters. Wounded and weary,
she plans one last battle, hoping to stop the man who has
made an alliance with the vampires. She never expects him
to be so much more . . .

*USA Today

penguin.com

M663T0510

Don't miss the brand-new series from
#1 *New York Times* bestselling author

CHRISTINE FEEHAN

WATER BOUND
A Sea Haven Novel

*In the swirling tides of the ocean
she found a handsome stranger . . .*

The last thing Lev Pravenskii remembers is being lost at sea, off the coastal town of Sea Haven. Just as quickly, just as miraculously, he was saved—pulled ashore by a beautiful stranger. But Lev has no memory of who he was—or why he seems to possess the violent instincts of a trained killer. All he knows is that he fears for his life, and for the life of his unexpected savior.

Her name is Rikki, a sea-urchin diver in Sea Haven. She has always felt an affinity for the ocean and felt the seductive pull of the tides. And now she feels drawn in the same way to the enigmatic man she rescued. But soon they will be bound by something even stronger: each other's tantalizing secrets, which will engulf them both in a whirlpool of dizzying passion and inescapable danger.

M615T1209

Also from #1 *New York Times* bestselling author
CHRISTINE FEEHAN

On the trail of passion and betrayal,
she's following his scent . . .

Leopard shifter Conner Vega carries the scent of a wild
animal in its prime, and bears the soul-crushing sins of
past betrayals. Isabeau Chandler has never forgiven him—
or forgotten him. The mating urge is still with her, and
hotter than ever. Dangerously hot . . .

M664T0310

The new GhostWalker novel from
#1 *New York Times* bestselling author and
"queen of paranormal romance" (*USA Today*)

CHRISTINE FEEHAN

Street Game

Years ago, GhostWalkers Mack McKinley and Jaimie
Fielding were lovers. Now they've been reunited on the
violent streets in pursuit of a common enemy who could
destroy them both.

M618T1209